# DIAMOND LIES

BY

## JOHANN SORENSON

Goodfellow Press

Goodfellow Press
8522 10th Ave. NW
Seattle, WA 98117

Copyright © 2001

ISBN: 1-891761-09-9
Library of Congress: 2001-131463

Edited by Pamela R. Goodfellow
Jacket and book design by Rohani Design, Edmonds, WA
Cover illustration by Barbara Levine
Printed by Edwards Brothers, Inc. under the supervision of Tanya Eldred

This is a work of fiction. The events described are imaginary; the
characters are entirely fictitious and are not intended to represent actual
living persons.

The text is set in 11.8 point Weiss with 14.3 point leading, Castellar for
title page and chapter numbers, KochAntiqua for drop caps, and Weiss
italic for chapters.
Author photo by Suzanne Wyman.

acknowledgements

I WAS TOLD WRITING IS A SOLITARY PROCESS. THIS was true, right up until the time I got stuck. Many talented people helped me complete this book.

I thank Pamela Goodfellow for her editing, mentoring and friendship throughout the creation of this novel. I'm deeply grateful for the insights of the Monday night group who didn't let me get away with anything. I'm also truly appreciative of the efforts of the critique group that helped shape the final draft. Suzanne Wyman's editing support has been tremendously helpful in finalizing the book.

I thank my daughter Suzanne for her support and patience. I especially thank my wife Judy for her belief in me and her understanding, indulgence, love and late night snacks.

*To my parents who showed me the world
and to Judy who shares it with me.*

# PART I

1

ERIK LEANED HEAVILY ON HIS CANE AND LOOKED the Viking Queen over from the deck to the top of her masts. She was beautiful even tied to her moorage at Tiburon. He knew, once away from the dock and slicing through the water, she would be magnificent. One hundred and thirty feet long, the custom performance ketch combined the best of seaworthiness and luxury.

He considered changing his plans and simply going for a sail around the bay, but a painful coughing fit broke his train of thought and reminded him of why he was there. He took as deep a breath as his failing lungs would allow.

He turned his attention to the two crewmen who were delicately lifting his wife of sixty years out of her wheel chair. "Don't drop her boys, she doesn't bounce too well anymore." Erik smiled to himself as Melanie shot him a look. He followed as the crewmen took her aboard and gently placed her in a cushioned deck lounger. He saw her whisper something to Chris, one of the husky men helping her.

"What did she say? I couldn't hear her. Is she plotting a mutiny, my boy?" Erik coughed from the exertion of his speech. He held onto the side rail for support until the spasm passed. He

1

sucked as hard as he could to get air but his lungs were never satisfied anymore.

Chris approached Erik nervously. "Are you all right, sir? May I help you to a chair?"

Erik waved him off. With an effort he pointed to Melanie. "Is she paying you on the side, trying to take over the ship?" He grinned at the young crewman.

"No, sir, but she did say that if you don't mind your manners I'm to throw you over the side."

"Ah, there, see, it finally comes out. After all these years together she wants to turn me into shark bait. Well, the sharks and she will both be disappointed now that I'm on to her."

Erik shuffled to where Melanie was propped up in the deck lounger. Most of the color was gone from her once-smooth face. Lines of age creased her temples but he still saw her beauty. Her eyes were closed and her thin gray hair blew lightly in the afternoon wind. He picked up her hand and softly kissed it. She half opened her blue eyes and smiled weakly. Over the last few weeks her condition had deteriorated faster than he had imagined it could. He silently cursed the very word cancer and all the suffering it had caused.

That young Dr. Byron had been surprised too. If it had been up to him Melanie would be in a hospital right now with tubes sticking out of her. What a horrible way to die, dangling on the end of an IV tube while people who had no idea who you were tried to keep your feeble body alive. The doctor would surely be furious if he knew Erik had taken her to the boat. The live-in nurse had about had a fit when the ship's crew had arrived at the mansion to pick them up. He was certain a call had already been made to Dr. Byron. Well, none of that would be of consequence in a little while.

"How are you, my dearest?" He had to lean close to hear her barely audible reply.

"Happy to be with you. Happy to be in the sun again."

A crewman named Ivan approached them. "Mr. Erikson, may I get you anything?"

"Yes Ivan, see that large suitcase there? I'd like it stowed in the engine compartment for now. And be extra careful. It's very delicate."

"Yes, sir. I'll take care of it." The sailor easily lifted the black bag.

"And Ivan, please let the captain know I'd like to see him. Also, would you be kind enough to bring us some oxygen? All this fresh air is doing me in." He coughed and his whole body shuddered again.

"Aye, aye, sir." The crewman moved away briskly. As Erik watched him take the black bag aboard, he fingered the plastic remote control in his pocket. Coughing again he looked at the blue California sky. It was definitely a good day for a sail.

Erik leaned over to Melanie. "Ivan is a good man. Still makes me feel like a sailor." He looked about his yacht with pride. The sailing ship was rigged with the newest hydraulics, winches and the latest computers so he could have sailed around the world if he had ever desired. When he'd originally bought her he had captained her himself. But over the last five years, with his strength deserting him, he had hired a professional skipper and left the maintenance and sailing to him and the three-man crew.

Under sail one man could handle the vessel, but even with the advanced rigging that man would have to be a superb sailor. Under power, one man could easily run the ship. Erik had sailed the boat to Hawaii with only Melanie along for company once, mainly to prove he could do it. However, the last few years he found he preferred a crew and a cook.

He was pleased with the way things had worked out and considered the captain and his crew to be more than employees. They were like an extended family.

Captain Jones arrived within moments. Behind him came the crewman carrying two small oxygen containers with plastic masks.

"Jonesy, set us a course around Treasure Island and then head for the Golden Gate. Please rig her for sailing so I can run her from the aft cockpit. And please move my lady there also."

"Aye, sir. Right away."

Erik watched in quiet appreciation as the crew expertly got his ship underway. It was one of those rare hot days on the bay when the wind was light and the sun was thoroughly warming. Erik reached from his chair and stroked Melanie's face. She grasped his hand and held it gently against her cheek.

A little while later, The Viking Queen was sailing west between Treasure Island and San Francisco. Erik had the polished wooden pilot wheel in his left hand and sat contentedly watching the city pass. In the light breeze the boat seemed to glide in slow motion.

"Captain Jones." Erik called the captain to him. "I'd like you to take the crew and go ashore in one of the small boats."

"Sir?"

"I've not lost my mind. Melanie and I would just like a few hours on the bay by ourselves."

"I don't think that's such a good idea, sir. How about if I send the crew ashore and I'll stay aboard but go below? You won't even know I'm here." His tone was conciliatory.

Erik continued patiently. "You're a good skipper and you've a good crew. But favor an old man for an afternoon." Captain Jones pursed his lips. He eyed the sails and the calm water then hesitated before speaking.

"When should I come back, sir?" Jones was not happy with the prospect of leaving them alone on the boat.

"I'll bring her close to the marina after sunset. You'll have to come back out and help with the docking." Erik hoped that would mollify him and was relieved when the captain nodded in agreement.

Jones shifted his weight from one foot to the other as if trying to think of a way to change his employer's mind. After a moment he sighed. "Aye, sir. But be careful, there's a strong ebb tide going out the gate and it'll be difficult to sail back against."

Erik smiled at him. "Thank you, skipper, duly noted."

Once the crew was gone, Erik stood in the open cockpit and let out a touch of sail to increase the boat's speed. The wheel was steady in his hand and the Queen gracefully responded to his every command. He enjoyed the way the hull sliced through the water with the waves gently rocking them. Expertly judging the wind, he sailed beneath the Golden Gate and into the Pacific Ocean.

Melanie sat beside him holding an oxygen mask that was attached to a small canister. She occasionally took a breath from the mask even as the breeze brought fresh air off the ocean. There was an identical canister by his side but he resisted the need to use the bottled gas. He wanted to smell the ocean as long as he could.

He briefly wondered what the crew would think tomorrow. Well, they'd move on. Besides, they would all get a nice envelope by the end of the week. Each envelope contained a letter of thanks for excellent service from the Erikson Company, a letter of recommendation for future employers, and a check for one hundred thousand dollars.

Once away from the swirling waters of the mouth of the bay, he again looked at Melanie. Reaching into his coat pocket he withdrew the bottle of pills he had obtained from an old college friend who had gone on to be a doctor. Originally there had been hesitation, but the doctor's wife had withered away in a rest home two years before. Erik had not had a difficult time convincing him that there was still a place for dignity in the world. He felt the rough edges of the cap with his fingertips, then slid the vial into his pants pocket. Melanie leaned over and tapped the slight bulge the vial made in his slacks.

"Is that something in your pocket or are you just glad to see me?" He could barely hear her and for an instant saw a flicker of a laugh in her eyes. She took a weak breath. "It's time, honey. But it's been wonderful hasn't it?"

Erik took the vial back out of his pocket. The wind blew a tear down his cheek. "More wonderful than I could have ever believed." He coughed so hard he had to sit down and hold himself with the hand that was not on the wheel. He wondered if his ribs might crack from the exertion. After the coughing subsided he noticed that the two portable medical oxygen canisters on their trolleys looked grossly out of place on the deck of his luxury yacht with its polished teak and gleaming chrome.

He locked the ship's wheel in place and with an effort collected one of the canisters and all its tubes and the mask. Even with the help of the trolley it took almost all his strength to get it to the side where he dropped the whole contraption into the dark waters of the ocean.

Back in the cockpit Melanie had gathered her canister and tubes and was trying to push it towards him. "This too."

When he saw the splash of the second container a rush of freedom pulsed through his veins. Seeing Melanie's smile after it dropped was nearly intoxicating.

Returning to his place behind the wheel, he took the bottle of champagne the crew had set up for them and struggled with the cork. Melanie laughed weakly and he made exaggerated faces until he finally forced the cork to pop into the air toward San Francisco.

"My favorite sound." Her voice was a whisper on the wind.

They toasted and Melanie looked up at him. "Is everything taken care of?"

"Everything is fine."

"Will the children be okay? I worry about Enya."

Erik adjusted the rudder to catch a slight shift in the wind. "Enya is one of the best business people in the company. She'll do well."

"I know she'll take care of the business. I just hope she gives herself a chance to live." Erik could hear the effort that every word cost her.

"When will Johnny get the map?"

"Tomorrow or the next day. I'm convinced that's the right place for it to be. He'll know what to do with it."

She placed her hand over his. "The map. Do you suppose we would have been as happy if we had not followed it?" She focused her eyes on his.

"Melanie, you and I both knew from the time we met we would always be happy as long as we were together."

"I hope John understands that part of the legend. I think the time in Europe has been good for him. I just pray he recognizes the one." Melanie squeezed his hand. "Do you remember the time when Enya was eleven and she fell out of that tree and broke her arm?"

Erik had to smile. "She always claimed it was John's fault but he never believed it. He said the branch just broke."

"She was really mad, but she forgave him. Do you remember what happened next?"

Erik took a drink of his wine. "Of course I do. About three weeks later some older kids were picking on John and Enya showed up and saved him. Whacked one of the bullies with her cast. Once he got over being saved by his big sister, he appreciated her a lot more."

Melanie pressed his hand again. "I'm glad they still help each other out. It's funny, but I think they'll both learn how to be happy. I hope they forgive us."

"They will. We tried to show them how to live and gave them their independence. I think that's the best we could do." The setting sun brought a cool breeze and a chill crept into his bones. Erik zipped his light jacket and pulled Melanie's blanket up to her shoulders.

She held her hand out and Erik poured what he knew was a lethal mix of drugs into it. She looked at him again. He filled his own hand with the same prescription. They clinked their glasses then took the pills in unison and washed them down with champagne.

He pulled the black plastic box from his pocket and switched the digital remote on. He pressed the button marked ENGAGE and a timer started counting backwards from 120 minutes. He watched momentarily fascinated as the seconds ticked off. A boating accident would be much easier for those left behind to deal with.

The Viking Queen passed under a darkening sky picking up speed. "Would you like to go below and lie down?" Erik looked at his nearly sleeping love.

"No. I'd rather have the wind in my face and you by my side."

Erik kissed her gently on the forehead and pulled her to a position so that he could sit and steer with one hand and hold her with the other.

"I'm setting a course for the second star from the right. Don't forget to make a wish."

"No need, my love. All my wishes have already come true."

c h a p t e r

2

[FOUR YEARS EARLIER]

"**Y**OU CAN'T DO THAT."
John could tell by the tone of Teri's voice that he had successfully foiled her next move. He smiled at her and raised his champagne glass. "Sure I can and I get a double word score and that puts me ahead."

He studied her face as she looked at the game board on the floor between them. He put his glass down and stretched out on the thick Persian carpet.

"Only a former Army guy would come up with a word like 'salute' and it blocks the whole left side of the board."

"I wasn't just an Army guy. I was a Ranger and you're only mad because I'm ahead and you're still stuck with the Z." It was tough not to gloat. This was one of their favorite games and she usually won. Having the upper hand for once was a welcome change. As his fiancée concentrated on her next move she brushed blonde hair away from her face with one hand. He liked that she wasn't prone to giving up on anything, even something as trivial as this game. If there was a word to be made up out of the letters she had left, he had no doubt that she would find it.

He took another sip of the dry wine and sat up, crossing his legs in front of him. She thought for a long time. While she concentrated he tried to imagine what was going on behind those intense Pacific-blue eyes. As she stared at the game-board he admired the smoothness of her face and the way her sweater accentuated her lovely shape. Intelligence, wit and beauty all in one package. He knew he'd been lucky the day he met her.

Whatever she was thinking, it was probably something mischievous. John was just starting to hope she was stumped when she smiled and then very deliberately put her letters down.

"There now, Mister Ranger Rick, I think that just about does it."

The air went out of his chest. The new word was 'zebu' and the Z was on the triple word score. This was a complete disaster for him. There was no way he could match her points with his few remaining letters. "What the heck kind of word is zebu? I bet it's not real. We're going to have to look this one up." He doubted this weak attempt to thwart her victory would work, but it was all he could come up with. He had tried his best to make the challenge sound authentic.

"Spoilsport. It is too a word. It's an African animal. You should know that. You know all about Africa."

"Maybe there's something like a zebu in Africa. But I bet it's not in the dictionary. We'll have to check before you add up your score. All I have to do is figure out where to find a dictionary. Let's finish our wine and think about it."

Teri stood up, smoothed her skirt with her fingertips, and looked around the game room. "You're just trying to distract me. This place is the biggest house I've ever been in. If you don't know where a dictionary is, we could spend weeks trying to find one."

John realized she had a point. He had taken his parents' house for granted so long that he sometimes forgot that people who were not used to it could be overwhelmed by its size. He glanced about the room wondering if there were a dictionary in here by chance. There was a bookshelf in the wall by the billiard table but he knew that was filled with sports books and most of them were about golf.

There certainly would not be a resource book on the shelf by the big television and the books by the wet bar were all humor and mixology. Mother was a stickler about having the right things in the right place. Then, with a slight increase in his heart rate, he thought about the one place in the house where a dictionary would be for certain.

John stood and stretched his legs. Sitting near her on the floor was more intimate than being across a table so he had put up with the slight discomfort. He stepped over the board and took Teri's hand. As he did he caught a whiff of jasmine perfume. It was a fragrance she had suggested she might like for her last birthday. When he'd bought it for her he had no idea how much he would come to enjoy it.

For a moment he considered forgetting the game and moving on to something more interesting, but the determination in her eyes told him this issue had to be resolved first. There was a point to made here. She had called his bluff and fair play dictated he had to respond. Besides, it occurred to him that getting the dictionary might be an adventure in itself. "I know where we can find one, but you have to promise not to tell anyone."

Teri raised an eyebrow. "Not tell anyone? Is this some kind of special dictionary that only has secret words?"

He laughed. "No, of course not. It's where it is that's the secret."

"You mean your parents' house has hidden rooms and passageways? Does it have a dungeon, too?"

He smiled to himself. Her imagination and sense of adventure could make even the most mundane things seem entertaining. "It was going to have a dungeon but there was some kind of hang-up with the permit. They had to settle for a sauna. Bring your champagne glass. We're going to go to my dad's study." John picked up his glass and the bottle of champagne in one hand then led Teri out of the game room and into the long hallway.

"I thought you told me you weren't allowed in your father's study. I don't want to get on your parent's bad side if we go in there."

John felt the warmth of her hand as they walked down the hall leading to a part of the house he seldom visited. "Don't worry, there's nobody here but us. When we were kids Enya and I saw where dad's assistant, Walter, hid his key. I wonder if it's still there."

Teri tugged gently on his arm. "I don't get it. Is it okay if you go in there or not? I mean, your father must keep the door locked for a reason."

"He didn't like Enya and me in there when we were kids. But we haven't talked about it for years."

"Does it bother you that he never said it was okay to go in?"

John slowed his pace and suppressed a surge of disappointment that his father had not seen fit to relax his rules on this. "Maybe I'll ask him when they get back from China. But now my curiosity is piqued. I've wondered about the study for years. Besides, it's the only place we'll find a dictionary. Let's see if old Walter's key is still in its place."

John stopped in front of a mahogany table in the wide hall and reached up underneath it. A little dust fell away and the unfinished wood was rough on his fingers. After a moment he located the key on the ledge where he had found it years before. He pulled it out and held it up triumphantly to Teri.

She looked at him and pursed her lips. "This is kind of creepy, I feel like we're sneaking around where we aren't supposed to be."

"Sometimes that's what adventures are like. Want to turn back and give up the game?"

She squeezed his hand tightly. "Of course not. And don't try to scare me out of it."

"Okay, here we go. Just remember not to tell anyone."

"Like who?"

"Like my sister, or my folks, or Walter, or your cat."

"Come on, Johnny, give me a little credit."

He stepped to the door and verified that it was locked. There was still something forbidden about it. John had the suspicion he'd never had the full confidence of the man he admired most and sometimes wondered what he would have to do to win it.

He slipped the key into the lock. His heart raced and he knew sweat was seeping into his shirt. He was accustomed to following rules, and entering this room gave him the sensation of being a thief. An exquisite feeling both exciting and dangerous like being on a tightrope. It made him feel alive and he wished he had it more often. Having Teri with him only heightened his enjoyment. He told himself this was truly a harmless activity. They only wanted to look up a word. However, the old taboo still haunted him.

John felt the lock to his father's library door click as he gently turned the secret key. He tested the polished brass doorknob and was rewarded with a full turn. The door swung open and invited him into the forbidden territory.

"It worked!" Teri's whisper was triumphant. Why they were being so quiet John wasn't sure. His folks were on the other side of the world. Getting caught breaking into his father's study was not something that was going to happen because the intruders spoke too loudly.

Turning on the light, he got the same pulse-quickening sense of wonder he'd had the first time he'd come in uninvited. He'd been twelve and had entered a world he did not comprehend. The only difference between then and now was that he was older and had gained even more respect for his father's accomplishments. He understood the business now that he was part of it. However, the way his father made his initial fortune was still somewhat murky in John's mind. He had always tried to convince himself that this detail would be forthcoming when his father was ready for him to know it. But he was thirty-five now and it seemed overdue.

"You're pretty sneaky for such an old guy." She kissed him on the cheek and laughed. He detected a hint of champagne in her voice. As he stepped inside the room Teri brushed by him in excitement and gasped.

"You said this was a study. I've been in libraries that aren't this big."

He had to agree the room was huge. Even measured by the rest of the estate, it was impressive. The air smelled of rich leather with a slight hint of lemon furniture polish. Every wall was lined with bookshelves that went from the floor to the vaulted ceiling fifteen feet above the rich carpet.

He was surprised to realize that this was the one place that still made him uncertain of himself. Maybe not as much as in his first unaccompanied visits, but it was as if the knowledge and the business transacted in this room were still something beyond his grasp.

Dad had been a pilot in the Second World War and after that founded a brokerage firm that had been staggeringly successful and later expanded to other enterprises. He was proud that his father had built wealth not only for himself, but also for many clients. His knack for making the right deal at the right time and for being able to read the market was remarkable by any standards. John considered himself intelligent, but he didn't believe he had the same business acumen his father possessed. The thought that his father felt the same way often gnawed at him.

"When I was a kid I always wondered what was in those books." He held Teri's hand as they moved deeper into the study. He pointed at the books on the uppermost shelves. "I snuck in here a few times but even with the ladder I couldn't reach the highest ones."

"Did you ever get caught in here?"

"No, Enya and I were too careful. The rules were pretty simple. If Dad were here and the door was open, we could come in. If the door was closed, and it usually was, it meant he was working and we were not to disturb him."

He could picture his father talking on the phone that rested on the great mahogany desk by the full-length stained glass window. "We were allowed to look at any book we could reach. If we couldn't reach them they were off limits. If Mother or Dad weren't here, the whole study was off limits. It never occurred to us to question the rule. It was just part of being a kid."

"It's almost spooky." Teri's voice was still a whisper.

"When we were little, sometimes Enya and I would make up stories about what went on in here. We came up with some very mysterious goings-on. Eventually we got bored with the stories and quit talking about it altogether." John had occasionally wondered if his father might be involved in some kind of nefarious business practices, but then had laughed at the notion. Dad was too astute in the business world and he had nothing to gain by doing anything illegal. He was also too honest to consider anything outside the law. Still it was odd and from time to time John found himself wondering what his father could possibly have to hide.

He speculated that the origin of their family's wealth was something his father did not want known. Loot from the war was the thing John thought made the most sense. Perhaps it would not be technically illegal, depending on what form it took, but it would not be something to brag about. His mother had always avoided the subject too. Though she was not actively involved with the firm, she and Dad were very close and appeared to share everything.

Teri looked around the study in awe. Her blonde hair danced across her shoulder as her head turned from side to side while she quickly read the titles of books. "*The Seven Pillars of Wisdom,* by T.E. Lawrence, *The Sea Wolf,* by Jack London, *The Jungle Book* by Kipling. This place is remarkable even for a family as rich as yours."

Teri's comment startled him. One of the things he liked about her was that she had never given an inkling that his wealth had any influence on their relationship. Did that comment reveal something she'd been hiding? No, of course not. He chided himself for letting the thought crawl into his head. His father never had to worry about things like that. His parents married long before there was any wealth. Their relationship was based on true love, or so it seemed to John.

"Your father is one of the kindest and most generous men I've ever met. You're lucky to have him." Teri pulled a book from a shelf, she flipped the cover open and inspected it. She closed it, replaced the volume and took out another. John scanned the area around the desk where he knew the reference books were shelved.

Lucky indeed. He loved his father and considered him to be nearly a saint. Still, being compared with him got tiresome. Having a successful father brought a certain burden of expectation with it. His father cast a big shadow.

"This is incredible. Many of these are first editions. This collection must be worth a fortune." Teri's excitement was catching and John watched amused as she examined the shelves floor to ceiling.

"Dad has a thing for originals. Art, books, cars, whatever. He even has his original wife."

"Lucky for you, silly. Lucky for them too. It's so rare to find a couple who has managed to stay together their entire lives. It must be wonderful."

John looked at her beautiful face as she intently searched the book titles anticipating another interesting discovery. "I guess you just have to find the right person."

She turned and looked into his eyes and whispered. "I guess."

A tremor ran down his back and she turned away before he could think of anything to say. Her attention was drawn to the highest shelf in the study where there was a very large hardbound book held in place by two bookends shaped like elephants. John's stomach tightened at the realization that this was what had her interest.

"Dad has always loved his books. He and mother are especially fond of the African ones. See, he has them way up on the top shelves. He only let me see the special ones a couple of times and that was when he held them and I just got to look. Now where the hell is the dictionary?"

"I told you not to bother. 'Zebu' is a word and I get a triple word score for it, which puts me in the lead and gives me the win."

"I don't think so. Hey, look at this. He's got a new computer and copy machine in here now. Dad's gone really high-tech since I was in here last." John continued searching for the elusive dictionary. When he turned around he saw that Teri had found the polished rolling ladder and moved it along its track to a position under the African books. The back of his neck started to tighten. "Teri, what are you doing?"

"I just want to peek at those books up there."

"We probably shouldn't."

Teri made an exaggerated face like a child deprived of an ice-cream cone. "Please."

The combination of her playfulness and his own curiosity prompted him to relent. As a child he had often wondered what was in those books and this presented him a perfect opportunity. He abandoned his search for the dictionary and watched her climb the ladder and stop near the top to examine the books in the African section. The ladder was not quite tall enough for her to reach the highest shelf. "Wow, look at the book at the very top. It's huge, I can almost make out the title."

John moved to steady the ladder. "It's too high. Leave it alone."

"No, I think I can get it."

On the uppermost rung of the ladder she stretched to reach the book. "It's called *Valley of the Rhinos*." Her fingertips just reached the base of the book and John's heart leaped several beats in alarm at her precarious position.

"Hey, lover, be careful up there!"

"Quit looking up my dress." Then she smiled at him. She stretched as high as she could and tugged at the book again. Without warning the volume slipped free and fell toward the floor. John quickly dodged the heavy volume as it crashed onto the thick carpet. The sudden movement caused Teri to lose her balance and she grabbed the bookshelf to steady herself. With her feet on the upper rung, all she could do was hug the bookshelf and hold tight with her fingertips.

John held his breath and climbed the ladder. Stopping one rung below her, he wrapped an arm reassuringly around her waist.

"I hate heights, so don't get fresh and just get us down." There was a slight quiver in her voice and he realized she was very frightened. In the years that he had known her this was the first time she seemed even remotely out of control of her emotions. He reproached himself for letting her get in this predicament. He should have gone after the book himself instead of letting her stretch for it.

He tried not to betray his own fears. A fall would probably break both their necks. "Darn, just when I had you where I wanted you."

They slowly moved down the ladder one step at a time. He kept his arm around her until they were almost to the bottom. Safely on the floor, they sat down as if even standing were too risky for the moment. They leaned back on the rich carpet and held each other. John's heart was still pounding. Seeing the most precious thing in his life, miles in the air, on the verge of falling, had taken his breath away.

"Don't do that again." He hoped it had not sounded like a lecture. Teri was already sensitive about anything that made it appear one or the other of them was controlling the relationship.

"I will if I want to." He could tell she was trying to hide a smile.

"I know, but don't, okay?"

"Maybe." She laughed nervously. "I think I scared myself. How about some more champagne?"

"Good idea." John retrieved the champagne bottle from the desk where he had put it. When he returned and filled their glasses Teri was sitting cross-legged on the floor with the large closed book in front of her. He poured the wine and took a seat on the carpet beside her.

"How's the book?"

"It looks okay. I'm not sure it's a book."

The volume was twice the size of a big dictionary. The cover was worn brown leather. The words *Valley of the Rhinos* were embossed on the cover in white. Beneath the title in smaller letters were the names of John's parents.

John saw that when the volume crashed to the floor it had spilled its contents onto the carpet.

"What's this?" Teri handed him an intricately carved object about nine inches long and polished to a high gloss.

"I don't know. It looks like a horn." John examined it in the light.

"It came out of the book. So did this." Teri held up a thick folded paper. John could see now that the book really wasn't a book at all, but a well-disguised case for the horn. The interior was shaped to keep the horn from rattling or moving about. Teri started unfolding the large sheet of paper on the carpet. "Look, it's a map."

John examined the brightly colored map. It was hand drawn with exquisite detail. Mountains and animals of all descriptions decorated the border. "This is someplace in Africa. I can't make out the language. Wait, look at the back here. It looks like my father's handwriting." He peered closer.

*"In the longest of years,*
*At the dawn of the day when sun and moon are faced,*
*This map knows a place where two who are one,*
*May find a treasure beyond the dreams they may hold,*
*the rhino's horn will show the way.*
*Adventurer be warned, one on his own,*
*or two who are two, will be cursed at this place,*
*In the way of this world."*

"Johnny, it's a treasure map! Your father has a treasure map."

He heard her words but they didn't register. He ran his finger around the edge of the map that was decorated with wonderfully drawn African animals. The document was obviously made to navigate with and the topographic features were detailed and precise.

John let his breath out. This thing might answer a lot of questions. He knew that his father had grown up, relatively poor, during the Depression. It wasn't until a few years after the war that he started to make his fortune. This map had to have something to do with that.

A car's headlights illuminated the window outside. John's pulse rate leapt and he moved to the window risking a quick look out. "It's Enya!"

"What's she doing here? I thought you said your sister was away for the weekend."

"That's what she told me. We have to put this away."

"Johnny, let's make a copy."

Teri picked up the map and ran to the copy machine by the desk. John flicked off the study lights and met her at the copier. She pressed the power button, illuminating the green light. A message glowed PLEASE WAIT. THE COPIER IS WARMING UP.

The dim light from the hallway was just enough for them to see by. The green control lights of the copier reflected off Teri's face giving her an ethereal appearance. Her eyes were wide in anticipation and she nervously licked her lips.

John tapped his finger on the copier. "Blast. We don't have time for this. If Enya catches us in here she'll flip."

"What's she going to do? She's been in here without permission too. You told me so yourself."

It took forever, but finally the copier message changed to READY. Teri had flattened the map on the glass and instantly pressed the gray copy button. A white swath of light passed underneath the map giving her face an unearthly bright white illumination as it went by. She quickly flipped the map over and repeated the process.

"I had to reduce it to make it fit. Let's check it."

"No time." John snapped the machine off, grabbed the map and refolded it along the creases that were already there. He quickly put it back in the book with the horn and hurried up the ladder. The room was suddenly hot and he had to pause to wipe sweat from his brow to keep it out of his eyes. At the top he made one lunge shoving the book into place.

He nearly jumped down the ladder and took Teri by the hand intending to race out of the door before his sister appeared. As they reached the door a hall light switched on indicating Enya's imminent arrival. They were trapped.

"Come on, I have an idea." Teri tugged at his hand and dragged him back to the leather chair behind his father's desk. She pushed him into it, placed their champagne flutes prominently on the desk then swiftly pulled off her sweater and unbuttoned the top two buttons of her green blouse. To his surprise she jumped into his lap, wrapped her arms around him, and pulled him close. He could feel the copy tucked inside her blouse. She drew him tight and kissed him on the lips just as Enya came to the door.

Her soft lips were hot against his. Big plus marks to Teri for thinking of this. It was probably the only thing they could be caught doing in the study that would throw Enya off.

"What are you two doing in here? I can't believe this. In Dad's chair no less. You're disgusting. You two will do it anywhere. Get out of here!"

John looked at his sister in mock surprise. "Really Enya, like you've never done it. Lighten up."

"I never did it in here."

John could see Teri's face starting to flush pink. He held up his champagne bottle. "Bubbly?"

Enya's stare was cold as she considered the question. Then she gave a thin smile. "Love some."

Teri stood and picked her sweater up holding it demurely in front of her. John retrieved a glass from the wet bar in the study, filled it and handed it to Enya. She looked at the champagne bottle suspiciously.

"Is this his?"

"Of course not. Cheers." They clinked their glasses. Teri was still flushed and Enya was looking around the study eerily lit by the dim light that spilled in from the hall.

"You guys find anything . . . interesting in here?"

John shook his head no. "Not even a dictionary."

As a group they walked into the hall with Enya pulling the door shut behind them. She held her hand out and John surrendered the key. Enya slipped the key in the lock and turned it. The tumblers fell with a click and she looked at him.

"You two better take off. Have fun."

John had to clench his teeth to keep from laughing as he and Teri hurried down the hall and away from his sister.

3

BARZAN LEANED OVER THE RAIL OF THE RUSTING
freighter as the hull slowly nestled against the dock. The
heat was oppressive and he wiped his forehead with a sweat-
stained rag from his back pocket.

On the pier below, the black Africans moved lazily in the
afternoon heat. They were in no apparent hurry to tie up or prepare to unload the ship. Barzan raised his head and scanned the
familiar shoreline of the harbor in Mombasa. The port was half-
full of ships in various stages of being loaded or unloaded in the
afternoon sun. Flags from a dozen countries hung limp on their
poles with no breeze to move them. He went to the other side of
the boat and after making sure the top of the dirty rope ladder was
tied fast to the ship's cleats he tossed the rest over the side.

The smell of the rotting jungle, mixed with that of open-air
cookstoves and burning rubbish, gave the air a distinctly foul
odor. Barzan silently cursed the slow-moving men and retreated
back to his cramped compartment. All he wanted to do was get
off this ship. He hated traveling by sea and only did so because it
provided more anonymity than flying.

By disembarking in the port, he could easily elude the Kenyan
customs officials and keep his presence officially unknown. Barzan
collected his heavy green duffel bag filled with his personal

essentials and returned to the deck. He looked out over the blue harbor trying to find the small boat that was to pick him up.

It was only a few minutes before a battered launch with two Africans pulled alongside of the freighter. Barzan gave his man Kip a slight wave of greeting. He didn't recognize the other man who was steering the boat and assumed he must be the owner of the rusty launch.

As soon as the small boat was close enough, Barzan tossed his bag to Kip and then quickly descended the rope ladder. The moment his feet touched the launch the pilot accelerated away from the freighter. The sudden jolt caught Barzan by surprise and he fell to the fishy smelling bottom of the boat cursing.

"Damn you infidel! Watch what you are doing."

The pilot smiled and nodded. "I was hired to pick up a valuable cargo. No mention was made of a clumsy one."

Barzan shot a look at Kip who avoided his eyes and scrambled to pick up the duffel bag. There had better be a reason he had hired such a fool. Barzan managed to right himself and find an uncomfortable rough wooden seat in the back of the boat. He looked at the driver with contempt. "You will not think me so clumsy when I cut the tongue from your mouth."

"And you will not ask about what I am doing when I deliver you to the authorities. You see there, directly ahead of us?"

Barzan turned and his breath froze in his chest when he recognized a Kenyan customs patrol boat heading almost directly at them.

"Ten more seconds, Mister Cut Your Tongue Out, and they would have seen you getting off the freighter. It would have been a very sticky situation for you, I'm sure." The African laughed. "Maybe I will double my fee."

Kip nearly hissed at the driver. "You will be paid more than generously, as we agreed, but only after we are safe onshore."

Barzan forced himself to look away from the patrol boat. "Being a sound businessman, I'm certain you understand the value of living up to your deals." He struggled to keep the fear that gripped his heart from showing in his face. The heat of the sun was even more oppressive here than on the ship. He could feel sweat soaking his shirt.

"Yes, Mister Cut Your Tongue Out, I understand, and you can be assured I am every bit as honest a businessman as you."

This was not at all reassuring. In fact it almost sounded like a threat. Barzan recognized the world for what it was, an oyster to be cracked and devoured by those who had the nerve. Honesty was only something that was useful when convenient. It was Allah's will that he was able to know when he should use it and when he should not.

The driver turned his back to Barzan and steered the boat closer to the shore. Kip looked uncomfortable in the front, his long legs cramped in the small space. On his own rough seat Barzan tried to find a position that offered as little discomfort as possible. He could hear the approaching patrol launch. Barzan knew smugglers who collected on both ends of a deal. They would get a hefty advance from a man coming into the county, then turn him over to the authorities to collect a reward. The hapless soul invariably found an untimely end in a filthy Kenyan jail cell. This was in some ways an admirable plan, but Barzan found it shortsighted. The thieves who did this could not stay in business long for soon their reputations damned them.

Barzan could only sweat and hope that Kip had promised this man that his fee would be paid only upon safe delivery. He briefly wondered if Kip might have planned to keep some of the money himself, but then decided that would make little sense because Kip knew he would make more money staying by his side. Still, he knew that at times even a little money could turn a man against an old ally.

The odor of rotten fish and engine exhaust swirled past his face and his stomach knotted as the skiff drew closer to the patrol boat. Barzan looked to the customs boat for any sign that something unusual was happening. In the front of the skiff Kip, who when standing was almost seven feet tall, gave Barzan a half-smile and pulled a cigarette from his khaki shirt pocket.

The launch was almost even with the patrol boat now. The uniforms of the crew were clearly discernible. The pistols on their belts and the submachine guns on their shoulders were more than Barzan had any hope of being able to overcome. He smiled at the customs men. The pilot of his boat slowed the engine. Barzan swallowed hard, his body went rigid. He was helpless and he hated it. Was this a betrayal? He fought off a wave of panic.

He touched the knife under his shirt. The handle was rough against his sweating palm. He might not be able to avoid the customs men, but he would have the satisfaction of gutting his boat driver and Kip before he was captured.

The pilot waved to the customs boat. "Jambo!"

The crew of the patrol looked at him and the other two in the launch with bored faces. One soldier raised his hand and gave a half wave to them. Then the patrol boat passed on the port side and continued on its course toward the freighter.

Barzan slowly exhaled in relief. He turned to Kip. "A cigarette. I would like one please."

Kip gave him a cigarette but Barzan could scarcely hold it straight enough for him to light it. When the boat driver saw his trembling hands he laughed out loud. His heart pounded and a seething rage burned inside Barzan's skin. He took a deep drag off his smoke and let it out. Soon they would be on land. Soon they would be off this infernal boat and he would be free to walk as a man should. And then, then this parasite of a boat owner would know what it was like to be afraid.

"So tell me, Mister Honored Client, did you have a fear back there? I thought for certain that you rhino poachers had no fears. That any man who could survive in the bush and kill the great rhinos would never give a poor customs boat a second thought."

Barzan took another drag from the cigarette. "For such a little man, you have a very big mouth. Perhaps you will shut it before it makes you sorry."

Kip wiped sweat from his forehead and looked at the driver. "You might do well to listen to my friend."

The driver laughed again. They rode in silence for the next few minutes. Barzan's thoughts returned to the port of Mombasa. This, he knew, was a truly dangerous city. Not only was it home to a huge population of displaced Masai, but it was the departure and embarkation point for all manner of cutthroats, thieves, poachers and pirates who used the waterways of the Indian Ocean. From here there was unlimited access to the shores of the rich oil sheikdoms of the Persian Gulf and the interior of the African continent.

Here a man's reputation was essential to his survival. Any slight must be dealt with swiftly and decisively or he would be besieged by those seeking to prey on the unfit.

Barzan did not particularly mind that Mombasa was dangerous, as he considered himself to be one of the men who made it that way. Mombasa was like the rest of Africa, a bad place for the weak or unwary.

The boat slowly went up a shallow side channel, lined with reeds and overgrown by the jungle. They reached a ramshackle dock and the pilot tied a worn rope to a broken piling to secure the launch. A building, little more than shack, leaned against a palm tree at the end of a long wooden walkway.

Barzan noted with satisfaction that the dock was isolated and out-of-sight of the rest of the harbor. It was perfect for his anonymous arrival. The driver climbed onto the dock and Kip handed him the green duffel bag. Barzan noticed a pair of ancient pliers resting by the engine. When the insolent driver started up the dock Barzan slipped the tool into his pocket, he then hauled himself onto the dock. He stumbled, quickly recognizing that his unsteadiness was due to 'sea legs.' He cursed ocean travel and looked forward to the next day when his legs would be steady again.

The driver dropped the green bag on the walkway. "Are you going after rhinos, or is the Chui going after the treasure of the rhinos?"

Barzan seethed. The infidel had said two things that infuriated him. First he had called Barzan, the Chui, the Swahili name for a leopard. This referred to someone who killed without warning. It was a name he had been given on his first trip to Africa. That time he had stolen a load of rhino horns from another poacher he had killed. It was a name he was given behind his back and held the connotation of one who wouldn't face a fight. Second, the man had mentioned the legend of the rhino's treasure.

If the treasure existed, it would make a man wealthy beyond his dreams. But because it was probably a myth, anyone who looked for it was presumed a fool. Barzan was not ready to admit he believed in it, but its promise of riches beckoned him.

This common boat driver had managed to call Barzan, the terror of the black market of Aden, a murderer and a fool in one sentence. After the indignity on the launch, it was too much for him. A man living in Mombasa should have better sense than to show such disrespect.

"I told you to still your tongue while it remains in your mouth."

The driver laughed as if he could calm Brazan by making a joke of this. He started backing away from him. "Remember, Chui, only one who has love can search out the rhino's treasure. All others are doomed."

Kip stepped behind the driver, cutting him off from escaping up the dock. Barzan moved toward him. "What do you know of the treasure?"

The boatman looked between the towering Kip and Barzan nervously. "I only know that an English took the map during the big war. Nothing more."

All this insect had to offer was worthless news on top of insults. Barzan could no longer tolerate the sight of the trembling man in front of him.

Barzan motioned to Kip. The tall African immediately grabbed the startled boat driver from behind and dragged him down the dock into the broken-down shack.

Kip held the man in a headlock, his forearm nearly squeezing the driver's throat shut. His eyes were wild with fear. Barzan and Kip quickly tied the struggling man to a beam inside the decaying building.

Barzan reached inside his pocket and took out the pliers. He jammed them through the man's teeth, pinched the tongue and pulled it out as far as he could. With his other hand Barzan reached inside his shirt and withdrew his knife with the eight-inch blade. He held it in front of the squirming man's face.

"I hope the fish that eat your tongue do not choke on it." Barzan slashed the tongue off and held the bloody red lump in front of the boatman's eyes. The infidel howled in agony splattering blood over Barzan's face and shirt. Kip jammed a cloth into the bloody mouth and held it in with his hand. In a fury Barzan went to the window and threw the tongue and pliers into the brackish water.

Barzan stepped back and made sure the driver could see him smile. He then plunged the knife into the driver's belly and ripped it up until he felt it jam against the ribs. The man grunted in agony and blood poured out of him onto Barzan's hands and clothes and onto the floor where it was instantly slippery under his feet.

The driver gurgled blood out of his mouth with his last breath. Barzan's heart pounded and he thought he felt part of the man's life essence pass through the knife into his own body. He yanked the blade out of the clinching muscles of the chest and wiped it off on the driver's clothes.

Breathing heavily he smiled at Kip as he put the knife into his belt. "Perhaps others will benefit from this lesson."

Kip lowered his eyes. "Yes, Bwana."

"Be sure that they do." Being referred to as Bwana, signaled to him that his position was clear. It was good to be back in Africa.

A few minutes later, wearing a change of clothes, Barzan led Kip, who was carrying his bag, away from the dock. He was confident his man would spread the news of the price one paid for crossing the Chui.

c h a p t e r

4

JOHN SHOVED HIS LEATHER BRIEFCASE INTO THE overhead compartment of the plane and took his place in his first-class seat. He let out a deep breath. Friday night, finally. Time to get back to Teri. They had been apart for five nights, much too long a time to be reasonable. He tried to calculate how fast this plane could load its passengers and get up the coast to San Francisco. He figured that if the plane left as scheduled he could be with Teri in two hours and eighteen minutes. Still too long.

She was all he could think about the last few days. He closed his eyes and swallowed hard when he remembered a meeting he had been in and how he was caught totally off guard by a question when his thoughts had drifted from the discussion at hand. It was a good thing Les had been there to bail him out. Dad owned the company, but John liked to stay on top of things. Some of these people actually thought he didn't know his job. It always amused him to straighten them out.

John was thankful that his friend and confidant, Les was on the team. Les didn't need the work, but he enjoyed the deals and thrived on making business operations better and improving profits. It was like a game to him and the higher the stakes the better he liked it. Les was one of the few people John had ever met who could remotely understand how he felt. Les' family had made a fortune in the newspaper business. He had confronted many of the same issues that bedeviled John when he was growing up.

They had met when they were both cutting class from high school and surfing south of Santa Cruz, trying to blend in with the locals. It didn't take long before they recognized that neither of them was going to make it as a surf bum and they became fast friends. They ended up going to college together at the University of California at Santa Barbara. They turned down Stanford, too snobby, and Berkeley, too close to home. Santa Barbara had a reputation for women and parties that turned out happily, to be well deserved.

These trips were all starting to be the same. He, Les and a couple of trusted lawyers and accountants would show up, give a subsidiary and its senior managers a thorough grilling then decide if a change was needed. Once John and his staff had learned to work together they became pretty effective. John enjoyed that most of the men and women they met were honest and hardworking. However, his team had quickly developed a reputation for finding what, or who, needed fixing. When the word had gotten out that they could not be buffaloed, and that they didn't screw around with incompetents, they got the respect and cooperation they needed. Representing his father well was the most satisfying part of the job.

Since his team had already slain most of the obvious dragons, John had recently come to regard the whole effort as little more than waving the corporate flag just so the local executives wouldn't forget who was king of the hill. After all, if there was a real problem it would show up in the profit and loss column and none of Dad's operations ever had a loss column, for long. Yes, this job had become a bore. He'd have to ask if there was something more challenging he could do, something that might be more meaningful.

Starting up his own profit center might be good. Maybe he could find a way to bring in some new revenue. Even in this saturated market there might still be room for some innovative e-commerce. Though he didn't have the Stanford M.B.A. most of his father's staff had, he thought his time as an officer in the Rangers helped put him on equal footing in almost any situation.

Months of leadership training, commanding troops in the field, and being in a position where his word was law was something that was not taught in any business school. He would just have to figure out how to get ahead of all the M.B.A.'s based on his performance.

The flight attendant took his drink order as the coach passengers started to file into the back section. As was often the case, he noticed that as they shuffled by most of them pretended not to notice the first-class seats. At the same time his seatmate, Les, and the rest of the entourage buried their noses in books or work notes and pretended not to notice the throng of people squeezing past them inches away.

John felt neither smug nor superior to be sitting up front, this was simply his natural place in the world. He knew he was extremely fortunate. He closed his eyes and rubbed some of the tightness out of his neck. Maybe lucky was the word. Yes he was clearly lucky, an accident of birth and here he sat at the front of the bus through no real doing of his own. And now there was Teri. Lucky was the word indeed.

When he opened his eyes, the flight attendant had returned with the bottle of sparkling water he had requested and a glass of ice with a twist of lime. She had a nice smile. He thanked her and she turned back to the galley.

The last of the boarding passengers finally managed to get seated and when the door was shut and locked he checked his watch again. Nuts, they were going to be late pushing back. He adjusted his safety belt and tried to get comfortable in the seat. He noticed his right foot was tapping a rhythm on its own. He drank his water, consuming almost the entire glass at once. It was cold and fresh and the sparkling bubbles reminded him of champagne.

He wondered if Teri would have any champagne at her apartment when he got there. Sure she would, after all, they had three things to celebrate. First the weekend, second his return from this ridiculously long trip, and third the unveiling if the map.

He had to figure out what the map represented and how and if it could have had an impact on his parents' lives. A slight shiver went down his neck and he adjusted the overhead air vent. Getting a good long look at that thing would be an event they'd make into an occasion. Over the last few years they had developed their own rituals for little occasions, or big ones. Having someone special, simply to have fun with was nice.

The plane started to roll back, prompting him to check his watch again. More time had gone by. More wasted time. That was it, the bottom line. Time away from Teri, away from that smile, that wit, that wonderful body was simply wasted time. He'd been in love before but this was different. He had never imagined he could feel so strongly about a woman. It was unsettling.

He thought about calling her right now, then remembered she was volunteering at the women's shelter tonight. Once a week, sometimes twice, after work, she would spend four to six hours working with battered women. He was never really sure what she did exactly. Sometimes it was answering phones, other times it was some kind of counseling. Either way it always seemed to leave her wound up, but she never talked about it with him.

He admired that she did the work and he even wrote the place a couple of big checks she didn't know about. He had a slight suspicion that her giving so much of herself to women who had been victimized made her suspicious of all men. Her endless questions about the nature of their relationship, the rules and boundaries that she constantly needed reassurance of, made him think she had a fairly low opinion of men in general.

Diamond Lies 35

She certainly was not alone there. Most guys were decent folks and given the chance would try to do the right thing. However, John knew a lot of men were little more than walking hostility, who felt they needed to prove something at every turn. He loathed these types and was certain the world would be a better place without them.

Or maybe Teri was leery of men's motives partly because her father and her brother froze her out of the family business. She had told him they rarely talked to her after she went to college, instead of staying home to take care of them. John sat back in his chair and watched the lights on the runway go by as he continued to put the Teri puzzle together.

That guy she was dating before was a jerk. Dumped her to go running back to southern California to open a surfboard shop with his buddy. Maybe if you're a surfer, girls are so easy to come by that you can toss one off now and then. The guy had tried to get her back, but too late. She would have nothing to do with him anymore. Too bad for him. His loss was John's gain. Only a fool would let this woman go. In the broad sense, her relationship hang-ups were only an annoyance and sooner or later he was sure he'd get them under control.

Her occasional tendency to question him about the relationship, a habit he laughingly referred to as the Spanish Inquisition, was not worth getting too worked up over. He was just glad she did not get that way very often.

Finally the plane turned onto the runway and the engines revved up as it took off. Once the plane was in the air he took a deck of cards from his pocket and dealt himself a hand of solitaire.

———

John opened his eyes to Teri's darkened bedroom and the pleasant sight of her smile. She was standing by the bed and leaned down to softly kiss his cheek.

"Come on sleepy head, let's go look at the map."

She seemed amazingly energetic considering the extended lovemaking session they had just had. John briefly wondered if he were just getting old. No that was a stupid thought. Women always got up first.

The sound of the rain on the window had been replaced by a CD playing one of Teri's favorite jazz singers. He realized she must have been up for a long time. She had already showered and he guessed she'd had two cups of coffee. She gently shook his arm and knelt down to let her hair fall against his face tickling him so he had to brush it away.

"Come on lover, time to get up. You've been asleep for hours."

"So what? I'm one of the last of the idle rich."

"Only if you could stand to be idle. Let's check out the map. You've made me wait all week and now I want to see it. I'm so excited." She danced off the bed in time with the music and swirled her red silk robe in a billowing circle. Her exuberance was catching. It made him want to get out of bed just to keep it going.

He threw the bedclothes off and scrambled to get his robe on.

"If that's what it takes to get you excited, I'm finding some more maps."

"You are so bad." Teri kissed him again and disappeared down the hall that led to the kitchen.

Every time they had talked on the phone during the week she had mentioned the map. They had speculated half-seriously, half-jokingly, that it could lead to either the secrets of the Erikson fortune or just a wild-goose chase. John was not sure which answer he wanted to be right. He had always enjoyed the notion that his father was a brilliant businessman. But if he turned out to be an adventurer who made his own luck, well that was not so bad either.

After a refreshing shower he followed the pleasant scent of warm cookies to the kitchen. Teri sat expectantly at the table, a glass of red wine by her right hand and a plate of chocolate chip cookies by her left. She had the afternoon newspaper, open to the fashion section, spread on the table in front of her. The kitchen smelled of simmering spaghetti sauce, rich with garlic and black pepper. On the stove beside the red sauce, a pot of water was coming to a boil in preparation for the pasta.

The place had an intimate cozy feel. It was small but not uncomfortably so. With Teri here, it was his favorite place to be. He enjoyed the irony that he had found proof you didn't need truckloads of money to have a happy home. John gave her a kiss.

He selected a bottle of whiskey from her modest liquor cabinet and poured a shot over a few cubes of ice from the freezer. He sat at the table with her and hunted for the sports section of the paper.

"Can we look at the map as soon as dinner is over?" Teri folded her section of the paper and started clearing the table even before he'd had the chance to spread out the sports page.

Her smile was as fresh and eager as a child's the day before Christmas. Except for the brief glance they'd taken the night they found the map, neither of them had looked at it since. The idea crossed his mind again that they might find something he didn't want to know. The map had been hidden by his father for a reason and the thought of discovering something that could be deep and dark about his father caused his stomach to knot. The idea of treading into forbidden territory caused his heart to pound a little harder.

Teri started setting the table and John automatically got the dinner dishes out of the cabinet. Setting the plates on the table he noticed she had put the knives facing the wrong direction, he flipped them over so they were set correctly.

Teri laughed at him. "I guess I'd better get that right before we invite your mother and father over. I wouldn't want them to think I ain't got no breeding."

"I don't think they would give it a second thought, I'm probably just too picky. Did you take a peek at the map while I was gone?"

She put a plate of steaming pasta and sauce in front of him. "No, I was good. It was hard to resist but I wanted to wait until you were here."

Watching the anticipation in her eyes, he knew that making an occasion of the unveiling had been a good idea. It would be a splendid way to spend a Saturday night. "Thanks for waiting. You know I hate being away from you." He took a bite of dinner and then a sip of the red wine.

"I hate it when you go away too. I hope you don't have many more of these long trips coming up."

"There is one condition for looking at the map."

"Oh, come on. You already promised."

"You have to go out to your car and get it." He smiled at his own tease. He enjoyed the way she reacted to things that were totally off-the-wall.

She laughed. "Dreamer."

"But it's raining out."

"You're the guy."

"Is that an admission of feminine weakness?"

"Do you want to sleep by yourself tonight?"

After they were finished eating, and John had cleared and washed the dinner dishes, he retrieved the map from her car, getting only slightly wet. Teri opened another bottle of wine in celebration and filled her two best wineglasses with a cabernet they had purchased for the occasion.

"Too bad we don't have a drum roll." With a dramatic flair, John spread the two-page copy of the map over the wooden dining table. Teri smoothed the document with her hands and they almost bumped heads when they bent over to look at it.

It was immediately obvious that the copy had not picked up the nuances of the original. Two of the edges were not captured and many of the words were unreadable. The vivid colors he remembered were not nearly as sharp on the copy. Even so, he was intrigued by what he saw.

The map detailed an area with exotic names that he had only read about in books. It mainly covered the Serengeti Plain of Kenya, Tanzania and Masilan. The area near the borders gave reference headings and distances to Dar es Salaam, and Mombasa on the Indian Ocean, as well as to Lake Tanganyika to the west.

Near the center of the front of the map was an area marked as the Olduvai Gorge, the birthplace of man. John put his finger on the concentric lines showing the elevation of the area around the gorge. A brief shiver went down his back. His parents must have been interested in something near here.

"Look at all the animals." Teri ran her fingers around the border over a series of hand drawn figures. There were elephants, giraffes, lions, hippos and many, many rhinos.

She pointed to the right edge. "Look how different these rhinos are."

He recognized the different species. "A few years ago, after their last safari, Dad told me about the rhinos. The ones with the long curved horns are the black rhinos. I think they're almost extinct. The few that are left are supposedly protected now. The ones with the shorter horns are the white rhinos. There are more of them still alive."

Teri continued to study the rhinos. "The black ones are still endangered? I thought they were safe on game preserves."

"They're poached for their horns."

Teri rubbed a picture of a rhino with her finger. "I've heard of that, but I never understood why. I get the value of the ivory from elephant tusks, but what would you do with a rhino horn?"

"Mysticism mostly I think. The Japanese think the horns can be used to make aphrodisiacs." He glanced at her face and their eyes briefly met. He suppressed a smile.

Teri blushed. "That's one thing you'd never need."

John's loins tensed. "Not with you around anyway."

They both took a sip of wine and turned back to the chart. "I also think the Chinese believe ground horn has great medicinal value. There's even someplace in the Middle East where they use rhino horns for dagger handles." John ran his fingers over the front page of the map. It was smooth paper. The texture of the original had been rougher.

This copy would never last a day being dragged around outside, folded and unfolded a hundred times with sweaty hands, in the rain or whatever. And it was definitely not as clear as he remembered the original.

It was becoming obvious to him that this version of the map was not going to surrender the secrets he had thought it might hold. His disappointment was tempered by Teri's total fascination with it.

Teri kept staring at the pictures on the borders. "That is so sad about the rhinos. Sometimes people are so ruthless it's disgusting. How can they be like that?"

The sadness in her voice didn't surprise him. She was so easily touched by the unfair. "I'm not trying to justify it, but these animals are in dirt poor countries. I think the value of these horns is huge in terms of the money that can be made from them. Maybe it's a question of who survives, the animals or the people."

He checked her face to see if he could gauge a reaction. He had tried to sound offhand because he knew she didn't like being lectured. As smart as she was there was still a lot about the world he had picked up that was out of the realm of her experience. He was relieved when she shook her head and replied. "I'm glad I don't have to make those kinds of choices."

He leaned close to the map to examine the topographic lines near the center. "These lines didn't copy very well. It looks like the crease from the fold caused some distortion. You can see it all through here, and look at the edges, some of the writing didn't make it."

Teri put her face close enough to the map for her hair to lightly brush it. John could smell the light herbal fragrance of her shampoo. He liked her feminine side, but he also liked that she was intelligent. She had a fresh innocent energy about her that countered his own boredom with most of the world. For a moment he considered forgetting the map and taking her back to bed, but her voice interrupted his thoughts.

Teri pointed to a city named Arusha on the map. "What do you think this is?"

She traced her finger over a faint line that left Arusha and ran at angles that changed frequently and moved toward the middle of the map. At each place the angle changed there was a number. "And what are these numbers?"

John's heart rate accelerated. "It's a plot line."

"A what?"

"It's a navigation course. It's what you follow. It's why the map exists."

She ran her finger to the end of the line, which was in a portion of the copy that was particularly poor. "You mean if you follow the line, then X marks the spot?"

John squinted to try to make out the symbol at her fingertip. "It's not an X."

"But it is a spot."

John looked closer and his breath left him. "No, it's a diamond."

He sat back in his chair as a flood of realization washed over him. His suspicions had been right. Somehow this damn map was tied to the family fortune. It was an honest-to-God treasure map. He had been right from the start. He wished his father had let him in on this. He leaned over the map looking for the coordinates that would go with the plot lines.

After a moment he found what he was looking for. He grimaced with disappointment. The map key that would give the compass headings and distances to the plot line was in a corner that had not copied. Only the first two headings were evident.

Teri looked at him. "Is it good enough to follow?"

"No, I don't think so. The best I can make out are general places. It looks like it leads to a place in Masilan but the lines are too wrinkled to tell the exact spot. There's a lot of territory here. This is useless for navigation without the key."

Teri put her finger on the words written in John's father's hand. "What do you think this legend means? The part about two who are one?"

"Siamese twins obviously."

Teri straightened up and whacked him on the arm. "You rat. What do you really think it means?"

"I'm not very good at riddles."

"Well, I think it means two lovers who are one, together. Like us."

John avoided her eyes and kept his focus on the map. He hoped this would not start the relationship inquisition. His shoulders tensed and he pressed on trying to prevent an opening to that line of questioning. "Then the rest of the legend is a warning. It must mean don't go with somebody else or disaster will follow."

"That's exactly what it means. If you go there with someone besides me you'll be in big trouble, buddy." She moved behind him, rubbed his shoulders with her strong fingers and kissed him on the back of the neck.

The warmth of her breath and the touch of her hands relaxed him again. He closed his eyes and tried to make sense of the riddle. The whole notion was preposterous, but it was fascinating. He tried to imagine what it would be like traveling into the heart of Africa with Teri. It could be heaven. Or it could be something else entirely.

"This is interesting, but I have to admit I'm a little disappointed. I really wanted to solve the puzzle and plan an adventure. I've been looking forward to this all week." Teri's thoughts mirrored his own.

John let her continue to rub his neck. "To solve the puzzle we'll have to have a better copy than this."

"That means another trip into the library. I don't know if I like that. Your sister was really mad at us and I don't want her to turn against me this close to our wedding."

"Don't worry about Enya. I can deal with her and you know she likes you. She told me."

"I hope so, but how can we get the map again? If we had it for a couple of days I could get a professional reproduction made."

John thought about it for a minute. He was becoming more intrigued with the thing every time he looked at the black and white animals and African masks along the border. "There's something weird going on with this. It's a mystery that must have to do with my father's fortune. Dad was an Army Air Force pilot in the Second World War. It was only after the war that he became wealthy."

John leaned down to the map again. On the edges were words in a language he didn't recognize. Near them, and running off the copy, were translations in his father's handwriting. He couldn't quite make out the words. He tried to read a passage in a corner by a white rhino. His heart skipped a beat when he suddenly recognized letters in his mother's long script. All he could read was 'The journey starts' and the rest ran off to an area that had not copied.

His father hadn't been the only one to follow the map. His mother was there too, wherever there was. That made perfect sense. His parents were as close as any couple he had ever met. For his whole life they had been virtually inseparable. If his father had followed a treasure map, there was no way his mother would not have gone with him. A surge of elation charged through him. Maybe Teri was right and the legend was true after all. Maybe Teri was the one and finding the map had not been such an accident. The thought made him lightheaded, or maybe it was the wine.

John sat up so fast he nearly bumped his head into Teri's nose. "I can get the map the day after tomorrow, once Enya has gone back to L.A. but we have to put it back in perfect condition, before my parents return from China."

"WHAT DO YOU REALLY WANT?"

Teri posed the question so innocently and out of the blue that it caught John completely by surprise.

He eased the red convertible into the right lane of the Golden Gate Bridge so they would be in position to take the first Sausalito exit.

"I don't know. The usual stuff." He was buying time, trying to think of the right answer.

"Like what?" Her voice had that playful 'I want to get into your head' tone. His hands tightened on the steering wheel and he braced himself for what would come next. She would give him the relationship quiz, and he would try not to stick his foot in his mouth.

He hated this game. He glanced at her and saw the sun reflecting off her dark glasses. Her blonde hair was nearly perfectly in place in spite of the open top of the car. Taking a deep breath he smelled the clean ocean wind.

"I'd like to be successful in my own right. You know, in spite of my father's money."

"Is that why you joined the Rangers?"

"That was more to prove something to myself."

"Prove what? That you're a big macho stud?" She licked her lips and smiled.

"That didn't actually need proving. It was self-evident all along." He hoped the light response would move the conversation in a different direction. He was not sure why, but the 'what do you want' questions made him feel off balance.

She laughed and squeezed his leg. "Okay, so you've been there and done that. Now what do you want?"

He shifted gears and the convertible accelerated smoothly under his command. He was glad some things were easy to control. The wind was refreshing on his face, he glanced at Teri but could not read her expression. He knew he had to come up with an appropriately sensitive answer, or this conversation, and the afternoon, could take a bad turn south in a hurry. "I guess I'd like a comfortable place to live, a respectable job and a stable relationship. Why? What do you want?"

Even before he finished the last sentence he knew he'd blown it. He had neglected to put her at the top of his list. He gritted his teeth then stammered out the first recovery line he could think of. "I mean, I'm planning on you being with me."

His whole body tensed as he waited for her response. She was quiet for a long time. He took the first exit off the bridge and turned up the road that would take them to the green cliffs above where the ocean met the entrance to the bay. The scent of eucalyptus trees mixed with the salt breeze off the ocean. When she spoke, her words were measured and soft.

"I want you, Johnny. I want you more than anything and I want you to want me. I don't want an ordinary life. I want us to be special. I want us to last a lifetime."

He took his eyes off the road for an instant. Even with her sunglasses on he could see her staring at him. His cheeks felt flush and hot. His hands were sticky on the wheel. The sensation of falling nearly made him dizzy. For some reason, the word lifetime suddenly had taken on a new meaning for him. He kept his voice even. "Well, I want you, too. You know that."

"Do you?"

"Of course."

"Then why didn't you say so?"

God, not this again. All he really wanted right now was a nice champagne sunset, not another rehash of the whole relationship. She always wanted to talk about love and commitment and all that stuff on the covers of the magazines at the checkout counter. He never was sure why he always ended up on the defensive. Exasperated he hit the accelerator and the car jumped at his command.

Her response was immediate. "Slow down, Johnny, you're going too fast."

Reluctantly he slowed, then momentarily took his hand from the gearshift and stroked her hair. "I'm sorry it came out wrong. You know I put you, us, above everything."

"Sometimes I wonder if that's true. There are times I think I should reevaluate what we're doing." She had that tone in her voice, as if she knew those words alone would rattle him.

He sensed that this was a ploy to get his full attention, but the idea that she would back off from the relationship was a possibility he was not prepared to consider. The very thought turned him cold inside.

John picked a place to pull over and stopped the car on a bluff facing the sun setting over the Pacific. He shut the engine off and turned to her. "Why? Why do you have to start this now, less than seven weeks before the wedding?"

She stared out to sea and leaned away from him until her shoulder pressed against the passenger door. She crossed her arms as if the moist sea air had given her a sudden chill. "Johnny, you can be a little intimidating. We're so different, sometimes I can't help thinking you don't take me seriously. Every

man I've ever been close too, or felt deeply about has, well, disappointed me."

Her lips were tight and she had a slight catch in her voice.
John immediately recognized he'd pushed the wrong button. It
was time for immediate damage control. He knew a little reassurance would go a long way. He interrupted her before she could
continue.

"Listen Teri, I know we have different backgrounds. And I also
know that you struggle with trusting men. But remember this, our
different backgrounds are part of what makes us so good together. And more importantly, I'm not any of those other guys, so
please don't confuse me with them. I intend to be the one man in
your life who doesn't disappoint you."

John pulled a bottle of champagne from the cooler behind her
seat. He detected slight tears at the bottom of her sunglasses. He
looked around to make sure no cops were in sight and took the
foil off the top of the bottle. "What do I have to do? What caused
this? Here we are less than two months from our wedding, at one
of the most beautiful places in the world, and you have to bring
this up again. What's really going on?"

John opened the bottle and it made a satisfying pop as the
cork flew over the hood of the car and down the cliff towards the
foaming breakers below. Teri took two champagne flutes from
their padded place in the glove box and held them up while he
filled them. A smile started to form on her lips.

They clinked glasses and she took a sip of wine. She arched
her right eyebrow conspiratorially above her sunglasses and lowered her voice. "You have to promise not to laugh if I tell you
something."

This had a decidedly better sound to it. John was hoping the
little moment of crisis was over. "I promise."

"Last Friday Beth asked me to give her a ride to her psychic.
While I was there I figured, you know just for fun, I'd get a reading too."

John could almost hear alarm bells going off in his mind. He had only met Beth a couple of times but had the distinct impression she did not like men in general and him in particular. If Teri had been running around with her, there was no telling what kind of female idiocy she had put into Teri's head.

Teri continued, "The psychic told me that if the one I love didn't consider me first above everything else, then this wasn't the love I'm destined to be with. She also said I should break it off sooner rather than later."

"Where did Beth find this nut? You know she doesn't like me, she probably put the psychotic up to this." John strained to keep the laughter from his voice. This was a new wrinkle and even Teri was going to have to appreciate how silly it sounded.

"No she did not and you're making fun of me. This is serious, I'm worried." She pursed her lips but he could tell she was trying to keep from laughing too.

"You never like my friends. And what about your buddy, Les? Sometimes I'm sure he thinks I'm a ditz."

John laughed. "Never mind him, he likes you plenty. Hey maybe we should hook those two up." He was pleased to hear the sound of her laughter and see the smile back on her face.

He raised his glass for a toast. "To us and to the future."

She added, "To our future."

They touched glasses and took a sip of the sparkling wine. The sun streaked gold through the bubbles in his glass. She held her glass between them and let the California light dance on the liquid. He knew she was dreaming up something exotic behind her sunglasses. "If you don't believe in psychics, how can you believe in the legend of the map?"

The question was simple enough but it brought a tinge of reality to mind: psychics, legends, treasure maps, the one. He knew if he thought about it too long none of it would make sense. When he spoke he tried to sound offhand. "They're different. A legend is from the past. It's almost the truth. Psychics on the other hand, are nonsense. No one can tell the future."

"Do you believe in destiny?" Her expression was partly hidden behind her dark glasses.

He glanced at the sun lowering on the horizon. "Yes."

She leaned to him and kissed his lips. He nodded toward the ocean and slipped his arm around her shoulder. She snuggled next to him. The sometimes pungent wind carried the scent of seaweed and distant lands and the sound of waves piling onto the beach. The red-gold orb slipped below the horizon.

Teri took her sunglasses off and looked him in the eyes. "I can tell the future. I'm your destiny. Take us to Africa."

chapter

6

BARZAN STOOD IMPATIENTLY IN THE SHADE OF an acacia tree. He could see the mother rhino and its babies clearly and wanted his man to hurry and kill it. She had a fine horn, and even though it wasn't the big prize he hoped to find, it would still be worth plenty on the market in Yemen.

Barzan scanned the horizon for a dust plume that would be the telltale sign of an approaching ranger truck. He was acutely aware that every second they were here was an invitation to death. The Masilan rangers had reverted to their old orders. Any unescorted people found within the confines of the national parks would be shot on sight. He fanned himself with the cowboy hat he had bought on his last trip to Nairobi. The government and conservationists were such stupid people. Willing to kill humans just so rich western tourists could come spend money to stare at the animals.

Why hadn't the Afrikaner taken the shot yet? The animal was in plain sight. Even though Barzan was accustomed to the heat of his homeland in Iraq, there was something about the Serengeti that made him hot and uncomfortable. Sweat covered his shirt front and back and the band on his new hat was soaked. He hated waiting like this. He wanted the rhino dead, it's horn collected, and the poaching party on the way to the border as soon as possible.

The mother pawed the ground with a mammoth foot and raised her head looking in Barzan's direction. Her ears rotated forward and he wondered if she would flee. He was surprised by the touch of a hand on his shoulder and jerked around to find the blond Afrikaner standing behind him.

"We should leave this one alone. It has a couple of calves."

Barzan couldn't believe he was hesitating. "What do you mean leave it alone? Are you stupid? Is that why you lost your country? I hired you to kill rhinos for us. Now kill it. Quickly."

The Afrikaner shook his head. "Don't you see what a waste this would be? Sure I can kill it now, it would be easy. But the two little ones won't last a week without the mother. Before they starve a lion or the hyenas will take them for sure."

Barzan's blood pounded through his veins. Adrenaline shot into his system and he grimaced to keep from screaming at the imbecile in front of him. "The little ones are not your concern. Just kill the big one. Now, before the rangers come or she decides to run."

"A man as wise as you surely understands the necessity of leaving seeds to grow fruit for the future. There are few enough of these beasts left as it is."

Barzan burned with rage, but forced himself to appear calm. If only one of his men were halfway decent with a rifle he wouldn't have this problem. In the old days they just would have used machine guns to blast the beast and that would have been all there was to it. Nowadays, because of the stupid environmental people and the idiot laws they'd passed, he was forced to hire mercenaries with large-caliber rifles with great sound suppressors on them.

"Take the shot and I will double your fee."

The Afrikaner let out an insolent hiss and turned to look at the animal. He knelt down on one knee and shifted his rifle to the firing position. The .50 caliber was one of the longest-range and deadliest of all the big game rifles. There were not very many who could use it as effectively as this mercenary. Barzan wondered if the man had honed his skills shooting men in the civil wars in southern Africa.

Barzan considered the Afrikaner to be a thoroughly dangerous man. Not the kind to turn your back on, but a necessary evil for this job. Barzan suspected the shooter did not have the intellect to match his and made up for it by moving through the world with brute force. He was like the rhinos they were stalking, big, menacing and difficult to predict. He needed to be handled with respect.

The mother rhino had her nose in the wind and a tick bird flitted between her ears. Her horn rose into the air as she looked, this way and that, in a vain attempt to see an adversary. The men were two hundred meters away by Barzan's estimate and there was little chance she would see them through the brush the men were hiding behind.

His biggest concern was that she might smell them. If she bolted, they would have to risk a chase and that was something he definitely did not want to get involved in this close to a ranger outpost. If they had to run the animal down, the trucks would kick up huge plumes of dust that could be seen from miles away and would give away their position.

The Afrikaner steadied his rifle and Barzan watched him freeze in place as he took aim. The sound suppressor on the barrel made the weapon look impossibly long. The gray animal stood motionless in the sun, the tick bird busy picking flies out of her ears. The two smaller rhinos were asleep in the tall grass a few feet away.

The rifle went off with a dull thud. The rhino startled and for an instant Barzan thought the shot had missed. Then the beast collapsed to her front knees, paused, and fell onto her side slowly thrashing her legs in the grass and heaving for air.

He heard the five poachers who had been waiting in two four-wheel drive trucks behind a scrub bush turn the engines on and race to pick up Barzan and the Afrikaner. As they arrived the Afrikaner got to his feet and smiled at Barzan.

The tan trucks barely slowed to collect them and Barzan was jolted roughly against the metal door as they roared to the still kicking rhino. When they got within fifteen meters, one of the men in the truck opened fire with an automatic weapon with a silencer. The bullets peppered the dying animal and little black spots of blood appeared on the soft underside of the gray skin.

The vehicles came to a stop and Barzan directed the men to make sure the creature was dead before they approached. When he was sure it was safe he went to the nose and with a tape measure checked the length of the horn. As he had thought, it was a good one, almost a meter long and worth more than its weight in gold. He smiled knowing Moto-san would surely be pleased with this.

Kip approached with a fine toothed saw and Barzan showed him exactly where to cut. Some poachers used chain saws for this. Although they were faster, he considered them crude and destructive. After all, they weren't taking anything as vulgar as ivory.

Satisfied that the sawing was proceeding as ordered he looked for the Afrikaner. The blond man was leaning against one of the trucks smoking a filtered cigarette. He offered one to Barzan as he approached and Barzan accepted it. He enjoyed the taste of these fine South African smokes. He took a deep drag and instinctively scanned the horizon for any sign of the rangers.

"Too bad about the little ones. In a few years we could have collected from them too." The Afrikaner spit as if to emphasize his distaste for killing the mother.

"By the time a few years passed, either someone else would have killed the mother and taken her horn, or the rangers would have tranquilized them all and sawed off the horns for their own profit. You must take what you can, when you can." Barzan took another drag on his smoke.

The Afrikaner grunted disagreeably. "Look, there they are." He pointed to the dry grass about fifty meters away. Barzan could see the two confused orphans staring at them. He guessed that the larger one was about two years old and the other almost new born. They were clearly afraid and waiting for their mother. He stepped to the side of the truck and reached in a window, withdrawing a rifle with a scope and a silencer.

The Afrikaner was an excellent shot but he didn't understand business. Barzan deftly hoisted the rifle to his shoulder and centered the larger of the two calves in the cross hairs of the scope. Holding his breath, he squeezed the trigger. The rifle gave a small pop and kicked his shoulder. He quickly shifted targets and zeroed in the other infant. The animal was startled by the odd behavior of its older sibling, which had fallen convulsing to the ground.

Barzan took another bite of breath and squeezed the trigger again. The last of the rhino family fell dead to the ground. Now the animals would not have to suffer a terrifying death at the teeth and claws of a predator. Perhaps the mercenary would appreciate that.

The Afrikaner spoke to him in what sounded like a hiss. "Why did you do that you stupid wog? There was no need. You've got your bloody horn."

Barzan looked at the man, surprised at his reaction. "Only moments ago you, yourself, said they were as good as dead without their mother. I just hastened the job. Allahu Akhbar. God is great."

"Allahu Akhbar my arse. You wanted to kill them."

"No. You are wrong. I killed them because, as you said, without their mother they were doomed anyway. I saw no advantage in letting them suffer over a long time. I thought you would understand that. I am a businessman first and foremost. My business is trading in a rare commodity for my employer. There was a time when we feared scarcity. But now, we embrace it."

The Afrikaner seemed puzzled. Barzan did not feel like going to the trouble of explaining the economics of the horn trade to this crude man. He did not think the mercenary would appreciate the lessons Moto-san had taught him of western economics, as simple as they were. Besides, the day was hot and Kip should have collected the horn by now.

The Afrikaner stamped his cigarette out on the ground. "I think you're bloody crazy. I'm glad this trip is almost over." His tone was low and had an edge to it that suggested he meant more than he said. He reached into a pocket and pulled out a silver flask and took a long drink.

Barzan watched the mercenary and his neck tightened reflexively. The man was being insolent to the point of hostility and now he was becoming unpredictable. Barzan made up his mind quickly, it was time to get rid of the Afrikaner who was revealing himself to be a potential adversary.

He forced his most polite smile. "I am glad the trip is nearly over also. I am gratified that I will no longer be needing your services."

"That's for the both of us." The Afrikaner turned away from Barzan and walked toward the back of the truck. Barzan saw his opening and once again raised the rifle. When the blond head filled his scope, he squeezed the trigger and blew it off the infidel's shoulders.

7

TERI STOPPED HER CAR IN FRONT OF THE GATE TO
the Erikson mansion and lowered her window impatiently
so she could punch in the security number on the keypad.
Streaks of rain shown in the headlights and she kept her head
inside the car to avoid getting wet. The rain cover over the
keypad prevented her from getting soaked but even so she ad-
monished herself for forgetting the remote control to the gate.

When the code was entered she quickly pressed the button to
raise her window, but not before a blast of wind off the Pacific
blew a face full of rain on her. She cursed to herself and peered
through the slapping windshield wipers as the iron security gates
slid open. She dabbed her face with the back of her coat sleeve
hoping her makeup wouldn't smear in the process.

When the gates opened she drove up the long circular driveway slowly. She didn't want to take a chance on hitting any of
the peacocks that roamed the grounds, though she doubted
they'd be out in this wind-whipped storm. She stopped in front of
the entrance to the house and turned the engine off just as John
came out through the double doors. He rapidly descended the
four brick steps to the car and knocked on the passenger side
window for her to unlock the car door.

She found the master door lock in the dark and heard the electric click when it released the locks. John opened the door and jumped in the passenger seat. He barely fit in her small sports car and the seat was all the way forward so he had to cram his long legs in while he struggled to move the seat back. He swore under his breath and slammed the seat to the rear when he finally found the release. She almost laughed, but after seeing the tight expression on his face, bit her lip instead because he was clearly in a foul mood. She was a little surprised, normally he was even tempered.

Teri's pulse quickened and her back tightened. She was irritated herself at being asked to come over in the middle of the night. The road to the coast was windy and treacherous in this storm. She would have been very content to stay cozy and snug by the fireplace in her apartment, but John had insisted she bring the map back tonight, ahead of plan. His unsmiling face was dripping wet and his shirt was half soaked even though he had been in the rain a short time.

"Don't stop here. Go around to the kitchen entrance."

"Why?"

"Just do it. I'll tell you once we get out of the light of the front porch."

The tone of his voice was sharp and demanding. She clenched her teeth and refrained from telling him not to give her orders like some flunky. She'd remind him later when he was less agitated. For the moment she hoped things would become clearer if she did as she was told so she drove around the house to the side entrance.

"My parents came back tonight."

A shiver teased her back and she immediately understood the reason for his behavior. "But they aren't due for another week."

"I know. I guess mother was bored and they came back early. I didn't get any warning. I'm just glad I was in town when they arrived. Otherwise this could have been a disaster. Park over there under the tree so they can't see your car from their bedroom.

Teri parked the car and shut off the lights. "Do you think they suspect we have the map?" It would be awful if John's parents knew she was involved in tampering with their property, no matter how harmless the intention. Her stomach felt suddenly hollow.

"You know Walter, my father's secretary."

"Of course."

"About an hour after the three of them arrived home, he called me at the club and insisted I come right over. I was afraid something terrible had happened so I drove over here like a maniac. When I arrived my parents were already in bed, but Walter looked like he had just seen a train wreck. I've never known him to be so upset."

"So what was the matter?" A sinking sensation started in her chest because she was certain she knew the answer.

"I'm getting to that. Walter said something was missing from the house and that when my father found out he couldn't predict what would happen."

"The map? How would he know?" This wasn't making much sense to her.

"Apparently Walter usually checks on the map every few weeks and since he travels with them he always checks it first thing when they get home from a trip. When he looked for it today, it was gone. He was so shaken I thought he was going to have a heart attack. I had to tell him I had it. I'm not sure if he was more relieved or angry."

"How does that old guy get up and down the ladder?"

Teri tried to picture the gray-haired secretary teetering up the ladder, the vision was scary and comical at the same time.

"I don't know. But he also said that the map is my father's most prized earthly possession. Whenever he returns from a journey he always looks at it personally first thing the next morning. If Dad looks for it tomorrow and doesn't find it, or if he suspects we've tampered with it, I don't like to think about what might happen.

"You're being silly, Johnny. What's he going to do, cut you out of his will? And if the map is such a big deal, why doesn't he keep it in a safe?"

"I don't want him to discover we've violated his trust. He values that above all else in his relationships. The study is the only place he ever forbade us to go. If he knew I'd not only gone in there, but had removed something he values so highly . . . well I don't want to find out what might happen. More than that, I don't want to hurt my, or our relationship with him. You know how fond he is of you."

He looked at her quickly and then back out the windshield where the rain splattered his dim reflection. The lines around his eyes were tight and his voice was almost a whisper. It was obvious he was sorry he had started this.

"I don't want to find out what he might do either." Teri had liked Erik from the first minute she'd met him. He'd always treated her with courtesy and respect a combination of things that few men ever mastered. Erik had a Groucho Marx sense of humor that often left her laughing in surprise at his quick wit. She'd never left a visit with him without a smile. She tried to imagine him being cross or angry with her but couldn't make the picture work.

"Did you make the copy okay?"

"Yes, Shirley did a great job, the copy is perfect. It captures every detail of the original." At least that part of the plan had worked. However, she doubted it would be worth their trouble. Her stomach turned at the thought that Erik might find out that his future daughter-in-law was involved in a deception and one that involved his personal property. And how would Melanie, her future mother-in-law, react? And Enya? Even though she suspected Enya did not totally approve of her, she hoped to be friends and certainly didn't want to put anything between them.

The two of them left the car and moved quietly through the side entrance into the house. She knew his parents' bedroom was directly over the library and she became anxious about their chances of successfully returning the borrowed item. If they were caught how would they explain themselves?

Raindrops on John's wool sweater glistened as they reflected light from the entryway chandeliers. John carried the map in the waterproofed leather case he had bought for it. Leave it to him to think of that kind of detail. She had come to respect and admire his sometimes surprising resourcefulness. She was glad he'd thought of the case because the outside was soaked from the rain and the unprotected map would surely have been damaged. They crossed the entrance hall, and the receiving room, with hardly a sound. John paused and opened the map case.

He removed the contents and then slid the case out of sight under an overstuffed couch. Taking the key from its hiding place he motioned her to follow. They crept silently to the library door.

Her pulse was throbbing and she could hear every breath she took as if it were amplified a thousand times. He inserted the key in the lock and the slight scraping of the metal sliding against metal was the loudest quiet sound she had ever heard. He leaned to her and putting his lips to her ear whispered words so lightly they were little more than transmitted thoughts.

"After we get in, close the door behind us. Quietly."

She hissed back at him. "What do you expect me to do, slam it?" Sometimes he gave her so little credit she could choke him.

She watched him slowly open the door and step inside. Her heartbeat pounded in her ears. She entered the library and reached for the brass doorknob. In the dark she turned it to retract the latch and gently pressed the door closed. When the knob was released completely she let go of it. Relieved that there was no sound she leaned back on the door only to jump when the latch finally clicked shut. In the stillness it seemed as loud as a gunshot.

John grabbed her elbow and put his finger to his lips to shush her. Her cheeks flushed and her sweater suddenly seemed unbearably hot. Her breath came in rapid bursts and she had to fight herself to regain her composure. In the dim light she could see John move deeper into the library. She followed him.

He moved quickly to the ladder, which was positioned under the book that normally held the map. Walter must have left it there. John started up the rungs and she put a foot on either side of the bottom and braced it. When John was about half-way up Teri's heart skipped in fright as she heard the unmistakable sound of the doorknob turning. John froze in place and they both stared at the study's entrance in horror.

———

John's heart sank as the library door swung open and his father, wearing a silk smoking jacket and puffing on a cigar, appeared in the doorway. Erik Erikson flicked on the light and stepped into the room in a cloud of blue smoke.

"Is that my map?"

His father's question hit him like a rock and John's voice deserted him. He felt as if he were the lowest kind of sneak thief. The library lights seemed brighter than they had ever been, like spotlights illuminating him halfway up the ladder with the stolen document in his hand. He leaned into the ladder too dumbfounded to speak. His father turned to Teri.

"Teri, maybe you can answer. Is that my map?"

John was so startled and embarrassed for an instant he had almost forgotten that Teri was holding the ladder a few feet below him.

"Yes, sir. I mean, yes it is."

Teri's voice was so soft and full of remorse John almost didn't recognize it. He cursed himself for bringing her along and getting her involved.

His father moved toward them and then John saw his mother come to the door. "Do they have it?"

His father turned to her. "John isn't speaking dear, he's just standing there like a booby. Teri still talks though."

"Yes Mother, I borrowed it and was just returning it. I'm fully responsible for this, Teri had nothing to do with it." John's mouth was dry and sticky, he lowered his eyes.

His mother smiled. "That's a relief. You had us so worried. I thought poor old Walter was going to have a stroke when he found it had gone missing."

John slowly descended the ladder. Even now it amused him that she would refer to Walter as old. Only his mother could make him feel better just by her unfailingly pleasant demeanor.

"She's right you know. I thought he was going to have the big one right at our bedroom door." Erik met John at the bottom of the ladder and held out his hand for the map.

John looked at the floor as he handed it over. "I apologize, I had no right to take this. I'm sorry." The words felt hollow and inadequate.

"Wait." Teri's voice surprised him. "This is my fault. We found it by accident, but when I saw it I begged John to take the map so we could look at it. It's fascinating. I can't tell you how sorry I am."

Melanie entered the library briskly. She had on a silk pink robe that flowed behind her. It made John think of something the old Hollywood movie stars might have worn. Her gray hair was brushed back over her forehead and was topped with a pink pin that matched her robe. He had to remind himself of her age now and then because she did not look or act it. He wondered if Teri would age as gracefully. His mother spoke softly but with authority. "I don't suppose there is any point in fretting over this. No harm has been done other than throwing a fright into Walter."

Erik took the map and spread it on his desk to inspect it. "It would have been better if they had asked. But I like the way they stick up for each other. Tells me a lot. Maybe they'll learn something from this escapade."

John couldn't believe the reaction they were getting. He had imagined his father would be furious. On the other hand, he couldn't remember the last time he had seen his father angry.

"I'm so sorry." Teri was on the verge of tears. "We never should have done it. I didn't know it was so valuable. I'm really, really sorry and so embarrassed." She started quietly crying and John put his arm around her.

Erik looked up in concern. "Melanie, look what we've done, we've made her cry."

His mother went to Teri and put her arms around her. Taking her from John and leading her to a chair by the desk she spoke in a soothing tone. "There, there my dear. It's okay, you'll just have to be more careful about what you let that knuckle-headed son of mine get you mixed up in."

"Oh Melanie, it's so sweet of you not to be angry."

His mother stroked Teri's hair. "Honey, one thing we've learned is that being angry is a pitiful waste of energy."

His cheeks were still hot with chagrin as he approached his father. "I don't want to pry, but where did you get this, Dad?"

Erik looked up from the desk, apparently satisfied that the document was undamaged. "It came from Africa."

He puffed on his cigar, then tapped it in the ash tray as if to end the conversation. John had not expected such a closed answer. Now that he'd been found out, he decided there wasn't much to lose so he decided to press his luck.

"Why do you have it? How did you get it? Is there any value to it?"

Melanie laughed from her seat beside Teri. "It all depends on how you define value."

Teri looked up at her. "Is the part about true love for real?"

John was still perplexed and looked at his mother. "What am I missing here?"

"We'll tell you when the time is right." She dabbed Teri's face with an embroidered handkerchief then put it away.

His father spoke with the cigar clenched between his teeth. "Dearie, it might be time to tell them now."

"Erik, we agreed that we would wait until after their first anniversary."

"I know, but so what. I think we should tell them now since they've already figured part of it out."

"Figured out what?" John was completely confused.

His father flattened the map on the desk with wrinkled hands. "That this map is the key to our family's good fortune."

John let the air out of his lungs and his pulse quickened. He had been right about the map. "Are you serious? How?"

Erik looked to his wife. "It's time."

His mother nodded approval. "But before you start," she pointed to John, "run get us some bubbly from the kitchen." She clapped her hands. "I just love this story."

———

John and Teri sat together on the leather couch in the study. His mother sat in the overstuffed chair near them while his father took a seat behind the desk puffing his cigar, thoughtfully watching the smoke curl in the light.

Erik started his story slowly, as if he were remembering every detail. "It was Christmas Day, 1944. I was stationed on a remote island in the Mediterranean thinking the war was passing me by. Early in the morning we received an alert that a Lancaster coming in from somewhere in Africa was under attack. We had two P 51 fighters on call, Bernie Sterling and I were the only pilots. We scrambled in minutes but Bernie had engine problems and had to turn back. I had no choice but to press on alone.

"I had never been in combat before and my heart was beating so hard I thought it was going to leap out of my chest. I was so excited, and I have to admit, scared, that I could hardly keep the wings steady. Still, all I could think about were those poor bastards on the Lancaster. I didn't think they'd have much of a chance against a German fighter attack."

John leaned back on the couch and closed his eyes trying to visualize his father's story. He listened to every word and imagined the scene as his father described it.

———

From the controls of his fighter flying at top speed near 5000 feet, Erik could see the oily black smoke of an airplane in trouble staining the sky. There was only one plane that could be leaving the smoky trail and that was the British bomber. The big plane had a crew of seven and Erik's stomach turned at the thought that it might go down. He scanned the sky for *Luftwaffa* fighters but didn't spot any. The fight was already over.

Erik pushed his microphone button. "RAF inbound this is Tango two, what's your situation?"

A broken transmission came through his headphones. "Tango this is RAF. Thanks for the help. We're in a bit of a mess. The flight-engineer is dead. Crew is mostly too shot up to bail out. One engine gone, one on fire, and not a bloody lot of control. With a bit of luck maybe we can make the airstrip. I suggest you land first just in case I muck it up."

Erik pulled up alongside the bomber amazed it was still in the air. He was close enough to see the pilot in the damaged cockpit. Erik gave him a salute and was surprised that he got one in return. He figured the RAF pilot would be fighting the controls with both hands. Maybe he was and it was just the English coolness in the face of fire he had heard about. He pressed his microphone button. "See you there." He couldn't make out the garbled response.

Minutes later Erik stood in the back of a jeep by the fire crew near the edge of the runway. He had cranked the Mustang up to full speed and landed well ahead of the struggling British plane.

Through his binoculars, Erik could see that the Lancaster looked even worse from the ground than it had from the air. The four engine bomber was barely hanging in the sky. With all the damage it had sustained it seemed to be defying the laws of physics by staying aloft. He tried to assess the chances the pilot had of successfully landing the crippled war bird.

The inside port engine was feathered and the outside starboard engine was on fire, leaving an ugly trail of black smoke in the morning sky. The tail seemed intact but the rudder was missing a big chunk off the top. The Brit had reported that the wheels wouldn't come down so he was going to have to land it on its belly. Even if he was going to give odds, Erik wouldn't take this bet.

The big plane dropped in a downdraft and Erik's heart jumped. Sweat soaked his shirt and flight jacket. He had known the RAF pilot only a few minutes but felt somehow kindred.

A gust of wind blew sand across the end of the runway obscuring the Lancaster from Erik's view. The radio on the jeep crackled. The voice of the British pilot came through the tinny speaker. "Tower, inbound RAF here. These controls are a bit of a worry and getting worse. I've got some badly wounded men on board. My apologies in advance if I ruin your airstrip. Over."

Erik listened as Willie, the kid from Texas, answered from the control tower. "RAF this is tower, we'll talk about the bill with you at happy hour tonight. Over."

"Right-o mate. I'll take a whiskey, neat. Out."

The radio hissed once after that but Erik knew that was the end of the conversation. The pilot would be too busy struggling with the controls to talk anymore.

The Lancaster blew through the dust cloud and over the end of the airstrip with surprising speed. The plane skimmed the sand, its two good engines roaring at maximum power. The flames on the starboard side were bigger now, almost engulfing the entire outboard engine. With the plane only a few feet above the ground he heard the engines throttle back and held his breath as the damaged bomber skidded onto the dirt runway.

The plane made a wrenching, tearing sound and the port wing dipped into the sand. The wing tip snapped off but not before spinning the plane to the side. The engine noise abruptly stopped as the propeller blades dug in and stalled in the sand. The plane skidded fifty yards on its belly passing in front of Erik's jeep breaking into three large pieces as it went by him. The port wing sheared off with a sickening grinding of metal. The fuselage cracked open aft of the cockpit and again behind the wings. Sand and smoke filled the air obscuring the wreckage from view. An unexpected silence enveloped the airstrip.

The noise of the roaring engines and ripping metal was replaced by a whisper of wind carrying the sound of an airplane on fire. Erik realized he had been holding his breath. He leapt from the jeep and sprinted to the Lancaster. The fire crew went to the fuselage, he knew he had to reach the pilot, his compatriot, get him out before the plane burned around him.

Erik pulled a light rag around his face to keep from gagging on the acrid smoke that filled the air and stung his eyes causing them to water. When he reached the cockpit he was stunned by the carnage. The flight-engineer's face was half shot away. Blood spattered the interior and the controls. The pilot was barely conscious, a huge gash in his right cheek and a gaping wound in his abdomen. He had bright red hair and a thick mustache. His green eyes held a smile even as death stalked him. He clutched his wounded midsection and forced a grin.

"Well, laddie, guess I'll be missing that drink."

"Save your breath while I get you out of here."

"Laddie, shut up and listen to me, man." He grabbed Erik's wrist and forced him to look into his eyes. "I saved some of the boys on my airplane now didn't I?" Erik nodded.

"Be sure you see to them, they're brave lads."

Erik tried to reassure him. "Don't worry, we'll take good care of them."

The pilot let out a low groan and continued, "Now that makes me a wee bit of a hero doesn't it?" Erik nodded again. "Will you tell my father for me? He's a farmer and I'm all he's got. It will mean a lot to him. Promise me you'll tell him for me? That I did the best I could."

"Sure, I'll tell him in person. This plane shouldn't have even been flying. It's a miracle you landed it at all." Flames were creeping toward them and the smoke was starting to thicken in the cockpit. "Let's get you out of here."

"Laddie, reach into my inside pocket and pull out the map." Erik did as he was told. "This is my payment to you for telling my father I went out a hero. Now I'm a dying man and I've no call to mislead you. Follow the instructions on this map and you'll find a fortune beyond your wildest dreams. But hear me, follow the instructions exactly. Otherwise you'll end up like me." He looked at his bloody hand barely holding his insides in. "Watching yourself die."

———

Erik finished his story and took a puff from his cigar. He gazed into the smoke again as if there might be an answer to a difficult question in the blue haze. Melanie broke the silence. "That poor man. I never met him but I've always kept him in my prayers."

Teri relaxed her grip on John's hand. "What did he mean?"

Erik took another puff on his cigar. "I've wondered. I can only think that he went there. I mean, he followed the map without the one."

Melanie nodded in agreement. "He must have gone without the one true love. We believed the war tested our love in the most difficult ways imaginable. When we followed the map we were very confident in each other. That's why we decided not to give you the map until the first anniversary of your wedding."

Erik looked at Teri. "Nothing personal mind you, but these times are so strange and things change so fast. We thought it wise to give you the chance, the opportunity, to experience life before you had to think about something like this."

John shifted in his seat, he was uncomfortable hearing his father apologize for nothing more than being prudent, especially since he and Teri were the ones who should be apologizing.

Teri squeezed his hand tightly. "Oh, I completely understand and that makes perfect sense. I just want you to know that it's not an issue for us. John and I are going to be together forever."

John found the room suddenly small and full of smoke. He needed some fresh air in a hurry.

# 8

K IP STOOD BY BARZAN AS THEY SCANNED THE
horizon searching for any sign of rhinos. Kip had never
liked the man, but Barzan paid well and that is what
mattered.

Kip thought about when he had joined Barzan on his first
rhino hunt seven years before. He remembered he had been
standing on a corner in Mombasa along with two dozen other
men who had been forced from their lands by the relocation of a
herd of elephants.

To him it seemed the government thought it was more important to protect these animals than to allow the tribes who had
hunted these lands for generations to keep their homes. He had
tried to live in the government settlement area, but in reality it
was nothing more than a slum. He left his parents and sisters to
try to discover a way to make more money.

Kip drifted to Mombasa with a few friends in the hope of
finding a job on the docks. This was a big joke played on them
he decided. There were so many men looking for work that the
wages could barely pay for the cost of a bed and food for himself.
He still could remember the laugh of the foreman on the dock
when he gave Kip his first day's pay. Kip had wanted to kill him

with his bare hands. He was, after all, in his heart, a warrior. He had passed the test of Masai manhood. He'd stalked and killed the leopard, the elephant, the cape buffalo, the gazelle and even a lion with only a spear. Of course it had been illegal, according to the Masilan government, but he was true Masai and his family had held on to the traditions of the past.

Kip had left the docks and found various odd employments that allowed him to feed himself, but he never made enough money to send some to his parents. Then one day he was standing on a corner hoping to be picked for a laborers job when Barzan drove up in the back of a big taxi, the kind the Europeans rode in.

Barzan had on a white cowboy hat and a white coat and pants. When he asked for men who knew the bush, Kip pushed his way to the front of the crowd and told him he was the one man here who could be trusted. Barzan had only smiled and told him to get in the cab.

Kip had lost track of how many rhinos they had killed over the years. The more the better he decided early on. If they could kill enough rhinos, and then the elephants, maybe the tourists and the Europeans would go away and his family would be allowed to return to their lands. Perhaps it was a false hope, but it was the only hope he had.

The money Barzan paid him was more than a man could spend. He was able to buy his family a house and to keep food on their table. Still, he lived in constant fear that the government would somehow discover what he was doing and put him in jail. Possibly his family as well. He made the choice early on that it would be better to live, and perhaps even die, as a warrior, than as a servant in a European hotel.

Kip lowered his binoculars and wiped sweat from his face. He turned to Barzan. "It is not good here. We must go farther into the park."

Barzan did not look at him but nodded as he continued to scan the horizon. Kip walked to his truck knowing his employer would follow.

———

Teri stepped off the cable car behind Beth, joining the throngs of people crowding Union Square in San Francisco. She heard the bell clang as the car moved off and she and Beth crossed the street to the bridal shop. The sidewalk was filled with tourists and shoppers all seemingly in a hurry. This part of town always had an exciting energy that made it fun to visit even if she wasn't shopping. Today was special though, she had a purpose and the thought of picking out a wedding dress was making her almost giddy.

They stopped in front of a window display, which featured a mannequin in a gorgeous flowing white gown with an exaggerated train. Teri pointed to the price tag that was strategically turned away from view. "I bet this one costs a fortune."

Beth nodded in agreement. "What do you care? Money is no object for you. You should start getting used to it."

It was a cool afternoon and even though they were standing in the sun Teri had a sudden chill. "It's not like that. I didn't even know he had money when we met. You remember."

Beth gave her one those wry smiles that meant she was not going to let Teri off easily. She could be fun, but she could be edgy too. "Refresh my memory, honey. I seem to recall you following armored cars around writing down the addresses where they stopped."

Teri had to laugh a little. They both knew that was as far from the truth as anything could be. "Oh come on. We met that day the receptionist called in sick and we couldn't get a temporary right away so everyone in the office took turns sitting out front, even the managers. I was at the desk when John came in to deliver some documents. I just thought he was one of those dot-com guys with a nice car. Anyway, we talked a little and he invited me out for coffee. I didn't know he was. . . ."

Beth interrupted. "Loaded."

Teri ignored the remark. Beth made it sound so crass. "That he was well off until weeks after we started going out."

Beth tugged on her elbow. "No need to be so defensive. Let's go inside. I wonder what would have happened if I had been at the reception desk that day. Maybe I'd be the one looking for a wedding dress."

"Maybe you would, but not with Johnny. He and I are meant to be."

Beth opened the door to the shop. "Please, don't make me ill."

Going inside, Teri was enveloped by the warmth of the store and smell of potpourri. "I mean it, I just think some people are meant to be together. Don't you?"

Beth took her sunglasses off and looked at her with a raised eyebrow. "You don't really believe that, do you? I think you've seen *The Princess Bride* one too many times."

Teri took a short breath and glanced around the store filled with white dresses, hats and veils while she formulated her answer. "Yeah, I think I do believe it."

Beth was staring at her now and Teri had the sensation of being suddenly open, almost naked in front of not only her trusted friend, but also herself. "So what happens if John doesn't marry you? Do you end up an old maid?"

"John is going to marry me. He must."

"Hold on there, princess, that sounds a little obsessive."

The word obsessive hit Teri like a slap in the face. "Oh God, I can't be sounding like that. It's just that I've put so much of myself into our relationship. I've never been so open or so intimate with anyone. If he were to break the engagement I think I'd die. We're so good together. If I could just make him understand how much I love him. . . ."

Beth stepped closer to her. "Wait a minute Teri, back up there. Did you say he might break it off, leave you with a diamond lie?"

Teri shook her head. "No, no he wouldn't do that. I'm getting anxious and maybe I'm pressing too hard. I might even be getting a little clingy. I can feel him backing off sometimes and it makes me nervous. But we'll be fine. I'm sure it's just pre-wedding jitters."

A sales clerk with spiked blonde hair and pierced eyebrows approached them. "May I help you today?"

Beth looked at her and spoke for both of them. "I'm not sure. What's your return policy?"

———

John was nearly asleep lulled by the sound of the rain softly drumming on Teri's bedroom window. In his mind's eye he had the image of the dying pilot and could almost hear his father's voice. 'He went there without the one.' John tried to make the ugly image go away, then he heard Teri's voice.

"Tell me the truth now." Teri's words pulled John away from the sleep that was seducing him into unconsciousness. His head rested snugly on one of Teri's down pillows. He was warmed by the feel of her bare skin next to his in her too small bed. She pulled the purple comforter over his shoulders and he opened his eyes just enough to see that she was peering at him to see if he was awake, or faking being asleep.

This was a habit of hers he never had quite managed to break. The post-lovemaking interrogation. They'd spent the last two hours of this wonderfully rainy afternoon engaged in what, even for them, had been a passionate session. He was marvelously exhausted. The thought of surrendering to a nap, so they could wake up and continue, seemed a perfect idea. But no. She was going to hang a question out there that would inevitably lead to another long involved discussion about the relationship. He'd rather answer to the Spanish Inquisition than go down this path. He took a deep breath and waited.

"Johnny, do you believe in the one true love?"

Oh God, this question was about as loaded as they came. The right response could be yes. On the other hand, the whole thing was kind of a silly notion. At least he had thought that before Teri. "Of course I believe in it. Don't you?"

"You know I do. I think everybody has one person out there who is their perfect match. What I don't understand is why so few people find their soul mate."

John recognized a chance to score some points and seized it. "I think people just get too impatient. They get blinded by lust and pretend that it's love. Or, maybe they just settle for convenience. Find somebody who is comfortable and quit looking for the perfect match." He thought this sounded very relationship correct and was pleased with the spin he had put on it. He checked her blue eyes for a reaction and was relieved when she gave a slight nod of agreement.

"I think you're right and it's so sad." Teri reached over his chest and took her wineglass off the bedside table. Her breasts rubbed warmly across him and he watched her in appreciation. She was definitely the most desirable woman he had ever known. Even if she were occasionally a little quirky.

"Sometimes I wonder about us. I wonder if our relationship is only about sex."

Alarm bells went off in John's head. His muscles tensed and his skin was suddenly hot under the blankets. Better cut this train of thought off fast. "You can't be serious about that. After all, we are engaged."

He watched her absentmindedly check her engagement ring in the candlelight. The yellow flame caused the diamond to sparkle. "It's true that we do have a lot of sex, compared to most people anyway, but so what? That's when we're closest to each other. That's when I feel most connected to you." He gently stroked her smooth leg with the palm of his hand.

Teri sat up now, with her back against the padded headboard. She struck a match and lit a stick of her favorite incense and placed it in a carved wooden holder. The smell of the sulfur from the match quickly gave way to the spicy scent of the incense. John tried to gauge her reaction.

"You're so sweet. I guess I should feel lucky. After all, how many girls get to spend endless days and nights in bed drinking expensive champagne with one of the sexiest and richest men the world?"

He kissed her on the arm. "I'm the lucky one." He wished she'd drop the references to his wealth. It disturbed him that she even considered it something worth bringing up. His heart sped up in irritation. He had spent a great deal of his life trying to distance himself from his father's money. He'd ended more than one relationship because he got the jitters about the girl's motivations for being with him. Enya seemed to have a keen sense for that. The money was like a curse in that respect. As hard as he tried, he could never get comfortable that people were not more interested in it than in him.

Teri slid back down into the covers beside him putting her face next to his. "Was it like this with the others? You know, the women before me?"

More alarms. The question enveloped him in a claustrophobic grip. Now she wanted him to compare people and situations that were completely different. He wanted to get away from it, but knew avoiding her would only bring more questions.

"No Teri, it was never like this with anyone else. I've been around a little, I've told you that before, but this relationship is special."

"How special?"

"There's something here I don't understand. When we're apart I feel as if something is missing from me. It's all I can do to contain myself until the next time we see each other and I can feel you next to me."

"Me too. It's as if the hours when we're apart are wasted time." She stroked his face. "So, why did it take you three years to ask me to marry you?"

He tried to keep her from seeing how hard he was breathing. The endless questions grated on his nerves. She needed to accept that he loved her now.

"Well, I wanted to be sure."

"You mean you weren't sure until I told you I was going to leave you if you didn't commit to me?" There was a hint of a tease in her voice.

"That's what made me sure you were the one. The thought of living without you was more than I could stand. I never considered the reality of losing you until that night you said you were serious about it."

Teri ran her fingers through his hair and rubbed his temple. Her massage started to relax his muscles. "I didn't want to go, but I didn't feel valued. I didn't like that."

The tension was starting to drain from where she was rubbing his temples. "That thought never crossed my mind. I wanted us to be together from the start."

Teri realized she wanted to believe him. She kissed him gently on the mouth. She posed the next question realizing it might sound ridiculous, but the notion wouldn't leave her mind and she needed an answer. "So, do you believe in the one true love?" She put her arms around his shoulders and gently kneaded his back with her fingers.

"You mean the one like in the storybooks and movies? That one whose destiny is forever intertwined with that of their soul mate?"

She let out a breath in relief that he had not laughed at her. She kissed him again. "Yes, that one."

"Sure, I believe." He wrapped his arms around her and she slid closer to his warm body. "And I believe you're my true love."

She had not realized how badly she had wanted to hear the words, how much she wanted to believe them. She was so excited that before she could even think she whispered in his ear. "Promise me you'll never leave me."

His body tensed beneath her and she knew he was closing her off. The word 'never' sounded clingy. She knew she shouldn't have said it. He continued to hold her tightly. She wished they could just stay together, right there in her bed, for a long time.

She was startled when he spoke. "So am I the one for you? Promise you won't leave me." Her heart was pounding against his. Was he serious or was he just playing the game? If she could only make him understand how much it meant to her. "Of course, lover. You're the only man I've ever really loved. There's nothing you could do to make me leave you."

He gave her a long kiss on the lips. She still wasn't sure he understood. She reached across him to the bedside table and retrieved the wineglass that rested there. She first gave him a sip, then took one herself. He reached up and playfully tickled her side, she pulled back spilling a little wine. Reflexively she tried to catch the falling wine drops just as he leaned up. The back of her hand accidentally brushed against his cheek and the diamond on her ring scratched across his face.

"Ouch." He jerked away startled.

"Oh, I'm sorry." She immediately kissed his cheek. She put the glass down and inspected his face and was glad there was not a visible mark. "Are you okay?"

He touched his hand to his face to be certain the skin hadn't been broken.

She looked at him, the candlelight reflecting in his eyes. Her diamond sparkled in the light and she thought it was time to take a chance. Time to bare her soul so he might truly understand. Time to let him know exactly how much he meant to her. And maybe if she opened the book all the way, she could draw him closer. "You know that if you ever leave me, Johnny, you'll scar me forever. You'll be cutting me with a diamond lie."

"With a what?"

"A diamond lie. It's the worst kind there is."

She could feel him wince under her and he looked perplexed. "I don't understand what you're talking about."

She raised herself and leaned on one elbow while she looked into his face. "A diamond lie is told convincingly and is very pretty to hear. Maybe it's even told with the belief that somehow it will eventually be true. But it is still a lie. And when it is found out, it cuts with a diamond's sharp, ruthless, unforgiving edge, to the very soul of the person who has been lied to. And because it was such a pretty lie, both the giver and the receiver end up with wounds that never ever fully heal."

She stared into his blue eyes intently but could not tell what he was thinking. He blinked and she forced herself to finish.

"These are open wounds that affect the way the people live the rest of their lives. They are forever wounds. Diamond cuts."

A chill ran down her back. His response sounded almost automatic.

"Don't worry. We'll be together forever."

She rolled over and shut her eyes tightly. God, she had sounded so needy. No, I'm not that person. Her mind raced to find the right words. Then she thought of them. She opened her eyes and leaned close to him.

"Johnny, we can be like your parents. They've been together their whole lives and they've always been happy. I want to go to Africa and follow the map to the rhinos' valley. I want to go to the place where only two who are one can go."

She kissed him again and rested lightly on top of him. She heard him whisper. "It takes two of us to be one, lover." The tenderness had returned to his voice.

She felt his hand gently caress her side.

"Take me, Johnny."

She softly stroked his thigh. He was once again warming to her touch. He whispered in her ear and the warmth of his breath sent a wave of pleasure over her entire body. "I couldn't go without you. I can't live without you. Of course we'll go. We'll leave right after our first wedding anniversary."

She wanted to hear it again. "Promise?"

"Promise." He closed his eyes and pulled her down to him pressing his lips to hers. The rain cascading on the window made a music she knew was theirs alone.

"YOU KNOW YOU'RE GOING TO HAVE TO LET
Teri go." Enya's words caught him by such surprise that
John almost fell off his horse. At first he could scarcely
believe she had said it, but then he recognized that it made sense.
He pulled on the reins and stopped the chestnut mare in the
middle of the trail. Enya rode a palomino that flipped its tail as it
passed him. She stopped as soon as she realized he had pulled up.

John looked at his sister in disgust. So this was why she had
asked him out for a ride. She wanted to give him some more of
that wonderful older-sisterly advice whether he wanted it or not.
She must have picked this activity to keep him from getting
comfortable. She knew he loathed horses. Always had, ever since
he had been thrown and busted his arm when he was ten. She had
been there at the time. He remembered how she'd laughed when
he landed on the ground and started crying. She'd thought it was
quite hilarious.

On the other hand, once she'd realized he was truly injured
she'd responded immediately and taken every measure to help
him. No one could have been more protective of him during his
brief convalescence. It was also Enya who'd insisted he get back
in the saddle as soon as the cast came off. He'd truly wanted to

have nothing more to do with the animals but she'd cajoled him into riding again.

With more work and time in the saddle than he'd ever wanted, his sister had eventually turned him into quite a proficient rider. He still didn't like horses though. Considered them to be smelly, furry, fly attractions.

Aside from the warm kinship he felt toward her, they had shared a lot growing up together and he had come to respect and trust her opinions. Her mind was sharp and she had a knack for seeing people for who they were. Her intuitions were usually dead on and her motives sound. However, occasionally he detected her talking down to him, as if he were not in the same league with her and their father. This had a grating affect on his nerves and he had to force himself not to let it color his judgment.

Beneath a canopy of sequoias he waited for Enya to turn her palomino and come back to him. Now the invitation to ride made sense. They had not talked since their parents had returned from China, since she had caught Teri and him in the library. He had hoped that she was going to let the matter drop. He realized that was a foolish hope.

"John, why did you stop? Come on up here."

He glumly kicked his mount and rode up the trail to where Enya waited. The early fall sun filtered through the trees and the morning shade made the ride comfortable. But John felt his temperature rising, his cheeks were hot and his palms were damp. He hated confrontations with his sister. She was difficult to argue with when she had her mind made up about something. She was very articulate and had a way of making him feel like his contrary opinions were immature and without merit. He wanted to get past being just the younger sibling and be seen as an equal.

Enya sat in the saddle with her back straight and her reins perfectly poised for control of her animal. That was Enya all right, always in control. Her deep green riding jacket fit her perfectly. Her short billed cap and blonde ponytail looked both prim, and sexy. He mused that she could easily be a model for either a fashion magazine or a men's magazine. Or better yet, maybe an S&M magazine. With the quirt poised expertly in her hand, she would definitely be the 's.' Woe to the poor guy who ended up with her.

"What's the matter with you. Why did you stop?"

John felt his fuse burning. "Because I thought I heard something stupid come out of your mouth and I was so surprised I had to stop and clean out my ears."

"Don't be trite. You know what I mean." Enya nudged her horse and joined up with John so that they were riding abreast on the trail.

"Enya, you can't possibly be serious. You can't mean you have any inkling that I'm going to do anything other than marry Teri." He tried to be final, tried to sound like there was no discussion to be had. He knew better though. He heard a snort and wasn't sure if it was Enya or her horse.

She turned in the saddle and looked at him. "John, I know you like her, but you have a responsibility here."

"Yeah, I have a responsibility to me and to her. And I don't just like her. I love her. We are going to get married and that's all there is to it."

Enya pulled the reins and stopped her horse abruptly. With surprising speed and deftness she reached over and grabbed John's bridle and yanked his mare to a stop.

"You've got to listen to me. This girl is a child. She has no concept of what's at stake here. She's a silly little plaything for you. Now you've had your fun and it's time you packed up her dolls and sent her back to the little world where she belongs."

"What's the matter with you? What have you got against her? Do you hate her because she's younger and prettier than you?" He jerked his reins out of her hands. "Maybe you have someone in mind for me? Someone who meets your specifications and criteria for acceptability?"

"Don't be so shallow, it doesn't become you. Think about it, John. You've done this before. First it was that little airhead from San Diego. Turns out the only thing she knew about you was the size of our parents' estate. Then there was the 'real love' from your gambling binge in Tahoe. I still can't figure out where you dug that one up. And what about that army lieutenant, weren't you 'in love' with her too?"

His horse tried to turn and he had to yank the reins to keep it in place. The sun was starting to filter through the trees and he felt as if the temperature had shot up two hundred degrees. "Okay, so what, I've made a couple of mistakes. You're not perfect either."

"We're not talking about me."

"Well what do you care anyway? Why does it matter to you what I do?"

"John, you know Mother and Father are getting older. When they leave us, and I hope it isn't for a long time, you will personally become extremely wealthy."

"So will you."

"Of course. My point is, you have a huge responsibility to watch over this fortune and the thousands of jobs and charities that benefit from it. I cannot stand by and let you risk it falling into the hands of someone who has no idea about what it is and means."

"She could learn to deal with it. You did. And is that what this is really about, the money? Screw the money, you can have it all. Besides, what do you think she's going to do, kill me? "

Enya was clearly frustrated and her mount was getting nervous underneath her. She controlled the animal with short tight pulls on either rein. "No she's not going to kill you, but I might if you don't wise up. I'd like to see you just try and live without the money. You wouldn't know what to do."

Her words stung him. "You know that's not true. I've lived without it before."

"Spare me, please. You've pretended to live without it a couple of times, but no matter what you've done, or how badly you screwed up, it's always been there to fall back on. I've talked to Walter."

She was right and it galled him that they both knew it. There was no way he could argue that he didn't appreciate the things their vast fortune offered. He had learned money couldn't make you happy, but at least you could be miserable in style.

"Before you get too pious, recognize you can't get by without it either."

"I don't pretend to." He detected a patronizing tone in her voice and it pushed him to lash back at her.

"Now let me see, sister dearest. As I recall you tried to play poor little church mouse when you went to Stanford. But that plan went astray when what happened? Oh yeah, you weren't going to get into the snotty sorority with Kelly Randal."

"You're being small, John."

"Oh, and what about the European hostel trip? Just a poor little white girl bumming her way around Europe to see the world. Let me see, wasn't it Walter who had to fly to Rome to get you out of that Italian jail after your boyfriend ripped you off for everything you had? Who were you supposed to be, little Miss Bohemian?" John kept digging at her to throw her off balance. He knew that was a cheap shot. She didn't know he was aware of that incident.

"How do you know about that? Did Walter tell you?"

Her reaction was angry and venomous. Her lips tightened and he could see her face was turning flushed. Their horses sensed the tension between them and moved nervously. Enya tightened her reins almost cruelly. John pulled hard on his to hold his horse still.

"None of that matters, we aren't talking about me." Enya was virtually hissing at him. She sat up straight in her saddle. He watched her close her eyes and take several deep breaths.

When she opened her eyes her face looked softer. She spoke in a calm, reasonable voice. "John, it's not the money but I admit it tends to color everything we do. I like Teri, I believe she could learn to handle it with time. But if you go through with this marriage I'm afraid you'll both be miserable."

He was furious with her. "What are you talking about? Why?"

"For pity's sake, I just told you, she's a child. Think about it. She's got you doing it in your father's chair. Quit thinking with your smaller brain and come up for air and see the light."

"She did not."

"She did too. Remember, I saw you in the library. It was despicable. And worse, she's already got you stealing things from my, our parents. She has no respect for you or this family. You can't do this. You have to let her go."

Now it was his turn to calm down. He realized Enya had Teri all wrong. Teri wasn't a thief or a gold digger and now he thought he understood Enya's concern. He swallowed hard, tasting the slight dust that was in the air. "Being in father's chair was her idea. It was meant to throw you off the track of what we were really doing in the study. Worked too, you didn't have a clue."

Enya's lips tightened and her voice took on a sharper edge. "I agree she's smart, but she isn't as smart as you think."

He watched her warily. He had pushed her too far and he knew she was ready to say something she otherwise would have held back. Might as well find out what it was. "What's that supposed to mean?"

Enya spoke in a voice that was soft and without malice. "She isn't smart enough to realize you don't really want to marry her."

The words hit him like a shot to the gut. He responded reflexively. "And you are?"

"John, I'm your sister. I love you and want you to be happy. But I know you. Every time the marriage word is mentioned you tense up and try to change the subject. I see how she cares for you but I don't see it going back the other way."

He wiped sweat from his forehead. "You don't know us, you don't see us when we're alone."

She persisted. "You're right I don't. But can you do this, can you sit there and tell me you want to be with her forever? Can you say to yourself that you want to be with her everyday for the rest of your life?"

The nerve endings at the back of his brain all seemed to fire at once hitting him like a jolt of electricity. He stammered, "Of course I can."

Her palomino reared back on its hind legs, surprising them both. For an instant he thought Enya would be thrown from her mount. Instead, she cast him a resigned look and expertly kicked the animal into a gallop. She rode down the trail leaving faint puffs of dust hanging in the air.

He adjusted himself in the saddle and called to her. "I want to . . ." and he heard his voice trail off. She was too faraway and probably couldn't hear him anyway.

———

"I hear you're playing hooky today. They told me you were bad, but I didn't really believe them. "

John smiled at Cynthia, who was giving him a sly look. She was an enticing woman. She was dressed in a black skirt suit that was San Francisco business chic, professional, and subtly sexy. If he weren't engaged he would certainly take the bait on this.

Still, it wouldn't hurt to talk a bit to the Director of Advertising. She had just come in the large glass office doors that opened to Market Street and he was on his way out. He stopped and she took off her sunglasses revealing mesmerizing hazel eyes. "I wouldn't exactly say I'm being bad, I'm just going out for a totally innocent round of golf. But I do know how to be bad."

She gave him a knowing smile that was a virtual invitation. "Oh, I bet you do." Her voice was almost a purr and it sent a rush down his back like he'd not felt for months. She gave him an exaggerated wink. "As for me, it's off to work, no time for play. Have fun." She turned on her high heels and walked to the elevator as if he no longer existed.

It took him a moment to realize he was staring after her. He quickly went out the doors to where the valet had pulled his car around. Standing in the cool air he glanced back at the office doors. Taking a deep breath he realized forever was a long, long time.

Driving down the coast towards Monterey he thought about what his sister had said the day before. She'd seemed so sure of herself and that in turn made him wary about his own judgment. Enya was right in one respect. Everytime Teri brought up the marriage he wanted to find something else to do or talk about. He hated talking about relationships. The subject always got so 'touchy feely,' as they used to say in the army. What he thought and felt wasn't anybody's business but his. He'd take his own counsel on this subject, thank you very much.

With the event only weeks away he realized he was less and less enthusiastic. The energy was draining out of the relationship but he couldn't put his finger on why. It was obvious Teri was starting to sense his reticence. She was increasingly anxious, which in turn caused him to withdraw. Maybe this was just the normal stuff people went through before any marriage.

He opened the window of his sports car and let the brisk autumn wind whip around the interior. Maybe they just needed more time. It would certainly be wrong to tie the knot if they were not both one hundred percent sure. That was the answer, it was so obvious he couldn't believe he had not thought of it before. He'd just suggest they needed to slow things down a little. He straightened his shoulders as if a huge weight had lifted. It was the best thing to do.

When he brought it up he knew she'd be pissed. She might even threaten to call the whole thing off. Well, she'd get over it eventually. After all, if she were truly the one, nothing could keep them apart. And if not, then they needed to know.

Besides, a spring wedding would be better than a fall one anyway. He could smell autumn in the crisp air. He turned the radio on and listened to a song about a man who didn't know his own heart. He looked at the radio and thought, you poor bastard. Yes, talking to Teri about delaying things just a little would be the right thing to do.

———

"I'm sorry, sir, but the course is full today." John gave the starter a nod and peeled a one hundred dollar bill from the money clip he took out of his pocket. Leaning over the counter at the pro shop at Sandy Beach Golf Course he pointed at the sheet that held the names of those people with reserved tee times. "Perhaps you misunderstood me. Isn't that my name there?"

The starter pretended to squint at the names and deftly palmed the bill. He pointed to his list. "No sir, perhaps this is your name here, scheduled for late this afternoon."

John's irritation with the man was growing quickly. What the hell kind of a world was this when you couldn't get a decent starting time for a hundred dollars? The starter wore a plaid Scottish hat and had a gin blossom nose. He had a sneer for a smile and looked at John as if he were just an ordinary hacker. John reluctantly shoved his hand back into his pocket.

Beside him, Les reached over the counter and pointed to the starter's sheet again. "My good man, I do believe my name is right there." John winced at the sight of the two C-notes that Les was showing in his hand.

The starter palmed these and smiled showing tobacco stained teeth. "Why I believe that is you, Mister . . ."

"Vargas, except you're mistaken again. We're on the tee next, before those other gentleman." He jerked his thumb toward the tee and indicated the next foursome, which consisted of a group of Japanese.

John was enjoying this now. Les was a big man, and one accustomed to getting his way. The starter was a weaseley little runt who had just pocketed a total of three hundred dollars in cash in addition to the greens fee. Les was going to make him work for it. The starter looked up and smiled. "You're right, sir. You are next."

John ignored the excited yammerings of the Japanese who were complaining to the starter as he drove his first shot two hundred and fifty yards down the center of the fairway. Les set his ball on a white tee and with a powerful drive hit his shot thirty yards past John's.

"So what are we playing for today John?" Les tossed his driver to his caddie and they started their walk down the fairway.

It was a gorgeous day for golf. The Pacific Ocean crashed onto the beaches and coastal cliffs to their right. The late morning breeze carried the scent of seaweed and salt air. This was one of John's favorite courses. Favorites places. But today even the sun and the manicured course couldn't distract him. His conversation with Enya hung in his mind like a lead weight. He had called and arranged the game because Les was the only person he ever confided in. Now that he was contemplating postponing the wedding, he needed to talk to Les even more.

"How about a quarter a hole and the loser buys the beer?"

John caught the caddies giving each other 'chump' looks. He laughed to himself. They set the game at a quarter a hole. It could have been a hundred dollars a hole and it wouldn't have mattered. What John truly enjoyed, and he always sensed Les did too, were the bragging rights to the game afterward.

They played even through the first nine holes and ordered hamburgers and fries at the turn. On the backside John had a two-stroke advantage as they arrived at the number sixteen tee. The wind off the ocean had kicked up making the drive especially challenging. This was one of the most legendary holes in all of golf, the sixteenth at Sandy Beach. The bold would try to shoot across the cliffs and ocean beach to a spot near the green, hopefully saving a stroke. The conservative played a longer route around the curve of the cliffs and avoided the risk of losing a ball to the ocean. More than one U.S. Open had been won or lost on this hole.

John had the honor and teed up first. Les was looking out to sea as John addressed his ball. John focused his mind, visualizing his shot sailing perfectly over the cliffs and beach and landing just short of the green.

"A diamond life is really tough."

Les' words drifted on the wind to John on his backswing and he was so startled he drove his ball and watched helplessly as it sailed into the Pacific Ocean. He turned to Les, incredulous. "What did you say?"

"Sorry, didn't realize you were swinging. You can hit another."

"No, that's okay. But what did you just say"

"I said a diamond life is really tough."

"What the hell does that mean?" John motioned for his caddie to throw him another ball. The caddie tossed a clean ball with John's name on it. "Diamond life, diamond lies. Are diamonds all anybody talks about anymore?"

"Face it Johnny, like it or not we have diamond lives. Most people would give their eyeteeth for the things we take for granted. And sometimes we have the nerve, the audacity, to pretend that somehow our wealth is a curse."

"I'm not following, I don't think I ever thought of it that way." John swung his club again and another ball sailed high to the left and nearly beaned a sea otter happily swimming in the surf.

"Come on, John. You remember back in college, how we tried to play 'poor kids' for a while? Well, it never worked because we couldn't stand it."

"You couldn't stand it. Ball please." John held his hand out expectantly. The long-haired caddie, who John sensed was beginning to understand the money he was working for, immediately tossed him another clean ball. John politely nodded his thanks.

"My recollection is," Les continued, "there were two of us who gave up trying to look poor about the same time. Anyhow, what I'm getting at is this. With wealth comes responsibility. Like it or not. And that means we have to be careful who we bring into the fold. We have to be certain that those from the outside, understand the implications."

"You're sounding pretty elitist here, Les, my friend."

"Don't get me wrong, if some guy works his tail off and earns his money that's one thing. More power to him. Someone like that probably has a plan and dreams he wants to follow. But you remember what happened to that guy my cousin hooked up with. He was Joe average, married into a ton of money, and didn't know what to do with himself. He picked up a complex, got a big fat chip on his shoulder, started drinking and the whole thing crashed around them. Now they're both screwed up. When he's not in rehab she is. Sudden unearned wealth can be terribly difficult to adjust to."

John swung his driver with a vengeance. He felt the impact of the club and twisted a full ninety degrees in a perfect follow through. The ball rocketed through the wind, over the cliffs and beach and landed safely five yards from the green. "I hope you aren't turning rich on me. You're starting to sound like Enya. Have you been talking to her?"

Les took his place on the tee. "No. What does she have to say?"

"She's on my case about Teri. Wants me to believe Teri isn't right for me, couldn't handle the responsibility that comes with money. And some other stuff." He didn't feel like admitting that Enya's comment about him not being anxious to get married was dangerously close to the mark.

Les took a practice swing. "Teri's pretty bright, I don't think there is much she couldn't learn. That's probably the only reason she let you get close. But maybe that's not the issue Enya is getting at. How is Teri anyway?"

John decided not to rise to Les' baiting. It was one of his more interesting aspects, a dry sarcasm that was second only to his own. "Her company set her up with an apartment in Tahoe because they want her to oversee a branch office a few days a week. I'm going up there after I drop you off. We're supposed to do wedding invitations tomorrow afternoon. But I have to admit, I'm not feeling that great about this marriage."

Les drove his ball to within ten yards of the green and John's heart started to sink. Les tossed his club to his caddie and joined him as they walked briskly down the fairway. John had to squint his eyes as the sun reflected onto the deep green ocean. The sound of the waves crashing on the shore carried on the stiffening breeze and he had to lean forward to keep his balance.

John's stomach was churning and he knew it wasn't because Les was going to win the hole. His concentration on the game was rapidly evaporating as he felt the realization of what he had just said. It was a stark, cold, suddenly alone feeling. Somehow he had just betrayed Teri. It was making him sick.

Raising his voice to be heard over the wind, John asked Les, "What do you think of Teri?"

"You know that I think she's a babe, a certifiable doll, smart too. But it doesn't matter what I think of her. All that matters is what you think. What you feel."

John trudged up the fairway giving a stray thought to his next shot. "Well, I love her and all that, she's something special, but I just don't know if she'd like being married to me. She loves her job and may not want to deal with our business and all those boring charity functions."

Les leaned toward him as if he didn't want the caddies to hear. "You're not making sense. All that stuff is set up to virtually run itself. How's the sex?"

"None better."

"Sounds to me like you're getting cold feet and you're trying to find some fault with her to give yourself an out."

A shiver ran through his body. It was the same sensation he had after talking with Enya. It was almost as if other people knew him better than he knew himself.

They arrived at Les' ball and his caddie handed him a wedge. Les took a short practice swing, then made a near perfect chip shot, sending the ball to within two feet of the cup. He turned to John. "I'm not much for giving advice, but you think about this. If you've got any doubts you'd better do something fast. If you marry her and then decide to divorce, that will cost you a ton of money. They haven't written a prenup yet that will prevent that."

"It doesn't matter. I couldn't ask Teri for a prenup. I couldn't hurt her like that. She'd see it as a lack of trust." John took the wedge his caddie offered, then changed his mind in favor of a five iron. He made a practice stroke, then asked for the wedge again. He addressed the ball and swung. He bladed the shot badly and sent the ball skidding over the green into a sand trap.

"You better make up your mind, Johnny boy. Breaking off an engagement isn't the worse thing that could happen to someone. But it'll be worse after the invitations have been sent. Imagine the humiliation that would cause."

"Who said anything about breaking an engagement?" John had to almost shout to be heard above the blustering wind.

"Maybe you should. Because the only thing worse than breaking an engagement is marrying somebody you know you shouldn't."

Les said something else after that but the words were lost in the wind. John's mind had tuned him out anyway. He hated hearing things he already knew.

———

"I don't want to get married. We can't do this." John's voice was flat, impassive. It frightened her. Teri tightened her grip on the flimsy box that held the fifty invitations to her happiest day. "I can't believe you said that. It's not funny."

It was the tone of John's voice, more than the words, that really shook her. He used that tone only when he finally really meant something. Her knees started to shake under her and her stomach turned queasy.

She stared at him, trying to think of what to say. Large wet snowflakes landed on his dark hair and after only a moment melted to be replaced by more of the falling stars from the sky. His blue eyes were hard and cold with none of the warmth she was accustomed to seeing there. Even in the dim evening light she could make out the tight muscles on his face.

Her thoughts reeling, she saw John reach for the box. Instinctively she pulled away, accidentally hitting John's hand. The box of fifty lovingly addressed wedding invitations on pearl white linen paper, with stamped RSVP cards on the inside, flew from her grasp into the air with the swirling snow.

Teri gasped as the envelopes fell to the wet ground. She dropped to her knees in the snow, soaking her jeans, and immediately started gathering them up. "Look what you've done!"

Four of the envelopes landed in a muddy puddle. The white contrasted sharply with the dirty water until the moisture absorbed into the paper and started to run the handwritten ink. The envelopes turned a murky brown. Teri quickly pulled the invitations for her Uncle Bob, Aunt Jennifer, her best friend Sally, and John's sister from the mud. "These are ruined. We can't send these. I think I might have enough extras."

"We can't send any of them. We can't get married. Not now anyway." He was standing above her but she could not bear to look up. The firmness in his voice seared her ears.

Still on her knees, she continued to gather stray envelopes. "Help me pick these up before they're ruined."

"It doesn't matter. We don't need them now."

Teri fought down the panic that welled within her. The chill night air and the smell of winter was like ice against her burning face. She felt small and desperate scrambling after invitations to a wedding that she feared wouldn't happen. The whole day had been wrong. All afternoon while she'd addressed the envelopes, John had been acting like a man condemned. Instead of being happy and going hand in hand to the mailbox to take turns depositing the envelopes one by one, he had only trudged after her when she made it obvious she would go without him.

Having collected all of the invitations, some brown with mud, some stained from wet snow, a few with only a minor blemish, Teri stood and faced John. Her chilled fingers fumbled to get the top of the crummy cardboard box back on to protect what was left of the dreams she held for them. With her vision blurred by tears, and her heart filled with anger, she looked into his eyes. "If we don't mail these invitations now there will never be another time."

"Don't talk like that." It was the calm reassuring voice she'd heard so many times before. This time it was too much. All of her senses came alive and it was as if a white light flashed across her eyes. Anger pumped through her veins. Her mind raced. She could barely control herself.

"Don't talk like what? Like someone who is fed up with your indecision? Don't talk like someone who has a life and dreams of her own? What do you expect? I've waited for you for years. We've done the long engagement, it's been ten months. Just like you wanted it. On the twelfth month we get married. Now is when we send the invitations."

"I just need a little more time."

"Time! For what? What about me? I'll be thirty-one this year. I don't have time to wait anymore. We've had this conversation too often for you to start this again. I've waited too many years to wait one minute longer to finally start our life together. I don't have enough tears to wait any longer. We either go forward, or end it now."

John was visibly taken aback by her outburst. When she paused for breath he stammered. "You'll appreciate this later. It's just not right now."

Her mind reached for a reason for this. Any reason. "It's another woman, isn't it? Damn you. I knew there was somebody else."

He looked stunned. "No. There is no one else."

"I don't care. I don't believe anything you say. Everybody told me you'd do this. Beth said it. So did my other good friends. I didn't listen to them. I defended you all the way. I've waited, I've given you my heart and soul, I've prayed for you. I've chosen to believe everything you've told me. Now it's time to do it or not. We either mail our wedding invitations right here and now, or it's over."

She started for the mailbox but stopped when it was apparent he wasn't going to move from his position between her and the postal drop. Her desire to fight the good fight for them had vented with her rage. It was gone. She felt nauseous and hollow, her legs weak.

She heard calm reasonable words come out of the night in a voice she no longer recognized. In a voice she no longer wanted to know.

"We can't mail these like this. They're dirty and wet. Let's wait and get new ones."

Teri lowered her eyes and watched the snow falling past her box of wedding invitations, her soiled knees, her black boots, and onto the ground, where it was starting to stick. She chose her next words slowly and deliberately, and delivered them with resignation. "You have destroyed us."

"What?"

"You have destroyed me."

The wintry air bit into her face. Tears were flowing on her cheeks, stinging as they froze. She drew a deep breath and managed to clear her vision enough to stare into his beautiful blue eyes one more heartbreaking time. "I love you more than I can tell you. I hope you have a wonderful life. And I never, never, want to see you again."

With that she turned, still clutching her box of invitations announcing a life together, and walked away from him.

chapter

10

I T HAD BEEN SIX MONTHS SINCE JOHN HAD watched Teri disappear into the snowy Tahoe night. It hurt like it was yesterday. He opened his eyes in the grim light of the small apartment he had taken to try and get away from all things familiar. Things that would remind him of her, of them together.

He had a dull ache between his temples that he recognized was the result of too many whiskeys on the rocks and not enough sleep. What time was it? What day was it? Who gave a rat's ass anyway?

Street noise carried through his window. Drivers gunned their cars' engines to climb the steep hill on which his building was perched. A foghorn moaned lowly on the bay. San Francisco was awake and busy. John put a pillow over his head and tried to ignore it.

What would she be doing this morning? Maybe today would be the day she'd finally call. He'd sent the last letter exactly four days ago. This would be the telling day. If she got it two days ago, that would have given her a day to think about it, and now a day to respond.

On the other hand, if she ignored it, tossed it, or if the postal service screwed up, he'd never know. He had already decided that he would leave that part up to fate. If she actually took the time to write back, to respond to his apology point by point, he could still be left hanging for a couple of days. God, this was miserable.

He tried to swallow but the inside of his mouth was sour and sticky. The aftertaste of stale cigarettes was like glue on his lips. The idea of a glass of water was appealing. The thought of a shot of whisky to cut through the filth he tasted was better.

Today was another workday in the city. She'd have on one of her prim outfits that looked like it was designed for her. Would she still be working at the same job? No doubt the sales guys would be sniffing around her skirts already. Did she have another guy, maybe some dot-com type? She must. He had to believe she must. Somewhere reality needs to kick in, dimwit. She hadn't returned a call for six months, had returned every letter sent to her unopened, refused to talk or communicate with him in any way, shape, or form. For pity's sake, how long could she keep this up?

He still couldn't believe he had been so stupid. What an idiot. John flung his pillow to the floor and managed to sit up in bed, his muscles aching. He focused his eyes on the tiny undecorated bedroom and located his cigarettes. After fumbling with a match he inhaled deeply. Smoke curled around his face and filled the little room slowly. What a filthy stinking habit. He took another drag and scratched his three day old beard. Maybe he'd shave today.

An hour later, having managed to force himself to shave, shower and dress, he paced impatiently back-and-forth in front of his window. Fortified with two shots of whisky he waited anxiously for the white and blue mail truck to appear outside his apartment. It normally arrived between 1:30 and 2:00. Sometimes it came as late as 3:00, but almost never after that.

His stomach was tight and felt as if it were trying to digest itself. The whisky hadn't helped that, so he tried a beer. The carbonation might take the edge off. Two floors below on the street, cars chugged up the hill and out of his field of view. He knew there was a stop sign up there, one that forced the drivers to brake on an impossible incline. But that was the city. You had to love it to live here. He could not imagine a circumstance that would cause him to live anyplace else.

John checked the clock over the television. It flashed 1:42. Still no sign of the mail truck. She had to write back. No, she had to call. She couldn't be serious about never seeing him again, she was smarter than that. She had to recognize that what they had shared was a special love, a once in a lifetime love. If only he had seen it.

Her failure to reconcile or confirm this tore at his insides. He'd never experienced such helplessness before. Never been so desperate for someone who was almost out of reach to save him from falling into the abyss.

Not an ordinary love. That's what he had said in the letter. And the one before, and the one before that. She simply would have to read one of those and know that he was right. Know that the two of them belonged together, no matter how badly he'd screwed things up. This was a love worth fighting for, worth suffering for.

He laughed at himself. He had the suffering part down. If she didn't write he'd have to learn to deal with it. No, that wasn't possible. He crushed the empty cigarette package into a tight little ball of red and blue foil. Maybe he should go and stakeout her apartment. Wait for her to come home. Talk to her, force her to see him.

No. That was a bad idea. He didn't want her to think he was some kind of whacked-out stalker, or worse. He had control of himself. She was just a girl and he was going to pursue her politely. She had said she never wanted to see him again. Well, she wouldn't have to if she didn't want to. That was the one gift he could give her. He decided he loved her enough to give her the space and freedom to go about her life without having to worry about him hanging over her shoulder. He hurled the wadded cigarette package at the window where it bounced harmlessly to the floor.

Lighting a smoke from a fresh pack, he heard another car coming up the grade. A red pickup passed by. He let himself fall back onto the lime green couch that had come with the furnished apartment. Sucking on a cigarette, watching the smoke swirl, he wondered if he were a coward for not going to her. For not making her say the words to his face that he so much did not want to hear. After that night in Tahoe he was sure he could not bear to hear them again.

His stomach turned over again. At the depths of his soul he felt an ache that drained the energy out of him. There was no point in living without Teri in his life. He could not possibly pretend that anything in the world had any meaning if she didn't come back to him.

He lay motionless, his breathing shallow. His body was bloated from the unending diet of junk food and alcohol. He put his fingers in his hair and realized he was months overdue to have it cut. He looked at the hand holding his cigarette and almost didn't recognize it. It was pale and shaking, with untrimmed fingernails and yellow tobacco stains.

The ash from his cigarette fell onto his shirt with part of the tobacco still glowing. He didn't realize it until he felt the burning on his chest. Startled he jumped up and quickly brushed himself off. This was perfect. Maybe he'd just set himself on fire and get the hell out of his misery.

Still smarting he went into the bathroom to see how badly his shirt was burned. Looking in the mirror he wasn't surprised to see the burn had ruined the shirt. He was surprised to see his own reflection. His face was white and puffy, his eyes sunken and red with dark smudges underneath them. He looked like hell. He went to the refrigerator and got another beer.

As he popped the top he heard the unmistakable sound of the squeaky brakes of the mail truck. Putting the beer down he went to the window to watch for the mail carrier to enter the lobby. The carrier today was the regular, a stocky black-haired woman who looked forty and had an easy smile. As he watched her he wished he had a place in the world too.

He tried to time his arrival at the mailbox so that he would not have to talk to her. All he wanted was to see if there was a letter. Going down the two flights of stairs he entered the lobby just as the mail carrier left.

He approached his bronze colored mailbox fumbling the key in his sweaty hand. Closing his eyes he held his breath, turned the key, and opened the door. When he opened his eyes his heart sank.

He reached into the small oblong box and withdrew the beige envelope he'd mailed four days ago. Teri's name and address were neatly crossed out, and the words, 'return to sender' were neatly printed with blue ink in her prim style.

"Perfect, my life's turned into an Elvis song."

John took the letter and dragged himself back to the solitude of his small apartment. Closing the door, he slid to the floor and sat against the wall. He pressed his face into his tobacco-stained hands feeling the letter against his cheek. In his heart he was completely alone. For the first time he could remember, he wept.

———

That night John made his way up the hill in front of his apartment through the cool fog that had rolled in off the bay to his newfound hangout. The two block walk was much more strenuous than he'd remembered. By the time reached the entrance of the Black Door Tavern he was out of breath and starting to sweat.

Pushing the scratched wooden door open he moved from the damp night air into the dry, smoke-filtered light of the bar. It was a small tavern with a polished bar taking up the length of one wall and a row of tables taking the space by the windows that looked out onto the street. It was dimly lit and had the usual neon beer signs and tacky bar paraphernalia. The walls were decorated with an assortment of leather clothes and sex toys favored by some of the more adventurous of the locals. John often wondered if the place had ever been popular.

He recognized a few of the regulars, the two gay guys in business suits who were evening habitués, holding hands while they poured over some legal documents. The three women in tight leather outfits who always left about midnight and of course Jerry the bearded bartender.

They all routinely checked him out when he came in, then seemed to forget he existed. Except for Jerry, who set up a draft beer and a shot of bourbon for him. John smiled and took his place on the corner barstool.

Two hours later John was still perched in the same place contemplating the smoke emanating from the end of his cigarette. He'd not been counting the number of drinks he'd had, but knew he would have lost track by now anyway. An obnoxiously loud country music song was blasting from the CD jukebox for at least the tenth time in the last hour.

Two guys in cowboy hats were playing the Somebody Did Somebody Wrong Song over and over and slow dancing with each other as if the music had been written for them alone. John started to weigh the merits of going over and kicking the living crap out of them or busting the jukebox open and ripping out the CD and throwing it into San Francisco Bay. Not only had he started to loath the song, it was so loud it was interfering with his figuring on how to get Teri back.

Before moving off the stool, he decided to think about it some more. He motioned to the bartender for another drink. He was a little startled when somebody came in and sat on the barstool next to him. He was really surprised when he realized it was Les.

John made out the look of disgust on Les' face as he looked around the bar. "How the hell did you find this dump?"

"I might ask the same question of you, buddy." John had a flash of embarrassment because he knew his words were slurring. "And it is not a dump. It has character."

"If it had any more character than this it would be Charles Manson." Les ordered a beer over the din of the blaring jukebox.

John's senses started to come into focus. The boozy fog he had been wallowing in was turning into a wary shroud of humiliation. He didn't want Les to know the true depth of the hole he had dug for himself. Besides, Les had no idea what it was like to lose Teri. For a while he had held Les partly to blame. Him and Enya. But as time went by he'd slowly recognized that like the song said, it was his own damn fault.

"You look worse than I thought you would. What are you doing here, trying to kill yourself?"

The question caught John off guard. It cut right to the chase. Cut to what he had only today started to wonder himself. He felt his face flushing in anger at being found out and interrogated so bluntly. "No. I'm just having a drink with my friends."

Les ignored him. "Are you still moaning over Teri?" His expression was placid, calm. It belied the violation of the question.

John's neck tightened and he resented that anyone wanted to know how he felt about anything. He took a drink. "Yes. I'm still moaning, as you put it, over Teri."

Les looked away in disgust, then turned back to John. "Forget her, man, it's over. You screwed up, maybe I even helped by giving you bad advice, but get over it, Johnny. There are plenty of other girls out there."

"None of them are Teri, can't you see that? She and I are, well, we belong together. I can't explain it." John wrapped his hand around his beer glass for comfort.

"What? Do you think you're the only guy to ever get dumped? Join the club, buddy, there are millions of us. You're obsessed with this woman. You need to get your life back. You need to forget her 'cause she's long gone and she ain't coming back."

"What am I supposed to do? Join the French Foreign Legion?"

"If that's what it takes. You're sure as hell killing yourself here, you might as well take a chance doing something else." Les sat back and ran his hands through his hair. John was starting to enjoy frustrating him. Suddenly Les leaned forward. At the same time the music stopped so Les dropped his voice to a near whisper.

"You ever been scared, John? I mean really scared?"

"What the hell kind of question is that?"

John's thoughts went to a night in a cellar in Panama. He had been terrified beyond words and still had nightmares about it. He answered slowly, not knowing where this was leading. "Yeah, I've been scared. Everybody has been."

Les persisted. "Are you scared now? Afraid you'll never see Teri again, afraid you'll never have that kind of love again? Well, get used to it because you won't. But you may find something even better if you try."

John could tell he didn't understand. "Les, let me ask you this. Have you ever been in love, man? I mean not just the like to see her, have the hots for her stuff. I mean, the really I'd kill for her kind of love. The kind that doesn't make any sense. You know you spend your whole life screwing around and acting like there's no tomorrow and all of a sudden you find someone who matters. Someone you care about more than yourself. You ever been that in love, Les?"

Les swirled the beer in his glass, averting his eyes from John. "No. Never been there. I'm not sure I believe it really happens."

"I didn't either. I was caught totally by surprise. I just thought she was another chick on the hit parade. I mean I knew she was special, knew we were special together, felt it in my heart." He took another drink and swallowed hard. "But, I quit thinking with my heart. Started thinking with my head. Started letting other people think for me. I told her things I meant, made promises I intended to keep, then turned my back on her. I didn't listen to myself, I didn't believe in myself.

"I never would have thought I could be such an ass. I don't know what's worse. What I did to her, or my having the nerve to be feeling sorry for myself."

The music blared again from the jukebox. Les leaned to John and had to raise his voice to be heard.

"Get over it, John. Self pity doesn't suit you."

Les would never understand. His love for Teri was a one of kind, once in a lifetime. It was something destined by the stars. Why couldn't Les and Teri and everybody else see that? John's rage started to flow. He realized now that he was scared of something new.

Les was right, Teri wasn't coming back. That meant that all the love and thoughts and talk of destiny were bullshit. There was no true love. This frightened him more because there was no way he could fight it. There was no physical manifestation to wrap his arms around, to punch or kick, to plunge a knife into and kill. There was only an ephemeral idea that if true, meant that he was utterly alone in the world.

John got to his feet shakily. "Piss off, Les. You don't know squat."

Les' voice was calming. "John, I've been afraid too, but this time I'm afraid for somebody else. I'm scared for you. I'm afraid you're killing yourself, buddy. You've got to wake-up and cleanup. Come with me. Let me take you to a clinic I know. They're real private and know how to deal with this kind of situation."

"Les, go to hell. You're not taking me to Camp Rehab. I'm just fine thanks, I don't need anybody or anything, and if you want to help me, just get out of here."

"John, what are you going to do? What do you want from life right now? Do you think if you sit here and drink long enough that somehow Teri is going to come walking through that door and suddenly make your life perfect again? Figure it out, buddy. She's gone, baby, gone. This show is over and the curtain has dropped."

Les shrugged and dug his hand into his pocket. When he pulled it out he had several one dollar bills in it. He held them out to John. "These are for you."

"Why?"

"It's three bucks. The bridge toll on the Golden Gate. Do yourself and the rest of us a favor and go jump off the thing so we don't have to suffer through the misery of watching you waste yourself away."

John refused the money and Les let the bills fall on the bar. "You've got a lot people who care about you, Johnny boy. Your parents and Enya are worried sick. You know she feels partly responsible for this."

"Give her a message for me, tell my big sister to screw herself."

"Let me drive you home."

"Go to hell, Les. Leave me alone."

"Do yourself a favor. Figure out what you want John. If you need anything, call me." Les walked swiftly out of the tavern.

John sat and finished his drink. He put the bills Les had left into his shirt pocket. He took a fifty from his wallet, slipped it under his glass and headed for the door.

Stepping out of the hot bar into the cool night he could smell the ocean in the air. The alcohol in his veins seemed to take hold all of a sudden. He staggered a few steps. His apartment, and the bay, were all downhill from here.

Minutes later John leaned on the wall outside of his apartment. A thick fog had rolled in off the bay and the night air was damp and cold. The streetlights glowed with yellow shrouds around them. A foghorn moaned on the bay. John could hear the distant sound of traffic on the Golden Gate Bridge. He started walking toward it.

The bridge wasn't very far from his apartment. He stopped at a liquor store and bought a small bottle of bourbon. Something to ward off the cold he told himself. He walked by the bay through the old Presidio and tried to focus his mind.

What had Les said? 'Figure out what you want,' that was it. Les must be blind. All he wanted was Teri. After that life was simple.

With an effort he climbed the stairs that led to the bridge deck and walked toward the south tower. At this hour there wasn't much traffic and what little there was whooshed by with their headlights making a piercing glow in the fog. The cars looked like spirits lost in a nether world of gray and black.

The bridge rail was about waist-high and the orange color was illuminated by gold lights that filtered through the damp air. John took a shot from the bottle and felt the bourbon burn its way down his throat. After he passed the first bridge tower he could hear the ocean crashing on the rocks below.

A seagull startled him as he leaned over the edge. Peering into the night he wondered how it would feel to plunge over the side, falling through the clouds free of the touch of anything solid. Falling, and turning, the mind racing to an end it had chosen. A few seconds of flailing legs and the wind ripping past his face then the hard slam into the cold water of the bay.

Maybe that would be the end. Then again, maybe there would be searing pain, broken limbs, icy water choking his throat. The last desperate effort as he would try to save himself, in spite of himself. The black water gripping him and dragging him under, suffocating the life from his body. He shivered.

What would they think when they found the body? They'd think he was stupid. They'd be right.

He took another hit from the bourbon bottle. Holding it over the water, he hesitated, then let it go. He watched it disappear into the fog and waves crashing below.

———

John staggered into his small apartment wiping the rain from his brow with the back of his hand. He ignored the mud on his shoes and closed the door behind himself. He felt his way through the dark across the sparsely furnished living room to the kitchen.

He switched on the light then closed his eyes in pain as the white light bathed him. With his eyes closed the dizziness brought on by too much booze came back so he opened them again and held onto the counter while the room steadied itself.

The raindrops on his cloth jacket caused the rank smell of cigarette smoke from the bar to cling to him like a reminder of his stale life. He withdrew a bottle of bourbon from a drawer, selected the least dirty water glass from the counter, and poured a shot. He quickly downed it, poured another, then lit a filtered cigarette.

Numb, that's how he wanted to be, but tonight the booze wasn't working. He was only drunk, and it wasn't a pleasant drunk. It was the kind of brain-fucking intoxication that caused kids to drive too fast and punks to start fights they were bound to lose. Anger seethed within him. He was angry at Teri, the bitch, for leaving him. He was angry with himself for driving her away. He was pissed at Les for rubbing his face in it. He took another shot and filled the glass again. It was becoming intolerable. Being lost in the world, being alone within himself, participating in his own self-destruction, the bourbon not working.

John picked up the phone book by the sink and threw it as hard as he could against the far wall. "Fuck it all!"

The outburst made him feel stupid. Unsteadily he crossed the kitchen and picked up the book. Opening it to the airline section, he tried to focus on the words. New World Airlines had the biggest ad with the largest print. He dialed the toll free number, turned off the light, then sat on the floor in the dark listening to the soft purr of the phone in his ear.

After three rings and a click, a pleasant female voice picked up on the other end. "New World Airlines. How may we help you?"

"I want to go someplace."

"That's fine, sir. We go lots of places." She had a nice manner about her. He knew he'd like her if he met her.

"Name one."

"We have a special to Amsterdam this month."

"What language do they speak there?"

"I believe it's Dutch, sir."

"I don't speak Dutch. Name me someplace where they speak English."

"Actually, I've heard that most everybody in Holland speaks English fluently."

"Okay."

"Sir?"

"Book me to Amsterdam."

"And when would you like to leave?"

"Tomorrow."

"And where will you be departing from?"

"Hell."

————

Two she-lions stalked through the yellow grass creeping up behind a herd of unsuspecting zebras. The striped animals grazed unknowingly, only yards away from impending death. A male lion watched only half interested in the hunt.

Suddenly one lioness broke into a trot heading for the unsuspecting zebras. The second lioness started to gallop after her. The zebras bolted and the chase was on. The other zebras in the herd scattered as the lions zeroed in on a baby that was away from the rest. A lioness leapt onto its neck and bit down hanging on with her teeth.

The second lioness raked a claw across the zebra's hind legs again and again until the beast collapsed under the first lion. She piled on and the male quickly arrived. The three of them began ripping and tearing chunks of bloody meat off the zebra while it was still kicking.

Teri pointed the remote control at the television and clicked it off. She put down her microwave dinner of lean spaghetti with tomato sauce in revulsion. She felt a tear running down her cheek and wiped it off with the back of her shirtsleeve. She was sorry for the zebra, but knew that wasn't what was making her cry.

Getting up from her couch she walked to the window of her apartment. She could just make out the near end of the Golden Gate Bridge. A thick fog blanketed San Francisco and the glow of the lights was eerie in the dark.

She let herself remember the last time she and Johnny had driven over the bridge and he had teased her about her psychic reading. God, what had gone wrong with them?

She'd known from the outset that getting over a love would be difficult. She'd done it before and had initially thought that after a little while this one would fade too. But now it had been six months and sometimes she still hurt as much as she had that night in Tahoe when Johnny had betrayed her.

She wanted to forgive him. So many times she wanted to pick up the phone when the answering machine screened him, wanted to read the letters that showed up almost daily for the first month. But she refused to let herself do it. She refused to be conned and cheated out of anymore of her life than he had already taken from her.

The years she spent working as a volunteer in the women's shelters had taught her one thing. Men didn't change. She wouldn't allow herself to get trapped in a relationship where the man would not keep his word to her. As far as she was concerned, it was almost the same as physical abuse.

That's what she had told herself for six months. That's what her friends and support groups had helped her to believe. She smiled in spite of herself. She imagined what Johnny would think about all of that. 'A bunch of air-headed femi-nazis, who think all men should be neutered,' is how he had described them to her once. She had to admit, there were meetings with her friends when she thought he might have a point.

She picked up her wineglass from the table by her dinner and smelled the tart bouquet. Turning the lights low she went to the couch and let herself sink into the soft cushions. She closed her eyes.

Life had become so desolate. She remembered that snowy night in Tahoe. She had returned to her apartment, packed and driven back to San Francisco after tossing the wedding invitations in the trunk like so much garbage. She had not even been sure if she'd locked the front door. Her only thought was to get out of there before Johnny showed up again. She could barely see through the tears that had streamed down her face and she nearly went off the mountain road at least a couple of times.

Somehow she made it to her best friend Beth's house without killing herself. Once there she collapsed into a helpless sobbing mess. Teri winced at how vulnerable she had been in front of her friend. But if it hadn't been for Beth, she was not sure she would have survived.

For a while she had a difficult time dealing with the reality. But each time she felt weak and had a notion to answer one of John's calls, or open a letter, Beth was there to lean on and talk to. Beth, who had been through a rough divorce only the previous year, had been a pillar of strength to Teri in her darkest moments.

Surprisingly quickly, her emotions turned to anger. She alternately cursed the day she'd ever met John and cursed him for ever making her feel happy. She had a hard time believing she'd just been used. He'd seemed so sincere when he said all those things about love, and destiny, and being together forever. Maybe it took a special type of rich, conniving monster to be able to break intimate promises.

And stupid! She could not believe she had been so stupid that she hadn't seen what was happening. She'd always been a little intimidated by the money thing. Also, John was a few years older and that had never felt quite right. But they had been so good together. That she let herself be led on for so long was what had rubbed on her nerves like a nail file for months.

She opened her eyes and stared into the fog outside the window. The clouds passed by, drifting on a wind that made them swirl in a gray layer of veils that were barely perceptible.

She sipped her wine, letting the tartness of it linger on her tongue. She inhaled the aroma again. It was one of the few pleasures she allowed herself now. She made it a point not to drink much, but when she did she wanted to savor it.

Normally she wouldn't have opened a bottle unless Beth or one of her friends were around. But tonight she was without any of her support group and was thankful for it. Being alone was finally starting to be okay. In fact, it was starting to be preferable to the company of some of those who had helped her for the last six months. Being alone was definitely a positive step.

Her friends were dear and well-meaning and she loved them, but lately she had started to feel overwhelmed. It was as if she now had to build her life to their satisfaction. Somehow her recovery from her crashed relationship with John represented a kind of redemption for them all. Teri knew this problem existed mostly in her own mind, but once the thought had formed, she couldn't make it go away.

It might have gone too far four days ago. She had been struggling with the notion that she wanted to talk to Johnny. Wanted to hear his voice, wanted to find some closure. Wanted to know something, maybe just how he was feeling, she couldn't put a finger on it. No, that wasn't true. She still loved him. Even after all the hurt and anger, she knew he was still in her heart. Over the last two weeks she had resisted the urge to call him on several occasions.

In the back of her mind a clock was ticking. A clock that told her how long she could go without contacting him before it might be too late. Before he might give up on her and move on to another woman. His phone messages had stopped months ago and what was once a flood of letters had trickled off to almost nothing.

The idea was insane. Considering that she had refused any contact with him since that night, it didn't make sense to try and reach him now. Yet, that was what she wanted to do. Her skin prickled at the thought she might miss him due to her own stubbornness. What did her love mean if she wasn't able to forgive?

It was time to set her pride aside and at least try to get some resolution.

Four days ago Beth had been waiting for her when she arrived home. They had plans to go to a movie but one of Teri's meetings had gone long and she was running late. She'd checked her mail on the way in and her heart had leapt when she saw the letter from John. She recognized the new address that he'd been using for the last few months. This was the first time in five weeks he had tried to contact her. Her palms were perspiring by the time she got to the door. She didn't know if she wanted to open it or not. Beth must have seen the look on her face.

"Johnny boy, again?"

Teri faked a smile.

Beth dug into her purse. "You want blue ink, or should we send the message in red? It's more meaningful that way."

Teri didn't want to send any message. She wanted to think about it. Beth looked at her expectantly and gave her a wink.

"Princess, you aren't thinking about reading that trash now are you?"

Teri felt a hot flash of embarrassment. "No, of course not. I'll take the blue. It'll match his eyes."

She took the blue pen and with strangely shaking hands printed, "Return to sender," on the envelope like she had many times before. Beth laughed and took the letter out of her hands.

"Let me do the honors."

Then before Teri could say anything, Beth went out the door and deposited the envelope in the mailbox.

The fog glowed lonely over the bridge in the distance. Teri drew herself out of the couch and went to the phone. Picking up the receiver she punched in John's parents' phone number. She wanted to get his new number. She prayed Walter would answer so she wouldn't have to speak to Erik or Melanie.

There were two rings and then Walter's smooth voice. "Erikson's residence, how may I help you?"

Teri's heart skipped a beat. "Walter, this is Teri." She drew a deep breath. "I was wondering if you could be so kind as to give me Johnny's new number."

"Ah, Miss Teri, wonderful to hear your voice again. Unfortunately I'm afraid I can't help you. It seems that John has suddenly left the country and he hasn't told us where he's gone. Is there a message I can give him should he call?"

She couldn't have been more stunned if Walter had punched her in the stomach. She forced herself to whisper. "No, no message. Thanks Walter, do take care." She put the receiver down as the tears began again.

PART II

chapter 11

BARZAN WATCHED AS THE RHINO BURST THROUGH the underbrush and thundered into a clearing. Standing in the back of the chase vehicle he yelled at the driver to close the distance. His hair blew in the wind and he leaned forward trying to steady himself as the truck bounced unpredictability over the savanna.

He cursed their luck. They'd almost had a perfect shot but something spooked the stupid beast into running, so they had no choice but to give chase in the two four-wheel drive trucks. They had been tracking for days without finding anything and Barzan did not want to give up on any of the increasingly scarce rhinos they found. He ducked behind the windscreen as they came perilously close to a long needled acacia tree.

The terrified rhino slammed into the thick brush near the river like a two thousand kilogram tank, stampeding over everything in its path. So far the poachers had only seen the back of the beast, but it was a big one. Barzan strained to catch a glimpse of the horn but could never quite see it as the animal raced away from them. The size of the animal alone would guarantee a handsome horn as a reward. Perhaps one valuable enough to make Moto-san truly appreciate Barzan's worth.

He was certain they had already collected enough trophies to satisfy Moto-san. However, they were not as great as in years past and he lacked the special one he wanted to present to his employer. One that would ensure his position as Moto-san's right hand. Barzan had almost given up in his hunt for an extra prize. The poachers had been on their way to the Somalian border when the sharp eyed Masai driver in the other vehicle had spotted the back end of the black rhino near the river. Now all they had to do was run it down and kill it.

The beast broke into the open again just ahead of the other vehicle. One of the men in the back opened fire at close range with an automatic weapon. Barzan cringed at the noise, but they were committed to this chase now, and damn the rangers. If they showed up, he'd kill them too, then slip over the border and be gone.

Barzan braced himself in the back of the careening truck as best he could and raised his rifle. All he could see was the gray backside of the rhino, so he fired at that. The animal slowed just a little, then started to stagger. In the open, the trucks closed on it quickly. Suddenly the dinosaur-sized beast stopped and turned to attack. Barzan was stunned to see the animal had no horn.

Several of his men continued to shoot at the rhino until it collapsed and writhed on the ground snorting wildly. Barzan watched as the convulsions stopped. The death of the animal was a complete waste. He slammed his palm down on the top of the truck in disgust. Not only was the animal's death of little use to anyone, but they had lost valuable time and risked being discovered by chasing it down.

When the truck stopped Barzan approached the rhino with Kip. He ground his teeth in frustration and lit a cigarette. Some stupid enviros had convinced the government that cutting the horns off would prevent poaching. Barzan silently cursed the infidels who started this practice. He knew of others who would kill a dehorned rhino just out of spite. Even if the poachers didn't get them, without a horn the animals were helpless to protect themselves and their young from predators.

Kip knelt next to the beast. "They go to a lot of trouble to save the animals from us. I wonder why they don't spend the money helping the people. Tourists don't want to pay to see disfigured creatures like this."

As usual Kip's insight was dead-on and it reminded Barzan why he had chosen the tall Masai as his second in charge. "You are right, it is a bad business all around. But I cannot believe they are that stupid. I think these people have found a way to collect horns legally. Then later they sell them on the black market and profit, all the while pretending they are saving animals. It is very clever. One has to admire such a plan, it seems to fool everyone."

Looking at the carcass, Barzan spat in disgust. He examined the smooth cut the rangers had made on the animal's horn. Idiots. Thieves. He swore at one of his hired Masai. "Get the chain saw and cut the root off its nose. We can sell the rest of this thing to the Chinese and still make plenty of money. The dehorning did not save this animal."

The poachers made short work of cutting the rest of the horn out of the dead rhino's face. Barzan didn't look back at the mutilated animal as they drove toward the border.

That night Barzan's hunting party camped several miles over the border into Somalia. The Masai men he had hired for this expedition had been of better than average quality. Kip had spread word of good pay and Barzan had learned how to select the best men. He required that they be tough, uncomplaining and follow orders. He was pleased with the way they had performed and was looking forward to rewarding them so that he might hire them again on his next trip. In comparison to the ultimate value of the horns, he did not give the men much, but compared to most Masai, he paid them a fortune. It was something Moto-san had taught him. A man was only rich or poor relative to his neighbors.

In much of central and eastern Africa, if a man could count on feeding his family comfortably and also have a few goods, then he was indeed fortunate. Barzan paid his men much more than they could expect to make farming or as unskilled laborers in the cities. At the same time he pocketed enough to live well in Aden. Not yet as well as Moto-san, but if he was successful on a few more hunts, that could change.

Tonight was a celebration of sorts. Barzan was happy to let them build a fire for the first time in weeks and they roasted a fine young antelope on a spit. The Masai told stories around the fire. Some spoke in English, which they had learned in their schools. Others told stories in various Swahili dialects. Although he did not follow all of these tales, he knew from their gestures and Kip's occasional explanations, they were mostly legends of brave hunters facing lions and leopards with little more than a spear and a shield.

Barzan appreciated that these men were true warriors in the oldest sense of the word. Anyone who would face a charging lion with only a piece of wood had to be a warrior. Or carrion. These men were much braver than many he had known in his homeland. They stood up and faced danger. Some of those at home hid behind false prophets and valued cheating their brothers more than standing up for themselves. That was partly why he liked the wild. Liked the Masai. He had found that if he treated them with respect he could trust them, a luxury he did not have with many of the men he dealt with.

The Serengeti was cruel but honest. The strong and cunning prevailed, the rest perished. It was brutal but simple. Barzan thrived on it.

The tone around the fire changed subtly. Barzan brushed a mosquito from his face and leaned slightly forward, tuning in to the storyteller. He was the oldest of the warriors and Barzan guessed he was fifty or more. He wasn't swift or strong anymore, but he was the best tracker Barzan had ever found and Barzan made a point to treat him with respect.

"In the valley of the sun, the biggest of the black rhinos may still live. It is a place so difficult to find that even the poachers have not discovered it."

Barzan's attention was immediate. A jolt of anticipation shot through him and he leaned forward. "Why not?"

The storyteller looked into the fire. "There is a jungle and a cliff by a river. That is all anyone recalls. The old warriors of my father's time knew the place."

"Where are they now? Can they still tell us?" Barzan's mind was racing. He had heard rumors of this place for years, ever since the poaching had started decimating the rhino population. Someone had made a map to it, but it was as elusive as the valley.

Old rhinos had been scarce for years. If there was an isolated herd someplace it would mean the breed would be pure. He knew that males with larger horns tended to dominate herds and that led to offspring with larger horns. Just a few trophies from such a group would be worth a fortune. His breathing was shallow. He tried to keep the interest out of his voice.

"No, those who knew of the place died in the tribal wars. There is no one left who can find the Rhino's valley."

Barzan laughed, trying not to appear anxious. "You and your legends. I must admit you had me excited for a moment. Do you realize that if we found such a place we could all feed our families like kings for the rest of our lives." He dug at the story-teller deliberately. He was well-aware of the sense of family the Masai had.

"No, it is not a legend." The storyteller barely changed expressions. "I saw a horn, as a child, that my father told me came from this place. We stood it upright and it was taller than I. Greater than any I have seen since."

The wind blew smoke from the fire toward Barzan and he squinted his eyes in the dark. He tried to provoke the story-teller to continue. "What of it? If you can't find it, there is no meaning."

"It is said," the warrior looked at Barzan with his eyes reflecting the yellow firelight, "that before the white man's war, an English made a map."

"A proper one?"

"A white man's map."

Barzan's pulse quickened. He forced himself to portray an air of indifference. Pulling a cigarette from his pocket he slowly lit it. "So what became of this map."

"A white man, an English, followed it, but did not heed the warnings. Then he flew away and was never seen again."

Barzan spit on the fire in disgust. His heart fell in disappointment. Always the same answer. Someday he would find out what happened to that map. If only he could find the right Masai. There must be someone left who knew. Perhaps he would talk to Moto-san about offering a reward. He threw his cigarette into the fire and watched as the flames consumed it.

————

John made his way to the number 16 train platform at the Amsterdam station and found the car destined for Paris. Holding his soft sided suitcase in front of him so it wouldn't bang on the sides of the car or seats, he located the first-class compartment and went in. He stored his bag in the overhead shelf, sat down and wiped the perspiration from his brow.

The heat was more than he had expected for this early in the morning. The long walk from the taxi stand to the train station platform had been invigorating. He only hoped he didn't start sweating enough to be uncomfortable during the ride to Paris.

He was happy he'd ultimately decided to go first-class. Reflecting on the last three years, he'd decided he was due for a little luxury. Overall Amsterdam had been a good place for him to come and clear his mind of the mess he had made of getting over Teri.

The train lurched forward as a man smoking a cigarette passed by on the platform. John felt his face tighten at the thought of a cigarette. That was one habit he would never go back to. Leaning back in the soft blue seat he watched the city go by as the train gathered speed.

The first two months in Holland had been the hardest. After arriving he had taken a flat in a rundown section of town. He'd made a deal with himself that he would not rely on the family fortune. All the money he had couldn't buy him what he wanted. In fact, it was easy to argue that it had actually cost him.

He'd found a job on a road crew that was working on a private project so they'd overlooked his lack of a work permit. He'd been shocked when they sacked him after he showed up drunk for work on the third day. That had been his reality check. Returning to his room that afternoon he had systematically dumped every drop of booze in the place into the sink.

After a week he ran into a man who hired day laborers for the busy docks at the port. This was where he worked for the next few years. He started at the low end, hauling boxes, moving pallets, carrying loads of goods on and off ships. The work was hard and menial, but he found he liked it in a way he couldn't define.

The great port handled all types of vessels from container carriers to cruise ships. John liked being near the water because it reminded him a little of San Francisco.

The men who worked on the docks were rough and vulgar, but for the most part they were also honest and direct. Initially the crew he'd worked with had some hesitation about having an American working with them. However, after he'd proven he could keep up and shown he wouldn't hesitate to take on any task no matter how challenging, they'd treated him fairly, then later like a friend. He liked being accepted for his work and what he could do and not because of who he was.

Over time he worked his way up to being a forklift operator, but given the chance he'd preferred to be on the deck using his arms and legs and the muscles he had once let get so soft. He held his hand up to the window and ran his thumb over the calluses on his palm. The veins on the back of his hand stood out and he was pleased with how firm and lean his body felt.

Often, after working on the docks all day, he would go home and workout just for the pleasure of it. He had quit smoking almost as soon as he arrived in Holland. He had only taken it up after Teri had left him anyway. Or was it vice versa? He kept forgetting who'd left whom and it wasn't worth worrying about anymore.

Laying off the alcohol had been harder than he had thought. However, the lesson on the road crew had distilled in his mind the consequence of his continued uncontrolled drinking. With an effort of will and determination, he weaned himself back to where now he only occasionally drank a little wine with dinner, or had a beer when he was out with the guys from the dock.

He'd never again shown up for work drunk, but in those first few months there were many mornings when he'd had a serious enough hangover that throwing himself under a passing truck seemed like a good idea. One morning when he was working near the cranes on the dock, a giant container full of textiles was being hoisted and a cable snapped. He'd been fuzzy-headed from drinking the night before and hardly had the wits to move out of the way. Fortunately another dockhand yanked him aside and he'd narrowly missed being crushed by a load of baby clothes. That had helped him back off his drinking quite a bit.

The train passed over a canal and John could see some live aboard boats lining the waterway. One of them looked a lot like the houseboat he had rented his first couple of years here. It had been suitable for a while, but he was glad he had finally moved into a larger, more comfortable flat. The sun sparkled on the water and he thought it would be a gorgeous day for sailing. Maybe he should have just stayed here and taken his small sailboat out into the harbor.

No, he had saved for and earned this trip. He was going to go first-class all the way. And every penny he spent would be one he had earned on his own. He smiled and thought Enya would hardly believe this when he told her about it the next time they talked. The first year he was in Amsterdam he only spoke with her a couple of times, but lately he'd been feeling better about things and the frequency and spontaneity of their calls had increased markedly. It was good to start putting things right again.

He thought of Paris with anticipation. Too bad he'd not kept Annette's address. She was something else. Annette was one of the few indulgences he had allowed himself and she had said she lived just outside Paris. It was probably just as well he didn't have her number anyway. He wasn't making this trip to chase skirts. This was going to be relaxation pure and simple. He didn't want to worry about expectations from anyone.

He leaned back in the comfortable seat as the train rocked gently and looked out the window. It was so pleasant just watching the world go by. He thought about his arrival in Paris and relished the idea of being in a new city. It would be nice to have a fresh start every morning.

———

Sharon Cameron checked her watch as she hustled out the door of the Hotel St. Michelle in Paris. The rest of her negotiating team had already left for this morning's meeting, but she had stayed behind waiting for the fax from senior management in San Francisco approving her final offer to the French consortium. Elated that she finally had it in hand, she needed a cab and she needed it now. Once she'd convinced her boss that the language of the contract needed to be altered to include, 'to the best of Seller's knowledge' and 'reasonable' and that the other changes were simply artifacts of different statutory requirements, they all decided they could live with it. It was remarkable how much time it had taken to work out the small details. But with the new agreement, success was imminent.

She motioned to the doorman and he pointed to a taxi that was just pulling up to the curb. She had her laptop computer case slung over one shoulder and she lugged a heavy briefcase crammed with hard copies of the documents. The doorman swung the door to the taxi open and she was halfway in before she realized it was still occupied. She nearly fell into the passenger's lap.

Her face burned in embarrassment and she fumbled with her awkward cases trying to exit as quickly and gracefully as possible. She was doubly chagrined when she realized the passenger was male.

"Pardon, sir. I'm so sorry. I didn't see you. Pardon, please." She was not sure if he understood her, which only increased her humiliation.

When she finally managed to get out and look at him, she realized he was well-built and remarkably good looking. Their eyes met for a moment and a flash of nearly electric excitement ran through her entire body.

He stepped out of the cab and with a wave of his hand offered her the now vacant seat. He smiled at her and said, "Charmed, I'm sure."

Speechless, she'd automatically sat down while he closed the door and walked away. She handed the driver a card with her destination written on it and sat back to catch her breath. Her shoulders tingled as if a cold breeze had just touched them. The cab pulled away from the curb and she looked at the front door of the hotel just as the passenger from the taxi went inside. It had been awhile since a man had caused that kind of an instant reaction in her. It was good to know it was still there.

As the taxi turned the corner, she reached into her briefcase for her digital phone. It was too early in the morning to be rattled like this. She tried to shake the incident off and compose herself. It was time to let her team know she was on her way with the final offer.

chapter

12

KISHU MOTO LEANED BACK IN HIS THRONE LIKE chair and looked out his window at the night sky over the desert in Yemen. He turned away from the desolation and mused over which of his many consorts should entertain him tonight. The Greek one was always interesting, but lately he found that the young Persian with the round brown eyes was increasingly on his mind. She had yet to see her eighteenth birthday but already was extraordinarily skilled at pleasing him.

Such a difficult choice. What was it the American had said at the bazaar in Aden last week? Life is choice. Make one and live with it. Moto had considered this for the better part of the afternoon. It was such a simple thought, almost worthy of a haiku verse. The idea had such wonderful, and terrible consequences, and they each were glaringly obvious. Too bad the man had made for himself a poor choice. This unfortunate fellow had thought he could steal from the proceeds of a deal that Moto had made for him.

In all regards the deal was a rather minor affair. The American had wanted a small quantity of opium in exchange for the latest in quiet high-powered rifles. Normally he would have had his man Barzan take care of this matter. The Chui was suited to this type of job and served him well. However, at the moment Barzan was on a rhino hunt and the timing of his return was uncertain, as usual.

These deals were common on the black market in Yemen and not at all difficult. Moto would not normally have involved himself in anything so trivial as this, but the man was recommended by a friend of the sheik and he always made it a point to please the sheik.

At the last minute the American had withheld the silencing portion of the weapon and demanded an extra payment. *Gaijin* fool. When the sheik found out about the transgression, he arranged for the fool to spend what was left of the rest of his life rotting in jail.

The thought of the smooth tongued American spending his life in a filthy cell brought a smile to Moto's lips. Life was, after all, choice.

Leaving his private office, Moto entered a long arched hallway and walked toward the dining room. He passed the tapestry depicting Arab horsemen on the attack and it reminded him once again of his friend the sheik. Al-Jamil was no more a sheik than Moto was the emperor. The man had simply been fortunate enough to have his tent pitched at the right place when the price of oil exploded. With his sudden astonishing wealth and his shrewd handling of politicians he'd grown instantly powerful. He insured his position by maintaining a low profile during the civil war and backed the right players. As long as he remained strong and an ally, as far as Moto was concerned he could call himself anything he wanted.

Looking around his palace Moto smiled in pride and tried to ignore a twinge of despondency. His choices had been made much too long ago to dwell on them still. But sometimes on a quiet night like this, the lost opportunities crept into his thoughts, haunting him.

The palace had been a gift of the sheik. It was smallish when compared to the great halls of the wealthy oil kingdoms, but it suited him perfectly. The interior was decorated with the finest tapestries that could be found in all of Arabia, also gifts from the shiek. Great porcelain vases and golden plates adorned fine wood tables throughout the hallways. Overstuffed embroidered pillows served as most of the seating. The sheik and his family were the descendants of nomadic tribes that dated back to the dawn of man and they never did care much for chairs.

Moto had never missed the chairs, as he was accustomed to sitting on the floor in his native Japan. He would probably never see his home islands again. Even with a host of consorts and the wealth he had accumulated dealing in rare and often illegal commodities, there were occasional times that he longed for a *geisha* house on the *Ginza* and the simple sound of his childhood language.

How long was it now? It had been forty years since he last saw Japan. He rubbed the stubs of his little fingers on his jaw. The *yakuza* had mutilated his hands back then. One finger cut off to join them, the second hacked off as a warning that he must never return without Kobayashi-san's consent. Moto realized now that Kobayashi-san had always hated him unreasonably.

He had fallen in love with Kobayashi's mistress, Nieko. She had been like heaven to him until they were discovered. Kobayashi-san was outraged and Nieko committed *seppuku* out of shame and fear as if taking her own life would restore her honor. After that his own punishment had seemed mild. However, as time passed Moto learned the true depth of his punishment. He paused at a window and looked out at the moon shining on the vast arid landscape. He always welcomed the night's relief from the intense desert sun.

A bitter taste filled his mouth and his jaw tightened at the thought of the archaic customs and outdated codes of behavior in Japan that had caused Nieko to take her life. Even now in the twenty-first century they persisted. He had read and seen on the television that his homeland was a modern country. Yet he knew that out of sight of the *gaijin*, the country still behaved as a virtual fiefdom. The *samurai* were now called corporate managers, and most people were merely vassals to the corporate *shoguns*. No, returning to Japan was no longer an attractive goal. He had a much better one in mind.

Entering the dining room Moto took his customary seat at the center of the table. The consorts started to arrive in twos and threes to take their appointed places. He lifted a silver wine goblet from the large table and held it out for a servant to fill. This was one of his favorite rooms in the palace. The centerpiece was the long banquet table. It was one of the few places where he preferred a chair, and so the table was surrounded by two dozen deeply padded chairs with rich decorations. At dinner he required that the consorts he selected be present and that they remain until he was finished.

He used the term consort loosely. They were really employees who were held to a strict standard of conduct or put back on the street. They all believed they were better off here than fending for themselves in the poverty they had come from, and were free to leave at anytime. If they failed to follow any of his strict rules, they would be removed from the palace but be given enough money to live for a month. Very few took either option. It pleased him to know he could command such loyalty.

He considered the rules to be fair but simple. Rule one was that each woman must please him, as they lived in relative luxury at his pleasure. Rule two was that each must get along with the others. Of course one could never get away from the petty arguments that occurred when women were together, but serious clashes resulted in both women being banished. Rule three, was that his word was final.

Dinner was served and the consorts started talking among themselves. He enjoyed the chatter between the women and liked to listen to the different languages they spoke. Many years ago he grew tired of trying to teach anyone Japanese. His language was so complex he reasoned that only the Japanese mind could comprehend it. It was simply too complicated for inferior races. Consequently he decreed that all of his harem learn both English and French. This way he could communicate with them, and they with each other.

After the last course the eighteen women, most under the age of twenty-five, fidgeted in their seats. He had only wanted the young ones tonight. He did not care to hear the bickering of the older women. In fact, he thought, perhaps it was time to move some of them to the outer areas of the palace altogether.

Moto sipped his wine, a red that he had imported from France, and set the goblet down. Servants cleared the remains of dinner from the table and the girls sat impatiently, all eyes on him, waiting. With a slight wave of the back of his hand he released them. As one they pushed their chairs back and started talking.

The girl he had bought from the Greek freighter captain approached his chair and took his hand. "Moto-san, will you please come and join me on my pillow bed?" Her eyes were deep and black and he was glad the gash that had been on her face when he saved her had not left a lasting mark. Before he could answer her the Persian with the round eyes took his other hand.

"No, no. You must sit with me tonight, you spend much too much time with her, Excellency."

"Perhaps it is possible that I will sit with both of you." He pretended not to notice the girls exchange cross looks and allowed them to pull his chair back and help him to his place near the center of the room that served as the viewing area for the night's entertainment. Although he rigorously practiced with his *samurai* sword two hours a day, and knew that he was very fit for a man in his sixties, he allowed the girls to help him like he was a doddering old man.

When he reached his accustomed spot the girls left him standing for a moment while they ran to collect pillows and blankets to prop around him. He was amazed at the speed with which they returned. He marveled at the firmness of their bottoms and he allowed himself to imagine their ripe breasts. This promised to be a memorable evening. After all, life was only as pleasurable as he made it. And he was an expert on what pleased him.

Once he was settled into his pillows, the lights were lowered and only candles remained to illuminate the great hall. They were strategically placed around the floor area that served as a stage to provide light for the performers. Sandalwood incense filled the air and mingled with the sweet smell of rich perfumes gracing the young lithe bodies. Moto pressed back into a pillow and allowed the Greek to place a fig on his tongue.

The Persian appeared before them in a most revealing costume. He guessed she had picked the design from one of his collection of old Hollywood movies about the Arabian Nights. She had a scant silk top with thin red pantaloons that billowed when she moved. Her midriff was bare and a thin white veil covered her face. Her only other decorations were five gold bracelets on either wrist and a long brightly colored scarf she moved with expert hands.

Several of the other girls tapped tambourines or drums and the rest clapped as the Persian started a slow seductive dance. Moto had seen her dance before, but never like this. She moved with a languid grace that was unearthly. Her eyes never left his and his desire increased with the way he knew she was looking into him. She slid her hands between her knees and slowly drew them up her body. He ached to be those hands, to feel the softness of the inside of her legs, to touch her warm young flesh. She was starting to arouse him when suddenly, a freezing liquid spilled onto his shoulders.

He leaped to his feet cursing and realized what had shocked him was ice water spilled on him by the clumsy Greek bitch. His suit jacket and coat were soaked. The girl with the black eyes fell to her knees begging for mercy. The others all stood frozen in place waiting for his wrath to strike. He coldly surveyed the room and decided that he must make this one pay dearly for her clumsiness.

A servant entered and excitedly approached with his head bowed and announced, "Excellency, you have a visitor."

Moto was in no mood for a guest. "It is too late for anyone to call now. Send them away."

"But Excellency, it is the Chui."

"Barzan?" The messenger nodded. "Very well. Make him wait for twenty minutes, then you may send him in."

"As you wish, Excellency." The servant bowed and backed out of the room.

Moto returned his gaze to the women. "Do none of you have enough sense to bring me a new coat and tie and shirt?"

The consorts moved as one toward the door that led to Moto's chambers and fresh clothes, each scrambling to get ahead of the others. He looked at the Greek girl who was still on her knees in front of him. "I will deal with you in my own time."

Exactly twenty minutes later Moto was seated behind the dining table in a clean shirt and coat with five of his favorite women. The Persian who had been dancing was on his right, an import from Thailand on his left. The Greek, with the black eyes, sat in a corner of the room by herself, as commanded. Each of the women had on a modest robe that revealed nothing of what was underneath. Wine goblets were full and a black-skinned girl from Ethiopia read aloud from an astrology book.

"Scorpio." She pronounced the words in English perfectly. "Power, passion, control. Attacks and paralyzes its prey with a powerful sting."

Barzan the Chui entered the room just as these words were spoken, precisely as Moto had desired.

Moto cast his gaze to Barzan and motioned the reader to silence. Barzan smiled and approached the table. Bowing slightly he raised his eyes to meet Moto's. "I have brought you great prizes from my expedition. I hope they will please you."

Moto doubted very much that they would. There was only one prize he was interested in now and Barzan was well aware of what it was. Moto had faint hope that he had obtained it this trip, but remained convinced Barzan was capable of finding it given a proper lead. It would be best to entertain him well tonight and to appear pleased with whatever he had brought. Moto wanted to be certain to retain his loyalty.

He made a point to pay Barzan well, but he had no doubt that Barzan kept back some of the horns from the hunts to pad his growing wealth. He needed to keep Barzan in his employ for at least a few more expeditions because there was no one else he could trust for the job.

"I'm certain your efforts will have brought satisfactory results. But that is business. You must be tired and thirsty from your journey. Please join us and the servants will bring whatever refreshment you wish."

Barzan sat directly across the table from him. Moto both liked and resented the Iraqi's bold style, taking a seat of power in the Japanese fashion. Moto pushed away a qualm of doubt about his ability to still control him, and noticed that the girls subtly slid away from the guest. Moto considered Barzan Al-Turfi, the Chui, to be a tough and resourceful man. He had been pure vermin and street filth when they had first met some twenty years ago in the bazaar in Aden.

At the time Moto had thought it was a chance encounter, but as he grew to know the Iraqi more, he deduced that it had been a clever ruse on Barzan's part. By the time he understood it, Barzan had proved himself to be a loyal and reliable employee. But an employee who must be treated with the utmost care. His independence was growing and Moto could not afford to lose him now.

Barzan was dressed in a starched western style white shirt with white pants held up by a black leather belt with a gold buckle. His boots showed they had just been polished and he held a cowboy hat in his hands. Moto was pleased the man had learned to cleanup before calling on him. He was also pleased the

Iraqi had given up on the drab attire of his fellow desert dwellers.

"Tell me of your travels. Where there any problems?"

Moto filled Barzan's silver wine goblet with a fine red from France. A bit of a waste he knew, but it would be rude to have the servant bring an inferior wine just for his guest.

"The travel has become much more hazardous than it used to be. I think I will no longer try to leave from Mombasa, but in the future try Mogadishu." Barzan took a long drink from his goblet.

"That means you will have to travel much more time overland in Somalia. Are you not concerned about the bandits?"

Barzan brushed his hand on the table as if chasing away a fly. "Bandits can be bribed or killed. The problem with Kenya is that the American and English infidels have filled the Kenyans' heads with notions of endangered species. For this they have ever stricter penalties and now even the customs and police inspectors are difficult to bribe. Africa is changing. Governments are faltering, poverty is growing everywhere, people are increasingly desperate and dangerous."

Moto carefully selected a cigar from Havana out of a gold covered humidor on the table, then offered one to the hunter who gratefully accepted. "Does it concern you?"

Barzan gulped down more wine and held his goblet to be refilled. "No. One simply must be on guard and plan carefully."

Moto sniffed the cigar and enjoyed the aroma of the Cuban tobacco. Then he thoughtfully clipped off the tip. "That is good for us. It means less competition."

"It is good for us in that sense." Barzan's eyes narrowed and Moto knew before the words were spoken what they would be. "But it also means my expenses are increased with the risks."

Moto smiled and laughed. "Of course my friend." He leaned forward with the cigar between his lips and waited while Barzan fumbled for a match to light it. Once the cigar was lit he sat back and puffed until big clouds of blue smoke surrounded him. "What did you bring me?"

Barzan motioned to a servant by the door and the man promptly disappeared. Moments later two men carried a large steamer trunk into the dining room and ceremonially placed it behind Barzan. He dismissed them with a wave of his hand and they bowed and backed out of the room.

The girls around the table stared openly and whispered among themselves. Moto always liked this part of the business. He loved surprises and presents and had come to enjoy watching the anticipation on his consorts' faces. If he was especially pleased with Barzan's efforts the palace would take on a holiday atmosphere for a week or more. For this reason he knew the girls appreciated it when Barzan returned from a hunting trip. On the other hand, Barzan's return also meant that he might be rewarded with one of them for a few nights. Moto had been told this was a fate they all abhorred above any duty they were called on to perform.

Moto knew that part of the reason for their dread was that whoever was chosen was never allowed back into his inner circle. In some ways he found it a little sad for the girl, but over time it had also proved to be an effective tool in encouraging the women to do their best to please him.

Moto pushed back his chair and went to the trunk to take a good look. The five girls from the table excitedly surrounded him and were all careful not to get too close to the Chui. The trunk was held shut with an oversized steel padlock. Barzan took off a gold necklace and revealed a key dangling from it. Bowing he graciously handed the key to Moto. Holding the key out on the chain, Moto teased the girls by dangling it in front of each one until he let it drop into the Persian's delicate hand. She squealed with delight and fell to her knees on the thick carpet in front of the trunk.

Moto and Barzan emptied their wine goblets and watched in anticipation as the beautiful girl slid the key into the lock and turned it. She quickly had the latch open and gave Moto a look before she opened the lid.

Moto's pulse quickened and his head became dizzy in anticipation. The evening's alcohol was pumping through his veins and a pleasant warmth engulfed him. The girl on her knees in front of the treasure chest swelled his sense of worth. He commanded not only her, but also the fortunes of thousands. She looked to him for permission to open the chest and he smiled his approval through pursed lips.

The Persian's soft hands opened the lid and the other girls gasped at the contents. Inside the trunk, against a background of form-fitted red velvet, were five of the finest rhino horns he had seen in years. They were all the long curved horns of the increasingly rare black rhino. The Persian lifted the largest and held it to Moto. He took it and weighed it in his hands. It was heavier than most others he owned. He estimated it might bring him one hundred fifty thousand U.S. dollars. It would make an excellent *jambiya*, a prized dagger handle, when sold on the market in Aden. A proud man might purchase it for himself, or perhaps for his son to show off his wealth.

Moto looked to Barzan who was watching for his reaction. "What else have you?"

Barzan grimaced and went to the chest. The girls scattered away as he approached and gave him plenty of clearance. Moto laughed to himself as they reminded him of birds scattering at the approach of a cat. Barzan reached into the chest and removed the top tray. He produced two knarled stumps of horns and held them up distastefully. "They are still dehorning animals in some places."

Moto almost bit through his cigar in disgust. "Stupid people, don't they know we can easily sell these for more than their weight in gold? The Chinese market is insatiable and all they do is grind them into powder and use them for their medicines and potions. They don't care what they look like to start with." He let his moment of anger pass, not wanting to show any lack of appreciation to Barzan.

Barzan nodded in agreement. "It seems a waste to me too."

Moto motioned for Barzan to take his seat again and he looked at the five complete horns.

"Are these the best?"

Barzan visibly winced at the comment. "It is getting very difficult to hunt. The animals are not as plentiful as they once were."

"Are these the best?" Moto repeated his question.

"These are the best."

"Good. This means that not many of the beasts remain. This will be an excellent addition to our cache. You have done well, my friend. When you leave this evening, please take this young Greek girl with you." He pointed to the girl alone in the corner of the room. "I'm certain she will please you." He noted the look of fear on her face. Perhaps in the future others would learn to be more careful in his service.

Barzan turned to Moto and whispered so that the others could not hear. "I have heard of the map again. The one that leads to the greatest of the rhinos. They say there are horns as long as a man is tall."

A servant filled their wine goblets and quickly left them. Moto felt his back muscles tighten and his pulse raced. If they ever found the map and it truly led them to the greatest horns, he could surely get what he desired more than anything in this world. Aja, the beautiful daughter of his protector. He lowered his voice so no one could hear but Barzan.

"See me in the morning and we will talk. As soon as you are rested you will return to the hunt. While you are my guest, enjoy yourself as you will. And of course, discuss the map with no one."

Barzan gave a slight bow. "As you wish." He motioned for the girl to follow, finished his wine in one gulp, and walked down the red carpet to the hall.

chapter

13

SHARON OPENED HER EYES AND SQUINTED AT THE digital clock by the bed. The red numbers indicated it was half past nine in the morning. She pondered this for a moment, then let her head fall back into the pile of luxurious hotel pillows.

At last, a day with no commitments. She stretched and snuggled deeper into the rich down comforter that covered her bed. When was the last time she'd faced a day with no place to be and no one to be there with? Maybe it was on one of those trips to New York to meet the eastern sales staff, or maybe it was . . . well who cared anyway? This was much too nice an opportunity to waste by cluttering her mind with trivia.

She tried to go back to sleep but soon realized it was a vain effort. The excitement of closing the deal with the French the day before, and the prospect of having three days in Paris with absolutely no plans, made her smile with anticipation. She had sent her underlings back to San Francisco with the details of the good news. Letting them present the package would give them visibility to the executive staff and she was confident they would give her the credit she deserved. Her senior vice presidency with Comtek was almost assured now. She had worked long and hard to get her due and was pleased she had once again proven she could swim with the big fish.

Now she was primed for a little well-deserved unwinding time. Even though she liked them, she was glad her business associates had left. She was extremely proud of her accomplishment but she wanted a chance to catch her breath.

Rolling over in the bed she stretched again with the luxury of it. She was accustomed to being alone, but mused it might be nice to have a companion. She closed her eyes and tried to picture the man from the cab. She ran the incident through her mind for at least the tenth time since it had happened. She could still feel the excited shiver that ran down her spine when their eyes met. She'd seen him in the hotel lobby a couple of times after that but he hadn't seen her. The one thing she had noted was that he was always alone.

Amused at herself for lingering on thoughts of this stranger, she slipped out of bed and into her dressing gown. Her richly appointed room featured a full-length window that offered a view of the Eiffel Tower and the city skyline. She considered Paris to be the essence of pure romance, probably from reading too many novels as a young girl. Too bad she had never been fortunate enough find out. Opening the night shades on the window she stood briefly behind the lace modesty curtains. The bright May morning demanded a better look so she drew the last of the curtains aside and was greeted with a spectacular view of the city.

From her vantage point on the third floor she could make out several of the major landmarks, including the twin towers of the Notre Dame cathedral. She had a momentary longing for Harold.

Damn Harold. It would have been so nice to share this with him. For a moment she imagined the two of them strolling down the avenue. She would be smelling flowers and watching the young lovers, while he would be looking into the windows of every electronics store they passed. On second thought, she was glad he wasn't there. This was the first time she had missed him in the three years since they were divorced.

She felt a twinge of regret, or maybe it was just her empty stomach. Harold had been a good man, but like so many in Silicon Valley he became obsessed with his work. When she realized she was living her life around him instead of with him, she knew it was time to leave. But enough of that. It was too nice a day to dwell on the unpleasant.

She took a deep breath and brought her focus to the courtyard of the hotel. Breakfast was being served at tables arranged around the colorful garden. Most of the tables were filled with couples who sat sharing the morning drinking coffee. She noted one young couple was holding hands and felt a bit envious. There were a few empty tables and one that was occupied by a single man who was sipping a coffee.

It was him. It was the man she had nearly knocked over getting into the cab. As she watched, a waiter brought him a tray with breakfast on it. Before he started eating he unfolded a newspaper and started to read.

That meant he'd be there at least a little while longer. On an impulse, and chiding herself for acting silly, like a schoolgirl with a crush on an upperclassman, she raced for the bathroom to shower and dress. Maybe she would try to meet him. And maybe she wouldn't, but the prospect was amusing and since she was in control, completely harmless.

Twenty minutes later Sharon approached the courtyard dining area wearing a print skirt that was light and summery, a pink blouse that showed off her shape but was not too revealing, and white designer tennis shoes, stylish but comfortable. She carried a navy colored sport's jacket, a small backpack purse, today's U.S. language paper and a tourist map provided by the hotel. When she arrived at the restaurant she casually scanned the tables and to her disappointment, and relief, discovered that the man she was looking for was gone.

The headwaiter offered to seat her but she politely declined. He couldn't have gone too far. She quickly walked to the hotel lobby then out to the street. There, standing at a corner waiting for the light to change half a block away was the tall stranger. She wondered where he might be going. It would be fun to find out. A little fantasy on the streets of Paris could be entertaining. She started walking in his direction.

The light changed, and he crossed the intersection with an old woman and her dog. The woman and the dog turned, but he continued up the street in the direction of the *Champs Élyseés*. Sharon had to scurry to cross with the light. She had walked behind him for several blocks when it dawned on her that she was in a foreign city actually following a man whom she knew nothing about, other than he was staying at the same hotel as she.

Well, so what. She could indulge in a harmless little game of 'follow the handsome man.' She and her roommate had occasionally played this in college and it normally ended up being hilarious. They never actually talked to their quarry but got a lot of laughs out of their pursuits.

As she followed she wished he would stop and get a cup of coffee. Her mouth was dry and still tasted of mint toothpaste. There was an idea. If he did stop maybe she would approach him. "Good morning, sir. You probably don't remember but we bumped into each other a few days ago. I was wondering if I could buy you a coffee to make up for any inconvenience I caused?"

Then he would look at her with those electric blue eyes and say, "Why Madame, I'm charmed that you recall the incident. Please join me, but let us drink champagne instead."

She forgot the imagined conversation when she passed a bake shop and the aroma of fresh bread nearly drew her in. Perhaps she was being foolish and should stop here and get back to reality. A crosaint would be good right now, but she let her feet keep moving past the bakery so she could keep Handsome Man in sight.

She thought that maybe if he stopped at the next corner she could catch him. "Sir, I'm a little lost, could you please direct me to Napoleon's Tomb?"

Then he would raise an eyebrow and say, "You will never find Napoleon's Tomb because it is at a place called *Les Invalides*. Please allow me to be your personal guide, a woman of your rare beauty should never be unescorted on the streets of Paris."

Sharon followed her quarry for what seemed like a long time. Fortunately it was a nicely cool morning and he had chosen a very scenic route. They wound their way to the banks of the Seine and he would occasionally pause to consider the goods at some of the street vendor's stands. The ones he looked at invariably turned out to be either painters or jewelry artisans. She wondered if he might be looking for a gift for a lady friend. That would be disappointing.

She was beginning to think he would never stop. Though he did not seem to be in a hurry he had a long stride and moved briskly forcing her to walk fast to keep up with him. She was sure she was hopelessly lost, but it didn't concern her because she knew she could always get a taxi back to the hotel if she needed one.

The morning faded away as the sun rose in the sky and the temperature and humidity increased perceptibly. She was no longer feeling fresh as a morning flower, there were prickles of perspiration under her arms and down her back. Since they had walked along busy streets most of the way her throat was getting scratchy from breathing the exhaust of so many cars. Her little adventure was running longer then she had ever imagined. While she walked she decided to stop half a dozen times and each time she invented another reason to follow him one more block, or around another corner.

If she were reading her tourist map right, and she wasn't sure she was, they were going in the general direction of the Eiffel Tower. She kept following rationalizing there was nothing for her back at the hotel and it was a gorgeous morning in Paris. And then there was that look they had exchanged.

She invented another scenario. "Excuse me, sir. I recognize you from a couple of days ago, would you like to join me for a refreshment back at our hotel? I'm in Paris for three days by myself and I'm dreadfully bored."

Then he would smile and nod yes. "Why Madame, no one should be bored or alone in Paris. Let me show you some of the places I know. We can make a grand adventure out of your time here."

A shiver of excitement ran through her. Something like that would be so unlike her. Three days with a stranger and no strings attached. Here today gone tomorrow. A little secret just for herself. She let the thought linger in the back of her mind.

She ached for a cup of coffee, an orange juice, and a muffin with marmalade to be delivered by room service to her cozy room. Maybe she should have tried to sleep just a little longer. That is certainly what she would do tomorrow to make up for this silly exercise. With each café they passed filled with people sipping drinks and smoking wonderfully strong cigarettes her interest in the man she followed lessened.

It was almost noon and she started giving thought to the idea of asking Handsome Man if he knew a good place for lunch. Then she could ask him to join her. She quickly dismissed that idea as being too real and too forward. Maybe she'd ask him to meet her for a drink at the hotel. That could be innocent enough. It was a public place, there would be no obligations.

When she realized she was actually flirting with the idea of making contact with him, she took a deep breath and decided it was time to quit the game before it took on a life of its own. Then he unexpectedly disappeared from sight around the corner of a red brick building.

Sharon rounded the corner thinking this was as far she wanted to go. She debated whether it would be better to stop at an outside café and keep herself from fainting due to lack of food, or to simply get a taxi and go back to the hotel, soak in a tub, and have room service cater to her every whim.

These thoughts evaporated when she realized Handsome Man had disappeared. He'd vanished so suddenly she stopped in her tracks. When she turned the corner she saw a large park filled with children and adults walking and playing on a great lawn shaded here and there by broad-leafed trees. The view was expansive and there was no other place he could have gone. But gone he was.

She could not see a glimpse of his blue shirt or the top of his head as he moved through the crowd. For the first time in an hour she recognized where she was. She was on the banks of the Seine on a street leading to the base of the Eiffel Tower which rose majestically towards the sky in the distance in front of her. It was a perfect place to be on a beautiful morning in Paris. Handsome Man clearly knew his way around the city.

As stunning a view as it was, she felt left out and frustrated. Sharon briefly wondered if he had caught on to her and ditched her the way her older sister used to when they were growing up. She hurried up the avenue hoping to catch a glimpse of him again. She passed a street full of restaurants with outdoor tables but none held her prize. She went almost to the tower before she gave up the chase.

Dejected, tired, perspiring, and feeling grimy she turned back down the avenue and moved sluggishly through the tourists and locals who were bustling about on the overcrowded sidewalk. She checked her watch and wasn't surprised that it was now past noon. She'd been walking for almost two hours. No wonder she was exhausted.

She mused that the little adventure had not gone quite the way she'd imagined. She almost laughed at herself. Just when she had decided to call it off her choice in the matter had been taken away by Handsome Man disappearing. Now she wanted to see him more than ever. It was one thing to call off a fantasy herself. It was quite another to have it taken away from her. Not having a choice in the ending left her feeling vaguely empty and out of control. It was disconcerting and not something she was accustomed to.

Deciding it was time for lunch and a glass of wine she started checking out the various cafés. Having lunch by herself would be fine, but not nearly as romantic as what she had imagined. She was just about to select a table near the avenue when a waiter making a great scene a little way up the block caught her attention.

The squat man with a black mustache was shooing people away from the very front row of tables at his café. There did not seem to be any real need for his loud talking and bristling style so she decided he must simply be announcing that his place was finally open for business. She wouldn't have given him another thought except as he unrolled a tablecloth and set a place, she saw Handsome Man patiently waiting to accept the table. Her breath caught in her throat and her hands clenched her newspaper and map tightly.

She stopped short of staring and resisted the temptation to run up to him and ask him where he had been. She had to remind herself that he still had no idea of her existence, or that she had been following him, like a stalker, for the last couple of hours.

She turned away and slipped into a fancy clothes boutique. A salesgirl approached and said something to her in French. Sharon shook her head no and took a compact out of her purse to check her look. The salesgirl muttered something else in French and gave her a disdainful look. Sharon was instantly aware that her casual summer outfit was a dead giveaway that she was an American and not even close to being stylish by Parisian standards. She wondered if she were reinforcing the stereotype that some French had of cheap Americans with no fashion sense. She smiled thinking she had accidentally dealt a blow to American-French relations. No time to worry about that, there was Handsome Man to consider.

Now that she had actually caught up with him, she wasn't quite sure what to do. Amused with her predicament, she wondered if this was the same way dogs felt when they finally caught up with a car they were chasing. *Well, there it is, now what should I do?* She briefly debated grabbing a taxi and going back across town, or confronting her fear of rejection and feeling foolish if he laughed in her face.

At least if she approached him she would have control. It wasn't as if he were some hormone-crazed jerk in a bar trying to get her attention. If she approached him she would have the upper hand and the ability to direct anything that did, or didn't, happen. There was nothing to worry about, she could handle herself. It wasn't like she was going to sleep with him. She was only curious about him. She put her compact away after dusting her face with the slightest hint of powder, took a deep breath and stepped back out onto the crowded sidewalk.

In a few steps she could see the café where she knew he was seated at a table. Her heart started to pound and she could once again feel the prickly sensation of perspiration on her back. Her breathing was shallow and she took small steps. Through the crowd she strained to see the table he had been waiting for. Finally there it was, and there he was seated at the table, talking to a stunningly beautiful blonde woman standing next to him.

She was so surprised she stutter stepped and almost turned around. *The bastard.* He came down here to meet another woman. It was like a slap in the face. Then she forced herself to remember he did not even know she was there. She almost burst out laughing at herself. She was mad at Handsome Man and he had no idea she was in his universe.

Sharon increased her speed as she drew near his table. When she was almost there the blonde left him sitting alone and walked confidently past Sharon. Handsome Man took a drink from his coffee cup and picked up his newspaper.

Half a block past him Sharon stepped into a flower shop
fuming at herself. She couldn't believe she was doing this. She
had worked years to gain the respect and admiration of her
coworkers and peers and was widely known as a confident and
expert negotiator and deal maker. She had been essential in
making millions of dollars in sales for the company by being out-
going and tenacious. Now she had allowed herself to be reduced
to schoolgirl idiocy in only a few hours in Paris. She had to talk
to this man. Mainly she wanted to satisfy her curiosity, but she
also had a gnawing doubt that if she didn't her self-confidence
might never be the same.

She took a deep breath and reminded herself that you only go
around once. Her father had often said, 'You're only as interesting as the people you meet.'

Sharon worked her way back up the crowded sidewalk that led
toward the Eiffel Tower. She remembered how just the word
Paris conjured up thoughts of romance and love. Now here she
was, in one of the most beautiful cities in the world, on one of the
most romantic streets in the city, approaching a stranger at a café.
She wasn't feeling romantic at all. She was now simply determined to talk to this man.

As she reached his table she was remarkably calm. She was
drawing closer and her mind was going blank. What should she
say? Something witty? Something polite? She could see the paper
he was reading was an American Today, the type that was available at all the major hotels. He had one coffee cup on the table
and a half-eaten croissant. She was relieved the table was only set
for one, which meant that other woman was not coming back.

His blue polo shirt was short sleeved and had a rich cut to it.
Though it was loose on his shoulders, she could see his arms were
well muscled and tan. He wore no rings or jewelry other than a
wristwatch. His sunglasses had a designer label and hid his eyes
from her view. His face was clean shaven and smooth and his hair
was short and combed perfectly into place. She had noticed ear-

lier there was no evidence of gels or mousse, something she personally despised in a man's hair. She knew he was about six feet tall, but even sitting he looked to be taller than most. His posture was nearly perfect and she wondered if it was from breeding or if he had been in the military. He was engrossed in his newspaper and did not notice her approach.

Almost before she realized it she was standing at the table in front of him. She hesitated slightly, took a deep breath then forced out the words. "Good morning, sir. Are you an American?" Her heart was racing and perspiration moistened her palms.

He looked up from his paper and peered at her through his sunglasses. There was a long pause and she had to bite her tongue to keep from blurting out something to fill the dead air.

"Does it matter?"

She struggled to come up with a reply. Was he being playful? Wary? She decided to play it straight. "Not really, I guess. But you do speak English. Would you mind if I joined you? It's so crowded here and I'm desperate for a cup of coffee."

She hoped that had sounded more nonchalant to him that it did to her. It was not exactly a fantastic opening line but it was pretty close to the truth. She wondered if the word desperate gave away her nervousness.

"Miss, no one as attractive as you are should ever be desperate for anything. Please have a seat. I'll get the waiter immediately." He stood up, pulled out a chair and seated her as if she were at a formal dinner. It was a custom her mother insisted gave you a true indication of a man's background.

She was so pleased by the compliment and his manners that she was almost speechless. He called to the waiter in French and then turned his attention back to her after he sat down.

"May I surmise that you only speak English, which means you must be an American?"

"Yes."

"Where are you from?"

"San Francisco." His jaw tightened and he took a moment before he responded. She concluded that might not be his favorite place and wondered if it were a strike against her.

"Really? I was from there once. I think I left something there. I'm from Amsterdam now." He smiled and she could tell he was looking her over. "Didn't we almost share a cab together?"

She blushed under his gaze and a rush of excitement passed through her. He'd recognized her. She wished she'd buttoned the top button on her blouse and hoped her perspiration was not showing through the material. "Yes, I guess we almost did share a cab. I'm so sorry, I was in such a rush."

"Think nothing of it. I'm glad we finally get to meet. What brings you to Paris?"

"I'm on a business trip. Actually the business part is over and I decided to stay on at the Hotel St. Michele for a couple of extra days just for fun."

"You're by yourself then?"

"Well, yes." Wait a minute. In four sentences this guy had found out where she was from and that she was alone. Maybe she was being paranoid. It was probably an innocent question but either way she needed to get back in control.

Her coffee arrived and she regrouped. He hadn't flinched when she had blurted out that she was staying at his hotel. She wondered how much she wanted to reveal about herself before she knew him better.

He smiled at her. "What do you plan to do for fun for the next few days?"

His manner was casual and easy. She decided to believe he was just showing some curiosity and making conversation.

"I was thinking I'd do a little sightseeing, visit some museums, hopefully meet some interesting people along the way."

"That sounds nice. Paris is a good place for that sort of thing."

"So far I haven't had much of a start." She sipped her coffee again. "Do you think I could get a glass of wine here?"

"Ma'am, this is Paris. Would you like wine or champagne?"

"Oh, champagne would be lovely. Will you join me?" She could scarcely believe this. It was almost as if he knew his place in her fantasy. It was great fun and she wondered how long it might last.

He scratched his chin thoughtfully. "Hmmm, normally I wouldn't, but it is a marvelous day, and you do have a captivating smile. How could I say no?"

He called the waiter over and ordered in French. The waiter smiled broadly and disappeared.

"If we're going to share a glass of wine together introductions are in order. I'm John Erikson." He extended his hand to her.

"Sharon Cameron, pleased to meet you." She shook his hand and he had a firm but polite handshake. Sharing a glass of wine with Handsome Man was more than she had ever truly imagined would happen. The notion excited her in a sensual way she had not fully expected.

"Sharon, that's a fine formal name."

"My friends call me Sherry."

"I prefer Sharon, you don't seem fluffy enough for a Sherry."

She wasn't sure what to make of that, but decided to take it as a compliment. The waiter returned to the table and to her surprise had a whole bottle of champagne. She could tell from the label and from the way he showed it off to John that it must be very expensive. She had only wanted a glass of wine, but what the heck, when in Paris.

The waiter opened the bottle expertly and started to pour the champagne into her flute. John motioned for him to stop and the waiter gave him a questioning look. They exchanged a few words in French and then both looked at her. John motioned for her to test the wine. Though she had performed this ritual countless times, with these two worldly men watching her she was nervous. She lifted the flute delicately, carefully sniffed it, took a sip, and considered the crisp dry flavor. Trying to look as grave as possible, she sat back, paused for an instant, then smiled and nodded.

Both John and the waiter burst into big grins pleased that she approved. The waiter filled their flutes with the fine wine and left.

She lifted her glass to John. "To Paris."

"To Paris."

They touched their glasses together lightly and sipped. This time she actually took a drink. It was extraordinary. Unquestionably the best she had ever had and she considered herself to be something of an authority. She wished she could see his eyes hidden by his small wire rimmed sunglasses. The waiter returned with an ice bucket for the bottle and a tray of delicate pastries and chocolates. He excused himself and left to tend other patrons at the bustling café.

She tried to think of something light to say and came up with, "You said you left something in San Francisco, what was it?" His body stiffened subtly. She had clearly touched a nerve.

He looked away from her toward the busy street. "Nothing really." He half smiled. "I left some . . . luggage there. I guess that sounds pretty corny. But that was years ago and it doesn't matter anymore."

It didn't take much to fill in that blank. She regretted hitting on the subject, although it did indicate he was alone. He still looked away from her and she wanted to say something that would bring him back.

"That's odd. I left some baggage by the bay too. But it was years ago and it doesn't matter anymore." She squirmed in her seat thinking they had both revealed a lot.

He turned back to her and smiled. "San Francisco is a beautiful city. But so is Paris and that is where we find ourselves today. I have an idea, let's play a game. You tell me something about yourself and I'll guess if it's true or not."

A chill crossed her shoulders. That sounded just a little intrusive and she wanted to set him straight from the outset. "I don't play games."

He hesitated slightly and his lips tightened. Her back tensed and she feared she had hit another nerve and put him off. He took a drink of champagne.

"Pity. I'm quite fond of games. Earlier you said you were hoping to meet some interesting people. What qualifies as interesting?"

She was pleased he had picked up on something she had mentioned. She tried to think of a playful answer to keep the mood light. "A lot of things make a person interesting. An exotic job, a checkered history, a keen wit. You never know when you meet someone if he will have that one thing that makes you want to spend time with him. And the vexing part is that if you do like him, are you then interesting enough for him, or her, depending on the case?"

John raised his glass to his lips and sipped his drink. He seemed to let the liquid linger in his mouth before he swallowed. He caught her watching him.

"Kind of silly I suppose, but sometimes I let the bubbles tickle the underside of my tongue. I guess I'm pretty easily amused. I don't bet that counts as being interesting though."

"I'm not sure. I'll have to try it." Taking a sip she closed her eyes and allowed the champagne bubbles to caress her tongue and the inside of her mouth. She tuned out the sounds from the street and the French voices of other patrons and let the wine linger. She swallowed and when she opened her eyes she realized John was watching her, apparently waiting for a reaction, and she almost burst out laughing.

Here she was in Paris, letting champagne tickle her tongue, with a totally charming stranger. It was beyond anything she had dreamed could really happen. It was perfect. "Amusing yes, but maybe not quite interesting."

"Blast. That might have been my best shot."

"That would be such a pity." She smiled to make sure he knew she was teasing.

John frowned and squinted his eyes behind his dark glasses as if trying to conjure up some little tidbit about himself that might keep her attention. "How about this? I'm one of the richest men in the world."

"Nope, sorry. Even if it were true, which it clearly isn't, it just doesn't do it for me."

"Okay, here's another one. I was a war hero, but it's a secret and I can't tell you anything about it."

"Sorry again. You don't look old enough to be a proper hero."

"But I've even got a scar, look." He pulled his shirt collar down a little on the right side and she could see a faint scar about four inches long at the base of his neck.

She involuntarily recoiled at the sight. "Oh my, how did you get that?"

"Can't tell you. It's a secret."

She laughed out loud. He poured another glass of wine and she felt a warm glow, not only from the sun filtering through the trees, and the soft spring breeze, but also from the champagne and the cavalier attitude this guy projected. The longer she studied him the more attractive he became. His features were sharp and his face clear. The smile absolutely caressed his face. His sunglasses were too small to hide the hint of lines around his eyes when he squinted that gave him the appearance of someone who had seen the world.

He rubbed the scar with his thumb. "I originally wanted this to be up here." he touched his cheek.

"Why on earth would you want it there?"

"It would be much more roguish, don't you think?"

She shook her head.

"Okay, you're a tough customer. Maybe no one thing does it for you, but how about the combination? Don't you find it interesting that I'm a fabulously rich war hero with a scar who can teach you about the finer points of champagne sipping?"

"You're really close, I think you have a wonderful imagination and an impressive scar, but I already know almost all there is to know about champagne sipping."

He took his sunglasses off and stared at her with eyes so blue she had to catch her breath. "I'll bet you don't know the very best place to sip champagne." She didn't know if it was his tone or not, but the thought was exciting and a shiver passed through her. Though they were at a table in a noisy crowded outdoor café, and the sidewalk was crammed with people going this way and that, she was totally captivated by this fellow, and it seemed as if they were the only two people in the world.

"Perhaps I don't know the best place. Maybe you could show me sometime."

"Aha. So I'm interesting after all." He grinned triumphantly.

He had her on that one and she was ready to let him have his moment. She didn't want to push this too far lest he get tired of it. "Okay, I'm convinced. You are actually a fascinating man."

He leaned back in his chair and put his sunglasses on. "Very well then. I'm glad I passed that test. Now it's your turn. What makes you so interesting?"

She was sure her heart skipped two beats. She should have known this was coming and she deserved the turn of the tables. She needed to establish her credentials without going overboard. She pulled a thought out of the blue. "I know a place in Jamaica where they serve roasted lobster on the beach."

He grinned. "Fascinating, you'll have to tell me how to find it. But first, what shall we do with the afternoon? Are you free?"

A wave of relief and elation swept over her. She tried to think of something exotic but her imagination failed her. After a moment she settled on what she really wanted, exotic or not. "I've never been to the top of the Eiffel Tower. Would you take me there?"

"That sounds like pretty ordinary tourist stuff."

"But I've never been there, it would be like going to San Francisco and not going to the Golden Gate Bridge. Besides, I am a tourist."

"If you put it that way, I'd be delighted. We can be tourists all day."

She almost pinched herself, the fantasy was becoming real, at least for a little while. "Maybe later you can show me where the best place to sip champagne is. That is, if it's in Paris."

He gave her an unnervingly sly look. "It is today."

J OHN RETURNED TO HIS HOTEL ROOM JUST BEFORE dawn. He fumbled with the electric card key and tried to think of the right word to describe Sharon. Captivating seemed close but not quite on the mark. She was witty, smart, charming, poised and self-confident. Over the course of the day and into the evening he'd found out a lot of things about her and was excited at the prospect of learning more.

Alluring was a good word, but still not the right one. Once inside he kicked his shoes off and turned on the light in the sitting room. Going to the window he could see the faint glow of the sunrise over Paris. His mind was a little fuzzy from lack of sleep and champagne. He hadn't had that much to drink since his early months in Amsterdam. This was different though. This was a light feeling. Not like the mind numbing, blinding drunks he'd hammered himself with in the old days.

He replayed the day in his mind. They had gone sightseeing around Paris like a couple of tourists who had never been outside Omaha. They had been to the top of the Eiffel Tower, to Notre Dame, Napoleon's Tomb and even done a speed tour of the Louvre. In his eyes Mona Lisa had not compared favorably with Sharon. And when he was with Sharon, almost nobody else seemed to exist.

At every other stop they had ordered a glass of champagne. He'd never felt drunk or even giddy. They'd simply enjoyed themselves. He peeled his shirt off and felt the cool morning air on his skin. He wondered what she was doing that very minute. Was she taking off that pink blouse and getting out of that flowered skirt? The thought started to make him wonder if leaving her was the right choice.

He had left her at the door to her room, which was two floors below his. He remembered how soft her lips had felt and how warm she was when she pressed against him. She was responsive and it was a difficult choice to let her slip into her room alone. But he thought it would be better to wait. He was going to approach this woman with his brain in gear and not get carried away by pure desire as he had sometimes done in the past. But he had to admit there was plenty of desire there.

He counseled himself to be cautious. The disaster with Teri had taught him a number of things. First, to think with his head. Second, be forthright about what he felt. Most importantly he needed to keep his emotions in check so the bottom of his world wouldn't fall out if things didn't go right. He knew he was getting way ahead of himself, but so what. He was going to see Sharon again and he wanted things to go well.

They had a lunch date tomorrow, which was actually later today, and plans to visit some of the out-of-the-way places in the city. Letting things develop slowly was the best idea. Besides, he didn't want her to think he was too easy. He laughed to himself. Lord, she was gorgeous. If she knew how to use that body as well as she wore it . . . he momentarily crossed his eyes then lingered on the thought.

He let his pants drop to the floor. He entered the bedroom and plopped onto the bed on his back. Perhaps the best thing about her was that she had no real knowledge of who he was. She had no clue about the family fortune and seemed quite content that he was an expatriate working in the shipping business in

Amsterdam. He hadn't told her much that was relevant about himself. He made a mental note to himself to clear up this white lie before too much time went by.

From their conversations he had picked up that she clearly was not someone who would put up with intentional deceit, even if no harm were intended. He liked the way she was straightforward in her conversations and expectations. It was refreshing to be with a woman and not have to guard every word he said for fear of saying the wrong thing.

She was self-confident and perceptive. It had been obvious from the start that she did not need or want for anything. He had the distinct impression he only had the pleasure of her company as long as he fit her fancy.

Smiling and tired he pulled the bed covers back and slipped between the soft sheets. He closed his eyes and tried to imagine what tomorrow, or rather the rest of the day, might be like. He could hardly wait for the morning to pass so he could get up and see what the new day would bring. He closed his eyes and let the image of her smile fill his mind.

———

Teri moved through the crowded hotel ballroom greeting the attendees with her warmest smile and thanking each person she talked to for coming. The annual black-tie fund raiser for the women's shelter had been a growing success for each of the three years she'd been involved with it. This year was the best yet and she had the personal satisfaction that it was largely due to her efforts. As the co-chairperson she had managed to get the society writer for the Chronicle to play the event up in the paper and it had mushroomed into a must attend event for the city's elite.

She took an ice water from one of the many waiters and found a quiet corner to collect herself. The program had gone very well and even her brief remarks before this exclusive group drew a round of applause that surprised and gratified her. She had been a little nervous, but now that it was over she realized she had an almost intoxicating buzz. She recognized that she was happier than she had been for a long time. She wondered what John would have made of this, but then the image of that night in Tahoe came back, as it always did when she thought of him.

It faintly saddened her that of all the time they had spent together their last shared moment was the one that was seared into her memory. If they just could have managed to understand each other a little better they would have been so good together.

The memory haunted her for a moment and a dagger of regret jabbed her chest. Damn Johnny for ruining them. The first year after their breakup the planning of this event had been a welcome distraction for her. Something she could throw herself into to keep her mind off her aching heart. When she realized the society angle was taking off, she had occasionally wondered if Johnny would show up. Sometimes she hoped he would, sometimes she prayed he would not. If he ever did come, she had no idea what she would say to him.

She took a drink of the refreshingly cool water and prepared to circulate through the dispersing crowd once more. She had no doubt that these people would give a lot to the shelter and never miss it. However, a little personal appreciation could go a long way. Especially when they sent the invitations to the event next year.

She caught sight of Richard and Katharine Cameron, the owners of a prominent real estate firm. She had been introduced to them the year before. When she started looking for a house, Richad had set her up with one of his senior brokers who'd found her an outstanding deal. They were very nice but a little on the formal side. She wanted to make a point of personally thanking them again. She started to move toward them when from behind her a vaguely familiar voice called out her name.

She turned and was stunned to see Enya approaching. She took a short breath and reflexively tensed up. Enya was gorgeous in a black sequined gown that looked like it cost thousands. She had a champagne flute in one hand and waved with the other. Teri was glad she had let herself splurge on the very stylish black dress she was wearing. She had spent a lot more than she should have, but had felt justified because she needed to put on a good show for the cause.

Teri held her breath as Enya stopped in front of her. Teri searched for words but came up momentarily blank. Enya broke the brief silence. "Hello Teri, you look simply smashing tonight. I want to congratulate you on helping pull off this wonderful event."

Teri tried to read between the lines. She doubted she looked 'smashing' compared to the rest of this group as she lacked bracelets and necklaces laced with diamonds. Was Enya being overly polite or just trying to break the ice? She had to say something and automatically replied, "Enya, so good to see you. You're much too kind, I think you're the one who looks absolutely wonderful."

Enya glanced around their immediate vicinity as if she were checking to see that no one could hear them. She answered in a lowered voice. "I'm sorry we haven't talked since . . . since ahh, you and Johnny parted company. I should have called you but we, that is Johnny and I, try to stay out of each other's affairs."

Teri's body remained tense and she gripped the water glass tightly. She responded in an equally low voice. "I really didn't expect to hear from you. That was a long time ago. How are your folks?"

Enya looked around again before resuming. "They're doing well thanks. I wanted to let you know that we all miss you. My parents were very fond of you. I had come to hope you and Johnny would . . . be successful together. I don't know the details of what happened but I believe Johnny was probably to blame. I just don't think he was ready for the responsibility of being committed to one person. I think his biggest flaw is that he's a male."

Teri looked at Enya who avoided her eyes. "Thank-you for saying that. I have always been fond of your family too. I always enjoyed your company."

Enya took a drink from her champagne flute and glanced around the room again. "Nice event."

Teri resisted the urge to break off the conversation. She was starting to think Enya was sincerely trying to put out an olive branch. "Thanks, but I'm always glad when it's over. These people are all so generous but being elbow to elbow with all this wealth makes me uneasy. I'm just looking forward to getting home to the house I just bought."

Enya's eyes lit up and she looked genuinely pleased. "You bought a house, how wonderful!"

Teri felt a flicker of pride. "I just closed the deal and moved in a few weeks ago. It's smallish, but it's perfect for me and my dog. The dog pretty much thinks it belongs to him and that I'm a boarder. But I think it's really cozy and I can see the bay from the upstairs windows." The tension in her back started to ease and she was glad she'd let Enya know of her success.

Enya twirled her drink lightly. "Small or not, buying anything in this real estate market is an accomplishment. So how are you? Do you have a beau?"

Teri was surprised and thought it a little forward of Enya to ask such a thing. It occurred to her that Enya might be checking up on her, she might even tell Johnny. After thinking about it for an instant she decided she didn't have anything to hide. "No, not at the moment. I'm so busy with work and the shelter, it's hard to meet people. How about you, anyone on the line?"

Enya smiled. "I know the feeling. You know what they say about this town, all the decent guys are either already married or they're gay. So far I haven't met anyone to take home to mom and dad."

Teri had to laugh, she knew the old joke and the frustration too well. She licked her lips and decided things were going well enough that she'd take a chance. "By the way, how's Johnny doing?"

Enya hesitated the briefest of moments as if trying to find the right words. "He's doing well, or at least better now. I spoke to him last week and he said he'd met someone in Paris a few weeks ago. He was kind of excited about it."

Teri's stomach did a small twist and she was surprised and annoyed that a pang of jealousy tightened her chest. She let it pass and forced a smile. "Good for him. I hope he's happy."

Enya's expression had changed slightly and she turned her glass in her hand nervously. Teri wondered if Enya was worried she'd offended her. Enya drank the last of her champagne. "I know you're busy so I'll let you get back to the party, I'm glad to hear you are doing so well. If I can be of any help to you, in any way, please call me."

"Thanks again for coming. Please give your folks my best, and tell Walter I said, 'Hi.'"

Enya smiled again. "Of course I will, and I'm serious, if you need anything please give me a call. Even if you don't need anything, we should do lunch sometime."

Teri's face tightened to a smile and she reached out to shake hands. "Thanks, Enya, that sounds like fun." For an awkward moment she had the impression Enya was going to hug her and was relieved when instead she politely shook her hand, winked and walked away.

Teri leaned on the wall and tried to sort out the implications of the conversation. She had always suspected John's family didn't approve of her. And now, totally unsolicited Enya had said they all liked her. Her thoughts swirled and a faint ache returned to her heart. She and Johnny could have been happy together. But it was too late now, he had pushed her too far and whatever they'd had died in the snow at Lake Tahoe, too many years ago.

She took a deep breath and turned around. Maybe she'd misread things all along. Maybe if she had felt more accepted by the family she wouldn't have pushed Johnny so hard. Funny that Johnny had, 'just met someone.' Even though she'd had no news of him, she'd made herself believe he was married, or at least in a long-term relationship so she could help herself not think about him.

'Just met someone,' was a long way from being married. A waiter in a white coat passed by carrying a tray of drinks. She traded her water for a glass of champagne and took a sip enjoying the crisp flavor and the tiny bubbles flickering in the light. She looked around the sea of unfamiliar faces and decided it was time to go home. She had a sudden urge to find a calendar.

———

John pressed the accelerator down just a touch and the blue convertible sped quickly onto the Golden Gate Bridge. He glanced at Sharon who peered at him through her sunglasses and smiled. With the top down the cool wind whipped over the top of his head. The exhilaration of being with her, and of being back in San Francisco was almost intoxicating.

Sharon peered into her compact and checked her look. "John, I'm a little nervous about meeting your folks."

"Don't worry, you'll love them. They've been anxious to meet you ever since I mentioned you. It's not like we're announcing anything."

"That's true." She flicked the compact shut with a firm snap.

He pondered when the right moment would be to bring up his idea. He had devised a plan he hoped would bring them closer together. He was pretty certain she would be receptive to it, but if she wasn't it would indicate their relationship was probably not going to last. The notion that she might turn him down made him nervous. Maybe he should just leave things as they were, and not risk trying to go further. No, he knew that wouldn't do. They had reached the make-or-break point and they needed to choose a path.

Sharon touched his arm. "John, do you know what day this is?"

The question caught him by surprise. He knew the answer was not the obvious one, but that was the only answer he could think of. He swallowed hard before responding. "Unless I'm wrong, it's Friday."

Sharon put her sunglasses down on the tip of her nose and grimaced in one of her mock scowls. "Oh, you're such a pooh. You didn't even remember that today is our third anniversary."

He was surprised she had brought it up, but she was being so cute he didn't want to let it drop. "It's our what?"

"It's our third anniversary. We met three months ago today and you don't even remember." She rolled her lower lip out in a big pout and crossed her arms feigning disappointment.

He slapped his forehead with his hand "*Secré blue!* How could I possibly have forgotten such a thing? You must think me such an imbecile. What can I ever do to make up for this terrible offense?"

She dropped her pretense and slipped her arm around his shoulder. "Just keep being you, John. I haven't been this happy in a long time and I don't want you to change." She kissed him lightly on the ear and her warm breath sent a pleasant shiver down his neck. This was nice. He put his hand on hers and she squeezed it lightly.

They passed the Sausalito exit that led to the headlands and for a moment he thought about the last time he had driven up there with Teri. Then he let the memory slide away and he focused on his present. "Has it really been three months? It seems as if we were in Paris only yesterday."

She stayed leaning close to him. "Well, technically it isn't exactly three months ago that we met. It depends on if we start counting from the time I almost fell into the cab, or if we count from the time we met at the café. But don't you hate those 'what day is it' questions? I know some people put a lot of emphasis on them, as if they were trying to gauge loyalty by what days someone remembers."

John changed lanes as they approached the exit for the coastal highway. The German built car was smooth under his hands and he enjoyed its responsive handling. "I agree, those kinds of questions are pretty annoying. I'm glad you don't play those games."

She rubbed his arm and let her head rest on his shoulder. The sun shining through the open top was warm and relaxing. "John, I wouldn't have even thought of it except I was going over my calendar this morning and I noticed the date. Then I started counting up the weeks we've known each other, and the weeks we've spent together. Do you realize we've only been in the same city for half the time we've known one another."

He knew perfectly well and wanted her to know it. He missed her every minute they were apart. "Sharon, by my count we've been together forty-two days."

She sat up straighter as the car took the exit. "This long distance romance is getting a little difficult to manage."

John's neck stiffened and he tried to glance at her face. This was a potentially alarming announcement and he feared it might be the prelude to something else. "I'm not too crazy about it either. I know we have a great time together, and it is fun being in Amsterdam, meeting in New York and all that, but the travel gets wearisome, and e-mail and phone calls aren't the same as being together. However, I believe we may know each other better than if we had been in the same town all this time. When our only contact is talking on the phone or sharing thoughts in letters there is a different kind of familiarity that develops."

John took her hand and gave it a light squeeze. "I know we've talked about this before but it's probably worth bringing up again."

"John, I like the way you think, but it's just so hard to tell. In some ways I agree I may know you better than if we lived closer. We do spend a lot of time on the phone and your letters and e-mails are pretty open. On the other hand when we see each other it's like a *Love Boat* relationship. We're always on holiday and the real world doesn't exist for us. On top of that I can't really expect to spend anymore time away from my job. It would be nice to have a normal relationship."

He adjusted the car's visor to block the sun that was dropping lower in the sky. "Normal? Us? I'm sure you don't mean that."

She smiled again. "Maybe normal isn't the right word."

He slowed the car onto the off ramp for the coast. "I know what you mean. It does get hard to sort out. But I think we have the real thing."

She looked at him as he turned the car onto the coastal highway. "John, I think I've really fallen in love with you. But . . .." Her voice trailed off and she stared at the road ahead.

John's thoughts raced in his head. This was wonderful to hear. He had meant to tell her that he was falling for her too, but had been afraid it might make her back off. He couldn't blame her for getting tired of the travel and long absences from each other. He was sick of it too and that's why he had planned to move back to San Francisco in two months. This was not the way he had wanted to tell her but now certainly seemed like the right time. If she didn't approve, well it was a chance he had to take.

The highway turned toward a canyon and the car tracked smooth and sure on the road. He took a deep breath. "Maybe I haven't made it clear, but I'm in love with you too." She looked at him but he could not read her expression.

He swallowed hard and continued. "I've started to make some plans to move back here full time. Mainly because, I mean, only because I want to be near you all the time. I want us to have a chance to see how we'd do living in the same neighborhood."

He held his breath waiting. Suddenly she threw her arms around his neck and almost caused him to swerve off the road. She whispered in his ear. "You would do that for me, for us?"

He got the car under control. "I'd only do it for you, for us."

She hugged him even harder. "John, that's the most wonderful thing you could have said."

Elation swept over his body and he thought his heart might never slow down. He pulled the car over to the side of the road and stopped. Giving his full attention to Sharon he took her in his arms and they shared a lingering kiss, one that made him hope they'd be together a long time.

———

John knew the road ahead twisted and turned through a steep canyon that would eventually lead to the ocean at Stinson Beach. Normally it was a slow drive because of buses, carloads of tourists, and trucks. But today it was wide open. Thrilled at the prospect of getting closer to Sharon and with no other cars in sight he pressed the accelerator and the car kicked forward in response. Taking a tight turn he was confident the tires would hold even as the weight shifted to the outside. Sharon held the dashboard and laughed.

"C'mon John faster, let's go faster."

They came to the next turn with too much speed and he had to brake hard to stay on the road, but when they came out of the curve he accelerated again putting the car through its paces. His hands gripped the wheel tightly and his palms were sweaty. He slipped the gearshift into the manual mode and the advanced transmission allowed him to control the gear selection without a clutch.

His heart was pounding hard and he raced into the next turn driving as fast as his nerves allowed. The rear end started to slip and he eased off the gas just long enough to get it to snap back under him, then he accelerated again. He glanced at Sharon holding on and smiling.

"John, is that the best you can do or do you want me to drive?"

He was surprised by the challenge and little wounded. He was a superb driver and was amazed she wasn't impressed. On the left side of the road was a five hundred foot drop-off and on the right side was a sheer canyon wall. A small screw-up would almost certainly be fatal. He jammed the car into another corner and could feel the tires barely holding the asphalt. One more RPM and the car would surely have spun out of control.

"Faster, John, faster. This is too tame. Are we normal after all?"

He grimaced as the car took off again. He used his best movie Mexican bandit voice. "Normal? This is not going to be normal. We don't want no stinking normal."

She laughed in the wind. "Okay, abby-normal will be better, but don't scratch the paint."

The white lines were a streak under the wheels. They came to a hairpin turn and the car shuddered as it slid into the corner. For an instant he thought they would hit the wall then he stomped the gas pedal and blasted out of the turn. Adrenaline pounded through his system and the car became an extension of his will.

He had driven this road many times and knew there was a narrow straight section ahead and after that was a severe left turn. He pressed the accelerator again and wound the car up to as fast as he dared. "There's a hundred. Fast enough?"

Sharon nodded and he could barely hear her over the wind. "Wonderful."

The next turn was on them and he needed to be on the brakes now. He gingerly pressed the pedal. He hadn't planned to cheat into the oncoming lane but they were carrying more speed than he had anticipated. He braked harder and started to drift into the other lane just as an oncoming bus came into view.

He held his breath. God, this was going to be close. He prayed the tires would hold, snapped the steering wheel a fraction to the right, and kept braking into the turn. The bus' horn was blaring and his brake pedal vibrated under his foot indicating the anti-lock function was operating. Horrified he realized the bus was cheating into his lane. The gray mass was on them in a heartbeat, he missed the front by inches. The canyon wall was only a whisper away from Sharon's door. He knew the road turned back to the left but he couldn't recall how sharp the angle was. The bus blew past in a cloud of dust and diesel smoke and John tapped the accelerator to put them into the next turn.

He slowed gradually and started breathing normally. His hands were trembling on the wheel and his armpits were soaked with sweat. He was grateful they were alive, but at the same time he felt foolish that he had almost killed them both. He looked at Sharon who was no longer holding onto the dash but was primping her hair.

She turned to him and smiled. "That was fun."

He gave his best effort at appearing relaxed. "I thought it was amusing too."

They both laughed. Sharon put her hand on his knee. "Okay, I admit, I was a little scared back there when the bus showed up. How about you?"

John put his hand on hers. "No, I was never scared. When I saw the bus I just closed my eyes."

She pinched his knee. "Liar. What is it the fishermen up in Alaska say? 'If you aren't living on the edge then you're just taking up space.' It's okay by me if we don't get quite that edgy too often."

John reached over and stroked her hair. "Agreed, we don't want to cut ourselves short on any time together."

She put her arm around his shoulder. "This is going to be fun." She kissed his ear.

They drove out of the canyon and the ocean came into view. The sun was red just above the horizon and a few seagulls dotted the sky. The sea breeze was cool and carried the scent of saltwater. Sharon still had her arms around his shoulders and he could not help but smile. Yes, they would definitely have fun together.

———

Sharon took another bite of the mouth-watering salmon as she looked around the Erikson's formal dining room. Things had been going better than she had hoped. John's parents were as charming a couple as she'd ever met, and his sister Enya, who was seated across from her, had a wry sense of humor and was fun to talk with.

Her one surprise was how old Erik and Melanie were. They both had sharp wits but age hung heavily on their bodies. By all appearances they were genuinely happy to meet her and they were very nice, unpretentious people.

That was a relief. She had visited enough wealthy families to know that some of them were suspicious of everyone, or that if you were not of the proper social station then you might not be the correct selection for dear sonny. All evening Erik and Melanie seemed completely indifferent to anything like that. Even so, during dinner, when the opportunity presented itself, she casually let it out that her father was a real estate developer. She was not surprised when Erik said he might have played golf with him sometime ago.

"John said you met in Paris, that is so romantic." Melanie's voice was soft and Sharon had to lean forward in her seat at the table to hear her.

"Yes, Melanie, we had the happiest of coincidences. John and I were staying at the same hotel and I nearly fell into the cab he was vacating. I was terribly embarrassed at the time, but it turned out to be a very lucky thing." She thought omitting the part about following him halfway across the city to the café would be prudent.

Enya laughed. "Are you sure he didn't trip you? I wouldn't put it past him."

Sharon laughed politely. Enya was someone she wanted to get to know. They had similar backgrounds and when it came out they had both been to Stanford within a couple of years of each other it opened up a lot of areas for conversation. Her dry sense of humor was not unlike John's.

"No, Enya. If I had been smart enough to trip her I would have caught her sooner. We actually didn't see each other for a couple of days after that." John winked at Sharon as if he was holding back some secret.

Erik cleared his throat and gently tapped his wineglass with a knife. "Either way John, we're glad she allowed you to bring her here." He raised his glass for a toast. "Sharon, delightful to meet you. Welcome to our table and we'd be honored if you would return many times." She felt her cheeks flush and for once she didn't quite know what to say.

Enya filled in the brief silence. "Sharon, that invitation is with or without John."

Both of his parents seemed to hold back a laugh and John shot his sister a bemused look. Sharon raised her wineglass and gained their attention. "I'm very pleased to have come to know such a fine family, thank-you for your hospitality and I look forward to getting to know you all better."

An assistant from the kitchen started bringing out small bowls of ice cream. After the rich dinner of salmon and rice she thought it would be a refreshing treat.

Erik cleared his throat again and this time coughed rather heavily as he had done several times during the evening. She was disturbed by it, as it seemed to shake his frail body. When he stopped coughing his voice was raspy and not much above a whisper.

"John, will you be following the map this fall?"

John put his spoon in his bowl. "I really hadn't considered it. I thought by now you would have given it to Enya."

Enya shook her head. "He offered to give it to me but I don't want it. What the heck would I do in Africa and who would I go with?"

Erik took a bite of ice cream then looked at John. "You know it's the year and you have a fine lady there."

Sharon recognized that she'd been given some sort of seal of approval and was pleased she'd apparently been so readily accepted by Erik and the family. She had considered the possibility of marrying John, but as appealing as the idea was, even if things worked out, she didn't see it happening anytime soon. But she was puzzled by the exact nature of what Erik was leading up to.

Sharon saw Melanie scowl at Erik. "Erik you leave those two alone. You know things have to work themselves out. I don't want you pushing anyone to do anything." This was the first time all night that Melanie's voice had sounded strong.

Sharon had only a vague idea of what they were talking about but somehow she was involved and wanted to know what she was involved in. "What map are you talking about?"

A silence filled the room broken only by John's spoon scraping the bottom of his bowl. He looked up from his plate and fixed his blue eyes on her. "My father has a somewhat rare map of Africa. It's kind of a treasure map and there's kind of a legend that goes with it. I'll explain it to you later."

Erik raised his voice in indignation from the end of the table. "Kind of a treasure map? What happened to you when you were in Europe, did you loose some marbles? That 'kind of a treasure map' may be one the most important things we own and I can't get either of my children interested in it."

Sharon's thoughts were spinning. What in the world were they talking about? A moment ago things had been going so well and now Erik seemed disappointed in both John and Enya over a treasure map. She wasn't sure this made any sense. The slight rancor was disconcerting after everything had been so pleasant, but her curiosity was growing by the moment.

Melanie spoke up again. "Are you done now? Because if you are I think we should move out onto the deck and have some bubbly and enjoy the ocean."

Erik coughed again. "Yes, that's an excellent idea. Sorry, didn't mean to put a damper on things. Put Miss Sharon's chair next to mine, I want to prove to her I don't really bite."

They all rose from the table and Sharon was glad they were going outside. The fresh ocean air would feel good. And maybe she'd have a chance to get John alone and find out what the heck was going on.

chapter

15

JOHN PRESSED HARD ON THE SUITCASE LID AND
pulled at the zipper hoping it would close. Someday he
would have to learn to pack lighter. He shoved one corner
down and succeeded, after much pulling and pressing, to get the
thing to close.

Packing again, what a bore. After the large bag was shut he sat
on his bed and stared at the small one. This was a trip he didn't
want to take. Going back to Amsterdam seemed like the wrong
direction. Sharon was here in San Francisco, and going halfway
around the world from her, even for a short time was completely
contrary to what he wanted to do.

After they had met in Paris he'd decided to surface again in his
old world. As soon as he did his father talked him into getting off
the docks and taking a position with an ailing shipping firm that
the Erikson Corporation had acquired through default. Pretty
soon Les and the troubleshooters showed up and before he knew
it John was deeply involved in a major deal trying to unload a
hundred million dollar company. It was good. He belonged again.

But now the work was threatening what should be the natural
development of his relationship with Sharon. He rubbed his temples trying to figure the best way to resolve it expeditiously. He

was clear in his mind that he was totally taken by her. It was also apparent that she enjoyed him, but she had an edge to her. Part of her charm was her confidence, her self-assurance. She handled their long distance relationship far better than he could.

This was different than what he'd been used to. With Sharon everything was open and on the table. With Teri he'd always felt he was a sentence or two away from being on her dark side. He wasn't sure if he had changed, but he was sure the women were very different.

He had a nagging suspicion that he might be more enamored with Sharon than she was with him and that if he didn't play his cards just right she would tell him to hit the road. It was important to him that he not screw up this time.

He stood and unzipped the small black suitcase. Time. He needed enough time to show her that they could be great together. In a couple of months he'd finish the job in Amsterdam and return to San Francisco. Sharon had managed the separation thus far. Surely she could handle a few more months.

He tossed his running shoes into the suitcase. He'd fled to Amsterdam to escape something he couldn't control. Now he wanted to stay, or maybe the better word would be 'return.' He wanted to come home to gain something, a relationship that he didn't want to control, but wanted to be a partner in.

Yes, that was it. He didn't want to run her life or have her run his. He just wanted them to share life. It was so obvious. He felt like a window had opened in his mind letting in a burst of sunlight. He dug his running shorts out of his dresser drawer and tossed them into the suitcase basketball style from across the room. "He shoots, he scores and the crowd goes wild."

Then he started talking out loud even though there was no one there to hear him. "I'll ask her to marry me. That's it. We'll be great together. But what if she says no? Well, I'll get her to change her mind. And if she really means no, then it's better to find out now and get on with life. I could just stay in Amsterdam."

He found his running shirt and used a jump shot to land it in the suitcase.

"Forget that, I'm not staying in Amsterdam. I'm coming back here, Sharon or not. But she's going to marry me. I am just so damn lovable she won't be able to resist."

———

Sharon faced the Pacific and felt the wind on her face. She inhaled deeply catching the scent of the salt air as the breeze swept over her. The sun was almost directly overhead and was the ruler of a cloudless California sky. Small whitecaps broke over the blue water and the waves roared as they crashed on the beach in front of her, the sound echoing off the towering sandstone cliffs behind her. Driftwood logs and sticks that had washed in from the sea littered the deserted beach. With the vast ocean stretching before her she thought about John leaving . . . being alone again. A cold gust of wind sent a chill down her back.

Turning around she went to meet him as he arrived from parking the car. She slipped her arm around John's waist and he pulled her close. He was warm and strong, being in his arms was one of her favorite places.

John found a driftwood log and they sat on it side by side and took off their shoes and socks. When she put her bare feet down she was surprised by the sensation. "This sand is really cold." She wiggled her toes burying them as if that would warm them up.

John laughed. "You were expecting maybe a heated beach?"

She zipped her coat up a notch. She laughed at the incongruity of northern California beaches. "Of course not smarty, but it's no fun being at the beach with your shoes on."

John knocked the sand off their shoes and slipped them into his day-pack. She watched as he carefully put them in a compartment separate from their picnic lunch. "Agreed. Going to the beach without getting sand between your toes almost doesn't count."

He swung the pack, with the blanket tied under it, over his shoulder and took her hand. Wordlessly they walked closer to the water where the sand was firmer, then headed down the coastline.

She held his hand and leaned against him. "What time are you leaving tomorrow?"

"I've got a ten o'clock flight direct to Amsterdam. The good news is this trip is only for a couple of months."

She had a sense of melancholy about his departure. She loved being with him, but the time apart was becoming more difficult. When they were together things felt so right and when he was away life seemed incomplete. It was a difficult way to live given they had only known each other for a few months. She would look forward to him moving back here full-time. That was a positive step and it would be worth waiting for.

A few sandpipers scurried in front of them racing in and out of the foam from the waves that reached toward the cliffs. She was not looking forward to the coming weeks. There were going to be many nights when it would be nice to have a partner around to go the movie with, or maybe the theater, or watch some dumb TV show. On the other hand, when he finally moved back she couldn't imagine being with anyone else.

They had been walking quietly for twenty minutes when John stopped and picked up something out of the surf. He wiped it off and presented it to her as if it were a rare jewel. It was a small bleached out sand dollar skeleton that was almost perfectly intact. He held it out to her. "Look, a treasure from the mermaids."

She took it from him and laid it flat in her palm. "It's beautiful. With all this pounding surf, a whole one like this must be really rare on this beach. I think this must foretell of good things for us."

She closed her fingers gently around the sand dollar and he lightly kissed her hand. Then he kissed her wrist, then worked his way up her arm causing her to laugh. When they were in a full embrace, he kissed her hard on the lips. She pressed against him holding on with all her strength wanting to keep this moment as long as she could.

Abruptly she was aware a wave was lapping at her feet and the shock of the cold water broke them both out of the moment. The wave slipped back to the ocean and he kissed her again softly on the lips. Their tongues found each other and she tried to press even closer to him. With her eyes closed he became her world. The competing sensations of the cold sand and his warm presence aroused her with an intensity that surprised her.

He let the kiss go and she rested her head on his shoulder. He backed away from her slightly and took his sunglasses off, then took hers off as well. His eyes were a deeper blue than the sky. Looking at her glasses he held them up to the sun. "Rose colored. Didn't think you were the type."

She was pleased with the compliment but wondered what he was up too. "Sometimes they help."

He kissed her forehead. "Like when I'm about to leave town again?"

She didn't look at him but nodded.

"Maybe I'll get some for myself."

He put both pairs of glasses in his coat pocket and withdrew a small velvet jeweler's box. Her pulse quickened as she instantly guessed its contents.

He flipped the box open and a diamond ring sparkled in the sun. He kissed her lightly on the lips then looked directly in her eyes. "Sharon, I love you and I'd be honored if you would marry me."

Her heart pounded in her chest and she had to convince herself he was really asking what she was hearing. Immediately she knew her answer. "Yes. I can't think of anything I want more."

Exhilarated she almost jumped into his arms but at the same time heard the sound of water crashing close to them. Looking to the sea they both saw a big wave coming that would surely soak them with the freezing Pacific water if they didn't move fast.

Almost as one they turned and raced away from the ocean, laughing so hard they could barely run. Once they were safe on higher ground they kissed again long and hard. He slipped the ring on her finger and she admired the light dancing on it for a moment and let her breath come back to her. Her pulse started to slow and a sense of well being and anticipation for the future enveloped her.

They walked happily down the beach for half an hour or so, stopping occasionally to admire the sea life in the tide pools or chase a flock of seagulls into the air. They talked about having a formal wedding or simply flying to Las Vegas but didn't bother with decisions.

She took the sand dollar from her pocket and held it up to John. "This is a wonderful treasure. I know exactly where I'm going to put it. Speaking of treasures, I have a question for you. What were you and your father talking about at dinner the other night? You said there was a treasure map."

John took her hand again and they continued their walk down the beach. "It's kind of hard to explain. There is definitely a map, I'll show it to you sometime. I'm sure Dad would be happy to let you see it. He used to be very secretive about it but he doesn't seem to worry so much anymore."

She was disappointed in his response. The notion of a treasure map seemed out of the realm of things that either Erik or John would delve into. "Is it a treasure map or not?"

John picked up a driftwood stick and tossed it toward the ocean causing a sandpiper to scurry out of the way. "Here's the story, this map purportedly leads to a lost diamond mine in some-place called Masilan. The mine is in, get this, the Valley of the Rhinos where there is supposedly a vast herd of rare black rhinos. Now here is the kicker, there is some mumbo jumbo that says a person can only go there with their one true love or something awful will happen. So if you believe in that sort of thing it's kind of an intriguing idea."

His tone was one of complete indifference to the subject. She was increasingly disappointed he was not more interested in it. After all, their relationship was partly the result of a fantasy. A treasure map might be fitting. "What did your father mean when he said, 'this was the year for it'?"

John threw another stick into the water. "For some reason you can only go on the autumnal equinox every fourth year. I think it's kind of a Stonehenge thing, you know, the sun has to be at a certain place and the dark side of the moon has to face the Earth and the rotation of the planets must align with the signs of the zodiac . . . ."

He was making her laugh again. "Stop it, you're being silly. I take it you don't believe in it."

"I don't believe in a lot of things anymore."

Clearly there was more behind that remark than he had let on. A gust of wind blew over the beach causing her to shiver. Her feet were cold in the sand and she hesitated, not sure she should ask the next question, but needing to know the answer. "Did you ever believe in the map, ever think about following it?"

He stopped and looked at her, but she had the impression he was really looking past her. "I thought about following it once, but I'm really not sure I believed in it."

She swallowed hard. She needed to fill in this blank. "Did not following it have anything to do with the luggage you lost in San Francisco?"

He looked directly at her now but she couldn't see his eyes because of his sunglasses. "You don't miss much."

She could only think of one thing to say. "It doesn't matter anymore." She knew she had gone someplace he didn't want to go and was grateful he'd let her. She reached out to him and drew him into her embrace. His touch warmed her even with the damp sand under her feet.

He whispered in her ear. "Following the map would be an edgy proposition."

His breath sent a warm sensation running all the way down her back. "You know I like to be on the edge now and again."

————

They decided to stop for lunch and found a spot against the cliffs out of the gathering breeze where they could watch the ocean. The sound of the wind and the breaking waves reverberated off the cliff walls. John built up a wall of driftwood logs and sticks that would keep the wind off them while she smoothed a spot on the sand and spread their blanket.

Before opening the lunch she took a moment and lay back on the blanket staring up the eroded cliff to the bright turquoise sky. John put one last log on the windbreak, which also shielded them from view of the rest of the beach. He gently lay down on top of her kissing her on the lips and holding her tight.

Her tongue searched out his and despite the cool air she was getting warmer with every breath. He rolled to his side and unzipped both their jackets. She reached down to massage him and found he was already aroused. He unbuttoned her shirt and slipped his hand onto her breasts. She momentarily recoiled at his cold touch but then came to enjoy the sensation as her nipples grew fully erect. He opened her shirt further and reached around behind her with one hand to unhook her bra. Then he slowly took each of her breasts in his mouth gently rubbing them with his tongue.

The effect was primal in the intensity it gave her. The wet exposed skin on one side and his hot breath on the other was almost maddening. She undid his belt reached in his pants and wrapped her hand around him. He was warm and hard and she wanted him now. He hunched down on his knees and unbuckled her belt and she lifted her bottom so he could pull her jeans down. He took them as far as her ankles but she didn't want to be constricted. "Pull one of the jean legs off my foot." He started to tug on her pant leg and she thought about the awkwardness of this particular maneuver. "You guys always have it so easy."

Still struggling to get the tight jeans over her foot he looked at her. "You think this is easy?"

She laughed and when her leg was finally free he kneeled and put his mouth over her panties where her legs were spread. Softly he let out his hot breath on her through the silk. Her body shuddered and she was instantly moist and almost out of patience. She lifted her bottom again as he slid her panties off. Then he unzipped his jeans and slid them down.

She reached up and pulled him to her. She gasped as he entered, then closed her eyes and started moving with him wondering if it was a sin to feel this good.

———

From the window of his flat, John watched the fading orange glow of the late summer sunset over the Amsterdam skyline. Cathedral spires spiked the air between modern office buildings and to the west he could see the lights from some of the giant cranes in the harbor. The evening was warm and with his window open he could hear music coming up from the street below as a band played in the square celebrating the start of another weekend.

He tapped the keyboard on his computer and the screen glowed blue as he reread Sharon's latest e-mail. They had finally decided on a late April wedding and she had selected her favorite winery in Sonoma for the location. He wanted a December wedding but she insisted on having it in the spring while the hills were still green and the chance of rain was minimal. He smiled at the irony. This time he was the one in a hurry to get married.

He opened his appointment book and flipped the pages to April next. This was going to be good. The date she had chosen would force him to juggle his schedule some, but as far as he was concerned if that date made her happy it would be fine. He took his hand off the calendar and the pages turned themselves back staying open to the current week where the binding was creased. The page did not completely go over but remained slightly bowed and raised revealing part of the dates for the next two weeks.

He was about to close the book when he noticed that in a couple of weeks there was a full moon and beneath it were the words, autumnal equinox. His hand shook slightly as he opened the page fully and counted the days from now until then. There were fifteen.

He got out of his chair and retrieved a glass of ice water from the refrigerator. He had thought about the map more than once since he'd returned to Amsterdam last month. Sharon had not brought it up again and he regretted not telling her more about it. He knew that somehow he associated it with another time and the unhappy events that eventually led to the disaster in Tahoe. But intellectually he recognized this was faulty reasoning and that maybe he should reconsider his perspective on the map. His father was right, Sharon was almost a perfect match for him. Maybe fate had dealt him a winning hand this time.

Clearly his father still believed the map had value. The Erikson Empire was huge and the family wanted for nothing. Perhaps his father thought of it more as a challenge. Maybe he thought there was something worthy in the pursuit of 'a treasure beyond the dreams one might hold,' or whatever the heck the legend said. Knowing how much he loved Sharon, the idea took on interesting possibilities.

He looked out the window at the stars beginning to twinkle in the night sky. He pictured the day just starting in California so many time zones away. He wondered what Sharon was doing and if she missed him as much as he was missing her.

Sharon might like the idea of the one. It would appeal to her abby-normal side, as they liked to call it. Part reality part fantasy, it would definitely intrigue her. Setting his drink down, he relaxed in his favorite reclining chair and closed his eyes conjuring up an image of Sharon's smile from his memory.

————

Somewhere in the distance John could hear a phone. The ringing grew incessantly louder until he realized the phone was on his desk in the next room. He opened his eyes startled at the darkness and wondered how long he'd been asleep. Shaking the fog from his head he listened as the answering machine intercepted the call. He waited while the greeting played silently then he could hear the caller's voice leaving a message. He closed his eyes again planning to ignore it.

Then he recognized Enya's voice. His stomach knotted in dread. It was too late for one of her infrequent social calls. He turned on a light and squinting at the sudden brightness hurried to his office to catch her before she hung up. As he approached the machine he could hear her saying, "Please call me as soon as you can. I need your help."

He reached the phone suspecting, no dreading, what she would have to say. Grabbing the receiver he pressed it to his ear. "Enya, it's me are you still there?"

For a moment there was only silence and he thought he had missed her. Then he heard the unmistakable sound of her sobbing. He tried to reach her. "Enya, it's me, John, I'm here. Tell me what has happened." His chest was hollow and he truly wished this call were not happening.

Over the line he could hear her trying to gather herself. "I'm sorry, John, I thought I was ready to call you. It's the folks."

John slumped into his office chair feeling suddenly tired. "Which one? How bad?"

There was a pause and he could hear her take a deep breath. "John, brace yourself, it's terrible. Yesterday they went out on the Viking Queen and the ship disappeared. The Coast Guard just reported they found the burned out hull this morning. They're both gone." Her voice trailed off into a soft sobbing. He could feel his sister's agony even this far away.

"What about the crew?"

"Dad had sent the crew ashore. They're beside themselves about this. Mom and Dad were the only ones aboard."

"I can't believe the crew left them alone." He leaned forward putting his elbows on the desk and rubbed his temples with one hand and kept the phone pressed to his ear with the other.

Her voice came through the phone softly. "They said Dad insisted they leave, they think he might have planned something."

A realization hit John and a sense of relief flooded him. "A Viking Funeral."

He heard Enya trying to catch her breath. The line was silent except for the hissing of the background. Finally he heard her whisper. "Are you suggesting . . . oh my, maybe you're right." Then she started crying again. "John, please come home as soon as you can. I need you here. I need your help."

John did not remember Enya ever asking him for help with anything. "Don't worry, I'm on my way. And Enya, I think we're going to need each other to get through this time."

c h a p t e r

16

BARZAN SAT UNDER THE SHADE OF A WHITE TENT with the sides rolled up watching Moto shooting pigeons that his servant released on command. Each time the old man shouted 'Hai' a pigeon was hurled into the air. The stunned bird invariably took a few seconds to catch air beneath its wings, and almost as soon as it did Moto blasted it into bloody pulp and feathers with the absurdly large shotgun Barzan had brought him from Aden.

Barzan's last hunt had been only moderately successful. The rhinos were increasingly hard to find and the legend of the map remained elusive. He was more than a little curious about why Moto-san had asked for this meeting, so early in the morning.

Barzan sipped at his tea, idly shifting in his seat and wishing his employer would tire of the activity soon. Even though he was in the shade, the desert sun beating down on the palace grounds already had him sweating. He distracted himself by admiring the view from where he sat. Moto-san had chosen the site of his palace well. It was on a small hill and the walls were high enough that no intruder could climb them without mechanical assistance. The stone walls were bleached white and reminded him of pictures of Mediterranean villas he had seen. He wanted to have wealth equal to the people who could live in such places.

If he were shrewd and worked with Moto-san carefully, he thought there would be a day when he would have a place of his own. Perhaps nothing this grand, but a large house populated with servants and beautiful women. A place where Barzan would be master and all would give ground to him. Moto-san was a worthy employer, but he was growing weary of working for another man and had started thinking about when the time would be right to leave the old man.

The interior compound had spacious grounds covered with elaborately decorated Japanese gardens. An artificial stream ran throughout the palace and here and there waterfalls, and small pools where brightly colored fish swam, were easily visible. Barzan thought this detail was something he would like in his home. It was pleasant to look at and showed others the power of the owner.

Moto-san had constructed this particular spot high enough so that he could sip tea and look down into his gardens, over the walls and out to the blue waters of the Gulf of Aden. There was no vantage point where anyone outside could look into the palace grounds. Barzan envied this place. In the beginning each time he'd come here he had felt small and inadequate. Now he looked forward to the time when he would command respect on equal footing with Moto-san.

"*Hai!*" Flutter, BLAM. Another pigeon splattered blood on the white wall. Moto-san laughed at nothing in particular.

Barzan's nerves were getting raw and his ears hurt. He wished Moto-san would stop. The best view of the entire palace was that of the elaborate swimming pool with its cascading fountains. Normally the women and girls from his employer's collection would be there wearing western style swimsuits with two pieces that showed off their ample breasts and round bottoms. When Moto-san started shooting they had all run inside screaming like frightened children. He scratched himself and regretted he had thought of bringing the shotgun as a gift.

*"Hai!"* Flutter, BLAM!

Barzan fanned himself with his cowboy hat.

Moto-san's voice startled him out of his reverie. "Perhaps you would like to go to America, my friend?" He pointed at Barzan's hat. "Maybe you are John Wayne."

"As for me," the old man continued, "I would like to go away from here. Far away and never return." Moto-san handed the shotgun to a servant and gave him instructions in French, a language Barzan did not understand. The servant bowed and backed away taking the weapon. Almost immediately two more servants appeared with ladders and buckets and started scrubbing the walls clean of the blood from the target practice.

Taking a seat across from him, Moto-san took a drink of iced coffee. "I know where your map is."

Barzan's back stiffened and he sat straighter in his chair. "The map of the rhinos? How could you? I have looked for it so long there were times I thought it was but a native superstition."

Moto-san fanned himself with his hat. "All superstitions come from someplace. Some even come from strange facts. In those cases, the facts are not always what they seem. I have been searching for this map for over ten years now. Ever since I became convinced it actually existed."

"I have searched as well." Barzan considered himself to be Moto-san's right hand. To have failed in finding the map, made his throat suddenly dry. The heat was getting truly oppressive.

"Do not be alarmed, there was nothing you could do. I was able to trace the map to a wealthy American who stole it from a dying British pilot." Barzan was doubtful, but very curious. "Ah, the map was taken by an English who flew away and was never seen again. That's what I heard on my last several trips."

His pulse quickened at the thought of actually finding the map. He also noticed the girls of the harem were returning to the pool and taking off their robes. "How could you find such a thing? I have searched half of Africa for this map but have nothing but superstitious legends to show for it. You have not left Aden in all this time. How could you know?"

"I went on the internet and found a detective for hire. He is a retired Interpol agent who was willing to trade, let us say, information. I led him to some minor drug dealers, who were a nuisance to us, and he led me to a rare map lost at the end of the war."

"The internet?" Barzan had heard the word but was still baffled by it. Perhaps it was Japanese.

"It has to do with a computer. But that is unimportant. He followed hundreds of trails, but eventually sorted through each lead and finally focused on one that matches the stories you have brought from Africa. It is my belief that the map to the great rhinos is in San Francisco, and that the owner has just died in a sailing accident. It is wondrous what you can learn with the help of one who has international resources."

Barzan lifted his iced tea and let the moisture that dripped from the glass cool his hands and then put one palm on the back of his neck. The slight chill was a welcome relief from the sun. "If the owner is dead, we can easily obtain it."

Moto-san took a handkerchief from his pocket and wiped sweat from his brow. "I think it will not be so easy. The family is not likely to be willing to surrender it, as not only does it lead to the great rhino's, it may also lead to an untapped diamond cache."

Barzan caught his breath. If Moto-san was right and not only were there rhinos, but also diamonds, his wealth would soar. Barzan could see the Persian girl who was Moto-san's favorite, preparing to dive into the water. Her light skin shone yellow in the sun and her tight bottom was barely concealed by the blue swimsuit. He wondered if she were as skilled as the Greek girl. If he found the map, a prize like that could be his.

"If you are to get the map, you must leave tonight. I have made all the travel arrangements and purchased the necessary documents."

Barzan switched his full attention to Moto-san. "Why tonight?"

Moto-san leaned forward and squinted at him through his round dark lenses. "There is an important matter of timing I do not fully understand, but I am told we must act swiftly or we may lose our opportunity."

Moto-san motioned for Barzan to come closer and then spoke softly so that Barzan had to strain to hear. "I am an old man and do not have many years left in this world. I desire only two things that I do not now possess. First, to leave this desert. I have purchased a small island near Fiji and I intend to live near the sea as I did as a child. I will enjoy leaving this wretched country and its barbarians." Barzan leaned forward in his chair as Moto-san was almost whispering his words and a little white pool of saliva formed at the corner of his lips.

Moto-san paused and took a breath then continued. "The second thing I want is Aja, the daughter of sheik Al-Jamil. She is the most beautiful and delicate woman I have seen in all my years. Until I saw her I did not know this heart could still have such desire."

Barzan was impressed that the old man could still feel such a way and he was surprised and pleased that Moto-san was sharing such a detail with him.

"I have made a deal with the sheik. He has agreed to give me her hand in marriage in return for the finest *jambiya* with a handle made of rhino horn in all of Yemen. I can only present him the *jambiya* once at a great feast he will hold for the occasion. I can take no chances on embarrassing him and risking his refusal of the deal. That means I cannot use any of the horns taken from the last few years' hunts. They are too small since the truly great ones have already been harvested." He laughed a little. "If I had known she would grow up to be such a creature, I would have saved a horn from the early years just for her."

Barzan held his breath. He had not expected this and was alarmed that his employer was leading up to something he had not anticipated. If his employer left Aden, where would that leave Barzan? He kept his face as impassive as he could trying not to reveal his sudden fears even as events were slipping out of his control.

Moto-san leaned still closer. The sun had moved and was now pounding down on Barzan's back making him sweat profusely.

"And you, my friend, you must wonder what will become of you."

Moto-san paused and continued to fan himself. Barzan took a shallow breath waiting for his employer to continue.

Moto-san spoke deliberately. "If you retrieve this map, and if you deliver to me a horn that I can present to sheik Al-Jamil, a horn for a *jambiya* greater than any ever seen, I will give you all of this."

Barzan tried to keep from gasping as Moto-san grandly swept his arm over the palace grounds, including the swimming pool now filled with his frolicking consorts. "And if there are diamonds?"

"Then we will both be richer. Of course you can refuse me, perhaps you can find another employer who can use your skills." He smiled that Japanese smile again.

Barzan was steaming under his shirt. He glanced at the servants still washing the blood off the white walls. He was concerned they were permanently stained.

Moto-san stood up. "Life is choice." He walked away from the table shouting at the servants to get some paint. Barzan was pleased with that. He didn't want his walls stained before he moved in.

Barzan stood up, straightened his back and swelled his chest. He put his hat on and looked at the pool full of women. He licked his lips in anticipation and could not decide which one he liked best. He wondered if American women were this interesting.

———

John slid the door of the family cottage open and the smell and sounds of the ocean filled his senses. This place held memories of his childhood, a time that seemed ages ago. He remembered racing down the beach with Enya and his father just to see who was fastest. The last time they had done it, his father'd still won.

He smiled at the memory watching moonlight reflecting on the breaking waves and he hoped the spirits of his mother and father were in the stars. Over the last four days he and Enya had convinced each other that their parents had, in the end, been lucky to be able to choose the time and place of moving from this world to the next. Even so, he had a hollowness in his heart and wished he could see and talk to them just one more time. He didn't even know what he would say, but almost anything would do.

He'd been relieved Enya had pulled herself together by the time he had arrived home. Initially they'd spent time crying in each other's arms and consoling one another. Then Enya had busied herself planning a private memorial service, scheduled for tomorrow, and working on a myriad of legal issues surrounding the change of leadership in the Erikson Corporation. Over the last year his father had been moving away from the daily operations and Enya had little difficulty in directing the transition team.

John attended a few of the meetings but he had been out of the business for so many years that he did not have much interest in the proceedings. It still bored him and he was glad Enya had a real passion for it. He was proud of the way she managed. He was confident she would be able to keep things intact.

He stepped out of the door and located the stack of firewood against the side fence. Picking up as much as he could carry he shook off the cold of the night air and hurried back inside. He was not looking forward to tomorrow. Even though the memorial service was small and designed to be short, he was giving the eulogy and was not certain he was up to it. The service should be an end point of sorts and at the same time a new beginning. He fervently hoped it would be. Maybe closure would help him feel less empty, but he doubted it.

He took the wood to the fireplace and losing his grip on it unintentionally dropped it in a heap. Sharon appeared from the kitchen. She came over and knelt down to help him put it in order.

"John, why don't you open some wine, I can take care of this. I think you should just try to relax. Coming out here by ourselves was a good idea. It's nice to be away from everyone for an evening."

He stayed and helped her put the wood in its box. "Some wine sounds nice. You know this is the first time we've been alone since I got back."

She stood and brushed her hands off on her blue slacks. "Yes I know. I wish you hadn't come back under such sad circumstances. I've missed you and I'm not sure how to act."

He looked at her and wondered if she had tears in her eyes or if it was just the light. "I'm not sure either. Lets just take it slow and easy and get through tomorrow."

She picked up the last stick of wood and threw it onto the stack. "If we were going any slower we'd be going backwards."

She was so indignant he couldn't help but laugh. For a moment she glared at him, then a smile crossed her face and she started laughing too. He pulled her into a strong embrace and she whispered through what was now a mixture of laughter and tears. "I didn't know them long but I loved them too."

He felt their hearts beating against each other and was grateful that she was there to hold him.

After dinner John pulled the couch up close to the fireplace. It was chilly inside even with their sweaters on so they snuggled together under a blanket as they watched the shimmering flames. Outside the wind had picked up. John could hear it blowing through the trees that stood near the cottage. Sharon was warm against him and the aroma of her perfume was a soft contrast to the slightly smoky smell of the fire.

John raised his wineglass letting the red liquid reflect the fire-light. He offered a toast. "To my folks, I hope they have found what they were looking for."

Sharon didn't raise her glass, but looked thoughtful. "John, don't you think they found what they were looking for a long time ago?"

He didn't follow her. "What do you mean?"

She looked into the fire and her green eyes glistened. "They seemed so happy. It was obvious to me they were glad to be together. You don't see a lot of that. How do you imagine they did it?"

How did they do it? John pondered the question for a moment and took another drink of his wine. It was a full merlot and the heaviness suited his mood. "A lot of people have said that about them and I have to agree they were happy together. But how they made it work I don't think anyone can say. Of course they would have said, 'it's the map.' Follow the map, son, and all will be right for you."

"John, are you being sarcastic?"

He paused again trying to examine his own feelings, his ambivalence about the damn map. "I'm not sure. I know that over the years they became convinced the map had some influence on them, but I honestly can't say if it was cause or effect. Would they have been just as happy if they had never followed it? We'll never know. Did something happen on that journey that tran-scended their other experiences? We'll never know that for certain either."

Sharon moved closer to him and put one arm around his shoulder. "Did you know your parents showed it to me?"

He wasn't sure he'd heard her right. A tingle ran down the back of his arms and all he could do was respond incredulously. "They showed it to you?"

"Yes, it was kind of strange."

"There's no doubt the map is not ordinary."

She shifted away a little bit. "True, but I mean everything was odd. About two weeks ago I received this call at my office and it was Walter. He invited me, rather he insisted I go to your folk's house for dinner, wouldn't take no for an answer. So I thought what the heck? It would be fun to see them and I didn't have any plans I couldn't change. So I went out there."

John poured them both another drink and let her continue. "I was surprised there were just the three of us. I had thought at least Enya would be there and perhaps some other guests, but I was the only one. I had a wonderful time but it was a little distressing because they both seemed so weak and frail. After dinner we went upstairs to your father's study for a cognac."

John sat upright and stared directly at her. "He took you to his study?" An inkling of jealousy flitted through his mind. His father had taken Sharon, whom he had not known very long at all, into his confidence and let her see the map. His intuition must have been to trust her. The moment of envy turned to pride that his father thought so highly of the woman he loved.

Sharon set her glass on the table and looked down at the floor as if she might be feeling guilty. "Yes, they took me to the study and he told me the whole story."

"He told you the story of the airplane crash and how he got the map."

"Yes, and he told me of the journey and of the promise they made to the Masai guide who helped them find the valley."

John took the blanket off of himself and stood up leaving Sharon sitting by herself on the couch. This was too much. His father had never said anything about the actual trip to him, and certainly nothing about promises to anyone. Why had his father shared this with Sharon and not him, or Enya?

Sharon looked at him with tears welling in her eyes. "I'm sorry. I thought you knew the story."

Puzzled and a little angry he stared at Sharon. "What was the promise?"

"He said the promise was that if they were led to the Valley of the Rhinos then they would, as long as they were able, help to protect them. At the time, back in the fifties, it didn't seem like a big deal. Over the last twenty years the Erikson Corporation has been funding conservation efforts all over Africa. But your father said they were failing, badly. He had just received a letter from his friend's son, a fellow named Mutombo, asking for help."

John's chest tightened. "What kind of help, money?"

Sharon sounded putoff. "Your father didn't think money was an issue."

John paced in front of the fireplace trying to put things in perspective. The corporation did lots of things and conservation efforts were certainly among them. He just could not recall rhinos specifically, but that didn't mean it wasn't happening.

"There's one more thing, John. He made me promise something too."

John stopped in his tracks and looked directly at her. Sitting on the couch, covered mostly with a blanket she seemed smaller and a bit more lost than he could ever recall seeing her. He realized he must seem angry but he wasn't. She was only the messenger, if his father had not trusted him with this information it was not her fault. "And you promised?"

"The letter took him by surprise and he said he was in no condition to act on it. Besides, he didn't want to leave Melanie. He made me promise to tell you all of this. He would have told you himself but he thought I would see you first. He told me if I believed in us, that I should ask you to help him keep his promise to his old friend. He wanted you, us, to go to the valley and see what is happening for ourselves."

John let out a deep breath. Of course, now his father's actions made sense. He couldn't make that kind of trip but did not want to try to explain it to him over the phone or in a letter so he entrusted Sharon with the information. "You mean he asked us to follow the map."

"If I believed in us."

"Do you?"

"Yes, John. I think you know I do."

John took another drink of wine and sat down beside her. "I'm not sure the map is a good thing. The last time, that is, the only other time I got involved with it everything went to hell around me."

Sharon put her arm around his shoulders again. Her cashmere sweater was soft on his neck. "What was her name?"

"Teri." John let out a long breath and a flicker of regret passed through him.

Sharon gently took his chin and turned his head so they were face to face. "Did you ever let her go?"

The firelight glowed against her complexion. He knew that he wanted to hold onto her more than anything. "Yes, she's gone."

Sharon leaned close and they touched lips. They both whispered in unison. "Then it doesn't matter anymore."

John pulled the blanket over both of them up to their shoulders. He slid his arm around her and closed his eyes. She felt so right, but now there was that damn map to consider. He counted the days, only ten until the equinox. He shivered involuntarily.

———

John drove home from the memorial service for his parents by himself. This was the first time he had been alone in a week. Turning onto the coastal highway he opened his window and let the wind blow over his face. He breathed deeply, smelling the faint hint of decayed sea creatures and salt carried by the breeze.

He missed the company of Sharon but she was driving her parents back to San Francisco. John had agreed that Sharon should go with them even though he would have liked to have her with him.

The memorial had been nice. Enya had orchestrated everything to perfection, as he had expected. She had kept the affair deliberately small.

John was pleased that he had managed to get through his eulogy without losing it. He knew he had distanced himself from the loss and the enormity of it. The empty hollow feelings hadn't caught up with him until he'd started his speech. As he'd talked he realized what he said was terribly inadequate. It was difficult to frame his parents and his feeling in words. "The best people I've ever known," hardly seemed worthy of them. He'd finished on the verge of tears vowing to continue his parents' commitment to conservation and wishing he had been more articulate in trying to capture the essence of their spirits.

The winding road demanded his attention and he was glad for the distraction. Sooner than he really wanted he reached the long driveway that led to his parents' house. His house now really. He still wasn't sure he wanted it. How empty it would seem without his folks to give it life.

He stopped in front of the iron security gate. He put his arm out the window and tried to reach the keypad just beyond his fingertips. Cursing he opened the door and leaning as far as he could pressed the keys with the entry code. He hit the last button and the gate made a satisfying clunk, then chattered as it pulled back on its track.

He squared his shoulders and hoped he was up to the responsibility of being asked to help out his father's old friend. If anything, being entrusted with the map was final confirmation of Dad's regard for him. Dusk had passed and the late summer air was getting cooler as night descended. It had been a typically hot September day on the other side of the hills, but here on the coast the damp ocean air chilled him. Driving to the front of the house, he noticed there were an uncommon number of lights on. He thought it odd that Walter, or any of the household staff, would have been so careless.

John stopped the car in front of the stairs leading to the double doors at the entrance to the house. He could feel his back muscles constrict as he saw that the doors were open. The staff never used these doors, and they had all been at the memorial anyway. He was positive he was the first one back.

He got out of his car and paused on the stairs leading to the entrance. He held his breath and listened for any hint of sound coming from inside, but here was only silence. His palms were suddenly clammy. He had the urge to get back in the car and drive away fast, but he pushed it down and slowly stepped to the doors. He hadn't been this wary of a situation since his last mission in Panama. He debated about whether or not he should go in. His breathing was shallow and he tried to convince himself there was an innocent and logical explanation for this.

He peeked inside. He could see nothing unusual and wondered if he were being a little paranoid. He pressed gently on the door so it opened enough for him to go inside.

The house was a disaster. It looked like an earthquake had hit. Furniture was scattered as if thrown from where it belonged to any random place. All the pictures were off the walls and the throw rugs that were not nailed down were all tossed about haphazardly. The place had been ransacked.

He clenched his fists in anger. He froze in place and sorted his thoughts. Why? The house was empty. All the members of the house were at the memorial, of course the house would be empty. Someone must have read in the paper about the wealthy couple's service and decided to raid the house while it was unoccupied. That would explain the pictures on the floor. They must have had visions of a wall safe of some sort.

He carefully entered the hallway gingerly stepping over pictures thrown on the floor and overturned cabinets. It would take time to inventory and determine what was missing. The family never kept any cash of consequence around and mother always kept her jewels in a safe deposit box. But nobody else would know that. Idiot criminals, they ought to license them so they wouldn't screw things up. John picked up a framed photo of the Viking Queen in the open ocean and put it back on its place on the wall.

His anger grew as he looked at the disarray. The whole family had been violated. He took his digital phone from his suit pocket and continued down the long hallway inspecting the damage. He punched 911 into the phone and listened to it ring. A chair had been pushed over and as he set it back up he heard a noise to his right. He looked up just in time to see a man with black hair, a mustache and dark skin smash a pistol into his head.

————

The word throbbing was taking on new meaning for John. He knew he was still alive because his head hurt so badly. Each beat of his heart brought another intense pulse of pain to the right side of his skull.

He became aware of voices around him. The vile smell of ammonia invaded his nostrils and he moved his head away and opened his eyes. Walter and Enya peered down at him.

Walter's white hair caught the light so that it looked almost like a halo. Enya persisted with the smelling salts. "I think he's coming to. Johnny, can you hear me? Are you all right?"

The ammonia was overpowering. He managed to push her hand away. "What happened? What did they take?"

"Never mind. Are you okay? The cops are on their way. So is an ambulance."

John focused on his older sister. She had been through a lot lately but even so he knew she would take care of him. That in itself was a comfort, given the pain on the inside of his head. "What time is it?"

With an effort, and Enya's help, John sat up and leaned against a chair. "What did they take?"

Enya dabbed a cool wet cloth delicately on the side of his face. It hurt like hell but he endured it. He was surprised by the dark red blood on it when she drew it away.

"It's strange. Walter looked around a little before he found you and couldn't find anything of consequence missing."

"Where did they go, I mean in the house?"

Walter shook his head sadly. "They nearly ruined the entire place. No respect for the dead. None at all, sir. I am pleased to report that they must have gone away empty-handed. You're a hero, sir, you scared them off."

John forced a laugh. "Hero? More like a speed bump."

Enya held his hand. "I'm just glad you didn't get killed."

His thoughts clearing John looked down the hall towards the study. "Did they go in the study?"

"Of course sir, they went everyplace. But they made a particular mess of the study."

John staggered to his feet. The pain in his head was searing. The man had attacked him from the right, as if he were coming from the study. He started down the hall.

"Johnny, sit down. What are you doing? Take it easy will you?"

He ignored his sister and made his way to the study with Enya and Walter close behind. It was a heartbreaking mess. Every book was on the floor. There was such a pile that he virtually had to wade through it. He checked the top shelf where the *Valley of the Rhinos* had stood for as long as he could remember and his heart sank when he saw it too was empty.

He sifted the pile with his feet trying to find some glimpse of the book with the map. In desperation he finally sat in the books and started moving them one by one.

"What are you looking for, sir?" Walter had been watching him as if the head injury were responsible for his peculiar behavior.

"You of all people should know. I'm looking for the map book. *The Valley of the Rhinos.*"

"I'm afraid you won't find it here, sir."

John's hopes fell, his worst fears realized. "Why not?"

"When your father left on his boat trip, he had me send the map to you in Amsterdam. The book, the map, the horn the whole thing. Said it might 'wake you up.' I believe that's the phrase he used. Didn't you check your mail before you left the continent?"

17

EVEN AT THIS EARLY HOUR THE SIDEWALKS IN Amsterdam were crowded with people and the streets were filled with autos and streetcars. Sharon stepped up her pace to keep up with John. They were only going to breakfast at a café she had seen on the corner, but he was in a hurry even so. Ever since they had landed the night before, he'd seemed on edge. For that matter his whole demeanor had changed subtly since the ransacking of his parents' home two days ago. Before that he had been easygoing, almost lackadaisical in his approach to things. Now he was focused, driven. It was a different side to him than she had seen before and she liked it.

The decision to return to Amsterdam to personally retrieve the map had been easy. They were both ready for a change after the depressing events at home. They'd agreed that since his parents had placed so much emphasis on the document they needed to get it in hand as soon as possible. As to whether or not they would follow it, now or ever, that was still unresolved.

They crossed the street at a busy intersection as the sun peeked over a cathedral spire she guessed had been built centuries ago. She hoped the day would warm up. She was dressed for weather a little less cool. Of course, at the pace they were walking she would soon start perspiring.

"Do you believe in fate?"

The question came from so far out of the blue that it took her a moment to answer.

"Yes. I guess."

"Do you believe we're destined to be together?"

"That's kind of a funny question coming from you, John. I already told you I'd marry you."

"But that's not the question. The question is, do you believe I'm your destiny?"

He took her arm firmly signaling her to hurry so they could cross the street ahead of a streetcar and two motorcycles that were coming down the road. The vehicles were closer than she liked and she wouldn't have crossed on her own but he nudged her forward. They had to run to be sure they got out of the way and the streetcar driver sounded his horn. She was close enough to see him sneer at them as they reached the curb.

She felt her face flush in embarrassment.

"Well?"

"Well, what?" They continued down the crowded sidewalk at the same pace, which she was now starting to think was unreasonable.

"Do you think I'm your destiny?"

That was enough. She pulled her arm free and stopped. He took a few steps before he stopped and looked at her. She waited for him to come back.

"What kind of a question is that? It's not even eight o'clock in the morning. We're on our second continent and third country in two days. We're going to retrieve a map we don't fully understand. A couple of days ago you were attacked and almost killed by God knows who. My rear end is now permanently shaped like an airplane seat. I haven't even had a cup of coffee yet, and you ask me that?"

She could sense the eyes of the people on the sidewalk checking them out.

John looked around noticing the other people for the first time. "Sorry bad timing. I'll explain later but we have to go now."

"Why?"

He tugged gently on her arm. "Somebody is following us. Come on."

"What? How do you know?" She let him lead her back into the crowd of people moving along the sidewalk.

"I know the same way I knew you were following me in Paris."

She looked at him incredulously. "You knew? I mean, I didn't follow you. It was a coincidence that we met. And how would you know anyway?"

They turned a corner. The idea that they were being followed had given her a burst of adrenaline. She quickened her pace to keep up with him.

"A long time ago I thought it would be good idea to join the army. You know, prove I could get by without the old man's money, that sort of thing. Well, somebody figured out who I was and I'm sure they thought they were doing me a favor. I got assigned to a Ranger team that pulled duty chasing drug lords around Central America, real prime duty if you're a career type. As for me, I hated it. Along the way I received some interesting training. Hence, I know when I'm being followed."

She did not want to let this issue go. "You didn't really know I was following you in Paris."

He gave her a sideways glance. "Not until this moment. I knew your showing up at the café was a pretty big coincidence, but now I'm flattered."

She could feel her cheeks turning red. "You brat, you tricked me."

She started searching every face they passed. She caught snatches of words and phrases in at least three different languages. She wanted to look over her shoulder and see what John had seen, figure out who was following them, but she resisted the temptation. She thought it would be too obvious and amateurish. On second thought, she was an amateur at this.

"Why would anybody follow us?"

"The map."

"Well why? We don't have it."

John stopped abruptly. "You're right. They want us to lead them to it."

She was a little proud of herself for making the point apparent. "Are you sure you had training?"

"I didn't say I paid attention."

"Now what?"

"Let's get some coffee. Maybe our friend will get hungry too, and leave us alone."

———

John sat at a small table at a sidewalk café sipping his second cup of coffee. Sharon had gone to powder her nose and he used the moment of solitude to mentally put things in order. He watched the streets in both directions, which gave him a view of avenues of approach, and also a view of the busy heart of Amsterdam.

The man following them was certainly after the map. Nothing else made sense. He was also a rank amateur because with his cowboy hat, he stood out like a duck in a hen house. John had already decided not to fetch the map from his flat himself. That would be too easy to track. He thanked his lucky stars they had stayed in a hotel last night and not gone straight to his place from the airport.

He assumed the package Walter had mailed him had been too big to put in his mail slot, so his landlady was probably holding it for him. He decided to have a courier pick it up while he and Sharon stayed far away. He wondered if his flat has been trashed the way his parents' house had. He'd worry about that later.

Sharon seemed to be holding up okay. Certainly this guy following them put a new twist on things and placed her in an unexpected danger. He loved being with her but had no intention of putting her in jeopardy. He was so lost in thought that he didn't notice the man in the cowboy hat approach until it was too late.

John felt him arrive more than saw him. By the time he looked up the man was at the table. John stood, instantly recognizing the face, and a flash of anger filled him. It was the face of the assailant who had pistol-whipped him at his parents' house, the man who must have ransacked the place. The bastard had his hands shoved deep into the pockets of a trench coat.

"Stay seated, or I will shoot you."

John looked at the slight bulge in the pocket. Maybe he had a gun and maybe he didn't. It wasn't worth finding out. He gritted his teeth and kept his face placid, forcing his anger down. He did as he was told. He hoped that if Sharon saw him sitting with someone she'd stay away.

The man sat across from him, keeping his hand in his pocket. John looked at him closely. He appeared to be Arabic and had a poorly trimmed mustache. His cowboy hat was of the variety favored by country singers and almost nobody else. The trench coat was new and cheap and John guessed it had just come off a rack in a store. As the man looked nervously around the place John guessed he was alone and without any backup. He seemed to be uncomfortable in the café, like someone who was out of his element. John could feel the back of his neck prickle. He was not fond of having guns pointed at him.

John rubbed the lump on his head from the pistol-whipping.

"You have something that I want." The English was thick and deliberate.

"I have lots of things lots of people want. Did you have anything particular in mind?"

"Do not try me. I am an impatient man and do not have time to be delayed."

"You're a common thief." There was a slight twitch of his adversary's lip. John began mentally measuring the distance between them and tried to decide if he could risk attempting to smash the table into him without getting shot. He seemed jumpy and unstable and John was not at all sure he wasn't about to get shot regardless of what he did or said.

At that moment Sharon returned to the table. She looked puzzled at the new arrival.

"Sharon, meet the man who has been following us. Don't be alarmed, but he has a gun pointed at me. I'm sorry, but I didn't catch your name."

"Barzan Al-Turfi." He motioned to Sharon. "Please sit."

Sharon sat. John pushed aside his thoughts of trying to overpower him for the moment. He could not justify putting Sharon at unnecessary risk. His mouth was dry and he hoped he wasn't revealing how scared he was. "Okay Mister Al-Turfi. Mind if I call you Al? What do you think I have that you want?"

"Do not be insolent with me or I will kill your pretty friend where she sits. You know that I have come to collect the map that was stolen from the Masai during the war. Give it to me now and I will leave you in Allah's grace."

"What makes you think I have such a map?"

"Your father was a thief and a coward. He stole it from a great warrior on the Serengeti to profit himself."

Anger boiled in John's veins. If this bastard didn't have a gun on him he would reach across the table and break his jaw. His mind was searching for a way out of this but he wore his best poker face. This was going to take patience. Even though this guy did not seem especially bright, he was certainly dangerous. John would have to let the comment about Dad go for now.

He glanced at Sharon wondering how he could get them out of this. She looked tense but calm. He hoped she'd hold it together. He thought maybe if he pulled this guy's chain he could rattle him a little. "What if I don't have the map. What if I don't know where it is?"

"Then you will die in the chair you are sitting in. Right after she dies."

He heard Sharon softly gasp and felt her touch his arm. His heart rate kicked up a notch. He dared not take his eyes off this bastard.

"Why do you want it?" Sharon's voice and tone surprised him. She didn't sound scared at all. She actually seemed defiant. Maybe she didn't take the situation seriously.

"A fair question. I am a trader in rare goods. This map, even though it leads to an ancient diamond mine, has another much greater value. You see, how do you say, my employer is a man of great wealth and he desires those things not held by common men."

"Diamonds are fairly common to the rich." Her tone was unforgiving. It increased John's agitation.

"Certainly true madame. The map also leads to the territory of the greatest black rhinos ever seen. This is what I seek."

John didn't get it. "Rhinos? What do they have to do with any-thing?"

"Horns John. Rhino horns. This man is simply a poacher after one of the most endangered species on earth." She looked at Barzan accusingly. "What kind of a man can justify killing a great animal like the rhino to make a profit of its horn?"

"A man with a gun who knows his place in the world. Rhinos are big and stupid and are not part of this universe anymore. When they are finally all gone, those who have the rare horns, will have great power in some lands. It is too bad you do not know more of the way of things. You look intelligent, for a woman. Now, where is the map?"

John decided to bluff. "I don't have it." He heard the unmis-takable sound of a pistol cocking under the table.

Fearing for Sharon, John backed down. "Wait. I can take you to it."

Barzan's voice was triumphant. "Then we must go. Now."

John saw an opening. "Yes. Now, right now. Get up Sharon, follow me."

John stood abruptly and pulled Sharon up by the arm. Barzan was surprised and stood as well, keeping his hand in the pocket of his coat.

John gently pushed Sharon in front of him and whispered as loudly as he dared. "Do exactly what I say."

She nodded slightly in agreement.

They moved quickly through the narrow aisles between the café tables. Barzan lagged behind then hurried to catch up. Just as they reached the exit a waiter called to them. John looked behind and pointed to Barzan. "He's paying for all of us."

Barzan brushed past the waiter and glared at John. The waiter grabbed Barzan by the shoulder.

John saw Barzan turn to confront the waiter. There were four rows of tables full of people between himself and Barzan. Glancing down the crowded sidewalk he guessed it was twenty yards to the next corner. It might not get better than this.

Barzan pulled away from the waiter. John flipped a table into the aisle. "Run!" He moved to push Sharon ahead of him but she was already at full stride. His heart raced as they weaved through the crowd for the agonizingly long twenty yards to the corner. He thought he heard a shot. Sharon reached the corner and turned. He was sprinting a half step behind her.

He spotted a taxi letting out a passenger. He pointed at it and Sharon dove headfirst through the door into the open back seat. John piled in behind her slamming the door shut. With panting breath he implored the surprised driver to, "Go. Drive! Fast damn it!"

The cabby shifted into gear and roared away from the curb.

———

That night John watched Sharon idly scroll through pages on her hand- held electronic planner. The soft blue glow of the color screen gently reflected off of her face and eyes. The hotel room was semi-dark as he'd elected not to turn the lights on until after the sun went down.

The events of the day had been startling and he was still trying to make sense out of what had happened. He rubbed the tension from his legs and stirred his glass of ice water with his finger. Sharon had been quiet for a long time and he was not really sure what she was thinking. On the surface she was amazingly calm. The fact that a few days ago he had been attacked by a man who apparently had followed them all the way to Europe to get the map was making him very uneasy. He had a difficult time sitting still and constantly peeked out the tenth floor window even though he could barely see the street below.

Since they had escaped from their predicament at the café he had constantly been looking over his shoulder. He couldn't get his nerves to settle down and a twinge of anxiety gnawed at the back of his mind. It was bad enough that he had been in trouble and hadn't seen it coming. It was much worse that Sharon was now in danger as well. He was not sure how he was going to protect her.

He got out of his chair and went to her and started gently massaging her shoulders. She straightened and closed her eyes leaning back into his hands like a kitten getting pets. She was firm and in great physical condition, an attribute he greatly admired.

"John, what are we going to do?"

The question caught him off guard and he had to think before he answered her. The safest thing to do would be to forget the map, and his father's request, and take Sharon home. The idea had a certain appeal to it but the thought of going that route made him feel guilty. On the other hand, following the map would be a journey into the unknown at best. The prospect of putting Sharon in jeopardy made his chest tighten. He wasn't sure what was best, even so he wanted to give her the choice. "Maybe we should go home and get our lives back together."

She pointed her stylus at her electronic planner. A calendar was on the screen and the next six days were highlighted in blue and the seventh day was in red. "I don't think we have time to go home and get back to Africa in time for the equinox. I think we need to leave from here."

The words startled him and stepped back from her. She was obviously serious but seemed as nonchalant as if she had just said they needed to go the market for a loaf of bread. He sucked in a deep breath and went to the table where the map was spread out. "I'm not so sure that's a good idea."

Sharon put her planer down and joined him standing by the table. She slipped her arm around his waist holding him lightly. "I didn't say it was a good idea, but I don't see how else we can get there in time."

She was talking as if the issue were already decided, and he was not comfortable with the notion at all. He would take a chance and tell his fears to see if that would sway her. If she thought he was a coward afterwards, then so be it. "Listen Sharon, there's something about this map that scares me. Everytime I've become involved with it bad things have happened. First there was. . . ." He hesitated, having second thoughts about bringing this part up.

Sharon's hold on him tightened slightly. "There was Teri, but was that the map's fault?"

He put his arm around her. "Hell, I don't know. The timing was just too weird." The admission made him realize again that the connection between the document and his failure to succeed with Teri was pretty slim.

He watched as she ran the fingers of her free hand over the map, tracing the contours of a mountain range. "What else is scary about it?"

He screwed up his nerve and his back tensed as he readied himself to show his true fears. " First of all, this map leads us to, if you will, deepest darkest Africa. I have no idea what we'll find there or who we'll get to help us. I spent time in Central America with the Army, and let me tell you, traveling around Third World countries can be pretty tough sledding."

She squeezed him tighter. On the map she ran her finger over a route marked with a broken red line. "That's okay, I like to sled."

He could tell she was not being dissuaded. "I don't even know how we'd get around out there, or who we could find to help us, or how we will find this African guy who wrote the letter."

She ran her delicate finger over the drawing of a rhino on the map. "We could hire guides. Money talks and there are plenty out there willing to take adventurers with money anywhere they want to go."

John could not keep himself from glancing out the window again, looking at the street below for some sign of Barzan. "What about your job?"

She stepped to the window near him. "I've arranged to take a leave. I've done a lot for the company and I've earned a break. I think there is something worthwhile at stake here."

He realized that she had been thinking about this more than a little. The idea that she was intent on going and had thought about the practical aspects was not only surprising, but intriguing. She had evaluated the risks in her own mind and still wanted to go. Her audacity spurred him on. She was not afraid to take things into her own hands. He knew he could not ask for a better partner.

He had been thinking of some of the realities too. "I can get Les to take over things for me. I brought him up to speed on the deal here when we were in San Francisco."

Even though he was sure she was aware of it, he wanted to clearly state his most obvious argument. "There is also some guy out there who is willing to harm or maybe even kill us for this map. Barzan didn't seem like the brightest bulb in the box but he did manage to track us to Amsterdam. It doesn't take much in the way of smarts to pull a trigger. I'm not wild about that kind of danger for myself and I'm especially not interested in putting you in jeopardy."

She turned to him and put both arms around his neck. "John, that's so sweet. I'm really touched that you are worried about me."

She kissed him hard on the lips. This was not the reaction he had been looking for but it was certainly welcome.

She let him go and turned back to the map smoothing it with both hands. "That guy at the café was a rhino poacher. Since your father first brought the map up I went on the internet and did a little research, it didn't take long to find out that black rhinos are virtually extinct. They've been nearly wiped out over the last thirty years for their horns."

She was speaking very matter-of-factly and leaning closer to the map. She tapped her finger on a drawing of a rhino. "That guy who was following us, he knows about the map so he must know about this valley. If it actually exists and he finds it. . . ."

John saw where she was going. "Then he can kill all the rhinos there, and become a rich man."

Sharon looked at him and the soft light shone gold in her hair. "Your father promised his friend that he'd help protect them."

John's pulse picked up and excitement filled him. "He always kept his promises. But what about the equinox? The only two who are one legend?"

She put her hand on his. Her palm was warm on his skin. "John, I think we may be uniquely qualified to go at this time. It must be a clue to something, otherwise it wouldn't be mentioned."

He turned her to face him, she was lovely. "Are you sure you want to do this? We could . . . we could get hurt, or worse."

She kissed his cheek. "We must go. I couldn't live with myself if we didn't go for us and for your father."

He kissed her softly and pressed his pounding heart against hers. "Me either. I guess we're off to Africa. What will we do when get there?"

"I don't know. You'll think of something."

18

T HE NEXT FEW DAYS WERE THE MOST EXCITING and bizarre of Sharon's entire life. Once they'd decided to go to Masilan the practical matter of getting there almost stopped them before they started. It took her a full day just to get visas and she burned through a lot of cash getting people to cut corners for them. While she worked on that, John was busy finding a guide. She was not surprised to learn it was difficult to do from Holland. John's success at finally locating a guide service and making travel arrangements gave her a boost of confidence for their endeavor. Once they had the right visas, and a slew of inoculations, they raced to catch a flight to London.

In London, they rushed through Heathrow to make a tight connection for a flight to Nairobi. When the 747 took off, Sharon let her seat back and massaged her temples. This was the first time in two days that she had not been in constant motion. She savored the moment to relax.

From his seat beside her John took her hand in his and fingered her diamond engagement ring. "You better take this off before we land."

Alarmed, she sat up straight in her seat not sure she had heard him right. "What on earth for? Don't you want people to know we're together?"

John raised her hand to his lips and gently kissed it. "Where we are going a ring like this is worth many years wages to most of the people. There are some who would cut your finger off just to get it. In fact, you should take all your jewelry off, necklaces, bracelets and earrings. People on the street may snatch them off you as they walk by."

A twinge of apprehension crept into her thoughts as the reality of the journey started to sink in. She turned the ring on her finger and the light from the reading lamp made the diamond sparkle. She leaned close to him. "Tell me about the plan again. I want to make sure I understand it."

John whispered so no one could overhear him. "We're going to have to improvise a little, but a few things are certain. We'll spend the night in Nairobi, then go overland to Arusha, in Tanzania. From there I've chartered a small plane that will take us to a safari camp in Masilan. It's the closest civilization I could find to the area covered on the map. We'll get there about forty-eight hours before the equinox."

He paused as a flight attendant walked by, then continued. "Hopefully, and this part gets a little murky, we'll find our African friend there. I never was able to talk to him but that is where his mail comes from and maybe someone there will know how to contact him. Either way, from there we'll have to try to get a vehicle and maybe a guide from the camp. Then we follow the map and live happily ever after."

She laughed, glad he still had his sense of humor. "The timing is pretty close considering we'll still have to travel from the camp to the valley."

"Really close. Who knows what kind of roads, or lack thereof we'll find. We'll just have to wing it." He sounded confident but the absence of firm details caused her shoulders to tighten. She held his hand as he settled back into his seat. Looking around the comfortable interior of the first-class cabin she wondered how different the world would be where they were going.

After an eleven-hour flight to Nairobi, they landed around midnight. They caught a couple hours of sleep in a hotel but when the wake-up call came she was certain she had just closed her eyes. She dragged herself out of bed and they were on the road to Arusha before dawn. She tried to sleep but the road was full of potholes and the driver was constantly swerving and slowing down to avoid damaging the van.

Occasionally she could detect the headlights of a vehicle behind them and she forced herself to resist the idea that someone might be following them.

The driver didn't speak much and it occurred to her that traveling with this stranger was a complete act of faith. She noticed that John, who sat in the front passenger seat, was wide-awake and watching the road intently. Reassured, she tried to get back to sleep but could not keep her eyes closed.

When the sun crept into the sky she was able to make out the faint snow covered peak of Mount Kilimanjaro. As the dawn shed light on the Loita Plains she could see cows and what turned out to be zebras roaming freely off the sides of the road. Zebras of all things. In the wild. It was too strange and wonderful to fully grasp.

The Kenya, Tanzania border when they finally arrived, was the scariest looking place she had ever seen. Every muscle in her body tensed and she stole glances at John and the driver to see if they were calm. John was alert as ever and the driver seemed to have increased his attention level too.

The border had a palpable tension to it. There was clear demarcation between Kenya and Tanzania and in-between was a no man's land. There were rickety shacks with hand printed signs on them and goods for sale stacked up against them. And there were people. Everywhere there were Africans in all manner of dress. Many wore the traditional red robes and handmade headdresses of the Masai, but almost as many had on western style clothes. They had one thing in common. They all had something to sell.

Sharon saw shoes, beads, stacks of red robes, carved statues of every animal in Africa, hats, chewing gum, writing pens, buttons, and things she did not even vaguely recognize, for sale. There were children barely able to walk selling wares alongside old women who tottered on sticks they used for canes. Here and there smoldering fires burned on the ground adding a smoky smell to the dusty air. Her first real look at the Third World gave the term a new meaning.

Sharon could see several vehicles similar to their van that were full of Europeans on their way to or from safaris. The vans were all surrounded by Africans attempting to sell some item or another to the people inside.

The driver parked the van near a building and turned the engine off. He turned to John. "You come with me please and missy must wait here. The fewer people the official see the easier things are."

She didn't like the sound of that but decided not to object. The driver got out and John gave her a smile. "Welcome to our adventure. I'll be right back."

The driver made it a point to lock the doors and instructed her to keep the windows up and doors shut until he returned. He and John stood outside the van talking for a moment.

A few uniformed men watched disinterestedly from the porch of a dilapidated building that had some official looking markings on it. She wondered if they were police or customs people. Her stomach tightened. What if the visas were invalid or illegal? She had not actually bribed anyone, rather she had paid, 'extra processing fees' for the quick response. If John were arrested what could she possibly do?

John gave the driver some papers from his pocket and they started walking toward one of the buildings behind the van. As soon as the men left, Sharon and the vehicle were surrounded by people selling handmade carvings, hats, spears, sandals, jewelry and pottery. They pressed their goods and faces up against the windows of the van and shouted through the glass.

"Missy, you like this? Today I sell you very cheap. Please miss, please look at this, it very good and I give you best price." By now the sun was fully up and it beat down on the van through the windows. It was stiflingly hot and she could barely breathe but she didn't dare crack a window. John and the driver were gone for what seemed like a long time. She resisted the urge to peek at the watch she had put in her purse because she did not want to show anything that would get more attention. She remembered John's warning too well.

She was beginning to think something had happened to John and the driver and could feel her chest constricting in fear. This was a rougher place than she had ever been. She'd never felt so out of her element.

As the people continued to press against the windows she recalled stories of tourists being ambushed and even taken hostage from supposedly safe base camps. She desperately wanted a way out of the van. She wanted to roll a window down and get air or throw a door open and race away from the people and the heat. Maybe she could make it to one of the cars full of Europeans but she didn't see any at the moment because her view was obscured by faces pressing against the windows. For the first time she felt vulnerable to things outside her control.

A teenage boy with several missing teeth rapped on the window to get her attention over the others. He held up a wooden dagger. "Hey, missy, you buy this. You might like."

Finally the driver and John returned and the driver shooed the peddlers away from the van. She was deeply relieved to see them and had to wipe the perspiration from her face. Once John and the driver got in they continued through the no man's land between the two countries and entered Tanzania. Finally they were driving relatively fast toward Arusha. She opened the window and let the wind rush over her face, glad to be away from the border, but leery of what lay ahead.

———

On either side of the road John would occasionally see a Masai dressed in red and carrying a spear. They drove past several villages that were little more than gatherings of mud huts surrounded by sticks tied together fort-like to keep predators out. The driver explained that many Masai had been driven from their homelands and were now forced to be farmers and cattle herders, but they still had to contend with the dangers of the wild. He told them the Masai wore red to be bold and frighten away lions and other predators. They carried spears in case the red didn't work.

John tried to imagine what kind of courage it would take to stand up to a lion with little more than a pointed stick. He was thankful it was a level of courage he'd never had to try out. He pulled his watch from his pocket, they were running a little late and he hoped the charter plane would wait.

Arriving in Arusha after noon, they drove directly to the airstrip. The hotel had packed a box lunch for them and he'd devoured what looked like a turkey sandwich and an apple. He supposed there wasn't a chance of finding a burger stand around here.

They boarded a small, single engine, propeller driven plane where he ended up sitting in the copilot's seat. The back seat of the plane was just big enough for Sharon and their two pieces of luggage.

They flew for about ninety minutes and he could see all the way to the horizon. Once they left Arusha he noticed something he had not fully considered before. For as far as he could see, in every direction, there were no roads. There were no fences, no buildings, no sign that man even walked this part of the planet except for the occasional cluster of mud huts arranged in a circle. A sense of isolation crept over him. He had brought Sharon to a place where they were dependent on strangers and their own wits to survive. He hoped it would not prove to be a mistake.

On the ground he would occasionally see what he thought was a herd of animals. The pilot was Greek and for the most part paid little attention to him. John was a bit unnerved when the pilot picked up what looked like a radio with digital numbers on it and started rapping it on the front. Not satisfied with whatever it was doing, he picked it up and asked John to hold it while he fiddled with the wires. This was a different way of flying. He wasn't sure what he would do if the pilot asked him to take the controls.

Up ahead he could see a volcanic peak rising out of the flat plains. It had the appearance of an up side down snow cone, except in this case, the snow was on the pointed end that reached into the sky.

The pilot leaned close to him and raised his voice to speak over the sound of the engine. "Sometimes it smokes." He pointed to the volcano. "Want to go closer?"

John nodded. The plane turned toward the gray peak and he could soon see a crater collapsed one side. There was snow around the edges but it was covered with soot and ash. The pilot took them in low enough that he could see billows of steam escaping from crevices on the side of the mountain. Yellow sulfur stained the surface of the snow in several places.

The view of this primal happening, this event that was a daily occurrence here brought him up short. Most of his life had been in the concrete cities where man had forced himself onto the environment and convinced himself he had taken charge. Here, people were only visitors. They were putting themselves at risk to pass through this place. He wondered about men such as this pilot and whoever was at the safari camp, men who chose to live in such a vast unforgiving place. It must take a special type and he was pretty sure that he was not one of them.

The fact that humanity's reach had somehow managed to harm even this remote place amazed him. His father had implored him and Sharon to journey here to see it first hand. The desire to help if they could, was almost overwhelming.

A burning odor filled the cockpit and he looked at the pilot in alarm. The man smiled and pointed to the crater. He realized that he was smelling the volcano. It occurred to him that if the mountain were to explode, he, and the airplane, would probably be vaporized. He resisted the urge to shout to the pilot to get the hell out of there.

The mountain passed under the plane and they resumed the course they'd originally been flying. The air quickly cleared and he welcomed the freshness. Apprehensive but also excited at the prospect of the adventure ahead, he took several deep breaths and turned around to look at his future wife. Sharon was leaning against the window with his camera, trying to get a picture of something on the ground. He touched her knee and she looked over and smiled.

A thunderstorm caused the pilot to alter course and the small plane was pelted with driving rain. John's stomach did a couple of flip-flops as they bounced in the air and he hoped they would land before he got sick. The pilot pointed out the Mara River below and a long black line of wildebeests and zebras stretching into the vast Serengeti Plain."The herd is on the move. The end of the migration is near."

The incredible and unexpected vision of tens of thousands of animals moving together made him forget his discomfort. He couldn't open his eyes wide enough to take it all in.

John wondered where the map was leading them. The safari company he had found operated a camp in Masilan about ninety miles from where he thought the Valley of the Rhinos was. Their story was that they were just tourists like anyone else who might contract with the company. Looking at the animals below he understood why there was a camp in such a remote location.

The plane set down on a dirt strip that looked like it was barely scraped out of the underbrush. The red color of the ground was a stark contrast to the dried yellow and brown grasses that surrounded it. As they landed he could see two safari cruisers waiting for their arrival. There was also a contingent of Masai. The pilot pointed to them. "They are just here to watch the airplane come and go."

Opening the door and getting off the plane, Sharon was greeted by a man who was so ruggedly good-looking he almost took her breath away.

"You must be Sharon Cameron of the Erikson party. More than pleased to meet you. I'm Frank Halverson, camp manager. Welcome. Are you up for a game drive this afternoon? There are still a couple of hours before sunset."

John shook Frank's hand before she could reply. "As you know from my communication we're in a bit of a hurry."

Frank's response was a little hesitant. "Oh yes, quite so. Well no one is going anywhere but to camp tonight, too late in the day for anything else so please take the chance for a drive."

Sharon hoped John would take a reasonable approach and was relieved when he agreed to the game drive. She extended her hand to Frank. "I'm Sharon, pleased to meet you."

He gave her a warm smile and she decided to hold off on asking about Mutombo. She did not want to be guilty of tipping their hand too soon.

Frank looked to John. "Ready for a ride then? Splendid, George here is one of our top driver guides." A tall African in the khaki and tan uniform of the safari company smiled and shook their hands. "He'll take you on a nice drive on the way back to the camp. I'll be taking the other vehicle and I'll show your documents to the customs people. It's pretty informal out here. Then I'll be meeting you back at camp for dinner."

John smiled. "That will be wonderful. This place seems really remote. How many trucks do you have out here anyway?"

"Just these two. These are the only private vehicles for three hundred miles in any direction. Worth their weight in gold they are."

They stayed at the airstrip and watched the plane take off again carrying some outbound tourists. John and Sharon climbed into the back of a cruiser and they were off driving across the Serengeti with a driver guide named George. He had the blackest skin of any man she had ever seen. His eyes were big and seemed to shine white against the darkness of his face. He impressed her as being warm and easy to get along with.

They spent the next hour driving slowly across the grassy savanna. George pointed out each new species of animal and bird with pride. Sharon was amazed at the vast number and variety of creatures.

George called out the names of animals she had never heard of before. There were statuesque topis, large antelopelike creatures with spiral horns and brown and purple coloring, and little yellow-brown klipspringers, who looked like antelopes but were barely the size of a dog. She had expected to see gazelles and zebras, but she had not expected to drive through herds of hundreds of them.

She laughed in excitement as the animals galloped and leapt ahead of the slow-moving vehicle. Once they were clear, a few of the bravest of the creatures invariably stopped and watched them pass looking at the truck quizzically as if to ask what its business was out here in their territory.

Sharon sat in the row of seats behind George and John sat behind her in the very back row. She leaned back to John speaking softly so George could not hear her. "John this is fabulous, but when will we try to get to the valley?"

John stroked her hair and kept his voice low too. "This is a commercial tour company. It's the only outfit I could find that could even get us close. I think we need to appear to be just like any other customers until I can get to the camp manager and enlist his help to get us to the valley."

She kissed him on the cheek satisfied that John felt they were on track. She was anxious to continue their quest, but she tried to relax and enjoy the respite from the frantic pace of the last few days.

George pointed to a group of elephants not far from the crude road. Four large ones faced the truck keeping a baby one behind them. "Look, see how the momma and females protect the baby. They are very good parents." As the truck passed by Sharon watched the elephants in awe.

Farther down the road she was astounded by the number of wildebeests they saw. These were strange, awkward looking animals. George joked that it was a creature put together when the gods had finished everything else and had nothing but leftover parts. With short pointy horns, the little ones had faces that looked like the devil himself. The adults carried wide curved horns, humped shoulders, and short black manes. They were everywhere. The Serengeti was alive with the greatest migration of land mammals on the planet and they were right in the middle of it.

The vehicle stopped abruptly and Sharon looked through the windshield. Fifteen yards away a bull elephant with huge tusks stood trumpeting angrily and flapping his wrinkled gray ears aggressively. She didn't know much about elephants, but this one was obviously ready to charge them.

She took her eyes off the elephant for a moment to see how the driver guide was reacting. Her pulse pounded even harder than it already was as George was clearly frightened. She looked back at the elephant that was now stomping and bellowing even louder. John reached up and put his hand on her shoulder. It was a small comfort.

Sharon whispered to George. "Why is it doing that?"

"Oh, he is a bull and he is very unhappy with us. I think he may charge any moment now."

"Why don't you get us out of the way?" John sounded a little anxious. But it was a good question, why the heck weren't they backing up at full speed?

"I do not want to move until I know why he is angry. Probably we are close to a baby. If we go the wrong way and move toward the little one, he may attack us."

Sharon saw him slide his hand onto the gearshift. She was starting to breathe hard. The situation had a surreal feeling to her and the image of this elephant on the verge of attacking them made her a little lightheaded.

Sharon winced at the irony of the situation. Back in another part of the world she was in charge of selling one of the most advanced products of the early twenty-first century. Now here she was about to get trampled to death by an elephant, along with John and a Masai guide who probably grew up in a mud hut. God sure had a sense of humor.

The elephant took a step toward them. George inched the truck back ever so slowly. "Do you see a baby anywhere?"

Sharon looked around frantically. She was perspiring from the heat and the adrenaline pumping through her veins. Most of what they had seen had been vast open plains dotted with acacia trees. But here there was a heavy brush that stood ten to fifteen feet tall. It was so thick it was almost impossible to see through. It was dense enough to could hide an elephant. Amazing.

She forced herself to stay calm. Her fingers were cold and her palms turned clammy. She searched for some kind of escape route. The safest place was in the safari cruiser, but as they faced the elephant, the vehicle was exposed as being small and fragile. She desperately wanted someplace to hide.

Her eyes were fixed on the bull and it trumpeted again. It was pawing forward aggressively. She imagined it could easily push the truck over with its head and stomp the cruiser into sheet metal with its great feet. The thing must be fifteen feet tall. She couldn't even begin to guess how much it weighed. Her muscles tightened into knots as she envisioned her head being crushed under the massive beast.

The truck inched back a little faster now. The elephant became increasingly aggressive. The animal's ears were fully extended making it appear even larger. It stomped the ground and made a bluffing charge toward them, stopping after only a few steps.

The dirt roadway, which was little more than two worn tire tracks, was narrow, hedged in on both sides by thorny trees and shrubs. The angry bull fully blocked the path ahead of them and the road behind them was winding and treacherous.

She glanced back when George shouted. "There's the baby."

Twenty yards to the rear of them a baby elephant came out of the brush onto the road. It didn't stand much higher than the door handles and under other circumstances she would have thought it was cute. As it was, the sight of the baby enraged the bull who trumpeted louder than before and was poised to charge them.

"I am sorry, this is very bad. We are between the big one and the little one. Please hold on."

The truck jolted, and to her surprise they went forward, not back. The bull was really charging now, there was no bluffing in this attack. It moved with frightening speed and was close enough that she could see long dark scratches on the huge tusks. Her stomach twisted and her heart pounded. George gunned the engine and swerved off the road and into the brush at almost a ninety-degree angle. She was thrown into the side of the cab. Pain shot up her arm as she banged against the unpadded door.

The truck bounced hard on the uneven ground. Brush tore at the sides of the vehicle making scratching sounds that reminded her of chalk squeaking on a blackboard. The elephant trumpeted again and crashed into the brush behind them. She was almost jolted out of her seat as they bounced farther into the brush. She couldn't see three feet ahead of them out of the windshield and suspected George couldn't either.

John tried to help her stay in her seat but he could barely stay in his. The elephant was getting very close. She held her breath. She wanted George to stomp on the gas and get them out of there.

George turned the wheel again, this time to the right. She realized he was taking them away from the baby and now had the charging bull behind them. How could he have been calm enough to think of that? What if they ran full into a whole herd? Her heart was racing wildly and she could barely catch her breath. She gripped the seat in front of her with all her strength.

The cruiser smashed through the brush and abruptly the bull stopped charging. She looked out the back and saw it raise its trunk in victory and let out one last bellow at the retreating cruiser. They burst out onto the road again and George slowed to a manageable speed.

She continued to stare out the back, half expecting to see the charging monster racing after them. Slowly she released her grip on the seat and caught her breath. Her fear turned to elation and she started to laugh in relief.

She was happy to hear John laughing too. Soon they were in near hysterics, laughing almost uncontrollably, so much so that George joined them as well.

She spoke casually, as if this sort of thing happened every day. "That was fun."

John collected himself and looked at her with a straight face, suppressing a smile. "I thought it was amusing too."

George turned around to face them. He flashed a pure white toothy smile and his eyes were bright. "Now you will have a story to tell at your country club when you get home. Are you each okay?"

They both nodded and started laughing again. She watched John's smile and knew nothing would ever be the same for them. The excitement she had in her life, the unpredictable nature of things would never have happened with her first husband. She thanked the stars she had met John.

"Look under your seat. There is a bag with drinks in it if you would like. And welcome to my home. Welcome to Africa." George let out a strong friendly laugh.

Sharon pulled the bag from under the seat and opened the zipper. She selected a bottle of spring water and John opened it for her. The cruiser passed from the brush onto a grassy plain. She was certain she could see so far that the earth curved away from them. Watching John survey the vast savanna, she tasted the water. It was the sweetest she'd ever had.

Half an hour later George stopped the truck near an acacia tree and shut the engine off. "Here we can stretch our legs for a moment, but we must stay close to the truck because there may be lions nearby."

They got out of the vehicle and Sharon was grateful for the opportunity to move about, but she also had a pressing need. "George, I don't suppose there is a ladies room about?"

George smiled and nodded. "I understand, Miss. You want to take a nature walk."

Based on their recent run in with the elephant, she wasn't at all sure she wanted to walk anywhere, but his meaning was unmistakable. "Yes, I think so." Looking around she realized there didn't appear to be any place to walk to. John had exited the truck on the other side and was now watching the two of them in amusement.

George took a long stick from inside the truck and she followed as he walked slowly toward a bush a little ways away. He motioned her to stop. "I'll check first."

He cautiously skirted around the edge when suddenly the bush shook. Her heart skipped and she jumped back, as did George. Two tiny klipspringers burst out from underneath and ran away.

George looked at her and smiled sheepishly. "I'm glad they were not lions. But since they were here, it means it is safe." He walked back to the truck leaving her alone. She stepped behind the bush not at all sure she liked this, but she was glad she had done plenty of camping in college.

Loaded in the safari cruiser again, they headed up a ridge that bordered the vast marsh where they had stopped. George drove at a steady rate and Sharon guessed they never exceeded ten miles per hour. The vehicle ambled along making little noise, gently rocking over the terrain. Occasionally George would have to come to almost a complete stop, put the truck into four-wheel drive and slowly negotiate a stream, or large hole that crossed in front of them.

He did this with infinite patience and care so as not to disturb his passengers. "George, where did you learn to drive?"

"All driver guides have extensive training, missy. These are very good jobs and we had to take special tests to get them." He smiled and she thought she detected a note of pride in his voice.

She was positive he must have been a star pupil at the driver training sessions. As they rode he constantly pointed out each new animal they saw. They passed two sleeping hyenas who scarcely gave them notice. Sharon's heart raced each time she saw a new creature.

A family of warthogs crossed in front of the truck and when they finally saw the vehicle started to run in a mild panic. The little ones skittered away rapidly, their tails high the air. The mother and father, both the size of large dogs waited behind, baring their white tusks at the cruiser. Once they decided there was no threat, they scampered off with their own tails comically in the air.

"George, why do they run with their tails up?" Sharon was fascinated and wanted to learn everything at once.

"That's a follow me sign, miss."

"What's that?"

"Each animal has a marking so that the others can follow it when it is running away. The warthogs have a tail that stands on end. Gazelles have different colored tails so that the rest of the herd can see them. Even lions have dark spots on the back of their ears that contrast to the grasses they hunt in."

"Wouldn't that help the predators?" It was John's turn for a question. He'd been so busy taking pictures that Sharon wasn't sure he'd heard what George had said.

"No sir, by the time the hunters are close enough behind to benefit from a follow-me sign, it is probably too late anyway. It is most crucial to keep the families and herds together."

Sharon had read about natural adaptations and species specific behaviors years ago in college. It occurred to her she had learned more about animal behavior in the last two hours than she had in

all of her schooling. It confirmed her long held notion that experience was the best teacher.

They passed through a small heard of zebras and wildebeests
spread on either side of the dirt path that served as the road. The
animals actually in the road scattered, galloping just enough to
get out of the way of the vehicle, but not wasting anymore energy
than needed. The dust they kicked up hung in the still air and
mingled with the aroma of the grasses and acacia trees.

She closed her eyes. She was having a hard time believing she
was really here. Really in Africa. She opened her eyes again, half
fearing it would all be gone. Just as she did, George stopped the
cruiser on a rise above the vast plains. "Look there, what do you
think that is?"

In the distance she could see a long line of animals standing
black against the golden grasses of the swamp. "Look how many
there are. I bet it's three hundred, they must be wildebeests."

"No ma'am. These are elephants."

Sharon did a double take.

"Elephants?" John was astonished. I didn't know there were
that many left."

"Yes, sir. This one is a medium size herd."

Sharon stood up and looked through the open top with John.
He gave her the binoculars and she involuntarily gasped as she
focused on the herd. This must have been exactly what the first
white explorers saw. Vast tracks of untouched wilderness filled
with strange creatures. She was so elated that she had to sit down
before she hyperventilated.

Sharon thought about why Erik had sent them on this trip.
"Do you think we'll see any rhinos?"

"Oh no, missy. Rhinos are extremely rare. When I was young
they were almost as numerous as elephants. But the poachers got
them and now they are almost gone."

Her stomach turned at the thought of the useless slaughter.
Even though she knew that before, the idea was somehow more

real here. She still wanted to know what else might be about. "George, do you think we'll see any lions?"

"Maybe miss, there were some in the camp last night. But I know where I saw a cheetah just this morning. Should we have a look?"

"Lions in the camp? How exciting."

"Yes, Mister Frank he had to chase them away in his truck."

"Oh my. Is it dangerous?"

"Only if you are outside when they are hungry."

She was certain she'd caught him smiling, but couldn't quite tell if he was teasing or not. She decided he must be. They wouldn't let the lions eat the tourists. That would be bad for business after all.

They cruised across the vast savanna passing a few solitary baobab trees as they crossed long stretches where the only color was the bleached bones of dead wildebeests and zebras. George explained that the main body of the migration had passed through here already. Those that had not survived littered the grasslands.

They eventually came to a small valley where a river wound its way through the brown grass. Here green leafy trees traced the river's course and Sharon could make out elephants and other animals, even a cape buffalo standing in the shade near the water.

The late afternoon was hot, but she didn't mind. She wanted to feel every aspect of this experience. The air was perfectly still and stifling. The motion of the truck provided a hint of a breeze over her arms and face. There was virtually no smell that she could discern. Perhaps this was what clean air smelled like.

John pointed to the far side of the truck and she was startled to see a huge black rain cloud moving over the savanna miles away. Lightning split the sky and she recognized the still air they were in as the prelude to thunderstorms. The air was muggy. The panorama was so vast she could see the leading edge of the storm cell as it rolled over the grassland.

George pointed at the clouds. "The season of the short rains has begun."

Looking back toward the river, a sudden motion caught her attention. Something, no, two things were moving with incredible speed almost on the horizon. At first she thought they were two birds, then realized they were gazelles. She couldn't believe anything that breathed could be that fast.

"Thomson's gazelles, second fastest animals in the Serengeti." George answered her question before she asked it. "They must move fast, they are the favorite food of the cheetah."

Sharon watched until the gazelles disappeared from sight. George drove them closer to the river and she could finally see an entire herd of the little Tommies, as George called them. Their short tails nervously swished back and forth while the animals grazed.

John leaned over her to take a picture. "When you watch all the nature shows on television you get the impression everything is one bite away from being eaten. All the animals we've seen look fat, dumb, and happy. What a life. You get up in the morning and look at your to-do list. Let's see, don't get eaten. Otherwise mate and hang out."

Sharon laughed and squeezed his hand.

"There, a cheetah." George pointed away to the left.

It took her a moment, but she finally located the spotted cat sitting on a termite mound that gave it a view of the surrounding grass. It had the appearance of an animal with its mind on an attack.

She followed the animal's stare and caught her breath when she saw a baby Tommy and its mother, unaware of the proximity of the cheetah.

Looking back at the cat she momentarily lost sight of it, then glimpsed it again. It was off the termite mound and on the hunt. Her pulse quickened. She had an urge to make George honk the horn, to have him drive to the mother and baby and scare them off, but she knew it would be wrong

She lost the cheetah in the grass. She bit her lip and held her breath, fascinated at the life and death struggle that was about to take place. Suddenly the cheetah appeared only a short distance from the gazelles. The mother gazelle bolted in a flash of hoofs and seemed to be only a streak of brown and black against the golden grass.

The baby made it only a few strides before the cheetah, which was roughly the same size, was on it, biting its neck and wrestling it to the ground. In a moment the gazelle was dead and the cheetah was ripping it open and spilling blood onto the dirt. Sharon turned away, her stomach churning.

Oddly, she didn't feel like crying for the victim. It was sad to be sure, but it was the way of this world.

George looked at her and smiled. "Africa is a beautiful place. But death comes quickly for those who are not wary, or lucky."

The reality of life and death hit her starkly. She looked back at the cheetah and its bloody prey. Following the map would take them someplace even the seasoned safari people didn't go. Following it had seemed like a much better idea in a warm hotel room in Amsterdam than it did right now as she watched the cheetah devour its meal.

# PART III

*chapter*

**19**

GEORGE DROVE SLOWLY ALONG THE BANK OF a muddy river that John knew was on the migration path of the great wildebeest herds. Sharon appeared comfortable in the middle row of seats and after two full days of traveling John was happy to have the rear seat to stretch out in.

The sun was going down and though it was still hot the temperature had dropped perceptibly from when they had landed. John had to raise his voice so George could hear him. "George, do you think there's a chance we'll see a crossing?"

George looked over his shoulder to speak to him. "Maybe tomorrow, sir. We are near the end of the migration, most of the animals have passed but a few herds remain. There was a crossing this morning just up the river here, I will show you."

Sharon turned to John and talked softly. "If the stuff about the equinox is true and we don't leave tomorrow, then we have to leave the next morning or we won't make it. I'm concerned about cutting this too close."

He put his hand on her shoulder. "I know. We still have to talk the camp manager out of a truck, too. It may not be easy."

George stopped the truck and pointed to the river. "There was a small crossing here this morning. You can see the bodies of the animals that did not make it. The vultures do not wait long."

It took John a moment to realize what he was seeing. He was shocked to see dozens of dead wildebeests and zebras strewn on either side of the riverbank and in the water. A bloated animal carcass drifted by and two vultures sat on it picking at it as if at a private buffet. Other vultures gorged themselves on the seemingly endless number of dead animals.

Sharon stared at the macabre scene with her mouth open. "My God. Is this normal?"

George pointed to the far side of the river. "Yes, missy. You see there, the animals came down that bank and waited. Many thousands but they are afraid to cross because of the crocodiles. Look there is one . . .."

John saw a huge crocodile glide into the water. The sight gave him a shiver.

"The wildebeests can smell very well, and the zebras can see very well so they travel together. None of the animals wants to be in the water first because if a croc is waiting then it will grab them and spin them underwater in a death grip. So the animals wait and wait until they are crowded together. Then if the leader thinks it is safe he jumps in. Then all jump in and swim to the far side. Where the bank is steep some trip and fall and others trample over them. It is very impressive." George's face was tight and his voice earnest, as if he were a teacher with an important lesson for his pupils.

John could only imagine the scene that took place. He recalled seeing a television show about it but reality was much starker. The smell of death drifted to them and left a sickening taste in his mouth. He was glad when George started the truck again and they moved on.

After they'd driven for a few miles John moved up and sat next to Sharon. He wanted to find out about the camp. "George, how many people are here at the camp now?"

George kept his attention on the dirt road ahead of them. "It is very slow at this time, sir. The season is almost over and the rains have started. There are only two other guests right now."

Sharon squeezed John's hand tightly and he knew she felt the same exhilaration he did. The fewer tourists the better and if there were only two then their chances of obtaining a truck were much higher. He had been forced to leave the details of this part of the trip sketchier than he liked. The company agents he'd dealt with in Amsterdam thought he would be able to get a vehicle, but they would not guarantee it.

He pressed George for more information. "Who else is in camp, are you expecting more clients?"

"I think not, but sometimes we get surprised. Mister Frank has a very difficult job and knows more about who is to come or go than I do."

Looking out the window John was startled to see a small two story concrete building. It was surrounded by a seven foot high cinder-block fence that was topped with razor wire. "What is that?"

Two men in uniforms waved at them and George waved back as they passed. "This is a ranger station. It was built to stop the poachers. Two years ago there was a big fight here when poachers tried to chase the rangers away. Since then they have built the concrete fort. Anytime we leave the camp and go to the south we must have a ranger with a gun with us."

John's chest tightened. He hadn't thought of rangers. The idea that they were in a heavily protected area had not entered into his plans. The territory on the map was clearly south of the camp and he no idea how to deal with this complication.

Sharon whispered to him. "Is it south?"

He nodded his head. "Of course."

Sharon leaned closer. "What do we do?"

John realized he didn't have a clue. "We'll think of something." He wondered if he sounded hopeful at all. This was the first time she had deferred to him and he didn't want to disappoint her. A tentacle of doubt tugged at the back of his mind but he ignored it. Once they arrived at the camp and he determined the lay of the land he would find a way to press on.

When they arrived at camp John was pleasantly surprised by the accommodations. Dispersed among the trees there were a dozen guest tents, each designed to accommodate two people. They had solid wood bases and floors, with verandas, on the front. Except for the canvas walls and tops they looked like cottages. In the center of the site was a large dining tent with a firepit in front of it. Away from the main camp were some larger semi-permanent structures where George said the camp attendants and driver guides stayed.

When he entered their tent John was happy to find it spacious and comfortable. An African attendant named Stephen showed them both the locations of the washbowls and the long drop that was conveniently in a separate area at the rear of the tent.

When Stephen left them alone Sharon stretched out on the single bed on one side of the room and John fell back onto the other one.

"John, how are we going to do this? Are we chasing windmills here? There are men, who know this country, patrolling this place with guns. Do we think we can do something more than they can?"

He was glad she had the same questions that were running through his mind. "If we could find this Mutombo guy, the one that wrote the letter, he might help us decide how to proceed. Hopefully we can find out something at dinner but we'll need to keep our cards close to the vest. We know this map has caused trouble before. Let's be cautious about who we discuss it with."

For the moment that was as good a plan as he could divise.

————

Sharon sat at the dinner table listening to John and Frank, the camp manager, continue to talk. She was tired and was growing impatient with both of them. They had been going over the same ground ever since the dinner dishes had been cleared from the table in the dining tent. The glow of the candlelight cast shadows across their faces and onto the olive green walls.

"If you don't tell me where you're going then I can't bloody well tell you how to get there, now can I, Mister Erikson?" Frank sounded as if he were getting exasperated and might cut the conversation short.

"Please, all I need is a driver guide and a vehicle. We won't be gone three days." From his voice she knew John was forcing himself to sound reasonable, but his request was getting nowhere with the camp manager. She bit her lip trying to decide if she should say something. She decided not to, for the moment, because she didn't want to put Frank even more on the defensive by having to deal with two customers.

An African tent attendant appeared wearing a white waiter's coat that contrasted starkly with his skin. He filled the wineglasses for each of them with a red that had earlier warmed her. Now she wondered if giving these two battling males anything else to drink was a good idea.

"Leave the bottle and bring another." Frank commanded the attendant and almost didn't lose his place in the discussion.

"Listen sir, don't think you can fly in here, wave a few dollars around, take one of two vehicles in a three hundred mile radius and just go lollygagging about the countryside. Where do you think you are, bloody New York City?"

"Is it the money? I'll buy you a new vehicle. For that matter I'll buy you two, as soon as we get back."

"Right. And I suppose you'll send the London Bridge as soon as you get home. Have a drink."

This made no sense. The conversation was a complete stalemate. Neither one of them would give in. She wondered if they were enjoying being bullheaded, or if this round of the discussion was purely for her benefit.

Sharon guessed Frank was about the same age as John and herself. He had a deep tan and the lines around his eyes were of the type acquired by men who spent vast amounts of time outdoors. His hair was short and black and brushed rakishly to one side. In his safari company short sleeved shirt and khaki shorts he was the picture of the big game guide. He was definitely an attractive man and he was proving to be both smart and forceful. She had a growing respect for him in spite of his not relenting on the truck.

The two men paused and filled their glasses. She was beginning to think they had forgotten her all together when Frank turned to her and offered to fill her glass.

"Madam, may I have the pleasure?"

She looked at his dark brown eyes. She felt the blood rushing to her face and had the vague impression there was more to that question than filling a glass. She was glad she was now engaged. Otherwise there might be a temptation to consider. Then again, maybe the notion was only in her mind. He had been exceedingly polite from the moment they met.

She wondered why a man like him would decide to spend so much time in the bush. She thought he must be dedicated to something besides money. That was a quality she didn't find in many people and was one she admired.

She held her glass out and saw John scowling over Frank's shoulder. She was amused that he was actually showing a hint of jealousy. Either that or he was just mad he wasn't getting his way.

Outside the tent a loud guttural roar broke the night. Sharon froze. "That was close."

Frank kept pouring the wine. Another roar answered the first. Then there were several loud and unmistakably angry roars in succession.

"Just a couple of lions quarreling. Probably over a bloody female."

He gave her a wink and smiled. A slight quiver went down her back.

He turned to John. "Or more likely a kill."

"Do lions really get this close?" That was a stupid question. She felt idiotic for blurting it out.

"Every few nights they come around. Nothing to worry about though, they won't bother you in your tent. Just don't go wandering around without a watchman. The Swahili word is 'ascari.' If you need to leave your tent after dinner, and I don't know why you would, just call out for an *ascari* and someone will come."

An attendant entered the tent and put a plate of chocolates on the dining table. Sharon selected one that looked like it might have nuts, and when she bit into it was not disappointed.

John returned the conversation to its original track. "We'll only need one vehicle for a few days. We'll be very discreet."

Frank sounded tired. "Discreet? What do you know about discreet? You'll be lion scat before you get a full day out. You've no idea how the bush can turn on you. If a lion doesn't get you, a croc, or hippo will."

"Give me a gun. I can take care of myself."

"Oh for pity's sake, you are crazy. You show a gun in this country and the rangers will bloody well kill you on sight. No questions asked. The only people with guns around here are poachers and rangers. And there aren't very many poachers carrying guns anymore. The ones that are still alive wised up a few years ago."

John let out a deep breath. "Why won't you give us the vehicle?"

This time Frank gave a more elaborate answer than he had before. "My company operates here at the pleasure of the government. We are situated in a national park that is designed to protect some species found almost nowhere else on earth. If I let everybody who came in here go willy-nilly wherever he wanted, I'd be out of business in a week. One of our main goals is to help with conservation, not to go running amuck."

John persisted. "Listen, I'll level with you. My parents came to this place almost fifty years ago. They told me it was the best journey they ever made. We're just trying to retrace their footsteps, it's kind of a family quest. The son of the guide they used, his name is Mutombo, recently wrote and invited us to come see this place for ourselves. The company I'm affiliated with is very large. There may be ways we can help with conservation efforts."

Frank sat back in his chair and thoughtfully tugged on his ear. Sharon saw this might be the place to help. "It's kind of romantic, and it may sound a bit silly to you but it means ever so much to the two of us. We've come so terribly far." For dramatic affect she put her arm around John and looked at Frank with pleading eyes.

Frank was quiet for a moment and seemed to be reflecting on something. Sharon's hopes started to rise. Frank ran his hand through his hair. "Long time ago, before she got tired of the bush, me and my missus had this place we used to go. It was near Victoria Falls and to us it was the best spot in the world and belonged to just the two of us. We had some times there I won't forget if I live to be a thousand. She left me years ago, I can't blame her. Wanted to be able to shop in London, and have a flush toilet, and not worry about getting eaten if she wandered out of doors at the wrong time. But I still think of that place. Everyone should have one."

He sat up and looked at them as if he'd just noticed they were there. "If it could be worked out, and that's a big if, when would you want to leave?"

Sharon almost leapt for joy.

John took a sip from his glass and started with a hopeful tone. "What will it take to get us, and a guide, to south of the mountains the day after tomorrow?"

Frank's voice had a new calmness to it. "I recognize that you and the missus have spent a great deal of money on this trip and it may be a once in a life time adventure. But you have to understand, I'm short-handed here, my partner's parents took ill and she had to return to Liverpool and won't be coming back. It's extremely difficult to find replacements out here. I could possibly spare a driver and vehicle, but I have other clients as well as your-selves to contend with. They have also spent huge sums on this trip. Before I even entertain that thought, I must know where you want to go."

John put his elbows on the table and rubbed his temples with his finger tips. " We're not totally sure where. It's maybe ninety miles south of here and is marked by twin mountain peaks. We were hoping this Mutombo fellow could help us out but we're not sure how to find him."

Frank sat forward in his chair. "I've never heard of anyone by that name around here, you might try asking the driver guides. I have a hard enough time keeping up with their Christian names. But there is something crucial you need to understand."

Sharon held her breath. From outside she could hear the strange laughs of a pack of hyenas in the distance.

Frank slowly took a drink and he looked John square in the eyes. "You realize you are asking to go someplace virtually no white men have ever been. A place where the last of a slaughtered species lives unknown to the rest of the world. Not to the gov-ernment, or the people from the nature shows, or to the poachers. Tell me you don't want to photograph these animals, and sell the pictures. It would certainly doom them."

John's voice had a trace of excitement. "You've been there. You've seen the great rhinos. That means they really exist."

Frank licked his lips. "I didn't say any such thing. But I know two people who go there better be damn sure of themselves and their motives."

Sharon thought her heart might stop. A rush of excitement went through her entire body. "You know about the legend."

Frank glanced at her. "A man gets to know about a lot of things out here, miss."

John put both his hands on the table and looked squarely at Frank. "Let me be clear. We're not after the rhinos. If you let us go I'll let you search the vehicle for cameras or whatever you want. In return I'll finance your operation for two years, and put a matching sum in the ecological defense fund of your choice. I'll also give my promise that neither of us will breathe a word to anyone else about what we see."

Frank leaned back in his chair. "And two new vehicles."

John nodded.

Frank smiled. "That's a big price for a romantic adventure."

John looked at Sharon. "It'll be worth it."

She felt her cheeks flush.

Frank leaned forward. "You've got the bloody map don't you? I'll be damned. I didn't expect it to show up on my watch. The flipping Masai were right. All this time I just took it for a legend."

Sharon remembered to breathe again. If Frank knew about the map then others would too. She couldn't tell if this new information would work for or against them. She squirmed in her seat watching John who sat stonefaced with small beads of sweat on his forehead. For several moments the only sound was that of a couple of mosquitoes buzzing around a yellow candle.

Frank spoke first. "It will cost you plenty to get permission to stay out in the park overnight, but I know the local ranger commander. I might be able to work it out. You'll also have to take an armed ranger with you. That's the law."

She could hardly believe Frank had relented. She was so relieved she wanted to hug them both but a lion's roar nearly shook the tent. Sharon jumped to her feet shocked by the close proximity. She looked at Frank for guidance.

He smiled. An *ascari* came in carrying the largest flashlight she had ever seen. Sharon remembered that George had told them they used the lights to scare off animals. The *ascari* spoke quietly and humbly to Frank.

"*Jambo, Bwana. Simba.*"

"*Ngapi?*"

"*Tano, Bwana.*"

"He says there are five lions outside. We'll run them off, then the other *ascari* will escort you to your tent. Did you bring a torch?"

John held up a small penlight he had in his pocket.

Frank and the *ascari* burst into laughter. "You won't scare many lions with that, *rafiki*."

John grinned embarrassed. "All I wanted it for was to find my toothbrush. I hadn't planned on doing any lion taming with it."

Frank laughed. "We'll finish this talk in the morning."

John smiled and held out his hand. "One more thing."

Frank hesitated. "Now what?"

"How the hell do you run off a lion?"

Frank took John's hand and shook it. "From inside a truck."

BARZAN PRESENTED HIS FORGED PASSPORT TO THE customs agent in Nairobi and tried to look as bored as possible. Thus far his documents had worked every place he had been the last two weeks, but each time he presented them it made him nervous.

The dark skinned man in the blue uniform was taking just a little too long. This was the moment Barzan feared most. Standing in the middle of the customs area with no weapon and no escape route he was as defenseless as a wildebeest being stalked by jackals. His collar was tightening around his neck and the sweatband on his cowboy hat was hot and wet.

"*Karibu!*" The agent smiled. Barzan was relieved to hear the Swahili word for 'welcome.' The official lifted his big stamp and slammed it importantly onto the fake passport, then looked past Barzan and waved up the next person in line.

"*Asante.*" Barzan mumbled the word for 'thank-you' and briskly strode out of the customs area. As soon as he had gone five steps he lit a cigarette, tried to breathe normally, and regain his look of detached interest. He wished his heart would slow down. The relief at getting through another obstacle was short-lived. He hoped his men in Nairobi had done their jobs. If they hadn't, his destiny of being appointed Moto-san's successor would be gravely jeopardized. Barzan planned harsh treatment for anyone who let him down.

He reached the outside curb and searched the faces impatiently. Even though it was a late hour the terminal was filled with people. Most were tourists from France who had just disembarked from the same crowded jumbo jet on which he had traveled. Others were greeters from hotels and safari companies here to pick up their clients who had money to spend on watching the African animals.

It was a profitable business and one Barzan hated. He spat in disgust as a fat Italian woman and her bald husband were crammed into a van, with their six pieces of luggage, by an eager tour guide. The tourists were one of the reasons poaching had become so difficult. Someone had finally convinced the governments of these dirt poor countries they could make money showing off their animals and collecting handsome sums for their efforts.

Vans full of fat tourists moving through the national parks served as extra sets of eyes for the rangers. These tourists were insulated from the reality of the bush by hired guides and were pampered with fancy foods and drink in their camps. Barzan wondered how the drivers could stomach being around such soft people.

Not long after Kenya showed success, other countries joined in to some degree. Once a steady income developed, the severe crackdown on poaching began. The business was now dangerous enough that Barzan was glad he was getting out of it. Glad he was going after his last rhino. Maybe the last worthwhile rhino anywhere.

As much as he liked the bush, it would be little sacrifice to stay at the palace and toy with the women while he sent others to collect his prizes. Rhinos might be gone, but there were still elephants, and even a few tigers he had heard. The anticipation of the unlimited pleasures of Moto-san's palace warmed him inside.

*"Jambo!"* Barzan jerked his head and saw Kip approaching. He was wearing a green shirt and shorts with hiking boots. He fit in very well with the rest of the crowd of people at the terminal.

Barzan did not like being kept waiting and wanted Kip to know it. "Where have you been?"

"Making arrangements. Your instructions came very quickly and took much organizing with little warning. Come, our car is this way."

Barzan followed as Kip moved swiftly toward the curb. "Do you know where they are?"

Kip did not break stride but reached back and took one of Barzan's carry bags from him. "They flew to a safari camp near the Mara where it crosses into Masilan."

This news was not what he had hoped for. "They flew? They are traveling very fast. I was surprised at how quickly they got from Amsterdam to here. I almost lost them in London, but fortunately there are only a few flights to Nairobi so I was able to warn you. How far ahead of us are they?"

"They arrived at the camp yesterday after the noon hour."

Barzan tried to formulate a plan but he was not thinking clearly. He was feeling a little groggy from the long flight. "Are they still there?"

They reached a van with zebra stripes painted on the side and Kip opened the back. "I think so. There is only one plane that services the camp. It normally arrives once in every three days."

Barzan's hopes for catching them plunged. "Three days is too late for us."

Kip placed Barzan's bags in the van. "I have chartered a small plane to take us to the same airstrip. It is thirty miles from their safari camp. Two of my trucks left Arusha yesterday and are now on the way. They will meet us there. We arrive near midday, then we will be in a position to watch them."

Barzan tossed his cigarette into the street and took off his hat as he climbed into the van. The vehicle was inconspicuous, looking like many of the other commercial vehicles. The night air was starting to cool him. Things might still be controllable. He breathed deeply and tried to rub tension from his neck as Kip got behind the wheel and moved the van into traffic.

Barzan reached into his pocket for another smoke. "How did you learn all this?"

Kip grinned but did not look at him. "I have worked for you a long time. These are big countries but business is small and information cheap."

Barzan once again congratulated himself on hiring a man as capable as Kip.

"But please tell me this, *Bwana*, why do we care about these two tourists?"

Barzan turned on the air conditioner and let the air blow into his face. He liked being referred to as *Bwana*. It showed he was being addressed with respect. "They are insolent thieves. But they will make us both rich beyond our dreams."

"What will we do with them?"

"I will kill the bastard infidel, and I don't care what you do with the woman as long as the authorities don't find her. Then we leave the carrion to the hyenas and vultures. *Allahu Akbbar.*"

———

John sat on the veranda of the tent drinking coffee watching the sun slowly erase the morning shadows. A tribe of baboons was making its way to a water hole. The older primates were deliberate and purposeful but in no apparent hurry. The little ones scampered about playing an endless game of chase with each other.

The bush was so different. He wondered what it would be like to live in such a place. He pulled his jacket tight to ward off the lingering chill. He could hear the noises of the camp coming to life. The tent attendant, Stephen, arrived with more coffee, muffins and juice. Stephen set his tray down and left just as Frank appeared.

"*Jambo*, Mister Erikson. I trust you slept well."

John stood and returned the greeting. *"Jambo.* Please call me John. I had a very nice rest after all that travel, thanks. Care to join us? Stephen left an extra cup."

Frank stepped up the two stairs to the verandah. "I'd like that fine. Is the missus about? I have some information."

The tone in his voice was not promising and John instinctively tensed. Sharon came out of the tent sounding cheerful. "Morning, all. What's the good news?

John poured coffee for everyone. Sharon took one of the two seats and Frank leaned on the porch rail. He paused before he started, making John think things had somehow changed overnight.

"I spoke to the ranger camp on the wireless this morning and found out that the local commander is on patrol and won't be back until this evening. No one else can give us permission to assign a ranger or let civilians stay in the park overnight." He looked at the floor of the porch not meeting John's eyes.

John swallowed hard trying not to show his disappointment. Leaving today would have been ideal but a delay might be manageable. The trip was not out of reach yet. "What about tomorrow? Can we go tomorrow?"

Frank kept his eyes down. "There's no way I can know until the captain gets back. And there is also this. The rangers have a problem and they want to use one of my vehicles for a few days starting this afternoon. It's an arrangement we've had for a while. We help each other when we can. It's life in the bush."

The back of John's neck started to tingle and he suspected there was something important that was still left unsaid. "That only leaves you one truck."

Frank looked up. "The math is pretty easy. My other two clients are flying out this afternoon. They'll drive to the airstrip to be dropped off and then the truck will go straight to the ranger post. The other truck will be going out to pick up a new client."

John held the side of his chair tightly. He could feel tension in his chest. "That's not the deal we made."

Frank put his coffee down. "Sorry, mate. I only found out about this new guest this morning. But maybe it'll work out. It will be just as easy to get permission for three to spend a night out as two. Still only one truck."

John clenched his teeth trying to sound calm. "You don't understand."

Frank took his hat off and wiped his brow. "Going to be hot today. You know you're right, I don't understand. Romantic adventure or not, I still don't quite understand why you want to go out there. Even if you find something, what are you going to do? We never did talk about that."

John's jaw went slack and his insides turned. He didn't know what he was going to do. So far it had all been about the journey. He tried to come up with something that made sense even if it was vague. "It's a bit of a whim, I know. But like I said last night, my parents assured me it will be worth the trip. But a third wheel is going to take some of the romance out of it. Is there any way we can avoid taking the extra person?"

Frank put his hat back on. "Not a chance. Anyway between you two, the driver and the ranger you're going to have a regular party. I don't think another client is going to detract too much from your romance."

John caught the look in Sharon's eye and she gave him a slight smile.

Frank turned to go and then paused. "You might want to take the ride to the airstrip this morning. Nice drive there and back. Lots of game to see. After all, that's what we're famous for. We'll fix up a lunch and you'll get a chance to meet your traveling companion."

After he left, Sharon put her arm around John's shoulder. "We'll make this work."

John kissed her. "I know we will." He looked in the direction Frank had gone. "Maybe you'd like to ride to the airstrip this morning. Maybe you'd like to get eaten by a lion this morning. After all, that's what we're famous for."

———

All morning George drove them through spectacular scenery and that helped Sharon settle her nerves. When the sun was nearly overhead they stopped to eat. She relaxed under the shade of an acacia tree on the edge of a vast marsh.

George had brought along a most remarkable picnic lunch. From the truck he produced a folding table which he covered with a white linen tablecloth. On this he placed silverware and china plates. Then he set up a small buffet that had fried chicken, sandwiches, fresh fruit, butterleaf lettuce salad with cucumbers, and quiche.

To top it off she was delighted to see he also had a bottle of red wine. He poured them both a glass and saved a cola for himself. They raised their glasses together in a toast. "To Africa."

Although she was enjoying the morning she wished they were on their way to the mountains. Waiting for a day was against her nature and the delay filled her with anxiety. The addition of an extra person to the trip was but a minor irritation considering they might not be allowed to go at all. She pushed that thought aside and decided to channel her energy into finding out as much about this place as she could.

After lunch John wandered to the edge of the marsh. Sharon's curiosity about everything around them was unlimited. She could hear the mooing of a herd of wildebeests, the sound carried on the light breeze that rolled across the grasses. It was warm in the shade and a nap seemed to be in order. She didn't want to sleep, however, because there was too much to see.

George had cleared the table and was sipping his cola quietly. This man intrigued her because he was clearly very intelligent and had a boundless knowledge about every animal they encountered.

"George, how did you learn to speak English so well?"

"Thank you, ma'am. It was not very hard. They taught it to us in all the schools. It's something leftover from the British colonial days."

"I see. How did you become a driver guide?"

"I wasn't always a driver. I used to have a farm with cattle near Arusha. I was a very good farmer, too. I was even allowed to travel to Frankfurt to attend a conference on farming in the region. You see, it is a little unusual for a Masai to be good at farming because historically we men were warriors and left growing things to the women.

"But I saw we had to change with the modern times so I moved away from my village and made a farm near the city. I also made my wife and daughters strong with the church. We tried to keep close to my sisters and their families but it was very difficult. When we would leave our house and go to visit, my daughters could not stand to sleep in the traditional Masai mud huts where the smaller livestock also sleep inside to protect them from predators.

"My children would cry and make me take them home early. Then my sisters would be offended and say bad things about my wife. They thought we were pretending to be better than them. They did not understand how different our lives were, living in the western way. They kept telling me I should come back and live the Masai way.

"As we grew older the differences became more apparent. My wife still looks young, but my sisters have aged from the hard work of living in the old way. It is sad for me."

Sharon was fascinated. "Tell me about your farm."

He smiled. "My farm was very nice. I made a way to reroute the water on my land and I was able to grow the tallest corn in our area. In fact, the President came to my property with the newspaper people and made a speech. He said all the farmers could learn from what I had done."

"That's wonderful, George. You must have been very proud." Sharon was coming to respect this man more with each new thing she learned.

"Yes, I was. Maybe a little too proud." He sighed and looked away.

"Why do you say that?"

"My neighbors poisoned my cattle and killed them. I think they were jealous like my sisters."

She was shocked. Her stomach knotted.

"I think they were just ignorant. The Lord tells us to forgive and I have. That is how I came to be a driver guide. I must support my family. My daughters are married, but I must still send money to my wife and sisters."

She looked at the savanna and realized the difference between her universe and George's was as vast as the Serengeti. For him living here was a matter of survival. For her visiting this place was almost a lark. The world was a much bigger place than she had imagined and she had never before felt so fortunate.

He stood and stretched. "It is good to be in Masilan. There was a time in Kenya, that if you were seen on foot in a national park they would shoot you on sight. I don't know what they are doing now."

"Oh, my. Because of poachers?"

"Yes. It has been very effective. In Tanzania they simply outlawed guns. At first it was a problem because they could not catch the poachers. Then they decided to arrest the families of poachers. That has been effective also."

Sharon thought again about the world they had entered. It was so beautiful, yet so unpredictable and dangerous.

"Mister John, sir." George called out to John who was now about thirty yards away. "Please come close. We are in lion territory."

She couldn't help but laugh as John scurried back to the truck.

———

Looking out the cruiser window John watched fascinated as two hippos opened their massive jaws and pushed at each other in the river. George stopped the truck and turned to face them.

"When I was small my father told me of an American couple he had met. They had a most unusual map and they paid him well to guide them. At that time there were rhinos everywhere, like elephants. But these people went to a special place that was isolated from the rest of the world."

If John could have made his ears point forward he would have. He sat completely still not wanting to miss a word George said.

"The three of them found a valley that had the largest rhinos he had ever seen. The Americans climbed farther up the mountain and when they returned he thought they were as happy as any two people he had known."

John could not help himself. "What were their names?"

George gave him a wide grin. "They were like yours Mr. Erikson."

Sharon interrupted. "Then you must be Mutombo."

George nodded. "Yes, I am the one who wrote the letter."

John's heart leapt. "That's wonderful! But why did you write now, after so many years?"

George's voice dropped and he squinted slightly like a man who had seen many sad things. "The world changes, it is the way of things. There are many good people who are trying to save rhinos and the other animals but I have seen with my own eyes they are losing. It is my hope because you are here now, at this year, you will look around and maybe your eyes will be opened.

"It is one thing to read of a problem, to know of it, but it is another matter entirely to see it. Maybe it will make no difference to you. Maybe you do not care. But for me, I must do whatever I can to keep the animals from vanishing. I don't know what you can do. But if you learn, maybe you will think of something."

Sharon put her hand on George's. "We'll do whatever we can."

John nodded and slumped back into his seat. He wished he had a solution. Or least a good idea.

George turned the cruiser away from the river. "When Mister Frank gets you permission, I would like to guide you tomorrow. To your special place."

John's hopes raised. "You said 'when' he gets permission. Do you think he will?"

George gave him a big grin. "Mister Frank gets most of what he wants. I think you will be going tomorrow and I would like to be your guide."

Sharon put her hand on John's leg. "We would love to have you drive us. It would be wonderful."

John could not agree more. "Yes. If we get to go we certainly want you to drive."

George put his attention back to driving and started humming to himself. John sat back in his seat and then gave Sharon a light kiss on the cheek. This was the most hopeful sign they had received since they arrived.

J OHN LEANED AGAINST THE FRONT FENDER OF the safari cruiser and scanned the Serengeti with his binoculars. A few hundred yards away two adults and one baby elephant took refuge from the sun under the branches of an acacia tree. They swayed slightly, flapping their ears lazily and blowing dust onto their backs with their trunks to stay cool in the heat of the afternoon.

Putting the binoculars down, John wiped a bead of sweat from his forehead and looked down the dirt strip that the driver guide called a runway. So far he had not spotted any zebras or gazelles crossing the strip, but he kept a lookout just in case. The animals had a remarkable knack for showing up just as a plane was about to land, which annoyed the pilot, and generally scared the hell out of the passengers.

This passenger would deserve it. He shouldn't be here anyway. The plane was two days ahead of schedule and he had told Frank specifically that he and Sharon wanted to be alone. The last minute addition of another traveler thoroughly annoyed him. And as if the intruder coming here weren't enough, he and Sharon had spent the better part of the morning bouncing around the back of the cruiser so they would be at the airstrip to meet the plane. It was either this or sit outside the dining tent and watch the baboons. He had done that for an hour before breakfast and that was plenty.

The driver, Christopher, had brought the other two guests to the airstrip. John and Sharon were both relieved they did not have to share a vehicle with them this morning as the other clients were lawyers who seemed intent on impressing each other by how many names they could drop in one sentence.

His apprehension about getting to their goal on time had caused his back to tighten and had put him in an irritable mood. It also made today feel like lost time. He was resigned to make the best of it though. The Serengeti was a stunning place and Sharon was a wonderful companion to share it with.

John squinted into the blue white sky putting his sunglasses on. Sharon reached out from inside the safari vehicle and touched his shoulder. The auburn hair around her shoulders and her dark glasses highlighted her lovely profile. "Be patient, Johnny. It'll get here eventually. Who knows, this could be an interesting person. Maybe he'll have a secret map, too."

"Maybe you're right. I just hope we don't get stuck with a lawyer like the two yahoos who are leaving."

"Agreed. If a lawyer shows up, your job is to hijack the plane and get us out of here."

George opened his door and looked into the sky. "I can hear it now. They will be here in only a few minutes, I think."

John didn't hear anything but the wind and the mooing of distant wildebeests. However, he had learned not to doubt the Masai guide. George hadn't been wrong yet.

Moments later John heard the drone of the single prop that was pulling the small plane into alignment with the runway. He spotted the familiar green safari company logo on the side as the aircraft descended and settled onto the airstrip, kicking up a cloud of red dust behind it.

The pilot shut the engine down as he drew close to the cruiser. Sharon stepped out of the vehicle to join John and George forming an impromptu welcoming committee for the new arrival. This, they had learned, was part of safari etiquette. They were going to be stuck with this person for the next three days so they might as well try to get off to a good start.

The front door of the aircraft swung open and the pilot hopped out and opened the passenger door. To John's complete and utter shock, the pilot helped Teri Clark step out of the plane onto the dust of the Serengeti, and back into John's life.

She was beautiful, and perfect. She looked exactly as she appeared in his dreams and nightmares. Her white tennis shoes showed just enough dirt to be appropriate. Her khaki shorts showed just enough leg to make him remember. A tan blouse matched her small carry bag and a blonde ponytail trailed out the back of a stylish baseball hat. Fashionable mirrored sunglasses hid her blue eyes from him. Even so, he knew she was staring into him.

John's throat constricted and his mouth went dry. His stomach tightened and the heat of the sun seemed to suddenly increase causing his palms to start sweating. He uttered the only thing he could think of. "Uh-oh."

Sharon looked at him. "What?"

"Um."

"What's the matter with you?" Sharon looked at Teri, then at John. "Do you know her?"

"Uh, huh."

"So, now all you can do is grunt? How do you know her? Friend, acquaintance, school chum?"

"Friend."

"Good friend?" Sharon was giving him a hard look now.

"Was."

"Okay. Just how good a friend was she?" Sharon's voice was developing an edge. A suspicious edge.

John said the words as if he were at confession. "That's Teri."

Sharon stared at the attractive blonde incredulously. "You mean to tell me we are in the middle of the Serengeti, five hundred miles from anything close to civilization, on the other side of the world from where we live, and your ex has just shown up?"

"Uh-huh."

"Why?"

Teri picked up a small bag that matched her outfit and ran the distance from the plane to where John and Sharon stood. Sharon watched her as if Teri were the strangest animal they had seen yet. "Johnny! Johnny, I'm so glad you're still here. I was afraid I would miss you."

Sharon had a look of disbelief. "Uh-oh."

———

George drove the truck slowly along the trail that served as a road. John sat next to Sharon in the middle seat of the safari cruiser and Teri sat in back.

John's mind was a whirl. He thought Teri could only be here for one reason, but if she were following the legend she wouldn't have come alone. He couldn't keep a train of thought going in one direction long enough to make sense of anything. The heat was getting overpowering and his breath was short and shallow.

Teri couldn't be after him. They hadn't spoken in years and their last conversation had not ended well at all. She had to be after the map. She must have found them by talking to Walter. He always did favor her.

She couldn't be too happy to find him with Sharon. And Sharon was looking colder than he had ever seen her. She was definitely not pleased with this development. If looks could kill there would be at least one dead person in this truck and he was not sure who it would be. He wanted to say something to break the silence but no words came to mind.

John felt oddly guilty as if he had been exposed doing something dreadfully wrong. It was like some deep dark evil deed he had done had suddenly crept out of the past and plopped itself down behind him for all the world to see. He took a sip from his bottled water but it had almost no effect on his dry mouth and throat.

"Will we see any rhinos today?" That voice. Teri was still as fresh and full of wonder as the first time he had heard her. He glanced at Sharon and saw her jaw tighten and she rolled her eyes at him. Well it was a stupid question to them by now. Of course, he remembered asking it just the day before.

"No, I am sorry we will see no rhino today. Maybe never again." George talked as he drove but John didn't pay much attention as the disaster of the rhinos was repeated for the newcomers benefit.

"In the last thirty years of the twentieth century almost all of the rhinos were wiped out by poachers. They saved some white rhinos down in South Africa but there are almost no black rhinos left outside of zoos or private parks."

"That's awful. But I thought the poaching was stopped in the eighties and nineties."

"No ma'am. Those were some of the worst times. As countries became poorer people realized they could make very much money from elephants and rhinos. They slaughtered them with machine guns and hauled horns and tusks away by the truckload.

"It wasn't until the Kenyans made tourist parks and put out an order to shoot on sight anyone on foot in a national park, that things started to slow down. It is still a very sticky issue. You have people living in deep poverty, people who have families to feed who can make almost no money farming or in other traditional ways. And for one horn they can get tens of thousands of dollars.

"You have to ask, why should they save the rhinos? They are big and dumb, really an animal from another time. But the Europeans and the Americans say no, you must save them because we want to look at them, we want to preserve nature. Well, missy, please don't misunderstand me. I know we need to save the animals. But if you are a man who has a family to feed maybe you don't see the world the way a European does."

Teri pressed on. "I think it's wrong to kill any living thing."

John felt Sharon dig her fingernails into his knee.

"I understand about the elephant tusks, but what do they do with the rhino horns?" John wished Teri would shut up so he could think.

"In China, Taiwan, Korea and Japan they pay big money for medicines that are made from rhino horn."

"Is it true they are aphrodisiacs?" Teri laughed nervously.

"No. Many people think that, but it is mostly not true. The medicines are said to have restorative powers but it is certainly a false belief.

"It is very sad that such a great animal is wiped out for such a little reason. Even now, when there are almost no rhinos left the poachers come back. Some hope to get the last rhino horn. When they kill the last rhino, the value of all the other horns will go up."

John wondered at the insanity that could be created by the dollar. It was becoming clear his father had more than John and Sharon's romance in mind when he asked them to take this trip. John had been focused on the adventure part and pretty much considered the rhino issue to be a sidebar. He might have to reorder his priorities.

"Demand and no more supply." Sharon's flat statement hung in the air. John shifted uncomfortably and looked out the window at a solitary tree that occupied the vast plains to the right. He let the breeze from the open window blow into his face.

Now he fully understood Frank's hesitation that they might expose a rhino herd to poachers. He had not realized how close the animals were to extinction. He felt small that he been missing something so obvious for so long.

He wondered how much the polished rhino horn in his suitcase back at the tent was worth. He hadn't even thought to lock it up.

"Lions!" Sharon pointed out of the window at three lion cubs watching the cruiser with curiosity from the tall grass.

Teri pointed out her window. "Kitties! How precious."

John's neck muscles tightened at the sound of Teri's voice.

"We had lions in the camp last night. They were very close to the tent. It was pretty exciting." John needed to say something just to hear himself talk. The hostility he felt from Sharon towards Teri was making him uncomfortable.

"Oh really? I wish I had been there."

Sharon turned, smiled, and spoke in a charming voice. "Me, too."

John cringed in his seat. He looked to the sky thinking he had been really good for a number of years. He didn't think he deserved this.

———

John and Sharon entered the dining tent just after Teri. John had given serious thought to skipping dinner altogether, but ultimately decided he needed to show up to preserve an illusion of normalcy.

The table was large enough to accommodate twelve. John saw that since there were only three guests and Frank, all the place settings had been arranged at one end of the table with Frank at the head. Teri's place was by him on one side and John and Sharon were across from her. Frank was still directing activity in the kitchen but Teri's designated spot next to his sent a surprising ping of jealousy through John. He tried to ignore it.

Frank put an appetizer of bread, crackers and cheese near the center. "Sorry dinner is taking so long. I really miss a good partner. It works out generally very well when a man and a woman run a camp. There are some things that just need a woman's touch, you know. Please tell me if I'm missing anything."

Smelling the faint aroma of roasting lamb, John thought Frank might be apologizing a little more than was needed. Then again John didn't have to worry about keeping his clients satisfied. They all took their seats as the attendants poured wine.

"Frank, don't worry. You're doing a marvelous job." Sharon was being especially sweet this evening. She hadn't even mentioned Teri when they were changing before dinner. He had made it a point not to either.

Teri raised her wineglass. "I think everything is just wonderful. I've never been so excited on a trip before. Let's have a toast to Africa and new and old friends." She smiled at John and he could almost read her eyes. But not quite.

They all raised their drinks and the four to them clinked their wineglasses together as one. The red wine was the best thing that had happened to John all day. He savored the tart taste.

Sharon smoothed her linen napkin gracefully. "Teri, have you traveled out of the states very much?"

"Not a lot. But one of my favorite trips was when Johnny took us to Baja for a week one time. Remember Johnny? That was a wonderful beach."

John put his hand over his mouth and coughed. He wished there was a hole he could crawl into to get out of Sharon's line of sight and Teri's question. "That was a long time ago."

Frank grinned. "So you all know each other. Bloody marvelous. Small world and all that."

John resisted the temptation to say, 'Too small.'

Stephen and two other Africans in white coats brought in the main course of lamb, rice and a vegetable John didn't recognize. Once everyone was served they left the main room as the guests started eating. John was amazed at the excellent taste of his dinner.

At the head of the table Frank spoke between bites. "Since you know each other it should make your trip tomorrow much more enjoyable. You won't have to be traveling with complete strangers." Frank seemed genuinely pleased at the prospect of the three of them traveling together. John's heart sank and his mind became a jumble of thoughts again.

Frank took another bite. "Here are the arrangements I've been able to make. You'll be able leave tomorrow immediately after breakfast. Christopher will be your driver guide and one ranger will accompany you.

John held up his hand. "What about George? We'd really like to have him drive."

Frank shook his head. "Sorry, I need George here to help repair the generator. He's the only one for the job. You'll like Christopher, he's top notch. So, leaving after breakfast you will travel all day and reach the mountains from the west. Normally they are approached from the other direction, which may be why your place is still relatively undiscovered.

"You'll be able to stay one night, but after that the ranger commander requires that you leave before a different ranger company discovers you. There will be much trouble if that happens so you must be certain to return by the following evening. Without seeing the map, I can't help you any further."

"Johnny, I can't believe you haven't shown him the map." Teri sounded patronizing. It was that tone she used when she was always right.

Sharon shot John a look that was a sharp message. Teri was too close to Sharon's territory. A sudden chill went down the back of his neck.

They were all looking at him waiting for a response. John felt a little silly and melodramatic for not having let Frank see the map since he was the only person in the tent who had any knowledge of the country.

"I'll get it right after dinner."

With the dishes cleared and a fresh bottle of wine opened, John spread the map on the dining table. Frank whistled and leaned close to inspect it. He quickly closed the tent flaps. "No need to let anyone find out about this who doesn't have to."

Frank pulled a cigar from his pocket and bit off the end. He lit it and puffed thoughtfully while he studied the map. Teri waved the smoke away from her face. John spotted more cigars in Frank's pocket.

"May I?"

"Please be my guest."

"I'd like one also." Sharon reached out with her hand. "My father loved these. Taught me to appreciate the occasional after dinner smoke."

John lit the cigar and puffed on it with relish. He was amazed to see Sharon enjoy lighting up as Frank held a match for her. Through the smoke he could see Teri smiling at him even as she tried to keep the smoke away from herself.

Frank tapped the map. "You know, you just might have something here."

John's heart skipped a beat. It was the first time Frank had actually conceded real belief.

"You see, maps of this area don't show the third ridge here." He pointed to a topographic note on the chart.

"This is so out of the way there are no over flights, and with this swamp here, it makes the approach to the mountains virtually impenetrable. Besides that, no one thinks there is anything to penetrate them for. If this map is accurate, you may have a path to someplace almost no one has been before. It might actually be the Valley of the Rhinos."

An *ascari* came in and talked to Frank excitedly. Frank looked at the group and motioned them to step outside with him. On the dark horizon John could see a low orange glow.

Sharon gripped his arm. "It's huge."

Frank pointed at the spectacle. "That's a grass fire probably set by poachers. The buggers are probably trying to drive some zebras or antelopes to their traps."

John became aware that Teri was standing very close to him. She stared at the fire. "Whatever for?"

Frank took a long look at her. John thought it might be too long. "Food, miss. Some people poach just to eat. With this wind we'll be okay here, but the rangers will be busy tonight."

John watched the distant blaze and squeezed Sharon's hand. This was turning out to be a more desperate place than he had thought. He swallowed hard wondering if this trip were foolish. For the first time he took comfort in the thought of the ranger going with them.

He turned to go back in the tent and caught Teri watching him. Their eyes met for an instant before he averted his. He tried to ignore an old desire that was stirring in him. Poachers were the least of his problems.

*chapter*

## 22

THAT NIGHT JOHN FELL INTO HIS BED EXHAUSTED, but sleep wouldn't relieve him of his turmoil. He could hear the gazelles outside as they snorted at each other and ran past the tent in a timeless mating ritual. He rolled over in a vain attempt to find a comfortable position.

Seeing Teri again had thrown him into a tailspin. He wasn't sure if he loved or hated her. She was deliberately being coy and he was beginning to think he knew why she was here. He had to figure out how to deal with her pretty fast or the consequences would be anywhere from unpleasant to disastrous. Damn her for doing this.

He had deliberately avoided talking to Sharon about the situation and she had not brought it up either. He had the impression she was giving him enough room, or was it rope, to move in, but he was running out fast. After dinner she had changed and slipped into her bed with hardly a word. He could hear the sound of her breathing in the dark but wasn't sure if she was asleep.

He took deep breaths and tried counting sheep, then gazelles, but none of his falling asleep tricks worked. He needed to figure out what to say to Sharon. She was not a happy camper. Tomorrow they would be going to a mystical place, only concerned about the voyage. With Teri's arrival the entire trip had been brought into question.

He had imagined going to this place with the woman who was his truest love. He had convinced himself that Sharon had become that person and constructed rationales to make it true: the coincidence that they were at the same hotel in Paris, the extraordinary times they had together, their amazing compatibility, her agreeing to his proposal after only a few months together, the way he felt about her, and most of all the confidence he had in himself when he was with her. All those things made sense in a world where there was one love.

But now there was Teri. He had once believed that she was the one truly and firmly in his heart. They had made plans to come to this place together before Enya convinced him to leave her. No, that was bull. He had backed out on her and there was no one else to blame.

Now here she was, almost as if she were back from the dead. He had assigned her to the status of other missing people in his life that he had never expected to see again. She was still young and beautiful and wonderfully alive. She had moved from being a sometimes fond, sometimes painful, memory to being a warm living woman who now was only a few yards away in the next tent.

He tried to imagine what was she doing in there right this very minute. He wondered if Frank would pay her a visit. They had exchanged more than a few glances during dinner. No, she wasn't like that and he knew he better not think about those kinds of things or he'd make himself crazy.

He thought about Sharon again. He was sure he was in love with her. It wasn't like she was the first woman he'd met after Teri. He was certain he had not fallen for the first woman who came along. His mind went back to Teri. She could only be here for one reason and that was him. She must still love him and he realized he loved her too. He opened his eyes but couldn't see anything because the tent was pitch black.

Outside the tent, gazelles continued their mating dance. A hint of the grassfire smoke drifted in. He could hear the laughing of hyenas in the distance.

———

Sharon heard John's voice but it was soft and somehow distant. "Watch your step. This is precarious." His grip on her hand felt oddly loose and tentative. Sharon was not sure he would fully support her if she had a misstep when she got into the boat. The Mara River looked black, and cold, and her instincts told her evil lurked below the surface.

John pushed them away from the dock and used a long paddle-type tiller to steer the small flat-bottom boat into the swift current. She tried to speak to him but a sudden wind blew over the Serengeti and her words were lost in the air. She tried again. The boat slammed onto a rock and John fell to the bottom. She reached for him and as she did a splash caught her attention. Looking up she saw a huge crocodile bearing down on the tiny wooden vessel.

She tried to scream, but no sound came from her throat. She pointed and John raised himself up and saw the beast. Suddenly, he leapt from the bottom of the boat and drew a pistol. He fired at the hideous monster, again, and again. Her ears rang with the sound of the shots, her eyes stung from the smoke. The wretched beast kept coming, appearing larger with every inch it gained on them.

It hit the boat and she tried to scream again, but no sound came. Suddenly, in one swift motion, John leapt onto the rocks and kicked the boat free. For a heart stopping second she thought he would be left behind. Then he was beside her again, dripping water, but he was different. His eyes were no longer soft and clear, they were red and wild. He grabbed her and she felt weightless as she flew through the air and landed in the river.

The water overwhelmed her and she struggled to breathe. She fought to believe what was happening. Her eyes finally cleared and she could see John steering the boat away from her.

"John, no! For God's sake, no! Don't leave me! Please, please don't leave me!" Tears choked her throat, her arms flailed the water in hopelessness and despair.

Despair turned to terror. She had forgotten about the croc. Her spine froze with fear as she twisted in the water trying to catch a glimpse of the loathsome beast. It had disappeared from sight. She couldn't see, smell, or touch it, but she knew it was there.

Any second she would feel its jaws full of jagged teeth clamping down on her legs. Then the reptile would shake her like a doll and spin her in a death roll until she died and it could eat her at its leisure. Terrified, she slapped the water and swam madly for a rock. With each stroke she expected to be dragged under the water, but after forever she touched the rock and dragged herself up on it.

The boat was oddly close as she looked down the river. She could see John clearly but he wasn't alone. Teri was in his arms. They saw Sharon on the rock and smiled and waved to her, still drifting away. She cried out to them but still no sound came. They waved at Sharon in slow motion. Sharon's brain screamed. "Don't . . .." She looked to her right and stared into the gaping jaws of the crocodile.

Sharon woke with a start. Her sweaty hands clenched the bedclothes and she stared into pure blackness. Disoriented, she wanted to shriek in terror, if only to convince herself she was out of the nightmare. She heard a pack of hyenas in the distance making their hideous laughs as they hunted.

Breathing heavily, she groped for the flashlight by the bedstand. Relieved at finding it, she fumbled the light on and only then did the demons of the night release their grip on her heart. She flashed the light around the tent to get her bearings and finally turned it on John's sleeping face in his bed only three feet away from her.

She clicked the light off. "God, what am I doing here?"

For the first time in a long time, she prayed. She prayed for dawn.

———

The next morning Sharon sat at the small vanity near the front of the tent and delicately applied her lipstick. John wondered at the particular part of a woman's psyche that made her feel the need to be made-up, even for a drive in the Serengeti. John slipped on the pocketed vest that held the camera accessories. Frank had relented on that after John convinced him pictures might work in their favor. He glanced at Sharon as she checked her face in the mirror and he knew she saw him in the reflection.

"You didn't join me in bed last night." She had launched the statement like a leopard pouncing on its prey. There was no prelude, no warning, no chase, just a quick attack. John dodged the statement, which they both knew was a question. He felt like an antelope running for its life.

"You haven't slept well the last couple of nights and I thought you could use the rest."

"That's thoughtful of you. I'm glad to know you weren't distracted just because she showed up."

This was a demeanor she had not used with him before. He wasn't sure how to deal with it. Time for him to change directions, fast. "You know I really hate these European-style arrangements. Remember that night in Amsterdam when the twin beds were attached to opposite walls? It's kind of like here. We can't very well push the beds together in the tent. What would the attendant say?"

As if on cue, Stephen showed up on the veranda with the morning coffee and juice. He hailed them from outside. *"Jambo!"*

Sharon smiled at Stephen and returned the greeting. "*Jambo,* Stephen. Put the coffee on the porch table and could you draw some hot water please?"

"Yes ma'am, be happy to."

John smiled hello and silently thanked him for the distraction. Stephen entered the tent through the front and slipped past him, disappearing behind the straw partition that separated the toilet and shower from the main tent. With Stephen here she might get off the subject until it was time to go.

"So," she continued, "it wasn't because she arrived that you didn't join me?"

He was cornered. There would be no distracting her from this line of thought. The question landed like a set of teeth biting into his neck. The morning heat was suddenly stifling. The wisp of her perfume that hung in the air smelled like the warning of an approaching predator. His senses and thought processes sharpened into survival mode. This could be a mortal wound to them if not handled right. He wanted to race out of the tent and collect his thoughts, but he knew that would only make things worse.

Of course he hadn't slept with Sharon after Teri's unexpected arrival. It had been four years since he'd last seen Teri and he had never expected to see her again. That she was here now had been the only thing on his mind since she'd stepped off the plane yesterday.

"No, her being here had nothing to do with it." He hated lying, but he was not willing to admit anything until he had matters straight in his own mind. The muscles on the back of his neck tightened as he sensed the potential spiral of lies that would inevitably envelop him in a disaster if he didn't get a handle on this quickly.

"It just seems odd that for the first time since our engagement, you didn't join me. And that it happens to be right when this other woman arrives."

Other woman? How could she just reduce Teri to being another woman? She'd been his life for years. They shared secrets only the two of them would ever know. They were different women and he was different with them because of it. Teri stirred feelings in him he barely knew existed before they met. When she went away, part of him went with her.

"You could have come to my bed." He immediately regretted saying that. He could see her tense noticeably. No, that wasn't Sharon, a woman he had come to love deeply in a very short time. She didn't expect to have to go to his bed and he didn't think it odd she wouldn't. There was a refinement she possessed that allowed her to expect he would treat her as a lady.

Not that she wasn't amorous, and she certainly was willing to take things into her own hands when she wanted them. But here in this situation she knew that he knew what the right thing would be. He had failed miserably and they both were keenly aware of it.

"That's true. I could have." Her voice was calm and flat. He decided to ignore her response. He desperately wanted out of this conversation, but he didn't want to damage their relationship. He was being evasive because he needed a chance to sort his own thoughts out.

John snapped his vest shut, picked up the 35mm camera and pretended to inspect it. "It's been an exhausting trip and I really thought we both needed a good night's sleep. It's a long day today and who knows what we'll find by nightfall."

Stephen accidentally clanged the steel water pitcher behind the toilet partition.

Sharon turned on her chair and looked at John intently. He could feel her stare, but kept his eyes averted to the camera.

"Was she the one?"

What a question. He knew why Sharon deliberately picked that phrase and he almost cringed. Yes, she was the one. At least she had been for years, until he blew it. She was the one he could have been happy with. She was the one he had missed everyday of his life for years. Or thought he did. He pointed the camera at Sharon and looked at her through the viewfinder. She was beautiful. He knew he had been extremely lucky to find her.

"No, dear. You're the one."

Her tone of voice had an air of formality to it that he was unaccustomed to. "I know, but it must be difficult. You must have had strong feelings for her at some time and these quarters are so tight. Are you sure there's no problem? One you want to talk about?"

John knew he had to do a better job of burying the past and the truth. Whatever it was. He had never felt so torn before. He had promised, with every intention of keeping that promise, to spend the rest of his life with Sharon, whom he loved in a wonderful way. But now there was Teri and he recognized his feelings for her had never completely died. He put the camera down and fiddled with the lens.

"John, you know the legend says we can only go to the place on the map with the one. There can be no doubt or disaster will follow. Don't do anything for me just because you think it's the right thing to do."

"I know, trust me. You're the one. You're my destiny." He kissed her on the lips. Living up to this woman's expectations was going to be a challenge.

"*Jambo*, excuse me please." Stephen had to exit the tent by the front. He smiled, and slipped past them through the door.

Sharon blushed slightly at the interruption. She turned back to her mirror on the vanity. "Why do you suppose she's here? Is it for you or the map?"

John put the camera strap around his neck. "It must be the map."

Sharon gave him a hint of a smile. "What are you going to do about her?"

John sensed a rope tightening around his neck. "To tell you the truth, I don't know yet."

Sharon surprised him by leaning to him and kissing him on the lips. "Thanks for being honest. I know you'll think of something." He wished he had her confidence.

———

The trip started out uneventfully. John sat by Sharon in the middle row, right behind Christopher. The ranger had his customary seat by the driver and Teri seemed content in the last row of seats. John continued to mull over his predicament and they rode mostly in silence.

He checked his watch and examined the two maps he had opened on the seat between himself and Sharon. One was a local map and the other, his father's. If his estimate was right, they were only an hour away from getting to the detailed section of the treasure map. Depending on their rate of travel he calculated they would get to the mountains by mid or late afternoon. He thought that should still give them time to find the approach to the valley before dark.

After a few hours they approached the river and the driver pointed to a herd of gathering animals. John looked out the window of the cruiser, astonished at the sheer numbers of the wildebeests and zebras poised on the riverbank. He had not imagined this many animals existed unfenced anywhere in the world. The endless migrating animals offered this part of the Serengeti a veritable moving feast. During the migration everything got to eat, making the savanna a constant battleground between predators and prey.

Frank had told them that with the easy pickings of zebras and wildebeests injured or drowned by the river crossings, the lions and hyenas did not have to hunt so hard, and were able to breed and perpetuate themselves. Tens of thousands of wildebeests took safety in their own vast numbers and by following the water, kept the Serengeti alive.

John rolled the map up and carefully put it back in its case. Then he took out his camera to get some pictures of the crossing. Even though they didn't want to waste any time, this was an event he wanted to see.

John listened to the incessant mooing of the wildebeests and knew the lead animals were on the verge of plunging into the Mara River to attempt their desperate crossing. The musky smell of the herd blew toward him on the wind of the gathering thunderstorm. The short rains had arrived with the tail end of the migration. The late morning sun that minutes ago had been baking the cruiser was now obscured by thickening clouds ready to burst with an afternoon downpour.

———

Barzan was still tired from the hurried trip from Nairobi. He rubbed his neck and hoped the truck he and his men had seen leave the safari camp was the right one. They had taken a chance and driven ahead of the green cruiser, anticipating it would follow the river. He had his men cross the river and now they had been waiting for almost an hour.

He was starting to grow impatient when one of his men waved to him. The poacher stopped what he was doing and listened intently. Ever so faintly, over the moos of the nervous herd and the noise of the water rushing in the river, he recognized the sound of a motor. The wind shifted slightly and the motor became much louder. Alarmed, he looked across the river and saw a dark green four-wheel drive safari cruiser. He realized the truck had approached downwind of the herd so the tourists could watch a crossing. But he still wasn't sure if these were the right tourists.

He dropped to his belly hoping to hide from the driver guide and the inevitable ranger who would be in the front seat beside him. With their powerful binoculars they might have already spotted Barzan and his men and that meant they would be on the radio to get more rangers to capture him. And that meant death or an inhospitable jail at best and the certain end of his future property, his harem, his rightful place in the world. Barzan watched Kip raise to one knee and take careful aim at the driver with his rifle. Maybe they had not been seen yet.

———

John alternately looked through the telephoto lens, and above the camera. He was determined to get a shot of the first wildebeest as it leaped into the river. It was one of the most compelling sights on the planet. Thousands of wildebeests crashing into the Mara River risking death by trampling, drowning or crocodiles to follow their age-old migratory trail.

Christopher kept the safari cruiser moving slowly toward the herd. John was sure they were getting too close and would spook the lead animals and spoil the crossing.

"Christopher, shouldn't we wait?"

"Let him drive." Sharon whispered from beside him. "He's the expert."

Because of the imminent rain they had taken the precaution of closing the roof openings which made it hotter and gave John a sense of confinement even with the windows open. He caught a whiff of Teri's jasmine perfume and resisted the temptation to lean back for more. Sweat trickled down his back and he hoped he could make it through the next few days.

———

Kip squeezed the trigger and his first shot hit the driver. The shot was timed to coincide with a rolling burst of thunder. The sound of the thunder directly overhead frightened the lead wildebeest into the river causing the herd behind to stampede into the water. Barzan smiled when he saw the driver go limp.

———

John snapped the shutter on his camera again and again. Sharon was leaning over his shoulder straining for a good view and he could hear Teri taking pictures behind him. A thunderclap sounded almost directly above and he lifted his eye from the camera. He saw Christopher slump into the wheel. He realized that the truck was headed for the edge of the riverbank but it was too late.

John felt the left front wheel drop and pulled away from his camera in time to see the nose of the truck start to slide over the embankment. Teri screamed and John grabbed for Sharon with one hand and tried to brace himself against the back of the driver's seat with his other hand. The cruiser tipped straight down to the river, slamming front first onto a rock. The shock ejected the ranger, still clutching his rifle, from his seat through the windshield, bashing his skull on impact with the rock.

John crashed hard into the back of the driver's seat. From the corner of his eye he saw Sharon hit face first. He felt Teri tumble over him toward the front of the passenger compartment.

The truck teetered on its grill for a moment, then tipped into the river upside down, smashing John hard into the roof. He winced in pain and felt somebody fall on top of him. Water swirled into the truck splashing over John's face. Drowning. God, not drowning, please. He fought to lift his head but the water was rising fast. He pushed the limp body off him. With his right hand he grabbed the seat that was now over his head and pulled himself up.

He gasped for air. The water was coming in fast. He righted himself even as the water continued to rise. He quickly saw the others were motionless, unconscious. The water enveloped his neck. He took one last breath and the river covered his face. Feeling with his hands he located the open window and dragged himself down. His six foot frame was almost too big for the bent window and his shoulders stuck in the opening. He fought to keep panic from freezing him. With all his will he braced his feet on the back seat of the truck, pushed himself free of the window and shot to the surface with nearly bursting lungs.

His head broke the surface and he gasped for air. Rain was falling and it pounded his face. The smell of the terrified wildebeest herd stampeding across the river filled his nose and mouth. The herd was crossing thirty yards upstream from where the cruiser lay upside-down in the water. John saw the bottoms of the tires barely protruding out of the water and grabbed one as he drifted by. He realized the current was bringing some of the crossing animals toward them. He held the tire tightly.

He had to act fast. The river was full of crocodiles. He forced himself to hope they would be occupied by the wildebeests and zebras. His immediate concern was for the two women still trapped in the cruiser.

He had been on the surface less than ten seconds. Taking a deep breath he dove under the water. He wasn't going to lose anyone if he could help it. Not this way. He pulled himself down into the murky water griping the bottom of the window ledge with his hands. He pulled himself deeper towards the window.

Water stung his eyes as he reached in and grabbed the foot of the person nearest him. The cotton dress Sharon was wearing billowed in the water, making it difficult to see the rest of her clearly. He managed to get both of her feet together and he pulled her through the window feet first. He was scraping her arms on the metal, but he had no choice. He was running out of air and she had been under too long. When her head was free from the window he grabbed her right hand and pulled her to the surface.

He reached the top and again gasped for breath. Sharon wasn't breathing so he quickly wrapped his arms around her from behind and gave her a quick hard squeeze, trying to get her breathing again. After two attempts he was relieved to see her cough and vomit, and most importantly, breath. He propped her on the bottom of the cruiser against a mostly submerged tire and dove back into the water.

He tried to remember how long the brain could live without oxygen. Was it sixty seconds? Two minutes? How long had it been since the crash? When he got to the window he could see Teri was just out of his reach, the current pushing her against the back of the cruiser. He didn't want to put his shoulders through the window again so he stuck his head in and with his right arm stretched out he grasped her blouse and slowly drew her to him.

With an effort, and starving for air, he got both his hands under her arms and wedged her through the window and out into the river. He dragged her to the surface and gulped for air even as he held her head out of the water. He sat on the bottom of the truck for stability and held her in place half floating over his knees and gave her mouth to mouth breathing. Between breaths he caught his fiancée, who was still coughing and holding on to her tire for support, watching him try to revive his former lover. And the rain pelted down.

Sharon gasped. "Try CPR."

He racked his brain trying to remember the sequence. He felt her neck and there was a slight pulse but she wasn't breathing. He put his mouth over hers and tried to breathe life into her again. John's hope for Teri was fading fast when to his surprise and elation, she choked water into his mouth and started coughing and breathing.

He rinsed his face in the water and came up looking at Sharon. Her eyes were wide and she opened her mouth to talk but nothing came out. He struggled to catch his breath. Sharon's eyes were getting bigger and she finally shouted. "Look!"

John turned to see behind him. Dozens of wildebeests, carried by the current, were swimming madly in the direction of the truck. John looked to the near shore and for the first time saw that the bank of the river was covered with animals stampeding up the sides in a wild panic. The zebras and wildebeests tried to climb out of the river at every opening and some floundered into places too steep to climb and fell back into the charging herd only to be gored or trampled by the sharp horns and hoofs of others.

He remembered seeing the remains of a crossing two days before. John realized the only safe place was on the other side of the river. It wouldn't be a long swim, but the current was strong and the image of the fifteen-foot crocodile they had seen earlier in the day flashed into his mind.

He made the choice. "We have to go!" He pointed to the far shore. "That way."

Sharon's face was ashen white. She gulped and nodded. John tried to get Teri's attention but she was still coughing and trying to breathe. "Teri we have to leave."

She coughed. "Where are the others?"

John was certain the ranger was dead, but he wasn't positive about Christopher, the driver.

"Can you swim?" Sharon looked hesitant. A large bellowing wildebeest brushed the truck. The smell of the animal was thick and musky. Their horns looked a lot more deadly up close than they had from inside he cruiser. Sharon nodded emphatically. More animals bumped the truck. Soon they would be on both sides and there would be no escape.

John slipped Teri into the water and Sharon jumped in.

"I know how to do this. Check on Christopher and come on."

Sharon cradled her arm around Teri's head and pushed off swimming with one hand and towing Teri who floated on her back.

Another animal hit the truck and John almost fell into the water. He held tight, then lowered himself in, took a breath and dove under. The water was stirred up by thousands of hoofs slipping in the mud. Visibility was almost non-existent. He felt for the window and stuck his head inside.

The water stung his eyes worse than before. He could sense the feet of animals on the other side of the truck. Something brushed his arm and he realized it was his map case floating out the window. He caught the shoulder strap and put it over his arm.

He reached in the window and grabbed what he thought was a collar. He yanked it towards him and pulled Christopher's face into view inches from his. He was stunned to see half the driver's head was caved in.

He involuntarily blew the air out of his lungs and backed out of the window. He popped to the surface wanting nothing but air. He gasped holding onto the side of the truck and saw Sharon and Teri headed for the far shore. He was appalled to see more wildebeests between himself and where they had gone. He was cut off for now.

There were animals swimming terrified and drifting on either side of him and he had the sinking feeling they would mistake the cruiser for a rock and try to climb on it. It was the only safe place he had at the moment.

The herd of crossing animals was splashing on both sides of him. The truck was being constantly hit and all at once several animals tried to climb on to it. Faced with the sharp hoofs and horns of the thrashing animals he abandoned the vehicle and pushed off for the near shore. Once he reached land he staggered ashore, afraid to fall down for fear of being trampled.

Then, faster than he thought possible, the mooing and bleating of the animals quieted and he saw only a few stragglers headed downstream.

He was so relieved to see Sharon still towing Teri that he almost fell to his knees. But something was wrong. Sharon was towing as fast as she could when suddenly Teri turned over and they both started swimming hard for the shore. Then he saw the crocodile.

The prehistoric beast looked twenty feet long and was closing on them fast. He remembered the ranger's rifle and scrambled around in the mud trying to find it. He saw the body that had been trampled into a bloody pulp. The rifle lay nearby, it was dirty but didn't look broken. He grabbed it and his heart fell when he saw the barrel was caked with mud. It was useless.

He looked back at the women. The croc was almost on them. He couldn't tell who was behind. He wanted to tear his eyes away but could only stare hopelessly.

A shot rang out. Then two more in quick succession. The crocodile jerked in the water then turned over kicking its legs in agony. Sharon and Teri made the shore and first crawled out of the water then ran up onto the land.

John looked at the far riverbank. He was stunned to see two men standing there looking at him. One was an African in shorts and shirt with a baseball cap. The other was out of place. As out of place as John felt. The cowboy hat was unmistakable. His heart skipped a beat as the guy in the cowboy hat aimed a rifle at him. John dove back into the water behind the truck.

He tried to catch his breath. Tried to think. It was that guy. What the hell was his name? Barzan. He had followed them here. John cursed himself for the danger they were in. He had been imagining the adventure with the map the way his father had explained it. The map would take you on the journey of a lifetime. A journey that was an end in itself.

He should have realized by now that any document that purported to lead to a secret diamond cache or a rare animal with a horn potentially worth a fortune, would mean something else to others. Now there was somebody trying to kill him for it.

"Hey, Mister Erikson, can you hear me?"

It was that bastard from Amsterdam. No question about it. John made an attempt at acting nonchalant as he yelled across the river. "Good to see you again Mr. Barzan. Thanks for buying our coffee in Amsterdam."

John could not make out Barzan's expression but his tone was harsh. "As you can see, I have your whores here. Show yourself or I'll throw one to the crocodiles right now."

John took a breath and stood up. The African was holding Sharon and Teri at gunpoint. Barzan stood beside them, a pistol in his hand. John's heart was hammering in his chest. "What do you want with us?"

"You give me the map, I give you the women."

It was a long shot but John thought he might be able to call a bluff. "Keep 'em."

Barzan laughed. "You talk very brave, mister. I will kill this one now." Barzan raised his pistol to Teri's head. It was no bluff. Teri's eyes were wide with terror.

"Wait!"

"Why?"

John tried not to let his desperation sound in his voice. "I'll trade, whatever you want."

Barzan lowered his gun. "Bring me the map and you can have them. If you do not, I will feed them to the crocodiles."

"How do I get across the river?"

"That is your concern. You have until sunset. We will be waiting in the shade of those trees. And, Mister Erikson, if you fail, be certain as to the fate of these two whores. It will not be pleasant. *Allahu Akbbar.*"

Barzan said something to the African and he pointed away from the river. Barzan gave Sharon a shove and the four of them walked out of sight, into the brush.

John swallowed hard and felt the aches in his arms and legs for the first time. His stomach was a hollow knot and he struggled to keep his trembling legs under him. This was hopeless.

S HARON WANTED TO OPEN HER EYES AND WAKE
from this nightmare. Instead she bent over and vomited
again. There was no more river water to lose but the reflex
was so bad she thought her insides might come out of her mouth.

Maybe it was more than the river. Maybe it was the raw terror
she felt gripping her spine and tightening her muscles. The wave
of nausea passed. She stood shakily and wiped her mouth with
the bottom edge of her wet cotton skirt.

Ten feet away the man in the cowboy hat, the man she
remembered was named Barzan, was looking at a tall African. Teri
sat on a log a few feet away sharing the shade of an acacia tree
with her. Teri looked up when Sharon straightened. Teri's eyes
were glazed and her face was pale and drawn. She didn't look
nearly as young as she had when she bounded off the plane the
day before. Sharon wondered if she looked as ragged as Teri. No
doubt she did.

The taste of bile was sour in her mouth so she decided to risk
talking to Barzan. "Mister Barzan, may we have some water?"

"Shut up, whore. Only speak when asked." He turned and
glared at her.

He could not have shocked her more if he had slapped her in
the face. No one had ever spoken to her that way before in her

entire life. Almost before she knew it she blurted out. "Who the hell do you think you are, you bastard? Where do you get off pushing us around and treating us like this? "

Before she finished the last sentence he started toward her. She back-pedaled but too late. Faster than she thought possible he backhanded her across the face and knocked her to the ground, her senses stunned.

She curled into the fetal position putting her hands over her head. She felt a kick in her ribs, then another.

"Do not talk to me, infidel bitch, or I will cut out your tongue and feed it to you on a stick."

"Leave her alone you son of a bitch!" It was Teri. Sharon dared to look up and saw Teri throw herself at Barzan. He grabbed her arm and threw her to the ground. His eyes were bulging and his face flushed deep red. She was certain he was going to turn his anger on her again when the African pulled him from behind.

Barzan resisted at first, then relented.

"We should not bruise them, *Bwana*. Maybe we can sell them on the slave market."

Barzan caught his breath and stared at Sharon with eyes that were black and unholy. She felt herself shaking under his gaze but tried not to flinch. This man was totally different from the way she'd remembered him in Amsterdam. There he was bumbling and almost comical. Here he was clearly in control and potentially deadly. Her insides turned cold looking at him

Barzan focused black eyes on her. "Kip, have you not promised them to your men?"

"You decide their fate, *Bwana*. You are the master." Barzan was visibly calmer now.

"Yes, that is correct. I am the master. Perhaps the slave market would be good. But I think they are not worth the trouble to get them there. I will have more amusement watching them squirm in the jaws of the crocs. If we are successful on this journey I will get your men more whores than they know exist."

"What of the man who has the map?"

"What of him? We kill him as soon as he is close enough."

The two men turned their backs on her and Teri and returned to their former vantage point.

Sharon was afraid to move. She was certain that even the slightest motion on her part would bring back the wrath of the monster who had slammed her to the ground. She remained tightly curled in a ball in the dirt. Her breath came in sobs and she could not clear her head.

That she could be reduced to a quivering, desperate person, afraid for her life by a blow delivered from a near barbarian rocked the foundations of her belief in her control of her life.

The glass world where civilization protected her from the harsh realities of rule by physical power lay shattered with her in the dirt. Her mind would not focus and it was not until she felt cold water splashing on her face that she opened her eyes again.

Startled, she looked up into the face of the African she had heard Barzan call Kip.

"You must get up. You are not badly hurt."

Kip gave her the canteen he'd poured the water from. She raised herself enough to take it and swallow a mouthful. Kip knelt beside her and she tried to back away. "They call him the Chui, the leopard, but you must never let him hear that. If you can help us find the map, I may be able to help you. If you do not, you and your friend are without hope."

The African went away leaving the water in her hands. Sharon wiped her face and focused her eyes again. Her vision was bleary and she realized she'd been crying. She was still more frightened than she had ever been, but she resolved to not let it show.

A few feet away Teri was lying in the dust where Barzan had thrown her. Sharon forced herself to stand despite her trembling knees and went to Teri's side. Teri opened her eyes and made a tight smile. "If I click my heels together three times and say, there's no place like home, do you think it will work?"

"Sorry, your slippers aren't ruby. Thanks."

"No problem. You would have done the same for me."

Sharon wondered if she would have. Wondered if she would have had the courage. She sat down involuntarily, her body no longer obeying her. She was shivering uncontrollably and had never felt so hopeless in her life. Rubbing her aching jaw she was surprised to find no blood. She wanted to curl up into a ball and wait for all this to pass. Her insides ached and her side throbbed, but she would not cry. She wouldn't give that filthy bastard the satisfaction.

Teri sat up and put her arm around her. It was a surprising comfort. They sat on the ground for a few minutes catching their breath. Then they helped each other up and together moved to sit on a log where they could watch their captors.

After a few minutes the African approached with another canteen in his hand. He gave it to Sharon. "Here is some water, share it between you. I will get more if you need it." He reached in his pocket and pulled out two candy bars. He looked over his shoulder as if checking on Barzan. "Don't let him see you eat these. You must keep your strength up."

They each took one of the candy bars and hid it quickly. The African rejoined Barzan.

After a drink and the surreptitious consumption of the chocolate, she felt slightly better. She was shivering in her wet clothes and wondered if it were the cold or if shock was setting in. Her face ached from where she had been hit, but not as much as before. Her side still hurt but she didn't think anything was broken.

"I feel like a drowned rat." Teri pushed her hair back in a futile attempt to get it out of her face.

"I just feel like a rat. I've been pretty cold to you since we met."

"Can't say that I blame you. Who am I to crash your engagement party? I can't believe I did this. I am so selfish. When I read about your engagement I knew Johnny would bring you here. I mean, well not here, but on this trip. I felt like I was losing my last chance at something really precious. It was overwhelming. I panicked and came out here without thinking things all the way through." She put her head in her hands.

Sharon reached out and put her hand on Teri's arm. "It's alright. We need to start figuring out what we're going to do now."

Teri looked at her with tears in her eyes. "I feel like Lucy out of control. What have I done?"

Sharon didn't know what to say. She thought out loud. "Maybe John can get us out of this."

Teri laughed. "How long have you known Johnny?"

"I don't remember anymore. A few months. A lifetime."

Teri wiped her face with a corner of her shirt. "You've only known him for months and you're getting married?"

"I guess it sounds pretty wild, but it seems right."

"I can't believe I wasted so much time." Teri sighed heavily and looked into the distance. Then she turned to Sharon. "If we're going to get out of this, we'll have to do it ourselves. Coming back for someone isn't Johnny's strong suit."

———

Kip watched Barzan squint through the binoculars. "After we have the map, we can let the women go in the other cruiser. They are not of value to us."

Barzan lowered the binoculars. "I will decide what we do with them. If I say we feed them to the crocodiles then that is what we will do. That way they can tell no tales to the rangers."

Kip had no interest in killing the women. It was something he did not consider honorable so he prompted Barzan again. "These women are nothing. I am a warrior and it is not my way to kill females. If you chose to do it, you will be showing that you are a small man afraid of the skirts of a woman. I will not help."

Barzan's eyes widened and he showed his teeth in a sneer. "You will do as I say. After all, there is much to be gained by possessing this map. And remember, everything you have, you owe to me."

"I can never forget. You will never let me."

———

Sitting on a rock by the riverbank John watched the muddy water flowing around the crashed safari cruiser. He wasn't sure how long he had been there, but for the first time he noticed vultures landing near the shore.

Dead wildebeests littered the broad span between the banks of the river. Carcasses floated downstream or, pushed by the current, wedged against rocks. A few animals that were crippled and not yet dead mooed miserably. The air was thick with the smell of death and animal dung.

John pushed his wet hair back with his hands and sucked in a deep breath. His heart had finally slowed to something like a normal rate and some semblance of strength had returned to his arms and legs. The adrenaline surge that had propelled him while he pulled Teri and Sharon from the wreckage had worn off leaving him exhausted. He had decided to sit and catch his breath for a moment. Now it was time to do something.

If he were back in the Rangers this could be a problem on the officers training course. Two hostages have been taken, you have a four hour ultimatum, one filthy rifle that may not work, no food or water and only the contents of a wrecked truck and your wits to resolve the situation. And oh yeah, the hostages are across a river filled with gigantic crocodiles.

What would one of those Ricky Ranger lifers do? Check the truck for food and water. There had been bottles of water in the truck. He doubted they'd survived the crash. Whatever food there'd been was certainly soaked with river water by now. Besides that, there was no way he was getting back in that water after seeing the croc that had been chasing the women.

Maybe it was time to recognize that he needed to cut his losses and just try to make it back to base camp on his own. He doubted he could do much to help the women anyway. Even if he gave up the map there was no reason to believe Barzan would keep his part of the bargain. The odds were not good against men who were skilled at surviving in the bush. Maybe he should just leave them and try and get help. He was more tired and empty than he had ever been.

He examined the rifle again. It was an old bolt action thing that may not have even worked when it was clean, much less now when it was caked with mud. He decided to clean it while he thought about his next move. He checked the river for signs of hippos or crocs. Seeing none he went to the edge and immersed the rifle.

The bore was plugged and he found a stick and busied himself trying to clean the mud out. What would he do if he found that bastard Barzan anyway? He would let him have the map easy, he had no problem giving it up. He had never guessed it would be so much trouble. The only thing it was worth now was getting Sharon and Teri back. If he got the map to him and Barzan reneged on the deal or harmed either woman John knew he would have to kill him.

While he worked the mud out of the muzzle with his stick he thought about the drug dealer he'd had to kill in Panama. The hackles on his neck raised. He could visualize the scene more clearly now than when it had happened.

He'd been surprised in the basement of a narcotics traffickers' house that had supposedly been secured by his strike team. John had ended up in a knife fight and sometimes he still woke in the night feeling the blade ripping through the mans' ribs.

He got a medal for that. A medal for saving his ass. Funny world. As he lifted the rifle out of the dirty river he hoped he was not going to have to kill again.

He removed the bolt from the rifle and looked through the barrel to see if it was clear of even the smallest obstruction. The barrel was slightly bent. It was worthless. A movement in the water caught his eye. His heart leapt when he realized a croc was swimming just off the shore. He jumped to his feet and started running up the slope of the bank but the beast did not seem interested in him. Even so he didn't stop until he was well above the river.

Breathing heavily, sweat ran out of every pore on his body. His heart was pounding and adrenaline pumped through his veins. He stood beneath a tree and watched warily as the croc glided down the river with only its dark eyes showing above the water. Its tail made the slightest ripples behind it. He leaned on the acacia for support.

He tried to clear his mind. He wanted out of this place. Out of the bush, out of Masilan, out of Africa. He wanted to be home with Sharon, or was it Teri? Screw it, by himself would be fine just now, it didn't matter. He just wanted out of this place.

He looked up the river and could see nothing slightly friendly or familiar. Looking down the river he could see the vultures landing on the wildebeest carcasses. He watched fascinated as two of the scavengers fought over a particularly gruesome morsel.

He averted his eyes and tried to reassess his situation. That was easy, he was totally screwed. The worthless rifle was in the river where he'd dropped it when he saw the crocodile. The thought of the beast sent a shiver through him. He was at least fifty miles from the base camp, even if he could find it. Sharon and Teri were being held by that thug in the cowboy hat who had promised he'd throw them to the crocodiles if John didn't deliver the map.

He briefly thought of each of them being faced with a terrifying death in the jaws of a loathsome scaly creature that would rip them apart. The thought gave him the shakes.

He struggled to come to grips with his own mortality. Only hours ago the thought of dying wasn't even on his mind. They were simply on a grand adventure. Teri suddenly appearing had been the most complicated thing in his world. The unexpected resurrection of a past life had been a big enough event to occupy his mind full time.

Now, however, the problem of figuring out how to deal with Teri and Sharon was a trivial compared to the real delema of finding a way to live long enough to make it matter. He had learned how to live regardless of the women in or out of his life. Maybe that's what his father had sent him on this trip to figure out.

One thing was certain. He would no longer consider leaving without the women. They were here because of him and he wasn't going back without them. He felt his face flushing, embarrassed for even thinking he might leave them.

He took a deep breath and sat on the ground exhausted. His body was slowing down again. He tried to ignore the weariness in his limbs as he scanned his surroundings for any sign of danger. There were so many directions it could come from and it would probably come without warning.

The smell of the river made him thirsty, but he dared not approach it again. He listened to the wind for any signs that something could be approaching, but the sound of the running water masked any low noises. The nerves in his back tingled and he could not relax. He knew he was being hunted. From where, or by whom he couldn't be certain, but he was being hunted, that was a given. He needed to find a way to become the hunter.

He started thinking through the problem which seemed immense. It would be best to take it in small chunks. First cross the river. No, first find a weapon. Hyenas and lions are sure to be showing up soon. Then get across the river without being eaten. Find the girls, kill Barzan and his henchmen, take his truck and go merrily on our way. What will we do for the rest of the day? Sit on the veranda sipping bubbly and talking about the story we'll have to tell at the country club? Bloody marvelous.

He climbed to the top of the riverbank and surveyed the horizon. Heat waves rose from the brown grasslands in the midday sun. The humidity climbed as the land dried out from the thundershower. He could see stragglers from the wildebeest herd grazing on the nearly treeless savanna. God, this was a lonely place.

He turned back to the river and slowly started walking away from the crash site. John decided to try to find a place to cross upstream of where the stampede had been. He soon found a stick that looked sturdy. Maybe he could scare a lion with it. After all, the Masai had been surviving here with nothing but spears forever. At least some of them.

He laughed at himself. *This is perfect. I'm going to beat up a lion with a stick. I feel like Fred Flintstone. Hey, Wilma, bring me a brontosaurus burger.* He took a moment to examine his weapon. The stick was about five feet long and not quite as thick as a baseball bat. He whacked it against a huge baobab tree and was satisfied that it was solid. He held it like a bat and took a double-handed swing at the air with his weapon. *I wonder how this thing will work on crocs? Probably not at all.*

He traveled up the river about a mile before he saw a place that looked like it might be passable. Crouching near a sweet smelling bush he watched the water for any signs of movement. So far he had not seen any predators and he was happy with that. A tall leafy tree shaded a portion of the water and a couple of monkeys sat lazily in the branches giving him an idle lookover.

A warm wind blew in his face as he watched the potential crossing place. The air was thick with the fragrance of plants he couldn't identify. Then he heard the faint, but unmistakable sound of an automobile engine. He dove for the cover behind a large patch of brush.

Holding his breath he hoped he hadn't been spotted. Back at the camp, Frank had been emphatic that there would be no other people in this area. If that were true then the vehicle moving slowly just above the bank must be driven by Barzan, or some of his henchmen.

The vehicle was barely creeping along the riverbank. They were looking for him. Options, quick. The cruiser must have crossed someplace close, so all he needed to do was to find that place. Wait, what if the girls were in the truck? He had to find a way to take a look. What if they weren't? Maybe he could hijack it.

With a truck, half of his problems would be solved. How do you steal a cruiser with people in it? Hit it with a rock and hope they get out? No, that would alert them to his presence. Surprise would have to be the key. The sound of the engine was on the bank just above him now. In a few seconds it would be past. His muscles tensed and his pulse raced.

The truck was barely moving. Whoever was in it was obviously searching for something, and trying to keep as quiet as possible. He might be able to catch it on foot. Running up to the truck was obviously the idea of an overtired mind. It would be crazy. Crazy or not, it was the only option he could think of.

He would wait until they were a few yards past him, then peek over the bank and see how many people were in the cruiser. More than one would be a problem.

After an agonizingly long time the low rumble of the engine finally passed him and he crept up to the bank. Peering over he could see the camouflage colored truck driving slowly away from him. The driver was looking at the river and a man in the front passenger seat scanned the area with binoculars.

John's thoughts raced. If he yanked the driver out maybe he could whack the other guy with the stick hard enough to immobilize him. If that didn't work, well, screw it, he'd just have to improvise. Either way he was going to have to do this fast before they got too far away. It's this or face the crocs.

The truck was about fifteen yards away now. John jumped up onto the bank and sprinted after it. He felt like he was in slow motion. After a few steps he realized he was not closing the gap nearly as fast as he'd originally thought he would. Almost panicked, he wondered if he had been spotted.

So far neither African had looked back. He kept running and prayed neither of them would turn around or look in a rearview mirror. He only needed a few more seconds and he would be there. He was breathing hard by the time he reached the back of the truck.

Things happened faster than he had imagined. Suddenly he was at the driver's side door. They still hadn't seen him. Pumped full of adrenaline he put his left hand on the door handle and yanked the door open. The driver started to turn to him but John grabbed him by the collar and jerked him halfway out of the vehicle.

The truck stalled and the jarring motion slammed the passenger into the windshield. John brought his stick down hard on the driver's head. The stick made a dull cracking sound and blood spilled out of the man's skull. John pulled the stunned man the rest of the way out of the truck and dumped him on the ground.

The terrified passenger looked at him wide eyed. John smashed his stick on the top of the truck with a resounding slam. He tried to convince him he was confronting a crazy man. He screamed at the top of his lungs.

"UUUURRRRRRAGH I'm going to kill you all!"

The passenger scrambled for his door latch and bolted out of the vehicle. John threw his stick on the seat, got behind the wheel and started the engine. He made a fast U-turn and screamed at the two shocked men as he drove past them.

"And your mothers and little sisters too! UUUURRRRAGH!"

The truck accelerated up the riverbank and John drove as fast as he dared. He kept one eye on the rearview mirror to be certain that no one was chasing him. He had hit the driver pretty hard, but did not think he had killed him. It had not been his intention anyway. Too many people had died today.

It occurred to him that perhaps the men he had just stolen this truck from might not be connected to Barzan. Wouldn't that just be great. For all he knew they could have been a couple of rangers. That would just about make this a perfect day. Be ambushed by poachers, survive a stampede, almost get eaten by a crocodile, loose a fiancée then mug two park rangers and steal a government truck.

He shook his head. His luck just couldn't be that bad. But he still wondered who the hell those guys were.

———

"We have to get ourselves out of here. Johnny's not coming back for us." She tried to keep her voice flat and matter of fact. Teri hoped Sharon would understand, but she was getting impatient. Each moment they spent in the company of Barzan and Kip made her more uncomfortable. She watched Sharon for a reaction.

"You don't have much faith in him."

"I just know him too well." Teri's stomach was knotted and she hated to hear herself say disparaging things about the man she loved. Even if they were true.

Teri tried to make herself comfortable on the log they were sitting on. The log was hard and uneven but it was the only thing around to sit on besides the dirt. She felt like hell. Her clothes were dirty and she knew a thin film of grim covered her from head to foot. The swim across the river, and the mad scramble up the muddy bank, inches ahead of the croc had covered both of them in red mud. The heat had already dried out her clothes, but the faint odor of the river clung to her like an unwelcome veil.

She fanned herself with a frondlike leaf. Even though they were in the shade, the heat was overpowering. Teri lifted the canteen Kip had given them and poured a little water onto her shirttail. Sharon was still shaking from the blow she had received from Barzan and clearly needed some encouragement. Teri slid closer to her and started wiping Sharon's face with the shirttail.

"How well did you know him?" Sharon asked the question quite of the blue. Teri decided she should have expected it. It was a perfectly normal thing to ask. She wondered what it might have been like if they had met at a coffee shop and had nothing more to worry about than the time of day.

"We were going to be married, but he backed out. I sort of understood why. It must have made sense to him at the time. It almost ruined me. That is, I almost let it destroy me. I had not realized how much I missed him. I thought I was over him but then I heard about your engagement. I guess I never fully gave up on him. Lord knows I should have."

"Why didn't you? I mean, if you don't believe in him why did you come here?" Sharon's face was starting to look cleaner now. Although the pale color Teri had uncovered did not look too promising.

"Why did I come here? That's a great question. I think I might have had a momentary lapse of sanity." Teri liked the way Sharon smiled at that. They could both use a laugh.

Teri looked nervously around the makeshift camp. Barzan and the African, Kip, who had given them the water were still searching the horizon for any sign of John and the map. She hoped they would stay there, continuing to ignore her and Sharon. Her heart felt like lead. She decided she might as well give the real reason.

"That stupid map. That's why I'm here. John convinced me, or I let him convince me, that there is in each life, a one true love. I let myself believe for me, it was him, and I never let go of that notion. They say true love lasts forever and after Johnny left I fell into one bad relationship after another. You know, I'd either compare the guy to Johnny and he wouldn't measure up, or he'd be too much like Johnny and I'd get scared. Somehow I'd always managed to keep myself free because I thought there would be a time when he would knock on my door." She drew a deep breath and let it out slowly.

It occurred to her that John might have used the same one true love line on Sharon. Why else would she be here? But it wasn't really a line. It had meant so much more. A flash of jealousy hit her and she bit her lip to make herself ignore it.

Sharon took the water and moistened a corner of her own shirt. She started wiping Teri's face. It was strange to have another woman touching her, but the water was cool and the touch was soft.

"He told me he tried to get back with you for months after you broke up, but you wouldn't have anything to do with him."

Teri closed her eyes and let the cloth soothe her hot face. "I was young and had been deeply hurt. I didn't want anything to do with him. I didn't want his letters, I didn't want his calls I didn't want anything but to make him feel as alone as I did. It wasn't until the letters and calls stopped coming that I realized how much they meant to me. After that, well time is a strange thing. It kind of gets away from you."

"Do you still love him?"

Teri let the question hang while she thought about the right answer. After all, she was talking to the man's fiancée. A wrong answer here could be taken poorly and things were bad enough as it was. Even if Barzan didn't throw them to the crocodiles like he'd threatened, the alternatives were not very appealing.

Teri wanted Sharon as her ally very much. Needed her as an ally. On the other hand, she had the grim feeling they were close enough to death that even a pretty lie wouldn't be prudent at this time.

"Yes, I do."

Sharon didn't change expression. "Thanks for being honest. Now, do you have any ideas on what we should do next?"

Teri felt her muscles relax a little now that this truth had come out. "I think that depends a lot on how you feel." Teri didn't think that Sharon looked particularly strong in her present condition. She also had no idea of Sharon's physical capability in general. Teri had always worked hard at staying in shape and she was confident she could endure more strenuous activity than most women. But she admitted to herself that she was already drained from the stress of the swim to shore and the oppressive afternoon heat.

She considered their predicament again. She'd only counted four poachers, including Barzan. Two of them had driven off in a truck about half an hour ago, which left only Barzan and Kip.

Barzan had told them he didn't need to tie them up because they had no place to go. They would be lion food before they got very far from his 'protection.' Teri didn't think their chances of overpowering the two men were very good either.

Sharon had shown some spunk after they were first captured, but she looked pretty beat-up after Barzan had hit and kicked her. Still they needed to risk doing something. Waiting for John wasn't going to get them anywhere. Even if he showed up she didn't think Barzan would honor his part of the deal. A chill went through her body. Barzan was too sleazy to trust.

Teri looked at Sharon to try and figure out how much energy she had left. Even with her lip swollen and her hair matted she was beautiful. No wonder John had been attracted to her. Her eyes were telling. There was life there, defiance. Teri realized Sharon was not asking her for advice, she was asking if Teri had the nerve to join her in doing something about their situation. She was a kindred.

Teri offered the alternatives available to them. "I think we have two choices. One, we sneak up on these guys and bonk them on the head with a couple of rocks, or two, we just sneak away."

Sharon brushed her hair back with her hands. "I'm afraid I'm not much of a bonker. I think we can slip away, they really aren't paying much attention to us. But then what?"

Teri looked over the trackless savanna. The scattered trees that dotted the grasslands offered few places to hide. She sighed. "I don't know. Maybe find Johnny. Maybe we just have to hike back to camp. When we don't show up tomorrow night I'm sure Frank will come looking for us."

Sharon looked at the savanna warily. "Do you really think we can survive out here long enough to get back, or get found? You saw the lions and hyenas today. They're all over the place."

Teri realized just walking away was not going work. Her neck was tensing. "The alternative is to stay with these guys." She motioned with her head towards Barzan and Kip who still had their backs to them.

Sharon shook head. "Not an option."

Teri looked around the camp again. She noticed that the safari cruiser was parked under a tree very close to them. In fact it was closer to them than it was to Barzan and Kip. Much closer. "What if we drove out of here?"

Sharon raised an eyebrow as if wondering if Teri were serious or not. "You're suggesting we just wonder over, jump in the cruiser and drive into the sunset? I don't think that bastard Barzan will look favorably on our taking his truck."

Teri's heart sank. She was desperate to do something, anything, and she needed Sharon's help to have any hope of getting out of this mess. She had thought that Sharon had the nerve to try an escape. Maybe she had overestimated her. Teri's lips tightened.

"Do you think the keys are in it?" Sharon's question caught her off guard.

"I don't know."

"There's only one way to find out." Sharon stood up and walked slowly, as if still unsteady on her feet, straight toward the vehicle. It was only a dozen steps away. She was almost there when Barzan turned around and saw her.

Teri's body tensed and she didn't know what to do. She wasn't ready to take action without a plan. Sharon might get them both killed. But she admired that Sharon was at least attempting to see if they could get out. Teri was sure Sharon was just going to check the truck for keys.

Barzan glared at Sharon. "What are you doing?"

Teri held her breath. She was sure Sharon was going to be in for a beating at the very least.

"I'm going behind the truck because I need some privacy. Is that okay or do you want to watch that too?"

Teri bit her lip. She was certain Barzan would beat Sharon for that. And Teri only a few moments ago had doubted her nerve.

Barzan stood for a tense moment. Then Kip tapped his shoulder.

"Look, there are the others." He pointed to a place away from them, out of Teri's line of vision.

Barzan waved off Sharon who stood frozen in her tracks. She resumed her walk to the truck after he turned away. She went boldly to the driver's window and looked in.

Sharon checked on Barzan and Kip, then motioned to Teri to come quickly. Teri hesitated a moment before she stood and walked as fast as she dared. Her heart raced fearing that one of the men would turn at any second.

Sharon opened the door, got in and started the engine. Teri sprinted for the nearest door. She opened it just as Sharon put the truck in gear. Barzan and Kip were running for them.

"Hurry, hurry!" She could see Barzan reaching for the pistol in his holster.

The truck lurched and stalled. Teri's heart was in her throat. Barzan was almost to them. She heard the starter crank again. Barzan reached the truck and put his hand on the door.

"Get us out of here!"

The truck started to move. Barzan swung the door open and reached for Teri. She slid away from him, put her feet up and kicked him in the face. He fell back as the truck sped away.

Looking out the back window she saw Barzan raise a pistol at them. Kip shoved his hand away just as he fired. Barzan turned on Kip and yelled something. Suddenly he pointed his pistol at the African. She heard shots and Kip staggered backward falling into the dust. Teri's stomach rose in her throat and she almost retched.

"Oh my, God."

She turned and looked out the windshield. Sharon was accelerating into the vast grasslands away from the river. The wind blew in the open windows and the dust in the air had never smelled so good. Sharon turned to her smiling and raised her hand in a high five. Teri limply slapped palms with her.

"What was that shooting back there?"

Teri realized Sharon had not seen what happened. "That bastard killed Kip."

"We have to find a way to make him pay for that."

J OHN HEARD SHOTS AND GUESSED THEY WERE less than a mile away. What was going on? He was pretty sure no one was shooting at him. It didn't make sense for Barzan to kill either of the women before he traded the map to him. Maybe it was a signal to him.

In any event, he did not intend to be left unprepared again. The backpack he had filled with supplies from the truck before he'd crossed the river was in easy reach on the seat beside him. Inside were a pistol, ammunition and enough food and water for three days. He had also put a pistol in his belt in case he became separated from the pack.

All his senses were alert as he drove slowly across the dry grassland toward the sound of the shots. There was a slight rise in front of two acacia trees near the bank of the river. As he neared it he saw Barzan standing on the rise, cowboy hat in place. John was surprised he'd made himself so obvious. Then he realized that Barzan didn't know who was in the truck. He was expecting his two men to be in the vehicle. John slowed so he would not spook him by getting too close, too fast.

When he was about thirty yards away John stopped the cruiser and got out. His blood ran cold when he heard Barzan's sneering laugh.

"That belongs to me, Mister Erikson. You are an amusing man. Tell me how you came into possession of it."

"The guys who were in it decided to walk for awhile. They'll be along anytime now I'm sure."

Barzan let out that hideous laugh again. "It will do them no good. They have failed me. But you sir, do you have what I told you to bring?"

"I've got the map. If that's what you want." John held up the case for him to see.

"Good. Now put it on the hood of the truck and walk away from it."

"Where are the women?"

Barzan's voice had a reassuring tone. "They are fine, I assure you. But do as I say, or they won't be."

John's instinct was not to trust him. "Why should I believe you?"

"What choice do you have? If you don't do as I say, I will surely kill them. I may kill them anyway and you as well if it suits me. But you see, I really have no reason to. With the map I will be able to hunt down some of the largest rhinos that live, and having taken their horns, I will be able to get all that I desire. Killing you and your whores is of no particular interest to me."

This guy was one crafty son of a bitch. In Amsterdam he had seemed like a comic book character. There he had been out of his element, in a big city. Here in the bush, he was cunning and ruthless, an adversary it would be a deadly mistake to take lightly.

"What are you waiting for?"

John detected an edge in Barzan's voice. He didn't have much choice. He put the map case on the hood of the car and walked away from it at a right angle. He slung the backpack over his shoulder expecting Barzan to make him put it down.

When John was clear of the truck Barzan walked down from the small rise he had been standing on and went directly to it. For the first time John saw the pistol he had in a holster under his arm. Barzan checked the map in the case, got in the vehicle and started it.

He looked at John and grinned. "Your whores have already gone. They didn't wait for you." He laughed loudly and drove away. John stood in the dead grass and watched him go.

Once certain Barzan wasn't coming back John ran to the acacia trees, his heart pounding. Terrified he would find the bodies of Teri and Sharon, he ran over the rise. Instead he found the bullet-riddled corpse of an African.

"Sweet Jesus. What the hell happened here?"

———

John saw the vehicle approaching out of the shimmering grasslands. It was heading straight for him so he knew that the driver was looking for him. He wondered for a brief moment if Barzan might be returning. That didn't make sense. He decided he better be prepared for the worst anyway.

He took the pistol from the backpack and checked to be sure it was loaded. The heat was making him sweat and he wished for a cool breeze. Through the heat waves of the Serengeti Plain the vehicle looked surreal.

There was no point in hiding. He took a seat on a big rock, put the pistol in his lap, and waited. The sun was behind him and glared off the windshield. He could not see who was driving until the truck was almost to him. His jaw dropped when he recognized Sharon behind the wheel and Teri in the front seat.

The cruiser pulled up beside him and stopped with the passenger side nearest him. Teri looked at him as if he were a roadside curiosity.

"We're here to rescue you. Get in quickly. We're in a hurry."

He was too surprised to speak. Here in one of the most desolate places in Africa, his fiancée and ex-fiancée showed up to rescue him. He climbed in the back seat and almost before he sat down the truck took off again.

Teri turned around to talk to him. "We had stopped to get our bearings when we saw Barzan go by. He didn't see us because we hid the truck behind some brush. We figured you must have given him the map."

"Pretty clever, so you knew that I would be here and came back to get me."

Sharon and Teri shared a glance. "Well, sort of. We really wanted to follow Barzan to keep him from killing any rhinos."

Teri gave him a bottle of water. "But we were afraid you wouldn't do too well in the bush by yourself so we came back to get you."

He felt small and silly. He had imagined he was the one who was going to have to save them all. Now it was evident that they had not needed him in the least. These were some kind of women.

He could see Sharon's eyes in the rear view mirror. "Thanks for thinking of me."

"Not at all." Sharon smiled.

He took a long drink of the water relieved they were all safe and together. He felt the need to bring some order to what was happening.

"There's a problem with this plan. We need to get back to the base camp so we can radio the rangers. They're the ones who should deal with Barzan and his gang."

Teri gave him a look. "No time for that. We've already discussed it."

A sensation of being exposed coursed through him. "What else have you discussed?"

The women met each other's eyes and something mysterious and female passed between them. This was really bad. He longed for the comfort of a crocodile attack.

"We are the only ones in a position to stop him. If he kills the last of these rhinos it will be our fault. If we weren't here he would never have found this place."

Teri had that determined look and he knew he was destined to lose this fight. Especially if both of them were on the same side.

"What were you going to do when you caught up with him?"

Teri pointed to a high-powered rifle in the back of the cruiser. "Do you know how to work that?"

"You know I do."

"That's the other reason we came back for you."

"I'm glad you thought I could be helpful. How long ago did you say he went by you?"

"I'm guessing he has a half hour lead." Sharon was driving the truck with a skill that surprised him. He wondered what else there was about her that he didn't know.

"How do you expect to follow him?"

Teri pulled up her shirt and revealed a plastic pouch strapped around her waist. She peeled off the straps and removed it. From inside the folder size compartment she withdrew a familiar looking document. His mouth went dry as he recognized what it was.

John almost stammered. "It's the copy of my father's map."

She spread the document on the seat. "Yes it is. And we can follow it to the valley of the rhinos. Just like your parents. They're the ones who started the whole thing."

He saw Sharon watching him in the rear view. His mind flooded with mixed thoughts. His desire to climb the mountain with either of them had evaporated over the last twenty-four hours but feeling their sense of urgency about preventing the slaughter of the rhinos had infected him too.

Now more than ever he was sure there was something more important than climbing the mountain. The three of them had a chance to prevent a crime against nature.

A few hours ago he would have been content to simply survive the afternoon. Now he was concerned about helping an entire species survive. These two women were not going to let the rhinos be slaughtered without a fight.

He remembered a time when he'd told Teri that he would never leave her. There had been so many sleepless nights between then and now where he had begged the powers that be to give him just one more chance to be with her. And now, here she was. But this was a circumstance he couldn't have dreamed up in a million years.

He'd always thought he had cut Teri deeper than he had cut himself. The edges of the wounds in his memory were still ragged, not fully healed. But she had come back and there could only be one reason. Unless . . ..

Unless there was a dark side to her that he'd opened up when he left her. Perhaps she had come on this quest in an insane attempt to keep him from ever having happiness again. After what he had done, he couldn't blame her. There was some evidence to support this too. The countless unreturned phone calls, the unopened letters he had sent. Perhaps he had turned her into a vengeful shrew who only wanted to get even with him for ruining her life.

He glanced at her. She was watching the plains, her sunglasses once again masking her eyes. There was the hint of new lines around her eyes, but her complexion was still fair. He wondered what she was thinking. Wanted to know what it was that was driving her.

He laughed at himself. How could he even imagine she had an evil intent. That wasn't part of her character. She had a true heart and would, as long as she lived, follow a path that she thought would lead her to love. She was the kind of woman who would always follow her passion. That empty feeling in his chest came back. He could never allow himself to underestimate her again.

John looked at Sharon as she drove the cruiser. His fiancée. She picked a fine guy to fall in love with. He wondered if he could keep the promises he had already made to her. He realized he felt as strongly about Sharon now, as he once had about Teri.

It was different to be sure. It had to be different. Sharon was a deeply passionate woman who zeroed in on what she desired and went after it.

He knew if she had a goal she would achieve it. It was defining the goals that made her happy, knowing where she was, and where she wanted to be. The journey itself was but a means to the end. He envied her ability to know what she was about.

Thinking of what he had already done to Teri, John felt exposed as a fraud in her presence. He had not only betrayed her, but in the process had betrayed himself. When Teri had unexpectedly arrived he had been uncertain that he had any right to ask Sharon to take a chance on him. Now he was positive that he could take another chance on himself.

They drove through the afternoon toward the mountains over miles of terrain that was covered in brown grass and dotted with acacia trees. They saw few animals, but the remnants of the migration were everywhere.

The plain was trampled and overgrazed. The passing herds had left little that was edible behind. The bones of hundreds of wildebeests were scattered over the savanna. Sometimes John could spot the remains of a rib cage and the skull and horns of an unlucky animal. Mostly he would only see chewed over piles of bones.

The brown grassy plain abruptly gave way to a swampy jungle. John was startled by how quickly the terrain changed when they reached the tree line. From a distance it had looked cool, green, and inviting. However, once they arrived they were in the dense shade of a thick canopy of trees. The hot sun bearing down on them was replaced by a muggy heat filled with the odor of rotting vegetation.

John welcomed the change and his excitement grew. As the terrain continued to match the map he could sense the expectations of both Teri and Sharon increase. The mood in the cruiser was electric. He was not sure who was going to get shocked.

Strange birds sang out in eerie calls, and unseen animals rustled about in the foliage. He heard Teri and Sharon whispering, "Lions, and tigers, and bears . . . ."

The map gave very precise directions about which way to turn at certain landmarks. Without it they would have been hopelessly mired in the swamp that surrounded them.

John could see the occasional tire tracks of another vehicle. They must be close to Barzan. Every once in a while he asked Sharon to stop and shut the engine off so they could listen for the sound of another truck. What they heard was the sound of monkeys and birds disturbed by their presence.

It was late in the afternoon when they emerged from the swamp and arrived at the base of a towering mountain range. They easily spotted Barzan's parked truck, but he was nowhere in sight. John checked to make sure the high- powered rifle he had found in the stolen cruiser was loaded. They filled back packs with essentials they found in the vehicle, including food, water and ropes.

The mountains stabbed up into the sky with jagged edges. The rockface was a deep contrast to the trees and it took them almost twenty minutes to find the start of the trail that would lead to the top. Once they found it, it became apparent that they would have to travel single file. The trail was narrow, but fortunately not too steep.

Progressing up the mountain, the heights quickly took on menacing proportions. To his left, John walked with his hand almost brushing the rockface. On his right, the path gave way to a sheer cliff that dropped almost vertically to the jungle below. It would only take one missed step to send any one of them plunging over the side to certain death.

John had instinctively taken the lead when they started. He had the rifle cradled in his left hand in case Barzan chose to show himself. Tactically this was an extremely vulnerable spot. He stopped and motioned for Teri and Sharon to stop also. His heart was pounding more from the fear than from the climb.

"Why don't you two go back. Let me make sure Barzan isn't going to ambush us again."

"No way, John. We're better off staying together."

Sharon had not hesitated to speak. Teri was almost as quick.

"You aren't leaving me behind, again." She smiled. "Besides, I'd be too scared to sit in the truck by myself anyway."

Since they showed no fear, he continued. He wondered if this was what they meant by the saying every good man has a good woman behind him. At the moment he had two. Did it take a woman to make a man do daring things he would otherwise chicken out of?

"Okay, but let's get some distance between us. We'll be less of a target if we spread out." The women exchanged looks. He was relieved when for once they took his advice.

No more words were spoken as the trio climbed into the late afternoon.

———

The rockface was steep but John found the going was unexpectedly easy. Using the map they'd followed the game trail that would have otherwise been impossible to see. He was breathing hard. Teri and Sharon were close behind him and neither showed any sign of letting up. What a pair.

If the map were right it would take them to a cave like passageway that led into the next valley. When he got to the place indicated he stopped in disappointment. There was no sign of an opening.

"Is this the place?" Teri was panting, trying to catch her breath.

"I think so, but I don't see the cave." He felt along the wall with his hands, wasn't sure for what.

"Maybe you have to say 'open sesame'." Sharon leaned against the rocks and smiled.

She still had her sense of humor.

Teri pointed to an outcropping a few feet away. "You have to stand on that to see it."

John wasn't sure about this. "How do you know?"

"I've had the map for four years. I've studied it. How about you?"

He was too tired to rise to her jab. He looked at the outcropping. He guessed they were four hundred feet up the mountain. The spot was narrow and precarious. To one side was the rockface, on the other a severe drop off. Looking down he felt almost dizzy and had to step back. The place Teri had pointed to was only a few feet wide and stuck out over the edge. A slip would be fatal.

"You have to stand on that and look where the sun crosses the peak, only there will the passage be revealed." Teri sounded as if she were reciting something she had memorized. One thing was certain. It was a good thing she was here because he never would have figured this out without her. He was grateful for that. Not giving her the respect she'd deserved might have been a big mistake so many years ago.

Sharon's voice cut to the heart of the matter. "How are we supposed to know where the sun crosses the peak?" She was looking at the stony mountain face trying to ascertain the exact point the sun would cross the top of the ridge.

John put the rifle down and took off his pack. The sun was almost setting and with no trees to block the light the mountainside was bathed in a pink glow. "Maybe we're just supposed to look up."

Carefully he stepped onto the outcropping. He told himself all he had to do was stand there and not fall over. The height was unnerving and his knees were shaking making his balance unsure.

He looked up the mountainside. Nothing but sheer stone. He looked right, then left, still no sign of a passageway. "Are you sure this is the right place?"

"Yes I'm sure. Why don't you move and let me look."

He was relieved to step back on the game trail, away from the edge.

Sharon pulled a rope from the pack she was carrying. She gave one end to Teri. "Here, you hold this and I'll get on John's shoulders. You'll have to anchor us when we back out onto the ledge. Can you do it?"

Teri looked to him with an expression he could not define, then turned to Sharon. "Sure, I can do it. Just don't lean back too far. I only have a little leverage here."

Sharon climbed on his back piggy-back style and with Teri holding their lifeline John backed out onto the ledge again. When he got to the edge of the precipice he leaned back knowing Teri was the only thing keeping them from tumbling back over the cliff. He looked into her blue eyes and saw an image he knew only too well.

Sharon tightened her hold on him. "I see it. There's a ledge and an opening up there. No wonder nobody knows about this place."

John stepped back to the trail and let Sharon down. "I'm betting Barzan managed to find this too. We need to be careful. We may be getting close."

Climbing to the next ledge John found a small cave. He helped Sharon and Teri up, then led the way through a narrow passage. Wary of what he might encounter he held a flashlight in one hand and a pistol in the other. He was thankful that after a short distance he could see light coming from the other direction.

They emerged from the cave and saw a lush plain on the floor of a small valley. It was the crater of an ancient volcano. The mountains rose up in a steep ring around them. It was not nearly as big as the one he had heard about at Ngorongoro but the principle was the same. An almost closed ecosystem. He estimated it was only a few miles across. It was gorgeous.

A waterfall cascaded down the mountains a half mile away and fed a stream that wandered through the valley. Trees dotted the grassland and there was a jungle on the near side.

They were still three hundred feet up the mountainside and from this vantage point could see almost the entire valley. It was quickly becoming dark and long shadows covered the valley. John squinted in the dusk trying to see any signs of movement.

Beside him Teri used a pair of binoculars to look for Barzan. "Look, rhinos. There must be a dozen of them. And over there, that one is huge!" Her voice was clear, delighted.

John saw where she was pointing. Even in the low light he could see the herd of black rhinos, but his eyes focused on one particularly large animal. His heart jumped in his throat. The map had been right about the rhinos. That meant it was probably right about everything else too.

Excitement rushed through him. If the map were truly right in every respect, then they were close to the end of the journey. For an instant he worried about the warning on the map, to only make the ascent with two who are one. He had heard years ago that a man who doesn't know his own heart is lost to himself. The end of this day would surely tell if he knew himself or not.

"There's Barzan. He's going to kill it!" Teri's voice rose in panic.

On the valley floor below, John saw the unmistakable cowboy hat. Underneath it Barzan was taking aim at the biggest rhino with his gun. John quickly took his rifle off his shoulder and slammed a bullet into the chamber. He dropped to one knee and put Barzan in the cross hairs of the scope.

"Don't kill him." Sharon's voice was firm.

"Maybe you could shoot in the air and scare the rhino off." Teri was pleading.

This didn't make sense. This guy had threatened to kill both of them, and probably would have, and yet they didn't want to see him dead. Well, he hadn't planned to kill him anyway.

Just hold on Barzan, don't shoot yet. John felt his finger touch the trigger. He hoped the sight was zeroed, this was going to be close. He wished he had a chance to fire this thing so he would know how much trigger pull it would take.

He took a bite of air and held it. Each time his heart pounded it moved the target picture ever so slightly. The cowboy hat was square in the cross hairs. He moved the site up two feet to a small tree branch over Barzan's head. He squeezed gently until BLAM. The rifle kicked back into his shoulder.

The branch snapped falling on Barzan causing his rifle to discharge into the dirt.

"You did it! " Teri and Sharon grabbed him and hugged him. From the valley below Barzan looked up at them. The rhino turned and charged him. Barzan dropped his rifle and ran with the giant beast not far behind. John thought he would be gored for sure but Barzan made it to the rockface and scrambled up out of the animal's reach just ahead of the sharp horn.

John couldn't help but laugh. The nearsighted rhino put its huge feet on the rockface and shook its horn and snorted inches from Barzan's feet. The poacher flattened himself against the rocks, standing on a slender ledge on his tiptoes trying to get as far away from the raging animal as the cliff would allow.

John tried to contain his amusement at the irony. "We better go get him. If the rhino gets bored and leaves him alone, I don't want this guy running around loose while we're here."

———

Just before dawn, the moon lit the valley with silver light that was almost as bright as day. John stirred the small fire letting the coffee in his cup cool before he drank it. He was sore, but alive. They had washed off a layer of grime in the waterfall before going to sleep that night. It was nice to feel clean again.

They slept in the valley because they were too tired to risk the path down in the dark. Also, Teri had pointed out that it was the night of the autumnal equinox. The next morning would be the dawn of the map legend, and wouldn't come again for four years.

He sipped his coffee and wished she had forgotten about that. It was time to make the climb. He thought about packing it in. Waiting for sunrise and leaving. Just going home. Never mind the legend. It was too complicated with both of these women here.

"Are you ready?" Sharon looked at him across the fire expectantly. His pulse quickened.

"Almost."

"I'm going to take our guest some water. I think we should start when I get back."

He nodded. He was thankful for the reprieve. He stood up and stretched. Teri touched his shoulder from behind startling him. He turned to face her. The moonlight bathed her face in light. His heart raced and his palms were suddenly clammy.

This was the first time they had been alone in years. It was also the first time they had been alone since she had arrived two days ago. A lifetime ago.

"Johnny, you can't do this. You can't go up there with her."

"I can and I will. She's the one I came here with." A chill went through him and he crossed his arms over his chest trying to warm himself.

"Johnny, I don't want to hurt anybody, but you love me. You know what the legend says, if you make the wrong choice disaster will follow. I don't want you to make a mistake."

Damn her. How could she know what was gnawing at his insides? "Is that why you're here? To keep me from making a mistake?"

"No. Yes. I'm here because I love you. I want you, I want us to be happy again. I miss us."

John ran his hands through his hair. He had an urge to reach out to her, to take her in his arms, to say yes let's be together and be happy forever. But he didn't.

"Teri our time has passed. We had our chance and I blew it. I'm as sorry as I can be. I begged you to come back but you didn't do it. I agonized over you but that was years ago. You can't expect to show up now and change all that."

She moved closer to him. "I never stopped loving you. Don't you see? This love has survived the worst kind of treatment. This love I have for you has lasted all the years between us. You told me you'd never leave me."

His stomach was churning and he felt himself slipping into an abyss. She was so close he could feel her trembling beside him. His heart searched for the words that would make everything right, but they weren't there.

"No Teri, you're wrong. This love didn't survive. I cut it with diamond lies. I drowned it in alcohol and I tore it from my soul one shred at a time. I made myself believe this love could die. I convinced myself I could live without it. I no longer believe in our love."

The words spilled out like a confession. He saw the tears in her eyes and reached to wipe them away.

"Tell me you don't love me, Johnny. Tell me even if it's a lie."

"I do love you, Teri. I love what we had, what we once were. But we're separate now, you know that, you feel it too. Part of me will always love you, love us."

"You're going to end up like the rhinos, Johnny. You're going to be extinct unless somebody comes along to take care of you."

She kissed him on the cheek. Her tears were wet on his face. He wrapped his arms around her. She was soft and warm and familiar. She whispered in his ear.

"I know you're right. I knew our time was gone before I came. I just didn't want you coming here and making a mistake. I like her. I think she may be the only one, besides me, who can take care of you. I'll always love you."

She kissed his cheek again and hugged him tightly.

"Is this a hello or a goodbye?" He was startled when he heard Sharon's voice. He looked over to see her standing by the fire holding a canteen.

John wondered how she could be so calm. Here he was in an embrace with another woman and Sharon had simply asked to know what the score was. This was the woman he wanted to spend a lifetime getting to know.

Teri caressed his face and stepped away from him. "We were just saying goodbye. We never did it properly before."

Sharon smiled. "That's a relief. Since I met this guy I've crossed the ocean half a dozen times, was nearly shot on the streets of Amsterdam, been almost eaten by a crocodile and I've chased a poacher across Africa. I've never had so much fun. I don't know how I'd replace him."

John felt his face start to flush. They were going to be good together.

"He's one of a kind all right. Be careful with him though, he needs lots of attention. You two better get going, the sun will be up soon. I'll stay here and watch our friend."

John had the thought he was being passed off like a slightly used car. He wondered if Teri were going to give Sharon an owner's manual to go with him. That was okay. For the first time in a long time he felt everyone was making the right choice.

———

John and Sharon climbed through the darkness into the predawn light. Streaks of yellow and red crested above the highest peaks and John felt his stamina being tested as he rushed to get to the designated spot on time.

His legs ached and the skin on his fingers was warn almost raw from having to search out handholds on the rockface. Twice he had slipped and almost fallen into Sharon below him. If a tumble down the rockface didn't actually kill them, they would certainly be severely injured.

That might be worse than dying. To be badly hurt this far from any help would be the same as insuring a slow and lingering death. Or worse, they could end up as an entrée for some predator. He forced the negative thoughts from his mind.

Each time he thought he could go no farther he looked at Sharon. She followed him steadily and without complaint. Her breathing was labored and her face glistened in the predawn light. He reminded himself of the reason they had come here and he was determined that they would pass the test. They would prove this was a journey worth taking. A risk worthy of their best efforts.

John paused to catch his breath and look for a new handhold on an especially steep part. Sharon tapped his heel with her hand from below.

"Hurry up John, the sun is almost over the peaks. We've got to get there in time."

John was almost embarrassed. He was a trained soldier. He also prided himself in his physical conditioning. Yet Sharon was the one who was pushing him. Whatever thoughts he had about her stamina were completely gone. He smiled to himself. After what she and Teri had done to Barzan, he would never underestimate her again.

Reaching above his head he felt a firm handhold. He pulled himself up and placed his right hand into what he thought was another crevice. Instead he felt a smooth flat surface. He prayed he didn't find a snake or a scorpion or anything else unsavory. He grabbed an outcropping and pulled himself up again. His heart leapt. The flat plane between two peaks was what the map described as the final location. They had made it.

They reached the top of the mountain just before dawn. Following the instructions he put the polished rhino horn in a crevice that had been chipped out of the rock.

"Now what?"

"I don't know. I guess we wait for the sun to come up. It has to be a Stonehenge kind of thing. You know, when the sun is at a certain declination it shines on a particular spot." Just as he finished these words the sun peeked over the crater wall opposite them.

It rose between two peaks and a ray of light hit the polished horn and reflected on a narrow crevice just behind them. It was a beautiful sight and John recognized it as the signal they were waiting for. They went to where the light shone and were able to squeeze into a small chamber.

He flashed his pen light around the rock walls and saw nothing but smooth stone. His excitement started to drain as he watched Sharon run her hand over the surface.

"There's nothing here." He was surprised she did not sound disappointed.

Then John saw Sharon illuminated by the sun in the entrance. A smile caressed her face and the sun reflected gold off her auburn hair. He stepped to her, looked into her emerald eyes and pulled her close. She was warm against the cool of the dawn and when they kissed, her lips where soft and moist. He pressed against her and for the first time had the sensation that somehow they were both complete, both part of the same love.

He whispered into her ear.

"This place may not be worth any money. But I've found my treasure."

————

Two days later John and Sharon rode to the airstrip with Teri and Frank. George, the day's driver guide, called out the names of the animals and birds they passed. John listened to the deep but soft voice, scarcely hearing what was said.

"There's a fine waterbuck near the trees, and he had better be careful, the lions were running this morning."

John was grateful the last couple of days were over. When they'd returned to camp there was initially quite a stir. No one was happy about the ambush and the subsequent deaths. The ranger commander had threatened to jail everyone and the situation was in doubt for a full day. When the commander finally found out that Barzan was wanted across Africa and that he was going to be honored for sending a team to capture the notorious poacher, he became much more hospitable.

John, Sharon and Teri had agreed to keep the secret of the Valley of the Rhinos. Frank had been both disappointed and skeptical when they reported the map was useless. John was pretty sure he saw through them, but Frank had at least pretended he bought the story.

John stared out the open window of the safari cruiser, letting the warm African breeze blow over his face. In a short time he and Sharon would be aboard the small plane and lifting off for home. Leaving Africa behind was going to be harder than he'd ever imagined. What was going to be worse, was leaving Teri behind. This time forever.

She had been right all those years ago. When he had promised her he would never leave her, she must have somehow known how things would end. He realized now that her words were more intuitive than he could have believed. Bouncing along in the dusty truck, he knew that diamond lies cut forever.

John glanced at Sharon who was watching the wildebeests scattering in front of the truck. The sight of her lightened his spirit immediately. He squeezed her hand and felt the soft touch of her skin against his. He loved her and was certain that he always would. They had been tested together and survived intact. This was a love that could stand in the face of not only temptation, but also harsh adversity. If he walked away from this love, he would not only be a fool but he would be lying to himself.

When they arrived at the airstrip, the plane was already there. John had hoped it would be late, or maybe not come at all. The heat was oppressive and every step he took heavy and required an effort.

In spite of the heat, the pilot and George loaded the plane in what seemed like an instant. George shook Sharon's hand and then John's. "Thank you for coming. Please don't forget us."

John patted him on the shoulder. "We will always remember you and this place. You can depend on us to do what we can to help."

John finally had no choice but to get ready to board the plane. Sharon was already seated inside and the pilot was waiting for him. He looked at Teri who was standing beside Frank.

"Are you sure you want to stay here?"

She looked at him from behind her sunglasses. "Positive. This camp needs a woman's touch and I've fallen in love with Africa."

Frank tipped his hat. "We'll take care of her, or vice versa. And thanks for the donation to the wildlife fund. It will help a lot."

John shook hands with him. "Believe me, it's just the start. I'm heading up a new organization in my company to run our conservation efforts."

John hesitated for another moment. Seeing Teri with the rugged Frank sent a pang of jealousy up his spine.

He laughed at himself. He looked at Teri and knew he had been lucky to share part of her life.

Teri had tears starting down her checks. "Johnny, give me hug."

She took her sunglasses off and stepped to him. He opened his arms and held her tightly. She was so familiar. He squeezed her hard and she held him with what felt like all her strength.

He grasped her shoulders and held her at arms length. Her tears were making tracks through the dust on her cheeks.

John heard the pilot's voice.

"Hey, Monsieur, let's go. I have a schedule to keep you know."

John waved to the pilot signifying he'd heard him. "Teri, are you sure you'll be okay here?"

"Yes. I'll be happy here, I'm sure."

"Have you been talking to your psychic again?"

They both laughed and embraced.

John climbed into the plane and took his seat. He held Sharon's hand. She looked at him and her face was as calm and perfect as ever. In a soft and understanding voice she whispered. "Are sure this is the right thing for you?"

John squeezed Sharon's hand and turned to her. "I'm positive. This is the right thing for both of us."

The pilot cranked the engine up. Outside, Teri and Frank stood together watching the plane prepare to depart. The wind from the propeller blew her hair as he remembered it blowing in his convertible as they drove across the Golden Gate so many years ago. She put her sunglasses on and covered her eyes.

He opened his mouth to speak but realized he had no words. Then Teri turned her back to him and started walking away with Frank.

The plane quickly taxied to the end of the runway and rolled to the takeoff position. The pilot gunned the engine and they bounced down the red dirt strip. The craft climbed into the air before they reached the safari cruiser. The last time he saw Teri his heart was lifting and she was waving to him as he flew into the sky toward Kilimanjaro.

He sank into his seat watching the vast landscape pass beneath them. Holding Sharon's hand tightly he turned his thoughts to the problems of the disappearing rhinos and other animals. With Sharon by his side, perhaps he could find the courage to make a difference in the world.

Sharon leaned close. "Do you think your father lied about the diamonds?"

John looked in her eyes and smiled. "He never said a word about diamonds. We only interpreted it from the symbol on the map. It was always about the journey. We just had to learn that."

She leaned over and kissed him. He closed his eyes and wondered what other adventures they would share.

epilogue

SEVEN YEAR OLD GEORGE ERIKSON PUSHED ON
the door of his father's study. It was open! He motioned to
his sister Sherry to come with him. They crept into the study
alone for the first time.

George stopped near the ladder by the bookshelf and looked
up at the great wall of books. He pointed to the big one, the
*Valley of the Rhinos* on the highest shelf. "When I'm old enough, I
want to read that one."

# Goodfellow Press Catalogue of Titles

### The Quest
by Pam Binder.
Time cannot destroy the tapestry of
a life woven with love and magic.
ISBN 1-891761-10-2
$19.99/$23.99 Canada

### The Dalari Accord
by Matthew Lieber Buchman.
Memory is the alien within.
ISBN 1-891761-04-8
$19.99/$23.99 Canada

### A Slight Change of Plans
by John Zobel.
Sometimes the answer is right
in front of you.
ISBN 1-891761-01-3
$12.99/$13.99 Canada

### Matutu
by Sally Ash.
To find healing and love, an English
violinist and an American writer
must explore a Maori legend.
ISBN 0-9639882-9-8
$12.99/13.99 Canada

### The Inscription
by Pam Binder.
An immortal warrior has conquered
death. Now he must conquer living.
ISBN 0-9639882-7-1
$12.99/$13.99 Canada.

### Cookbook from Hell
by Matthew Lieber Buchman.
One part creation. Two parts soft-
ware. Season lightly with a pair of
love stories and roast until done.
ISBN 0-9639882-8-X
$12.99/$13.99 Canada

### Ivory Tower
by May Taylor.
Does the scent of lilacs herald
a soft haunting?
ISBN 0-9639882-3-9
$12.99/$13.99 Canada

### White Powder
by Mary Sharon Plowman.
It's hard to fall in love when
bullets are flying.
ISBN 0-9639882-6-3
$9.99/$10.99 Canada

### Bear Dance
by Kay Zimmer.
A man betrayed and a woman
escaping painful memories struggle
to overcome the barriers keeping
them apart.
ISBN 0-9639882-4-7
$9.99/$10.99 Canada

**Glass Ceiling**
by CJ Wyckoff.
Facing career and emotional
upheaval, Jane Walker makes a bold
choice to explore east Africa with an
unorthodox man.
ISBN 0-9639882-2-0
$9.99/$10.99 Canada

**This Time**
by Mary Sharon Plowman.
A man and a woman with differing
expectations and lifestyles take a
chance on love.
ISBN 0-9639882-1-2
$7.99/$8.99 Canada

**Hedge of Thorns**
by Sally Ash.
A gentle story unfolding like a
modern fairy tale, of painful
yesterdays and trust reborn.
ISBN 0-9639882-0-4
$7.99/$8.99 Canada.

# 2001 RELEASES

**Howl at the Moon**
by Polly Blankenship.
On a dusty country road in Texas,
a woman and a boy come face to
face with a nightmare.
ISBN 1-891761-07-2
$22.00/$25.00 Canada

**The Girls from Hangar B**
by Kristin Campbell Nail.
WWII, the union and men are no
match for four women when they
break all the rules.
ISBN 1-891761-08-0
$22.00/$25.00 Canada

**Altar Stone**
by Robert Hackman.
Ancient spirits stalk the unsuspecting
to live again in human form.
ISBN 1-891761-14-5
$22.00/$25.00 Canada

**Between Two Worlds**
by Suzi Prodan.
As the new nation of Yugoslavia
rises from the ashes of WWII, rebels
learn the price of freedom.
ISBN 1-891761-12-9

## AsYouLikeIt - A Goodfellow Imprint

### Rozner's Constant
by Jeffrey L. Waters.
Now that you have inherited the
secret of the universe, how do
you stay alive?
ISBN 1-891761-11-0
$19.99/23.99 Canada

### An Unobstructed View
by Jenness Clark.
Life's unobstructed views, while
desirable, depend on where one
is standing.
ISBN 1-891761-02-1
$12.99/$13.99 Canada

## Coming AsYouLikeIt RELEASES

### Midnight Choir
by Richard Clement.
In 1907, a Seattle nurse witnesses
a murder and becomes entangled
with the detective she fears may
be the killer.
ISBN: 1-891761-16-1

### Yellow Finch
by Ed Ratcliffe.
Two sisters in Peru, struggle to keep
loved ones together when their
family is fragmented by a terrorist
connection.
ISBN: 1-891761-19-6

### The Day the Music Died
by Florine Gingerich.
With the help of an unlikely ally, a
young gypsy woman faces the
horror of Nazi aggression.
ISBN: 1-891761-17-X

### Point of Departure
by Doni Pahlow.
Surprised by her ability to embrace
change, a successful forty-two-year-
old explores the secrets of her heart
and soul.
ISBN: 1-891761-18-8

## GOODFELLOW PRESS *Professional Services*

Goodfellow Professional Services is dedicated to the education of writers and the promotion of the written word, not only as a vehicle for pleasure, but as a work of art. To this end the following services are available.

- Editing Services
  Editing is done by Pamela Goodfellow, Editor-in-Chief of GP, or by an Associate Editor. All editing is done with two goals: supporting authors to reach their highest potential and aiding them in creating a work of fiction viable in the commercial market.

- Weekend Workshops and Saturday Seminars
  These two to five-day workshops offer students complete immersion in the writing process. Sessions are led by Pamela Goodfellow, GP authors, and a variety of guest speakers. This forum provides both new and experienced authors with a motivational boost. Saturday Seminars are a one day alternative to the weekend workshops.

- Ongoing and Private Classes
  Educational opportunities are available in several formats including: evening classes for groups of six or more, on-going weekly critique sessions monitored by a GP author or editor, and weekend seminars by request for groups of twelve or more.

- Speakers Bureau
  Authors, designers, and editors are available as speakers for classes, seminars, luncheons, and professional societies and conferences. Topics include all aspects of book creation, from writing to publishing.

**Goodfellow Press**
8522 10th Ave NW
Seattle, WA 98117
(206) 881-7699 / fax(206)-706-6352
info@goodfellowpress.com

## GOODFELLOW PRESS 2001
## EDITORIAL SERVICES RATE SHEET

| Editorial Services | Rate |
|---|---|

1. Four-sentence exercise.
   This is great for pinpointing a problem area and
   working through it. Make up your own or we can
   assign one specifically for you.  $ 25.00

2. One-page stand-alone scene (based on
   300 words per page in 12 pt. type with 1″
   margins, double spaced).  $ 50.00
   (Each additional page is $25.)

3. One 5-page scene (1500 words)  $125.00
   (Each additional page is $20.)

4. A short story of 10-13 pages (3000–4000 words)  $300.00
   (Each additional page after 13 is $35.)

5. A series of five 5-page scenes (each scene 1500
   words, total 7500).  $500.00
   (Each additional page is $20.)

6. Editorial Consultation (1-hr minimum):
   with an Associate Editor (face-to-face)  $65.00
   with Pamela R. Goodfellow (face-to-face)  $175.00

7. Editing of full manuscripts is done on a limited basis by individual review.
   Costs vary according to condition of manuscript.

Please specify what you want done and what you expect from us and send to:

**Goodfellow Press**
8522 10th Ave NW
Seattle, WA 98117
(206) 881-7699 / fax(206)-706-6352
info@goodfellowpress.com